THE BOY IN BLACK

Printed in Australia

Cover and internal design by Shawline Publishing Group Pty Ltd

First printing: July 2024

Shawline Publishing Group Pty Ltd

www.shawlinepublishing.com.au

Paperback ISBN 978-1-9231-7123-7

eBook ISBN 978-1-9231-7135-0

Hardback ISBN 978-1-9231-7147-3

Distributed by Shawline Distribution and Lightning Source Global

Shawline Publishing Group acknowledges the traditional owners of the land and pays respects to Elders, past, present and future.

A catalogue record for this work is available from the National Library of Australia

THE BOY IN
BLACK

J. J. POMYKALA

To my wonderful Pop, Mieczyslaw 'Mick' Pomykala
– I hope I have made you proud.

To those who never gave up on me; to those who never
stopped believing in me; to those who always supported me –
thank you.

PROLOGUE

November 9, 1938

It was cold that night. The frost swept in unexpectedly and settled gently over the lands. Father travelled into town, rather briskly. He refused to say what it was but demanded that we stay put in the house. We lived only a mile out of town, on a small commune with a number of other families. We heard distant noises coming from the town and anxiously stood up, peering through the window. I couldn't see anything as the low-lying frost impaired the nightscape. I turned to Mother and asked, 'What's happening, Mother?'

She looked at me and said gently, 'Something that has never stopped for our people.'

I was slightly confused but wary of what she meant. We had been taught, through family tradition and knowledge, of the history of our people – but sometimes it wasn't a history I wanted to hear. My younger sister, Edith, sat next to me on the window ledge. She swung her feet in the air and leaned in front of me on her elbow, watching my eyes squint.

'What is it, Johan?'

I broke eye contact with my reflection in the window and looked down at her.

'I don't know. Mother said nothing. She refused to talk about it.'
'I want to see what is happening.'
'Me too, Edith, but I don't think it's any good.'
Simultaneously, we turned to Mother, who sat with her hands placed neatly in her lap and her head turned to look out on the fields. Her lips were pursed as she continued to look through the window, her eyes still. I looked back at Edith.

'I'm going to go and see what is happening,' I whispered, still looking at Mother to make sure she didn't hear. 'You have to stay here.'

'But I want to go with you,' she demanded.

'No, Edith. If something bad is happening, I don't want anything bad to happen to you. Stay here, please.'

We looked at each other for a few moments before she replied, 'Fine. But be safe.'

I smiled. 'Of course I will.'

Mother went to the bathroom, and I used the opportunity to slip out unnoticed. I ran across the fields with the chill freezing my body as I ran. The frost was too thick, and as I came to a fence, I naïvely attempted to jump it, hooking my foot beneath the wooden beam, and violently hit my head on the other side of the fence. I moaned and staggered up, stumbling slightly as my feet tried to find a solid piece of ground. To begin with, I decided to walk, but adrenaline was coursing through my body, and I felt boundless energy. I decided to jog and headed for the town.

I stopped for a moment to catch my breath and continued on until the town's buildings were visible. Smoke rose and mixed with the frost to create an uncertain haze that lingered in the air. I was careful now. The screaming and shouting grew louder, and it wasn't until I walked slowly into the town's centre, aware of my surroundings, that I saw the fire. Flames licked up into the air, towering above the buildings and embers flowed on into the darkness. It was then I realised the shops there had been ransacked. The shopfront windows that encased the mannequins in breathtaking dioramas for passers-by to admire, had been smashed, shattered into thousands of crystals which now paved the streets. Mrs Königsberg's jewellery shop had been obliterated, and the dentistry run by Mr Kleeberg was no longer standing. I stopped and looked at the damage. Who would do this? Who would want to do this? I was bewildered. I looked for Father, but he was nowhere in sight.

'Father!' I screamed. 'Father!'

No answer. Every person who was on the street was already preoccupied with the chaos that had occurred. Screams echoed through the air as people fled in all directions. Mothers held tightly to their children; fathers prepared to defend their families. Wide-eyed and panicked, their faces bore the unmistakable marks of fear. Frantic footsteps echoed against the backdrop of the chaos surrounding us. The air was thick with smoke, billowing towards the heavens from every corner. I wondered if the end-of-days were upon us. I ran up and down the street, frantically searching for Father, but he was not there.

I continued walking east until the road split into a T and I went left, walking for a few minutes before I saw the synagogue. It was a beautiful building, built from a mixture of clay and limestone bricks, graced with intricate carvings that was a sight of wonder. It stood thirty feet high into the sky in all of its magnificence. The masterpiece was a symbol of pride for the town, and for our own community, with its beige walls neatly blending into the town's older buildings. Yet as I got to the synagogue, I saw the bright fire erupting from the building's rooftop, which had partially collapsed. The wood glowed red as it struggled to keep intact, straining to hold the entire rooftop up.

It took only five seconds. Five seconds and the roof caved in. Five seconds and the entire structure had disintegrated. Only seconds before, five men raced out of the synagogue, flustered, and panting furiously. The roof had caved with a large bang, and the wood continued to crackle under the fiery heat. One of the five men I instantly recognised. *Father.* I began to race toward him but stopped in my tracks as two men approached him, each wearing the distinct uniform of the *Sturmabteilung.* As they approached Father, I thought they had come to help him. The people who did this should be punished for it. But it was Father who was punished. One officer, a man of large build, grabbed Father by his shoulders and threw him violently. Father spiralled as he fell, hitting the cold stone with such force I could hear the crack on the ground as he hit it. I could hear the other officer yelling, above the thunderous crackling of the fire as it consumed the synagogue.

'What's the matter, old man? Having trouble getting up? Here, let me help you.' He reached out his hand to Father, who refused to so much as touch the man.

The officer pulled back his arm with a clenched fist and smashed it into Father's face. A swift blow to the left cheek, he had knocked Father to the ground once more. Blood flowed from Father's mouth, down his chin and dripped onto his trousers. I wanted to run and help him, but I knew I would be of no use – that's what my mind told me, anyway. Cowardice is for those who wish to live in darkness; I was in that darkness. It was my *father*. It was the man who raised me to be as courageous as the soldiers, to fight for my own freedom.

He would say to me, 'No man can fight for your freedom, but you. As long as it is your candle, the fire will keep burning until *you* blow it out. And if a wind blows it out, as life often does, then you are tasked with relighting it, son.'

I couldn't be sure, though. Did I leave Father there to be beaten up by the two soldiers, or did I intervene, only to have a high probability of getting beaten up myself?

I kept my feet planted on the ground and looked on from a distance. My lips trembled as I watched Father struggle to stay up. I couldn't look away, with the small amount of hope that persistently remained in the back of my mind that, by some miracle, Father would get out of this without any more trouble. I prayed. I don't often pray, only when Mother tells us to before we fall asleep – but I never do. Yet I found myself praying, hoping that this singular event would be exactly that – singular. Never recurring. *Please God, please. Please let him go. Don't let those men hurt him. Make them go away. Please.*

And that was the moment that would change my life. I witnessed the small, slender man stand over my father and pull out a gun from beneath his jacket. With the barrel of the gun pressed against Father's forehead, he yelled in his face. Father's eyes squinted, and I saw him cry for the first time in my life. He looked up at the soldier and said, 'God help you, Herr Oban. I forgive you.'

One shot. The sound echoed through the street, and for a moment everything seemed to black out. Nothing was real. I collapsed to the ground, and for a moment I thought I was Father, my head hitting the ground. My vision was blurred, reducing the two men to shadowy figures on a foreground of fiery destruction behind.

A few moments had passed, and I quickly stumbled to my feet. My head spun and I tripped, but nothing deterred me. A man tried to hold me back, but I screamed and shouted and fought my way through, and eventually he let me free. I ran to where Father lay and fell to my knees.

'Father!' I screamed. I put my hands on his shoulders and squeezed them. 'Father! Please! Don't be dead. Please don't be dead!' I shook him, but there was no answer.

His blood smeared onto my hands, still warm. I knew he was dead; I just didn't want it to be true. I cried that night. I cried more than I had ever cried in my life. It wasn't fair. My father was a doctor; he helped people. Why would someone take him from us? Mother said nothing. She cried, and so did Edith. We all did, but I didn't let them see it. I didn't deserve to cry. I was the coward who stood by and watched Father die. I did nothing. I let him die. And now his candle was extinguished.

At first, I didn't fully understand what that night was, but as I grew older, I knew exactly what it was. Our people were the outcasts of society for most of history – I was accustomed to it since birth. If Father had ever seen the boys at school and their treatment of me, he would have intervened. He would have set things right... and yet I couldn't pay him the same courtesy.

The morning light shone over the town – a wreck. Buildings had crumbled to piles of rubble, and those that stood were now windowless, the glass fragments raked up by shop owners. Each of the shops destroyed were owned by people in our community on the outer fields of town, and all went to the local synagogue.

They hated us, and we didn't know why. Many more people were killed that night along with my father, and I could never let go of the image that haunted me – the moment of my father's death. That night changed everything. They called it *Kristallnacht*.

CHAPTER 1

September 6, 1941

Operation Barbarossa. The Germans had launched the invasion into the Soviet Union three months prior. Even at nineteen I was still easily frightened. After Father's death, we left the village. Mother knew it was a targeted pogrom on the Jews, and if we didn't move on, we were next. We moved to a small village south-east of Berlin. We witnessed people systematically moved into smaller and smaller areas, known as the ghettos. We were mocked, beaten and spat upon, all because of how we were raised – of who we were.

Eventually, I ran away – cowardice was still the menace that haunted me. I ran from our small, crowded home, its derelict walls almost seeming to collapse around us. When I mustered up the courage to return, buildings had been burnt and reduced to rubble, just like those on that November night three years ago. Mother and Edith had been taken to another place, where most were taken to. I had only ever heard the stories of what occurred in places like that. But it became my mission. I was going to find Mother and Edith, and I would free them. I had to.

I joined the army under a different name – Hans Adler. A young German boy had died unexpectedly near the ghettos where we lived. I can only ask for forgiveness for what I did. I took his name, all that was part of him, and became him. I never knew what his family did, nor what his death meant for them – I thought myself cruel, almost like an agent of death, for what I did. But I wanted to live – to save Mother and Edith – all that I had of my old life.

With a new name and new life, I prayed no one would suspect my true identity as a Jew. All I wanted was to find my family, to return to the ways I had previously known. I knew it was naïve, but I continued to hold a sense of hope within me.

The men in the army were fierce, but I knew beneath the hardened exterior that exalted this war, there were hearts weeping to be home by the warm hearth that kept alive a roaring fire. This territory – unknown territory – had already proven difficult. In just a few months, the bleached white snow would blanket the landscape. The sky would blend with the snow-capped hills, and we would be trapped in a white abyss with no place of rest.

I looked around, taking in as much of the beauty that was before me while it was still clear. To my luck, two years ago, I had met a soldier, Oskar Bauer. A tall, strongly built nineteen-year-old who had a penchant for killing; I befriended him after he had saved my life, on more than one occasion. His humour was dry, his words often coarse and yet they held a ring of truth to them. He would often come across as a brute yearning to face death for his people. Yet, I knew there was more to him than one would originally perceive. I wanted to know him, to understand those like him, but I was afraid. I was afraid the words he spoke would be true, that my people were as evil as they spoke of. But fear only prohibits, and so I followed my heart and mind, beginning to understand those who surrounded me in their uniforms, fighting for the words which others spoke.

As I struggled to walk up the steep hill, I was startled by Oskar's hand grabbing my shoulder. I quickly turned my head and asked, 'What?'

He chuckled. 'Relax, Hans. I'm not waving the red flag.'

'It's you.' I sighed with relief. 'I'm sorry, I was just startled, that's all.'

'You'll be startled once those guns start firing, Hans. We all will be. You have to be ready. Remember, I've got your back.' He patted me on the back. 'Nothing bad will happen, okay?'

I nodded. 'Thanks, Oskar.'

He smiled at me and then looked forward, covering his eyes from the oncoming harsh sunlight.

After a moment's thought, I asked, 'Do you ever think about the men we kill?'

'No.' Oskar's answer was blunt. He saw my distorted face. 'Well, I mean, I try not to. It's our job to kill. It's our job to push forward.'

'But we could have different jobs. Jobs like there were before, without the war.'

'What jobs? There were no jobs, Hans. We had nothing. Now we're so close to having everything. Are your thoughts getting to you again?'

'No,' I said defiantly. 'No. I just can't help but feel frightened sometimes. What if I'm killed? What happens then?'

Oskar laughed a little. 'Hans, if you die, I'll die trying to help you. And if you do, you died for your country, right? You died fighting for our people.'

'No. I won't, Oskar. I will die fighting for Hitler. Like all of these men.'

'What did you say?' Suddenly, Oskar's face darkened; a menacing look that I instantly recognised from those at school, the scourge who would parade themselves triumphantly before all.

'I mean, I –' I began to stutter.

'Hans, this is *our* cause, do you understand?'

I nodded without saying a word. Oskar smiled a little.

'You're a bright kid, Hans. Sometimes I think that's a worry.' We both laughed. 'You know I'd never hurt you, right? We've been through too much together for me to shit down your throat.'

The image I received in the back of my mind almost made me sick, but I held it down and nodded, trying to smile.

'I know. It's just, sometimes you get that look and it's the same look I got years ago at school. I can't seem to escape it.' I thought about what he had said – "bright kid". Was I really as naïve as to be unknowingly patronised by someone so close to my age?

'You still think about those days?' he continued.

'Yes. Sometimes too much. I get anxious over the past.'

'We all do. I can still see my father staring at me with a disappointed look, saying that I will never become something. He hit me once – clean across the face.'

Silence carried over as I thought of what to say.

'That's awful. I'm sorry, Oskar.' *Idiot*, I thought to myself.

Oskar remained quiet for a moment, then replied, 'Don't be. He's dead now, anyway.'

'Sometimes death isn't the solution to a problem.' I thought about what I had said. Perhaps it was. 'I'm sure he loved you.'

'He loved no one but himself.'

I knew the subject was becoming uncomfortable when Oskar looked down awkwardly at his boots crushing the earth beneath as we walked. I decided to remain quiet rather than change the subject.

I stopped for a moment and observed the surroundings before me. The hills seemed to roll toward the east forever, meeting the horizon, and to the west, a forest with a patchwork of fields. It was of a magnificence I hadn't experienced in a long time. The sun gently shone its rays over everything that lay before us. Even the forest's morning dew glistened in the soft light. But I knew the impending doom of this pristine landscape – and us – was imminent. Soon gunfire would sound, tanks would roll in and decimate the glory of this part of the world. I refocused and realised Oskar was far ahead. I quickly stepped forward, but before I could steady my footing, the sole of my boot slipped on a rock that hid in the shadow of the sunlight, still wet from the morning's dew. I fell and my back slammed onto the pointed rock, and for a moment I was paralysed. I screamed in pain. One of the commanding officers pointed to me and bellowed at the soldiers, 'Shut him up!'

Before I knew what was happening, one soldier held me by my shoulders while another held a damp rag to my nose. Within seconds, darkness ensued.

≡

I awoke to gunfire. Men were racing around me, yelling orders as they readied their guns.

'Gunfire to the east! Guns at the ready! Soldiers at the ready!'

My head ached, and my back even more so. I sat up, grunting as a sharp pain shot through my back, but no one seemed to notice. I looked around and saw we were sprawled along the hillside, facing east. I turned to the soldier next to me and asked, 'Have we reached the Red Army already?'

The man chuckled.

'Look who decided to join us. You were out for at least thirteen hours. No, we haven't reached any army yet. Just a few rogue soldiers who want to do us some damage. Not to worry boy, we'll be moving in no time.'

Thirteen hours, I thought. It felt like only five minutes.

I crawled to the base of the hill where five men crouched out of sight. They all looked at me simultaneously, as though studying me like a painting.

'Your gun, Private Adler.' The commander passed me a Maschinenpistole 40. I was surprised he knew my last name, or what I wanted them to believe, anyway. Oskar must have told him.

'I thought it was only a few rogue soldiers,' I said timidly.

'Rogue soldiers?' he scoffed. 'These men are Russian soldiers. They know discipline, they know how to fight, and they know how to kill. They are, by no means, just a bunch of rogue soldiers. Which fool told you that?'

'I don't know, sir. Just another soldier. He was over there, I think.' I tilted my head to the left.

'Then he will be the first to be killed. Know your enemy. Know who they are, and you will know how to kill. It may not be a battle, but you never underestimate someone who points a gun at you. Now go, Private.' He looked at me with an expression of guilt, as though he was responsible for sending me to an impending doom. I nodded slowly, turned to face the enemy, and walked away with the heavy gun cradled in my arms.

I walked atop the hill and lay, my gun poised. I looked down the sight, aiming for anything that moved.

We had been positioned at Pskov for the last days of August, with no movement of the enemy. We advanced to Leningrad, with the definitive plan that we would rain destruction down on them. I was more than nervous about the endeavour of our division; I was objective to the whole thing. Never before had I inflicted pain on any living thing, and this war seemed to turn even the most sincerely compassionate into a cruel, black-hearted criminal. Somehow, every way I looked at it, it was impossible for me to grip the cold steel of a gun with any form of malice. I knew that every time I looked down the barrel of a gun, with the intention of killing, it wasn't so much cowardice that I would be feeling, but empathy. I empathised with these innocent people. If we attack, their homes are taken, just as my own had been. I would look down the barrel and observe their faces. Faces of determination. Faces of sorrow. All they wanted was to defend their home, and they had every reason to.

As we fought through the Russian lines, each foot was a foot closer to the heart of Leningrad. The tanks opened fire, obliterating anything in their path. Our tanks had outflanked the Russians more than once, and we were confident they would do it again. Only minutes after I awoke and remained atop the hill, the gunfire stopped, and an uneasy silence filled the air. They were dead – every single one of them. I looked at the corpses that were scattered over the field. Some of them had families. Some of them hoped to have families. But all of them were human – just like me.

We continued onward, the soldiers hardly containing their excitement as we moved closer and closer to Leningrad.

'I can smell it, it's so close,' said one soldier.

'We're so close to seeing it,' said another.

And they were right. I thought I was as naïve as any other soldier, but I realised these young men thrived on something so sinister. No, I was too aware to become as naïve as they. I knew the pain. I knew the suffering. I knew too much of the heart burning as families were ripped from each other.

We were almost seven miles from the city when our Führer gave orders for our army to change course. We were to lay siege on Moscow.

Concentration Camp

I let out a heavy sigh. Pity, poor people. They are sent to me all too often. They fear me and my siblings. Morning's light is almost here, and there is work to be done. Lots of work. Too much work for such small people. Skinny. Too skinny. Small, skinny people. They have no fat, just bones. Walking skeletons, waiting for hope. But hope never arrives.

The guards are not particularly warming people – in fact, they are animals. Cruel as they are, they keep me alive. As long as guards walk these halls, I am safe. I am a *Stufe III*; Grade III. Tough as I am, I will break any enemy of the Reich. Oh yes – they will wish they had served the Führer. The sick linger for a time, and then pass. The healthy become the sick, and new ones then come in. The cycle is infinite. Death is infinite. It is never ending. And they are made to do hard labour – tough, gruelling labour.

People say they fear the Führer. They do not fear him – they fear me. They fear that they will be sent to me. The Führer does not make them work; I do. The Führer does not break their spirit, I do. The faces of these people are peculiar. Saddened, but not frightened. Over the years I watch as faith lingers, holding on by a mere thread. Then, within seconds, it vanishes. The people's faith is gone –their physical faith in humanity, and often their faith in God. Humanity has failed them far too many times in history. They question their faith in God, and his power to stop this; yet others hold hope that the afterlife is far more pleasant. They are not frightened – their ancestors prepared them. But not for this, no. For this, history prepared them. Unfortunate it is, and I do feel remorse, but it is my job. This was what I was built for.

The new labourers came. Misery. Sorrow. These labourers are only men. No women or children – and yet they are as small as the children, withering away to nothingness. They walk slowly, their feet dragging along the dry dirt and the dust kicking up behind them. The guards yell orders; bellows of hate. The labourers – prisoners, more so – are made to work more in a day than they would in a year; condensed to one miserable day of the sweat, blood and tears they shed. It is a condensed hell. They dig trenches and holes; they build railways and roads – not those whose jobs it used to be. No, their jobs are gone. They are cheap – it costs nothing.

Blood drips from the walls. Thick, red blood. The blood of the innocent. It is abundant, almost a never-ending river. Screams radiate down the long, dark halls. Torture. Pain. Death. These linger on in the halls after one is gone, for one is not enough. Death is hungry, and it enjoys it with a side of pain, and a tall glass of torture. The guards are its demons, carrying out the routines with no thought of remorse or sympathy. Tick tock. Tick tock. Time is running out. Is it time, or patience? Their patience does not exist. And their time is far longer than hope. My time depends on them, and I will never cease. Never.

This is a place of hate.

CHAPTER 2

September 12, 1941

We were heading south, ready to walk the streets of Moscow. The men in my army were excited. They kept saying how they were ready to open fire on the Russians. But they were left disappointed when we received word that we wouldn't be going to Leningrad, just seven miles from the city. We had travelled for a long time, and all I wanted was to go home. The Russian territory was a cold place, and the bitter winds were more frequent as it got closer to winter. There was no snow yet, but soon thick, white blankets would rest across the landscape and the journey would become more difficult.

We were already exhausted from the long trek to Leningrad, and the change of course may have caused some excitement, but the relentless campaign seemed like a never-ending pursuit. And it was a pursuit of death – purity had no place in this war. Purity was never aesthetic. The Führer had a belief that this was the case, and it had led to death sweeping through like a plague.

The sun was setting, and we would be unable to travel at night. We stopped and set up camp. Multiple fires roared, their embers floating up to the sky and disappearing with the stars. I sat with Oskar and two other soldiers, Earnst and Felix. The night was cold, but the fire was enough to satisfy us, knowing that in a few months, no fire would take away the sharp chill of this place. Our bones would freeze, and it seemed with just a gentle touch, they would break into small fragments – *snap!* Earnst, Felix and Oskar had been talking while I was thinking. When my mind became clear, I decided to join the conversation.

'He seems angrier than usual, though. As though he's angry with the Führer,' said Felix.

'The Führer? Why would he be angry with him?' asked Oskar.

'For sending us south. We travelled for months, fighting to cross the border into Russian territory, and when we're just seven miles from the pot of gold, we're told to turn south.'

'South to *Moscow*,' I said.

All three looked at me, as though I wasn't permitted to speak.

'I didn't realise you had joined us,' said Felix. 'We thought you were still talking to your imaginary friend.'

'Leave him alone,' said Oskar.

'Why do you stick up for him, anyway? We all know he couldn't shoot dead a bear if it was one foot away from him,' said Earnst.

'I said, *leave him alone*.' Oskar's voice was stern, yet fierce. 'He hasn't done anything to you, so don't even think about doing anything to him. Understand?'

Earnst and Felix were quiet but nodded in compliance. Earnst turned to me.

'Sorry, Hans. I didn't really mean that about the bear. Or the imaginary friend. I was just playing around. To be honest, I'm just scared, I guess. I hate to admit it, but I am.'

I smiled a little, then it vanished. I looked at the fire, watching the flames dance.

'We're all scared. Whether we admit it or not, fear is there. It always is. There's every reason to be scared – we're in a war. I mean, look at us. We're in the middle of Russian territory, freezing by a fire in September, waiting to fall asleep while we all take turns on watch to keep each other alive.' I realised I was becoming far too vigorous in what I was saying and quietened.

'Hans is right. We're only here because of this war. I just want to go home,' said Felix. '*Home.*'

'So do I, but we can't. None of us can. We're in this, and we'll get through it.' Oskar looked at all of us. 'We're going to get through it.' He almost had the voice of a commander, determined to the bitter end.

We all nodded in agreement and sat in silence, watching the flames lick higher into the night sky. I lay down and looked up, wondering if this feeling would ever end – the feeling of hopelessness as we're on the cusp of chaos. Before I knew it, I was immersed in total darkness, falling into an exhausted sleep.

Dawn broke. It was early, and each day seemed to consist of the same thing. Push forward, little to no sleep, and push forward more. The engines rumbled to life and the tanks began rolling, the trucks following closely behind. I jogged over to Oskar.

'Manage any sleep?' he asked me.

'Enough of it. What about you?' I asked.

He shook his head.

'None. I haven't managed much since France.'

'You're still shaken by it, aren't you?'

Oskar nodded solemnly.

Two years ago, our panzer group was known as XVI Army Corps. We were a part of the invasion of France. On the edge of the city, we were fighting the French army in a bloody battle. We were slaughtering them, and even I had the audacity to attempt to shoot the opposing side, though failing in the process. Oskar and I were together, only having met a few weeks previously.

To win this battle, we were heavily relied upon to be mobile and highly effective in our killing skills. We kept close communications with every group, which was to our advantage – each time we would fight to take an enemy position, their slow mobility and poor communication meant we could advance quickly and gain the upper hand.

Everything was going well, until something unexpected and drastic happened – as unexpected in war as can be. Oskar and I had the enemy lined in our sights, but sight was a difficulty.

No scope was our aid when aiming for the other side. If you aimed toward the opposing side, you hoped it was at the right person. Sometimes, however, the enemy isn't who you think it is. Sometimes the enemy isn't the enemy, but those they hold hostage. The innocent, caught in a world of gunfire and disarray. Oskar found out the hard way. Looking down the sights of our guns, we both saw there were three figures, all of whom we assumed to be firing at us. We fired at the figures without any hesitation, Oskar directly toward them and me carefully navigating around so as not to be the one to kill them. But it wasn't until we approached them, that we saw what had been done.

Lying on the ground were three blood-spattered bodies. Bullet holes covered them from their necks down to their stomachs, the blood seeped out and soaking their uniforms. My stomach churned at the mere sight. The young girl was no older than ten. She wore a long, dark blue overcoat, her ruby red shoes almost glistening. Two young boys, who looked the same age as me and wore the uniform of the French army, lay next to her. They were twins. They had a bond of life, and with one shot, it was gone. That young girl had a life ahead of her, and within one shot, it was gone. That's all it took – one shot. Of all the soldiers that were killed in our campaign against France, they were the ones that left the scar on both Oskar and me.

You cannot liberate a nation with their own selfish interests at heart, without raining destruction on another. National interests create tension, but human interests create peace. And peace can only come when we accept that we are the same species, and our survival depends on acceptance.

It was then I realised I had become the very thing I despised; I had gone against what I was taught and attempted to take the life of an innocent. I had become the very monster that lurked in the back of my mind, its claws abrading my soul and devouring my heart.

'Oskar,' I began. 'You have to be able to forgive yourself.'

'Forgive myself? If I can't forgive the enemy for killing an innocent civilian, or for them killing a friend, then I can't forgive myself. I don't think I ever can, Hans.'

I looked at him. 'At least try. Please.'

He put his arm around my shoulder and showed the hint of a gratified smile.

'I'll try.'

We had been travelling for hours, and my bones ached. My joints grinded along as I forced myself, step by crippling step, to keep going. All the soldiers had become disorientated since the diverted journey south to Moscow. Just when I thought I would find myself being left behind the group, as I dropped to the ground dying, we stopped. The engines stopped. Every soldier stopped and looked either suspicious or cowardly for whatever awaited us.

In the air of silence, our commander screamed, 'Get down!'

We dropped simultaneously as gunfire erupted around us. We kept down until we were given further orders. Soldiers leapt into position, grabbing their guns and opened fire. Forming a semicircle around the artillery, we struggled to get into proper formation, bullets spinning past our heads. With great difficulty, we crawled into formation – a row that faced the oncoming gunfire.

The tanks started to open fire. Each barrage a great bellow of strength. I was next to Felix, and he smiled while looking down the scope of his gun.

'Time to kick some, right, Hans?'

I smiled nervously, and replied, 'Sure.'

An explosion twenty feet away from our position uplifted the earth and rained it over us. The sound was deafening – a constant high-pitched ringing in our ears.

'We're being flanked to the south!' yelled the commanding officer.

Felix and I began to crawl through the grass to where the officer was, along with fifteen other men. I studied the Russians' movements and realised they were attempting to encircle us. The officer saw it, too.

'Shit!' he said under his breath. 'They're going to come in on the north! Soldiers at the ready!'

Felix looked confused. 'They're not at the north.'

'They're trying to make a diversion,' I explained. 'If we're too busy with the east and south, they can come in from the north, trailing behind us and catching us off guard.'

Felix continued firing, swearing under his breath. Soldiers moved to the north, watching the grass intensely for any movement, even the slightest. If an animal happened to move while guns were pointed, it was its own funeral. They were on high alert. In an instant, everything went silent. No sound. Every man tensed, expectant.

The silence dragged on, until broken by a scream. 'Grenade! Get down!'

We buried our heads in our arms. The explosion sounded, followed by four more. Guns continued to fire as Russian soldiers swarmed from the forest to the east. I was certain we were going to die. But Death had other plans.

The tanks roared, and battered as they were, they advanced. The Russians knew the land, but we knew tactics. Designated soldiers threw several grenades toward the enemy lines. Once they exploded, the upheaval of earth created enough dust to cover us to move a few paces forward, unseen, until we were nose to nose with the Russians. They surged toward us, with steel knives of which the sleek metal reflected sharply in the sunlight. We – those who were in the frontline – drew our knives. The others continued firing. Most were shot dead immediately as they stood to run, but not all.

A large man ran directly toward me, his stomach moving independently from the rest of his body. I froze. He charged forward and lunged. Flinching, I held out a knife while turning my head. The weight of his entire body collapsed onto me, sending us crashing to the ground. His heavy body lay atop mine, crushing my small build body. The soldier's head looked up, and as he looked at me, blood poured from his mouth. His eyes locked into mine – it was like looking into a dark abyss. *I killed him*, I thought. *I killed this man.* I squinted, trying to hold back the tears in front of the others. Felix ran over and lifted the limp body from mine. As the weight was lifted off, I rolled to the side and pushed myself up from the ground. I coughed loudly and spat on the ground.

I looked at the soldier's face, who was still staring at me, trying to speak. He gargled as the blood built up in his mouth and poured down his chin. His head slumped to one side, lifeless.

'Good kill,' said Felix, with the hint of a smirk in the corner of his mouth. He hit me on the back. 'Good fucking kill.'

It was like hunting for wild animals in the forest – the glorified death of the animal, or person, standing opposite. But he was no animal.

I mumbled and turned away. I didn't want to see him – his dead body – knowing I had his blood on my face. I wiped it off with my jacket and grabbed my gun. My hands shook as I attempted to pick it up and aim. My mind turned to darkness.

You killed him.

You're a murderer.

You took his life.

Yours will be next.

An eye for an eye; a life for a life.

Your life.

It was no use. No matter how I tried to turn it, my mind wouldn't allow me to accept that the killing was necessary. I heard muffled noises amidst my thoughts and shook them away to see who was calling me. It was Felix.

'Hans! Come on!' He waved me over to his position.

I ran, half crouching, to where he was positioned. I dropped my gun and collapsed to the ground, kneeling in the dirt. Felix slid his arm under my shoulder and stood me up. He picked up my gun and pushed it to my chest.

'Pull yourself together, Hans. Come on, we have to push through. We have to keep going.'

I nodded and took a large gasp for air. We positioned ourselves as we were before, shooting down anyone that attempted to run toward us. Left, right and centre, soldiers were shot down. Their strategy was not as well thought out as ours. They would run toward us, while those in the forest lay in the grass attempted to give them covering fire. Some would make it to our lines, but few managed. And those that did were immediately shot down or stabbed – brutally. Some of our soldiers had been wounded and two were killed. But they had the numbers – every man, it seemed, attempting to charge toward us. What we weren't anticipating, however, was an attack from the western side.

The Russians had crawled through the long grass, while we were flanked from the north, east and south. It was just a diversion. Sergeant Shödler had spotted them only feet away before they emerged from the grass.

'Enemy to the west! Guns ready!'

Running to position, our soldiers faced westward and fired into the grass. Bullets shredded the grass, until it stood no more than a foot from the ground. The few remaining soldiers charged forward, only to be shot down almost immediately after emerging. A few, however, managed to run into our narrowly occupied territory and kill five of our soldiers. The Russians were dead almost instantly, before Sergeant Shödler held up his hand and bellowed, 'Wait!'

He walked over to where two of our soldiers had gripped the Russian soldier in a vicious lock. He stared at the man who struggled to get free, and his eyes became dark.

'He's going to help us.'

'What if he doesn't co-operate?' asked one of the soldiers who had hold of the Russian.

'He won't have a choice,' snarled Sergeant Shödler.

CHAPTER 3

September 13, 1941

I dreamed the previous night. It was the first time in a long time that I had dreamt. I dreamt of my mother. It was a strange dream, and I hope never to have anything like it again.

I was in a forest, shades of violet and beige bursting from the leaves of the surrounding trees. My mother stood at the end of a long, winding path that stretched beyond the horizon. I ran to her, my surroundings becoming a blur.

'*Mother!*' I screamed.

She turned; her face melted as her skin dripped from her sharp cheekbones. I stopped and held out my hand. She held out hers and screamed, 'Help me! Get me away!'

Dust crept up around her, and within a short moment she had become the dust. Dissolving away to nothing. She was no longer there. I turned and saw Edith amongst the trees. The leaves were yellow now, with plush bark of a cream blend. The sky was grey, and lightning struck in the distance. Edith signalled me to come over. I ran toward her, and she hid behind the tree. But when I looked behind it, she was not there. I looked further onward and saw her. Again, I ran toward her, but once more she vanished. I was chasing her but could never reach her.

'*Edith!*' I screamed.

I heard her giggle. But it was not just a giggle – it was an incessant giggle, an earache. Almost a screech.

'Help me, Johan!' It was Edith's voice. 'Help me!' She screamed so loudly; it was as though she had emptied the air from her lungs. I ran toward her and held out my hand, but she disappeared.

'*You killed me,*' whispered a voice from behind. '*You took my life.*'

I turned to witness standing behind me the man I had killed. His eyes dripped blood as he staggered toward me, the knife that I had thrust in his stomach, protruding from him.

'I'm sorry,' I said. 'I'm sorry!'

'*I had a family. I was going to go home. You took it from me.*' He continued to stagger toward me, stretching out his hand.

I shook my head. 'So do I.'

'*You invaded my home. I defended it for my family, from the monster – you. You're the monster.*'

Tears streamed down my face as I realised what I had done. Before I knew what was happening, the ground beneath me collapsed and I was falling into a dark abyss with no return. Falling infinitely, with no ground to land on beneath.

I awoke with a fright and sat up immediately. It was still dark, but the moon reflected enough light to allow me to see my surroundings. The soldiers were still asleep, except for those on guard. The fires had died to glowing embers. I stood up and walked toward the forest, when I was stopped by one of the soldiers on guard.

'Where are you going?' he asked.

'I just have to go to the toilet,' I said.

He examined me for a moment, his eyes squinting in discernment, before finally replying, 'Fine. Don't wander off.'

I nodded and turned, heading for the forest. When I was sure that I couldn't be seen, I turned and headed east. We had dumped the bodies of the dead Russian soldiers after the small battle. When it had ceased, it became the place of a mass grave. I carefully stepped on the ground, trying not to make any noise, nor lose my footing in the gaping hole that contained bodies. It was difficult to see anything with the trees blocking most of the moon's reflective light. I looked over to where we were camped and watched the silhouetted figures pacing up and down. My cover was still safe.

I came to the large crater where the bodies were dumped and felt my way around. I jumped down and got out my small torch. Hoping that no one would see, I turned it on and searched for the man that I had killed. I shone the light over the large pile of bodies. I couldn't see him on the top and deduced he must be in the middle or bottom of the pile. I quickly looked around one more time before determining that he wasn't there.

I climbed over the bodies and held the torch in my mouth. I pulled the top body off and looked beneath. It wasn't him. I grabbed the next body and rolled it over to see the face – not him. The next – not him. Each body that I moved seemed to roll their eyes to mine, an uneasy feeling sweeping over me, as though they watched. I didn't want to do this, but I knew I had to. I climbed down close to the bottom and pulled one of the bodies toward me.

He was heavy, smelling of sweat and death. With a grunt, I managed to pull him free, along with several of the others that weighed down on him. It wasn't him, but one of the bodies that had collapsed on top, was. I pulled his limp body out and looked him up and down. His eyes were now beads of white. The blood that had spurted from his mouth had dried against his pale skin, and his uniform was stained with thick blood on the front, almost blending with the brown wool. He was difficult to move, and I had flashbacks of his weight crushing my body, as he lay on top of me, the blood still warm as it ran from his mouth. I opened his jacket and reached into his pockets.

I felt a piece of glossed paper and pulled it out. It was a photograph. As I looked at it, bitter tears welled. I was bitter at myself, at this whole situation. The photograph revealed the man with what I assumed to be his wife and two children, smiling beautifully – picture perfect. I began to sob. I sat in the dirt with my knees clutched to my chest, curling my arms around my legs. I stared at the soldier's dead body, the warm tears streaming down my face. I stood up abruptly and kicked the ground.

'You idiot! You killed him!' I screeched, gritting my teeth. 'You killed him, killed him, killed him!' I screamed the words through my teeth, kicking the dirt each time.

I collapsed to the ground and cried. My body ached – I hated it. I hated everything. I punched the ground in anger, knowing I would never forgive myself for what I did. Ever.

A hand grabbed me by the shoulder, and I jumped quickly. I turned to meet one of the soldiers on guard. He stared at me, his eyes reducing me to a small, frightened boy.

'What are you doing over here?' he demanded.

'I was just… I think one of them had my knife still,' I replied.

'And you decided to cry about it? Don't lie to me, boy.' He grabbed me by the collar and heaved me from the ground, my legs dangling in the air. I shuffled awkwardly to try and feel for the ground. 'What are you doing here?'

'Nothing!' I spoke. 'Let go of me!'

He dropped me to the ground, sending me crashing with a loud thump as I landed on my knees. I whimpered in pain but turned my head away from his sight. He held my arm and pulled me forward to my feet, gripping me tightly.

'We'll see how well you answer to Sergeant Shödler.'

I was seated on a chair in front of Sergeant Shödler by the time the sun had risen. He stood in front of me, clutching his chair and leaning forward.

'Why were you going through the dead bodies, Private Adler?' he asked.

'I was looking for my knife,' I replied hesitantly. 'I stabbed one of them, but I never got it back.'

'Pity. You see, when my soldiers dumped those bodies, they didn't come across any knife. Now that's a bit strange, isn't it?'

I shrugged. 'It must have fallen off at some point.'

Sergeant Shödler laughed.

'Pathetic,' he said, grimacing. 'You are pathetic. Do you take me for a fool, Private Adler?' His voice heightened.

I shook my head. 'No, I–'

'You what? You just thought that, perhaps, I was going to believe your every word? Is that what it is?'

'No, I mean I didn't think you were a fool.' My voice was quiet, my throat tightening.

Sergeant Shödler was ghoulish. He looked at me and tilted his head. *This man is a maniac*, I thought. He walked over to me and stood against my shoulder. He placed his hands on my shoulders and crouched down. He brought his lips close to my ears and said gently, 'I am very disappointed in you, *Hans*.' Shivers ran down my spine. 'Very disappointed indeed. I have a taste for blood, you know.'

His breath was warm and reeked of smoke. Just as he began applying pressure to my shoulders, the commander walked in. He looked down at Sergeant Shödler and me.

'Sergeant Shödler. Private Adler. What is going on here?' he asked.

Sergeant Shödler stood attentively and saluted the commander.

'Commander,' he began, 'one of the soldiers caught Private Adler rummaging through the dead bodies we had disposed of earlier. I brought him in here to question his actions.'

The commander raised an eyebrow. 'And you thought that feeling him up was going to get him to talk?'

Sergeant Shödler's face turned to a bright crimson.

'No, sir. I was just–'

'You are sick and depraved, Sergeant. That's what you are. Now hand him over to me.'

I stood and walked past the commander, out of the tent and waited. I could tell Sergeant Shödler was brewing with anger. The commander followed to the entrance of the tent, then stopped.

'We'll take a walk, Private Adler.'

Before the commander followed me out, I overheard him speaking to Sergeant Shödler.

'You're on thin ice, Shödler. I never wanted you in my army, but I'm stuck with you. One more foot out of line, like last time, and you'll be dealing with me personally – alone. Is that clear?'

'Commander, that little shit–'

'Will be dealt with by me. I don't want some lunatic, such as yourself, to have a chance at breaking my soldiers. Do you understand?'

'Yes, Commander,' hissed Shödler.

The commander left the tent and walked beside me. We walked atop the hill that was near our camp, but far enough that we couldn't be heard. We stood, overlooking the camp and neighbouring forest.

'You went back to him,' said the commander. 'Why?'

I looked down at my feet, then back to the camp.

'I wanted to see if he had a family.'

The commander was quiet for a moment. He looked at me.

'You're a good man, Hans. I admire you for that. But remember, every one of these soldiers wants to be home, too. We have a duty to our Führer – to our people – and it cannot be abandoned because of what we feel, deep down. Regardless.'

'Commander,' I began, 'he's the first soldier I've killed in a long time. I watched as he died, slowly. He looked straight at me. He even tried to speak to me.'

'I know,' he replied. We both watched the soldiers pack up the camp. 'But he won't be your last for a very long time.' He sighed heavily. 'Hans, let me tell you something. You can go through this war without killing anyone, but that won't stop them from attempting to kill you. You are the type of person I wish I had as a son. Your father should be proud of you.'

'He's dead, sir,' I said. 'He died a long time ago.'

'Regardless, he would be proud of the man you are. You have a rare personality, and I like it.' I smiled humbly and looked down. 'But if you tell anyone that I said this to you, I'll deny it.'

He began to walk down the hill, toward the camp.

'Yes, sir,' I said, relieved.

CHAPTER 4

September 18, 1941

We had travelled without any quarrels or attacks since the day we were surrounded by the Russians. The soldiers, on the other hand, were becoming restless. The younger men tended to dispute amongst themselves, which was almost always easily solved within a few minutes after it had started. But today, they grew more and more tired, hissing at one another as hackles rose at the slightest provocation. Felix had been teasing another boy, Luis, who was more than tempted to silence his bully. But Luis kept quiet, allowing Felix to continue his insults. That was until Luis turned around with his right fist clenched, delivering a deadly punch to Felix's jaw. Felix fell straight to the ground, with an immediate red mark taking shape on his lower jaw. He kicked Luis's legs, bringing him crashing to the ground, where he landed sharply on his elbow. Luis screamed in pain and kicked sharply, clipping Felix's ear. The two boys were enveloped in a full brawl, until Sergeant Shödler grabbed both by their ears and dragged them off, yelling profanities from the top of his voice.

We all looked at one another uneasily, unsure of what to do next, or to how to approach one another. We were all cautious about how to act, to not step on anyone's toes. The tanks and trucks had stopped; our company came to rest. I was amongst a group of younger soldiers, testosterone mixed with a group of sexually frustrated and tired teenagers. Captain Alden approached us from the front of the group and announced, 'We stop here for camp.' He pointed at all of us. 'And if any of you step out of line, I'll throw you in the firing line of the Russians myself. Understood?'

'Yes sir,' we replied simultaneously.

We dropped our things and set up camp. Oskar walked toward me and sat down on the grass, his arms resting on his knees.

'Some fist fight, that was,' he said. 'Want to give it a go?' We both chuckled at the absurdity. 'You seem quiet. Quieter than usual, that is. Is there something going on, Hans?'

I sat down next to him.

'If I tell you something, will you promise not to say a single word about it?'

He nodded, but I had to make sure he knew how serious this was.

'I mean it, Oskar. If you tell anyone...'

'Relax, Hans. I'm not going to say a word.'

I sighed heavily, thinking carefully about what I was going to say.

'You know that guy I killed the other day? The one that I...' I motioned a stabbing movement. Hans nodded. 'He was the first man I have killed in a very long time. After France, I told myself I couldn't do it again. I couldn't kill again. I couldn't think about how many more innocent people I would kill, again and again. And I haven't been able to forgive myself for it, at all.'

A lump in my throat formed, and I could feel Oskar looking at me quizzically.

'I just don't know what to do.'

'You can't forgive yourself about France, either? And yet you've always put on a brave face for me. I had no idea.'

I nodded. 'I guess.' My voice had crumbled.

Oskar sighed in contemplation and looked forward. 'What does it feel like for you?'

I was puzzled by the question but answered regardless.

'I feel awful. Like I was killing one of my own. I keep picturing his face, as though when I stabbed him, I took away everything. Which I did, in a way.'

'When I killed my first man, I imagined it being my father.'

'Your father?'

'Yes. And when I looked into his eyes, it was him. He was finally dead. I thought that. I truly thought I had killed him – rid the world of his malicious intent. Rid the world of evil. I was wrong. Look around you – evil is everywhere. Wherever you look, evil lurks in every place, in every human being. It's whether you succumb to that evil.'

'Did you?'

'I did a long time ago.' The sentence made me shudder, but I continued to listen attentively. 'When I was young, I used to play in the forest behind our house. I lived on a large estate, and often I would wander off into the forest, chasing whatever animals I could see.

'One day, I followed a hare far out into the forest. I saw it stop and I crept up to it. Without any hesitation, I jumped on it and caught it before it had a chance to run away. But the next thing that happened wasn't what I wanted.' He paused for a moment, seeming to gather his thoughts.

He continued, 'I grabbed it. I just grabbed it and twisted its neck. No hesitation. No worries. Nothing. In one snap, it was dead.

'My hands were covered in blood. I remember looking down at them, mesmerised by the red liquid dripping from my hands and onto the ground. And then, without thinking, I wiped it on my face. Like a warrior. It was smooth on my skin. I sat there, watching the forest keep still – no wind, no sound.'

I became awkward. 'Do you... do you still do it?'

He looked at me, with the eyes of a predator. 'No.'

'That girl in France, Oskar...' I felt an impending sense of anxiety for bringing it up again, but I had to know if it was linked with this strange obsession.

'What of her?'

'What did you feel when you killed her?'

'What do you think I felt? You think I'm some sort of monster because of what I just told you?'

I became defensive. 'No, I didn't mean it like that. Don't twist my words, Oskar.'

He scoffed. 'Of course, you didn't, because you're the perfect guy who means no harm to anyone. You can't even kill a man without feeling guilty.'

Why was I to take this sort of resentment?

'It's empathy, Oskar. It's called being human. Maybe you should try it sometime.'

'Empathy? You call it empathy? And yet you *still* do it. You haven't stopped. Don't tell me I don't have empathy because I kill people – you kill people, Hans. You just can't admit it to yourself.'

'I can at least admit it's wrong. I don't *want* to do it.'

'And yet, here we are.'

My muscles seized. I felt vulnerable, as though anything could break me. He was right. I do – I *have* – killed people. I just couldn't admit that I do it. I didn't know what to think, or what to say. I remained silent. I stood up and walked away, to where Earnst sat.

'You two sounded like you were having a fairly heated discussion,' said Earnst.

I shrugged. 'You could call it that. He was the one getting heated, not me.'

Earnst chuckled slightly and replied, 'Uh huh, I see.'

I raised my eyebrows and shook my head.

'I don't want to talk about it. So, what are you going to do without Felix?'

'Not much, I suppose. The guy is a loose cannon, anyway. Sure, he's my best friend, but he drives me insane sometimes. He had it coming, *especially* from Luis.'

'That's true. The poor guy, having to put up with Felix's shit for so long.'

We both laughed and it was the first time I felt friendly enough with Earnst. I looked over my shoulder at Oskar, who scowled at me, his eyes burning. I smiled a little at him and turned away. I didn't want it to be like this. I hated fighting with Oskar, but if this war proved anything, it was that even the innocent were cruel on the inside. From truthful retribution to heinous joy in death. We enjoyed killing; it was who we had become. But I was never so sure that our cause was ever truthful, nor any recompense of past retribution. Our problem was greed.

I slept badly that night. Almost every hour, I sat up and looked over to Oskar. Most of the time I knew he was awake, but he avoided all possible eye contact. I threw a stone at him, but he didn't move. As stubborn as he was, he couldn't hold it for the whole night. Eventually, he sat up and looked at me. I flicked my head to signal him to sit next to me, and sure enough he stood up and made his way to where I sat.

'Can't sleep either?' I whispered.

He shook his head.

'Look, I'm sorry about earlier. I…' I cupped my hands and placed them on my face, sighing heavily. I slid my hands down my face and rested them under my chin. 'You're the only person that has ever stood up for me before. Apart from my father. But you're the only… well, only friend.'

Oskar smiled and ruffled my hair.

'Don't be so hard on yourself. I was having a rough day. I should say sorry too, for the way I acted. I know how hard it can be to hear something like I told you. But I told you because you *are* my friend.'

I nodded, a slight smile forming as he said that word. *Friend.*

'We all have those days. Just try and direct it to the other side next time? Or Felix.'

The moment he laughed, I immediately felt relief. He wasn't mad anymore.

'Hans,' he said gently. 'I'm no monster. I know this war can change people, and eventually make them monsters, but I'm not one of them. That girl – she reminded me too much of back home. I don't enjoy killing, but I do it because I must. I know you may not see it that way – that we have a choice – but I was taught to just follow orders. And if I did that right, then someday I would give the orders. But I never want to be a monster. Not now, not ever.'

I shook my head. 'I don't think you're a monster. Sometimes our past can haunt us – sometimes we think that it dictates who we are. But we can't let it take us over.'

Friends fight, and they can fight for as long as it takes to make their point. But friends do that, and they do it often. It's what happens afterwards that matters. And if that friendship is intact, it proves that it is stronger than most.

I knew Oskar and I would fight, and it wouldn't be an experience I would want repeated, but I also knew he would do anything to keep me alive. And that's a bond that would last a lifetime.

Concentration Camp

Who dares wake me from my slumber? Their screams are deafening. They do not cease. Their screams go on, and on, and on. It seems they don't take a breath. I can hear their words, clearly as I can see the blue sky during the day.

'Help me! Please! Please! No!'

Today, however, the sky is no longer blue. It is a dark, sickly grey. Thunder rumbles, but soon after, the rumbles turn to crashes, piercing the air as lightning strikes in the distance. Lightning strikes. A cliché, no? But what happens here is not a cliché, it is sickening to the human mind.

Tick tock. Time is running out. This human, screaming for mercy, has almost no time left. He begs for his time to halt, to cease forever. Perhaps I shall observe what is happening; why his incessant moaning has not stopped.

So, I observe silently. The wind makes my walls groan and creak with life, but it does not deter them from what takes place. I watch the man who screams. The officers are tormenting him, making him suffer. It is odd that I have never come across this man before. He has never taken a breath out of line, never sworn under his breath at an officer, nor started a violent dispute with any of his fellow inmates. Why is he suffering? So much pain.

'Do you want me to stop, boy?'

Boy? He is a mere adolescent. His face is contorted with pain. He grits his teeth. Tears drop from his eyes. Blood spills onto the ground, trickling from his body. The walls are marked with stains of previous innocents, tortured until their last breath.

The commander suddenly bursts through the door. The officer swiftly turns, and his eyes widen as he quickly realises who is standing in the doorway. He stands to attention and salutes.

'Sir!' he remarks.

'What is this?' asks the commander.

'He is a spy, sir. We are getting the information from him that we need.'

The commander gives the officer a quizzical look, then raises an eyebrow. 'He is but a boy.'

'He is a spy, sir!'

The commander's eyes widen as he glares at the officer with such fierceness.

'Do you question my authority, Private Laus?'

The officer shakes his head, quickly indeed.

'No, commander. Not at all.'

'Let the boy go,' says the commander. He leans in close to the officer's face, and looks deep into his eyes, threateningly. 'And if you ever question my judgement again, I will make sure it is you who is tormented inside these walls. Am I clear?'

The officer nods. 'Yes, sir. Sorry, sir.'

I watch the boy escorted down the halls, into the room which holds the sleeping men. He is limping and grunting in pain. He reaches for his bed, sits gently on it and moans. He lies down and rests his head in his cupped hands. There is a silence. He breathes heavily. I feel pity for the boy. Then I hear it. I hear a heavenly voice. And it is the boy.

He lies, singing. His angelic voice scarcely heard by the others around him, but I can hear it. I am everywhere. One of the men wakes up to the boy's singing, but he does not move. It is as though he does not want to distract him. Instead, he lays with his eyes wide open, and listens. Just listens. When he shuffles, however, the boy immediately stops, startled at the movement. The man sits up and looks at the boy.

'You have a beautiful voice,' the man says.

'Thank you,' says the boy, shyly.

'I saw them take you. What did they do to you?'

The boy lifts his shirt to reveal fresh bruising, the colour of plums. Every time he moves, he shuts his eyes tightly in pain, and grits his teeth. The man gets up and sits next to him.

'They are brutes,' states the man. 'All of them are brutes.'

The boy looks down. 'The commander, he... he stopped the officer.'

The man scoffed. 'Stopped it? Why would *he* stop it? He is just like the rest of them.'

'No,' says the boy, defensively. 'He did stop it. He told the officer to stop.'

'He wants him to stop so that you don't bruise too much. If

you bruise too much, you can't work. And when you can't work, what good are you in a labour camp?'

I often watch the men work each day, as they are tormented by the officers who, in turn, stand over them and watch intensely. As the labourers tire, the officers enjoy it more. Often, they will kick the labourer's legs, sending them crashing to the ground.

Death seems like sweet relief for these men. They dream of it. They beg for it. Life is nothing but brutal. They are at their end, and soon they will be united with Death. But not just yet. No. Life can still use them for now. But when the time comes, Death will suck the life out of them with no hesitation, and they will weep with joy.

CHAPTER 5

September 28, 1941

The sharp winds picked up. We marched on, persisting through the icy cold temperatures. The tanks were struggling to start up each morning, slowly groaning to life. My feet ached; beyond any pain I had ever felt. Every step I took, pain shot straight through, from my feet and through my legs. At that moment, I really did want it all to end. I wanted to see Father. I wanted to be held by him, just to feel his breath on my cheeks as he whispered, 'I love you.'

We had only been travelling for half an hour, an hour at the most, when we stopped.

'Why are we stopping?' asked one of the soldiers. He was not much older than me in appearance, but he was well beyond his age when it came to intelligence and wisdom.

An older man, Lieutenant Jonan, ran toward us. He was out of breath and struggling to speak, but his eyes were filled with fear, though he never showed it in the rest of his face.

'Get into positions, men!'

We dropped our things and grabbed our guns without hesitation. As I edged closer to the front, I froze for a moment. My heart seemed to burn as I saw what was up ahead. Lines of

Russian tanks were before us, too many to count at first. But I knew there were well over one hundred. *Father, help me,* I thought. Then we heard the call.

'Fire!'

The deafening sound of the tanks' erupting gunfire blanketed the air, and somewhere, the faint noise of our commander yelling orders. Oskar was next to me, firing away. Since the day I took that Russian soldier's life, I felt guilty enough to warrant not firing one shot, not even if it was into the trees. I couldn't bring myself to do it.

To the west were hills and trees scattered around large boulders. To the east was the end of a forest, and the start of farmlands, with broken wooden fences and stone walls around each of the fields. The Russians had come from the south-east. I stood up, about to walk off when I was pulled back by Oskar.

'Where are you going?' he demanded.

'I'm going to a better position,' I lied. Well, it was partly the truth. I was in fact going to a better position, but not to shoot down enemy soldiers.

'We've been given orders to stand our ground here. We have to maintain position.'

'Oskar, if the Russians sneak through those hills, we'll be outflanked.'

'I'll come with you,' he insisted.

'No Oskar, it's fine. Just stay here.'

Oskar put his large hands on my shoulders.

'I'm not letting you go on your own. I'm coming with you. I'll be your bodyguard, if you like.'

'All right, then,' I said with a slight chuckle, 'then let's go.'

We made our way to where the hills met flat ground. I braced myself for the hard bit of getting up the hill. I gripped my gun tight to my chest and took the first step upward. I moaned, the searing pain returning in my legs. Oskar turned and looked at me.

'Come on, Hans. Stop being such an old man.'

I rolled my eyes and gave him a look of disdain, followed by a small smile. 'Yes, sir!'

It was hard work, but eventually we made it to the top of the hill, and sat on a large, grey boulder under an oak tree. Everything seemed to transgress when I was walking up the hill. I stood atop it with a great feeling of satisfaction, my mood broken only by the gunfire sounding in the background.

Oskar lay on the ground with his gun at the ready. I sat on the boulder, overlooking the battle. Oskar was focused on the small figures moving on the ground, then turned momentarily to me, holding his gaze. He raised an eyebrow.

'What are you doing?' he asked.

'I'm sitting here,' I said sarcastically.

'Get down and help.'

'Help? With what? You know I can't shoot.'

'You can shoot, you just refuse to shoot people,' he said while looking down the barrel of his gun. 'Hurry up and get down here. If someone spots us, it's because you were careless enough to sit on a huge boulder, on top of an isolated hill. I'm not saying you have to shoot anyone; I just don't want you seen.'

'If anyone spots us, it's because you're shooting at them from a position where no other soldier is. So, when they realise there's gunfire coming from the hill, they'll turn to us, and kill us.' I admit I overreacted towards Oskar, but I was just as tired as he was.

I had always been an emotional person, so it was no secret that maybe, just maybe, he could tip me over the edge from time to time. And so was he. We both were, and I guess that's why we knew each other so well – how to annoy each other, and how to relate to one another.

'Okay,' he said. 'We'll do it your way, *captain.*'

I could tell by the derisive tone, he was no longer playing around. He was annoyed, and it made me even more frustrated to know that.

'Good,' I said, almost proudly.

We sat there quietly and watched the battlefield. Oskar was becoming agitated, I could tell. He would shuffle awkwardly, as though he was about to jump up and run down the hill, his gun firing at whatever moved.

'We should be down there, Hans!' he finally snapped. I knew it was coming.

'Well then go,' I said bluntly. 'I'm not stopping you.'

'What the hell is wrong with you, Hans?' His eyes were like daggers. 'There are men dying down there! *Our* men! People who fought to protect you!'

'Protect me from what? Our own destruction?' I stood up, my hands flailing, as I continued to yell at Oskar. 'There are other people down there that fight to protect people too, Oskar! And here's something, they wear a brown uniform and are on the other side of that battlefield!'

Oskar's face contorted in confusion and boiling enmity.

'On the other side? The *other* side? You know, you seem to be strangely guilty about killing someone who has no trouble in taking your life away! You're a coward, Hans! A fucking coward!'

I paused for a moment, then lowered my voice. 'I know.'

Oskar stood with his chest protruding, breathing heavily as he clenched his fists. His face had turned crimson. He pointed at me, but stood no closer. 'And sometimes, I hope you die knowing it.'

As strong as I thought I was in situations like this, I couldn't hold back the tears that began to well. Blinking profusely, I tried to stop but couldn't. I kicked the ground and held my hands on the back of my head. Oskar attempted to approach me, his hand outstretched, but I stood back. I sat down on the ground and looked up at him.

'I'm sorry, Hans. I shouldn't have said that. I didn't mean it.'

'Go and save them,' I said with antipathy.

'Hans...' he said, with an air of sincerity.

'Just go, Oskar!'

He sighed heavily and turned. Before he left, he turned his head halfway and said softly, 'I'm sorry. I love you, brother.'

Then he was gone.

I was now alone, atop a hill on the edge of a bloody battlefield. The wind picked up and the bitter cold made me shiver. I sat with my knees against my chest, arms wrapped around my legs, immobilised at the horror that stood below me. I reached into the inside pocket of my jacket and pulled out a piece of paper, crinkled and ripped. I unfolded and read it.

My dearest Johan,

You have no idea how much you mean to me. You are my world, as is your sister. You doubt yourself, but doubt only holds us back from our dreams. I do not know what your dreams may be, but all I wish is happiness for you. I love you more than all of the stars in the heavens, and more than anything in this world. You are a beautiful young boy, but more importantly, you are my beautiful young boy. You are destined for something great, and your father and I will stand by your side. We have never been more proud. I love you, with all my heart.

Happy Bar Mitzvah.

Love forever,
Mother

My hands began to shake. The ink smudged as tears dropped on the paper. I held it tight and looked up, pursing my lips, and shutting my eyes tight. I had kept this letter since my bar mitzvah, and every time I felt that giving up was easier than moving forward, I would read that letter. It was so easy to give up, believe me I know. To let everything go, and yourself along with it. The hardest thing was coming back from something and doing it with the love that you want to do it with.

Life offers twists and turns, and strength never comes from others – it comes from yourself. I suppose that's why my cowardice during war had never gone – because I let it stay. But my cowardice was that I couldn't kill someone, and that's never a bad thing – it just showed I'm as human as the next man.

Dear Father

Father,

Everything seems so hard without you. Sometimes, I would wake in the night, thinking your death was but a dream. But dreams can sometimes be beautiful, and this was reality. Having you gone is the hardest thing. I know I can never turn back time, but if I could, I would do it in an instant. I stood there and watched you die. I just stood there. I didn't flinch, I didn't move. I was a coward, and for that I am sorry. Father, I am so sorry. I should have run to you; I should have helped you.

Every night I look up, hoping you're one of the stars looking down on me. And every night, I say sorry to you, for leaving you. Mother always said I was just a boy, that you would never expect me to be humiliated or hurt for you, but I wasn't. I wasn't a boy. I was a young man.

I still remember when you would swing me around, holding onto your arms tightly and trusting you not to let go. How you would smile and say, 'We're going into the sky, hold on!' I would laugh, and I felt nothing could hurt me. You were my protector; you were my guardian. I knew that whenever I was with you, you would always make sure no harm would come to me, as would any father. But you were different.

The bullies that tormented me, you confronted. Instead of telling me, 'You've got to be tough, son,' you went to them. I don't know what you did, or what you said, but they never bothered me from that day on.

You did everything you could to teach me to be a man. But not just any man. A man that had the qualities of kindness, of compassion. You were my everything, and I idolised you. It took me too long to accept that you had gone. I cried each night, months after it all happened, hoping you would walk through the door and hug me once more. But you never did. And I slowly learned to accept that it was the young naivety I cherished, but knowing I had to let it go. You taught me how to do that.

I don't think I believe in God anymore; it's hard to, after everything that has happened. I'm struggling and I have no one. And sometimes I have trouble believing in heaven, but I'd like to think there was, for people with a beautiful soul like yours. Please Father, please help me. Whether you're in heaven, or in the stars, just tell me what I have to do. I have never felt so alone, and I have never felt so helpless. I let you down, but I hope you can forgive me. Somehow, I know you have. You're that type of man, and I love you for it.

I love you, Father. Always.

Love,
Johan

CHAPTER 6

September 28, 1941

I felt disorientated as I got up. I lay on the ground and cried for a long time after I read the letter from Mother. Even as the tears dried up, I still wept inside. I thought about what Oskar said, and I knew that sitting up here, feeling sorry for myself, wasn't going to make the problem go away. I stood up and walked down the hill, careful not to slip. Keeping out of sight of, not just the Russian soldiers, but my own fellow soldiers – so not to direct any negative speculation – I ran around our tanks with my head down.

I crouched behind a mound of dirt and rested my gun on the top. Oskar was far from where I was, and I didn't want him to see me, as though I was trying to make a degrading point to him. Instead, I took a deep breath and looked down the scope of my gun. I fired it. The force of the gun pushed back onto my shoulder, and I let out a painful grunt. *Come on*, I mumbled to myself in annoyance. I watched the Russian soldiers running for cover, springing up whilst shooting, then diving again behind the mounds of earth.

I had a clear view of the whole battlefield and, more than once, I witnessed soldiers meet Death; I had witnessed it that many times, I was sure he was waiting upon that hill, feasting with his eyes as he watched it play out. I shot, and I killed. I killed more than one. I felt sympathy, but my natural habits of freezing my muscle movement and an overwhelming sense of remorse were almost non-existent. Instead, I writhed slightly with discontent, and then kept firing.

I took a deep breath. I watched one Russian soldier advance over the open grass field, toward one of our own men with his back turned. I aimed and pulled the trigger. The bullet travelled across the field and launched itself into the soldier's left knee. He immediately fell, screaming in pain as he dropped his gun and clutched his knee. The soldier who had his back turned, was now approaching the screaming soldier, half crouched among the grass. When the German soldier raised his hand at the Russian soldier, I winced. My eyes were shut tight, and I turned my head. I then heard a voice next to me.

'What the hell are you doing?'

I looked to my left to see a middle-aged soldier, with a dark brown moustache and a prickled beard, staring at me. He widened his eyes, pushing for an answer.

'Wh-what do you mean?' I asked.

'Why are you turning your head like that? You should be looking straight at them, and firing that gun, not flinching. Pull the fucking trigger right between their eyes.'

'I know, I just got hit by my gun while firing,' I lied. 'I was in pain.'

'You'll be in more pain if those Russians cross that field, son.'

I stared at him, as I said menacingly, 'I am not your son.'

The man scoffed nervously. 'I didn't mean it like that.'

'Then don't say it,' I said, raising my eyebrows.

Stunned, the soldier turned and continued firing into the battlefield. I heard him swear under his breath, calling me names I would rather forget. I studied him up and down for a moment, then turned and resumed watching the events unfold in front of me. We had defeated many of the Russian tanks, but they had resisted somewhat and taken out seven of ours already.

The tanks continued to trade gunfire, offering enough sound to deafen a child in an instant. Our soldiers had begun to dig trenches along the north side, and that's when I knew we were going to be here longer than expected. We had begun building up our defences. The small contours on the land had offered minimal defence, but enough for a small attack from the Russians. Our soldiers were beginning to be outflanked, and we were feeling the defensive force of the Red Army.

'Adler!'

I turned behind to see Sergeant Shödler approach me. 'Sergeant Shödler, sir.'

'You are to go to the west side of our defences. Help to dig our trenches there. They need more men.' He then turned to the soldier next to me. 'Gefreiter Luden, you will go to the east side and help the soldiers there. Understood?'

'Yes, sir,' we said as one.

We both got to our feet, half crouched, and went in opposite directions. I ran to the west side, where soldiers were strenuously digging the trenches that faced southward. One soldier turned and looked at me, as I stood awkwardly watching them work hard without saying a single word.

'You.' He stood up and pointed to me. 'Drop your things and help here. We've been given enough covering fire to dig these trenches.'

I dropped my things and leant my gun against a mound. I jumped down, into the part of the trench that had already been dug and was given a pickaxe to hack at the earth. It was cold, but the work was enough to make me sweat within minutes of starting.

'Keep digging, men! We need to get our trenches dug and show these Russian soldiers who's going to win this!'

The yelling wasn't as inspiring as the soldier who did it thought it would be; rather it was an incessant rambling of who's the man with the most testosterone raging through his body or, enough to shoot bullets into those standing on the opposing side. I was able to ignore most of what was said, and instead focus on what I was meant to do.

Don't give up. Don't give in. Keep going. This is in your hands, and therefore you control it. If you give up, that's when cowardice becomes your haunting friend. When you persevere, you laugh in the face of cowardice, and embrace change. So, I say to you, don't give up.

I mumbled under my breath, keeping myself in control of what I was doing. It was hard work, and my small body, along with low energy levels, made for a mix of desperation and suspected failure. But I surprised myself as well as the other soldiers, as I dug deep, both literally and figuratively.

We had made progress along the north trench line. Our hard work was visible, and soldiers had begun to move into the trenches, out of sight of enemy gunfire. But our work was not the only thing that had progressed – the sun was beginning to set, creating a blanket of orange and pink over the sky, with dark grey clouds beginning to dominate the lower half.

A young soldier approached me, putting his hand on my shoulder. I quickly turned.

'We've been told to relieve you. You're to move north, behind the trenches for the night. Get some rest.'

I studied his face. 'We have to keep going. We can't stop now.' I motioned to an untouched area, where the trench was to extend. 'We've got too much to do.'

'You need to rest. Hans, is it?'

I nodded. 'Yes.'

He squeezed my shoulder. 'Get some rest, Hans. You need as much as you can get.'

'Okay, but make sure you finish the job.' I was adamant.

He chuckled. 'I will, don't you worry. And you make sure you get some rest. Got it?'

The thought of him laughing because someone of my stature bellowed an order, irritated me, but I suppressed the feeling and replied, 'Don't worry, I will.'

We nodded and turned in opposite directions. I made my way northward, to where a few of the other soldiers had dropped back and where our command post was. There were trenches already dug here, in case our soldiers had to unexpectedly drop back. Tents were set up for the soldiers, but no fire pits had been made; my guess was because they would easily give away our position during the night.

I was walking toward the tents to the east side when I was called by an unknown voice.

'Adler! Hans Adler!'

I turned to see a younger man, probably in his twenties, running toward me. He stood before me. He was extremely tall, over six feet, and his body bulged from his uniform. I stared at him for a moment, then replied, 'Yes?'

'You're wanted in the commander's tent.' I sighed and looked up momentarily. 'Is there a problem?' he asked.

'No,' I said quickly. 'Of course not. I'll go now.'

He nodded and walked behind me, all the way to the commander's tent. I felt uncomfortable. I could feel his constant presence near me but couldn't see him. I arrived at the tent, but before I entered, the younger soldier, who had followed me, brushed past and stopped me, his hand on my chest.

'Wait here,' he said firmly.

When he turned, I pulled an infantile expression. It was a moment of immaturity, but by the way he had spoken to me, and for someone as young as he, to which I wasn't accustomed, I had immediately taken a disliking to him. I knew I shouldn't immediately judge as soon as he opened his mouth; he was probably just attempting to act more like a soldier than before.

I made sure to smile at him when he poked his head out of the tent and signalled me in. It didn't go as expected; rather he just gave me a questionable look and then rolled his eyes.

I entered the tent, and before me was the commander sitting at a table facing directly toward the entrance, along with two other men. On his left sat a thin middle-aged man, with a long face that highlighted his protruding chin and sharp cheekbones. He had a long, curved nose, and his greasy brown hair was combed to one side. To his right was an elderly man, almost sickly-looking, who had a bleached white moustache down to his chin, and a large frame accompanied by a bulging stomach.

The commander looked at me. 'Adler. This is Colonel Hirsch.' He pointed to his left. 'And this is General Koertig.' He pointed to his right. I stood tall and saluted. 'I've asked you in here to give a report on the battlefield. You've worked hard. What did you see?'

'Me?' I began to stutter. 'What... what do you mean?'

'Adler, I'm not blind. I saw you and Bauer make your way up that hill. You're a smart and trustworthy soldier – an asset to us all. Now I'm asking you, what did you see?'

His voice was stern, something I hadn't experienced before. I supposed he was doing it for show to the others present, but nevertheless, it scared me enough to begin sweating while the temperature had dropped fast since the sun had set. I had never been called an asset before, which made me more anxious. Was it naivety, or hopeful vanity that I be called such a thing?

'The Russians have more tanks than we do, but only just. Their army was larger but guessing by the events I saw in the trenches, I would say their numbers have deteriorated, sir.' I took a deep breath and stared at them while I waited for a nod or any sign of life. None of them did. They kept waiting for me. 'I… I think that's it.'

'That's it?' General Koertig spoke up. 'You were on that hill for a lot longer than usual, and that's all you have to say? An asset to us, you say, Commander? Was that an attempt at humour, or genuine drivel dripping from your mouth? What exactly were you doing up there?'

Looking down at my feet, I closed my eyes and inhaled. I then exhaled slowly. *Breathe.*

'I went up there to…' I thought about what I was going to say. 'I went up there to get a clear view of the Russians' movements, but I was distracted.'

'Who ordered you up the hill?'

'I didn't have any orders, sir.' I knew I was treading dangerous ground and thought rapidly. 'It was too chaotic at the time.'

'What made you decide that a walk up a hill was a better tactic than firing on the enemy?'

Beads of sweat slowly dripped from my brow, but I suddenly became inspired.

'Sir, the enemy tactics in the other battles were to attack us on one side, while a flanking group used the distraction to come at us from another. When I looked round, I realised we couldn't see over the hill, which meant the enemy could be creeping up to catch us by surprise. There was no time, and no supervising officer nearby to tell, but I felt it was important to know whether the enemy were approaching over the hill or not.'

General Koertig nodded, seeming to be satisfied by this, allowing me to relax a fraction.

'I see,' he began. 'Appropriate thinking in what could have been a disastrous situation. But you said you were distracted – by what, exactly, Private Adler?' Colonel Hirsch had remained silent throughout the whole questioning process.

What was I supposed to say? I thought for a moment. 'Oskar Bauer.'

'Private Bauer? What did he do to *distract* you?' Colonel Hirsch finally spoke. His voice was deep, almost menacing. He stared at me with his head tilted slightly downward, and I could feel his eyes studying me. He knew if I was lying, he could tell.

'He wanted to come, so I agreed. But when we were up there, he wanted to shoot the enemy from the higher ground. I said no because it would give away our position.'

'And then what happened?'

'We began yelling at each other, and it didn't exactly end on the best terms. He walked off, back down to the other soldiers and fought. I stayed and studied the battlefield a little more before I went back down.'

Colonel Hirsch's eyebrows raised, and I could tell he knew I was lying. He sighed heavily and scowled at me.

'And why didn't you report what you had seen straight away?'

I attempted to swallow, but my mouth was dry.

'That was my intention, but I was immediately ordered to help dig the trenches.'

It was partly true, but had I not been ordered to help dig. The truth was that I was unlikely to report what I had seen on my own instinct, even in those circumstances.

'By whom?' queried General Koertig.

'Sergeant Shödler, sir,' I replied.

'*Christ*, that maniac,' said the commander. 'Of course, it had to be him. The man has been a pain in my side ever since he was assigned to this panzer army.'

'Are you sure it was him?' asked Colonel Hirsch.

'There's only one Sergeant Shödler around here, sir.'

'And the man is a fucking maniac,' hissed the commander. He cleared his throat and nodded at all that were present in the tent.

Colonel Hirsch raised an eyebrow. 'Very well, *Hans*.'

The hairs on the back of my neck seemed to stand on their

ends, as my face became flushed. I didn't know what to expect next.

'You are dismissed, Adler,' said the commander.

I saluted and turned. As I walked out of the tent, I could hear them discussing Sergeant Shödler. I exhaled, emptying my lungs. My heart was still beating too fast for comfort, but I dismissed it and made my way to the tents on the east side. I had partly lied in the questioning, and partly told the truth. Somehow, partly lying didn't seem too bad – it was plausible, and plausible stories make for safety. I was okay and content with that, for what it's worth.

CHAPTER 7

September 28, 1941

Sitting outside my tent, rain droplets ran down my face. It got heavier as time went on, and it showed no sign of stopping. The noise of the rain was overshadowed by the gunfire that had continued into the night. In the distance, the tanks had refused to cease gunfire, and our soldiers were lining the trenches, firing into darkness. The water felt refreshing on my skin as it washed down my face. I wondered where Felix and Earnst were, but not until now, had I even paid so much as a thought to Oskar. I hadn't seen him, and until he apologised, I didn't want to see him. I felt a lot of anger toward the scenario that had played out on the hill, and I couldn't suppress it once it had weaved into and dominated my thoughts.

He had the audacity to, not only call me a coward to my face, but to hope I'd die knowing it. Granted, I am a coward, and *I* know it, but never would I have thought that death would be hoped upon anyone. He was, I thought, my best friend. I was no expert, but I do think that wishing death on your best friend immediately determines that friendship as null and void. Nevertheless, I *wanted* to forgive him, but whether he proved it to be the right decision, only time would tell.

Thunder rumbled, but it almost blended in with the tanks firing. The only reason I knew it was thunder was by the lightning toward the north. As the lightning struck, it lit up the entire battlefield, and I was able to witness the entire fight in an instant. It felt surreal, and I had thought about dismissing it as a dream. But reality is dark, and dreams help to suppress reality as a more beautiful alternative. Reality is the true nightmare.

It was cold, but no fires could be lit for the obvious reason of visibility for the enemy. In an attempt to escape the cold, I went into my tent and lay for a moment. I was soaking, and the uncomfortable feeling of having to lie while the weight of a heavy woollen coat, soaked in the rain, pressing down on my body, was not what I wanted. A few hours of sleep is all I wanted, and to forget about the events of the day – although it was difficult with the constant gunfire. I took off the heavy woollen coat and stripped down to my underwear. The blankets we were all given were thin, and far too thin for the crisp frost of Russian territory. But it was all I had, so I wrapped myself in the blanket like a cocoon and hoped my body warmth was enough to keep me comfortable for the night. That was, until Felix and Earnst burst into my tent with adrenaline coursing through their veins, as they jumped on me and ruffled my blanket.

'Hans, what are you doing asleep?' asked Felix.

'Yeah Hans, what are you doing?' accompanied Earnst.

Earnst grabbed me by the waist and dug his hands in. I wriggled, trying not to laugh. But it was no use, and soon they were both wrestling me to find my weak spot, while I howled in laughter. After we had all calmed down, I sat up.

'What are you guys doing here?' I asked with anticipation.

Earnst shrugged his shoulders. 'Because we can,' he replied. 'We can't have you all alone now, can we? Who knows what you would get up to, you crazy bastard.'

I laughed. 'Is that right?'

'It is,' said Felix. 'We saw you looking down, earlier on. You just sat in the rain, like someone waiting for the love of your life. Oh wait, is she here?' He looked around playfully, then chuckled. 'But seriously, Hans, what's wrong?'

'Nothing. I'm fine. I'm just tired.' A pure lie.

'We know when you're lying, Hans,' said Earnst. 'That's bullshit, and we know it. Come on, you can tell us. It's not like we're going to shoot you between the eyes.'

Felix gave Earnst a conscientious stare, then gently punched him in the arm.

'Hans, you can tell us. We're your friends. What's wrong?' We looked at each other, then he tilted his head and added, 'Please?'

'Oskar and I fought.'

'What's new?' said Felix.

'This time it was bad. Really bad. We started yelling at each other and,' I rubbed my eyes, then slid my hands down my face, 'and then it ended badly. He said some things that cut me, and I guess I wasn't the nicest either. But he wished that I would die. Who does that?'

'I'm sure he doesn't mean it, Hans,' said Earnst comfortingly. 'He's under a lot of stress.'

'*He's* under a lot of stress? Earnst, we're in the middle of a war! I'd consider someone a god if they weren't going through stress at this point in the war. We all have our own problems, so don't tell me he has more stress because he is somehow immune to empathy or sympathy when killing someone.' I had run out of breath.

There was silence from both Earnst and Felix, and I felt guilty for raising my voice at them, especially when they were comforting me in my time of need. I took a deep breath.

'Sorry. I didn't mean to get angry. Especially since you guys came to cheer me up.'

'Don't worry about it, Hans,' said Felix. 'You know what we would do if we were back home? We'd take you out for a drink, and then go exploring in the woods. All the fun stuff, that we *would* be doing, if we weren't stuck here... in the freezing cold.'

'It is pretty cold,' I agreed. 'I wish we could light a fire.'

'You're almost naked. Of course, you're going to be cold. Where's your jacket?'

'It got soaked from the rain.'

Felix flung his head back. 'Of course. Because we all enjoy just sitting creepily in the rain.'

'It's one of my favourite pastimes,' I said sarcastically, while screwing up my nose.

'Wait here, we'll go and get our stuff,' said Earnst.

'Get your stuff? For what?'

'We're moving in!'

Before I could say anything, they had both left the tent and scrambled to theirs. I lay back down and put my hands behind my head, smiling. Sometimes all you need is true friends, and even though they once gave me a hard time, we were now all fond of each other and enjoyed the company. They were crazy, but sometimes life needed a little crazy, with good friends thrown in – the recipe for true happiness.

Dear Mother

Mother,

I hope you're not angry. I know that running away was not the best choice, leaving you and Edith alone. But more so, I hope you're not angry that I made the decision to join the army. I changed my name, but it isn't me. Sometimes, I still don't answer to the name 'Hans' when it's called, specifically to me; I just hope I don't forget the name you gave me.

I know it must have been hard to tell me as a boy what was happening to us, but that night I asked you, I wasn't a boy. You said that to comfort me about Father, but I know I wasn't. I was a young man, and it pained me to see you silent, looking through the window into darkness. It was the stillness. You just kept looking, and somehow, I knew you were aware something bad was coming. I just wasn't expecting this.

You taught me that heritage is everything. And it is. But the thing is, I can't tell anyone about it. I can't be proud of it in public. My new best friend, Oskar, doesn't even know – and I can't tell him, I know it. Felix and Earnst were, at first, hard to get along with. But now they've grown on me, and we have become close – but it's the same. I can't tell them, for fear of what will happen.

I don't know where you are, but I hold hope every day. To be honest, hope is a hard thing to have, and it's even harder to keep. You always told me that life is precious, and that has kept with me since. That's the thing, life is precious, and I can't take that away from anyone – not one person. I still feel guilt from that man I killed. I didn't mean to, I just flinched. But it hasn't left me, and it's a burden I've carried since. What have I done? This is the time I need your wisdom, and this is the time I just want to sit on your lap and hug you tightly.

I know you would forgive me for the things that I have done. But I also know you would be disappointed – you didn't raise me like this. And I don't want to have to ask for your forgiveness, knowing the mistakes I have made are for my own vanity.

I will get you out, I promise. And when I do, we will all live together again. You, Edith and me, together. I'll look after you, and Edith too. And I will never let anything bad happen to you again. Ever.

I love you, always and forever.

With love,
Johan

CHAPTER 8

September 29, 1941

Felix and Earnst refused to stop talking, but somehow, even though I incessantly asked them to stop, I secretly hoped they would keep going. Their ridiculous banter was comforting, strange as that may be. It made me feel comfortable for the first time. They talked about everything from what home was to them, to girls, to the war. And every time the topic changed, they would always turn to me and nudge me gently, making sure I was awake, and ask what my opinion was of it all.

It was the early hours of the morning though, and we became tired very quickly. Throughout the night, I would wake to Felix sleep talking, and Earnst would mumble some strange tongue.

'Don't make me, please,' said Felix at one point. 'I want cheesecake.'

I chuckled to myself, listening to the strange sentences he produced in his sleep. Then, soon after, I would fall asleep. The cycle continued every few hours, and before long the morning light shone though the tent and lit up. As soon as dawn broke, the tent seemed too bright to see in. Our eyes had trouble adjusting to the brightness, but after squinting for almost half an hour, we managed.

'Time for war again,' said Earnst.

'Do you think they'll let us stay here for the day?' I asked facetiously.

'And have the Russians jump on us?' said Felix.

'They could stay in bed too. There's no harm in sleep.' I ran my finger down the side of the tent. 'There's no harm in peace.'

'So profound, Hans,' said Felix in jest. 'You should be a philosopher.'

'Would be better than this,' I stated bluntly.

We dressed and exited the tent. Our bones cracked as we stretched widely and then made for where the food was. Breakfast was nothing fancy. We had dry crackers with a variety of tinned muck stuck on top. It never filled our stomachs, but I supposed it was better than nothing.

Once we had forced the tasteless, dry food into our stomachs, we headed for the trenches. The men who had fought all night were exhausted, and some that were sleeping had been pulled from their tents to assist. Their eyes were reddened, dark rings beginning to form under their eyes. They were a mess. Immediately, they sighed with relief as they were dismissed for rest, and we took over. I wondered what the Russian soldiers were like at this hour, if they were just as tired as we were, if not more. Looking down the barrel of the gun, I could make out figures on the other side, but they were too far to make out any facial recognition.

Felix and Earnst were focused solely on firing, their eyes fixated strongly on the opposing side. I could have offered them a mansion on thousands of acres of land, and they would still dismiss any word of it. I looked at the hill that I sat on the day before and contorted my face in thought. I wanted to go back up there, but the commander would know of it. Instead, I looked forward and fired into the distance.

As if by some miracle, Sergeant Shödler approached me and pulled me aside.

'I didn't want to disturb you,' he said flatly. 'You seemed purely fixated on shooting down the enemy, which is always a good sign, but this is important.'

I laughed inside at the sentiment, knowing that I was able to act well enough to seem as though I wanted them dead. I gave Sergeant Shödler an anxious look.

'What is it, Sergeant?'

'The commander wants to see you. Urgently.'

I sighed. 'What is it now? I just spoke with him last night.'

Sergeant Shödler raised an eyebrow. 'Is there a problem, Adler?'

I widened my eyes, realising what I had said, and shook my head ardently. 'No, of course not.'

'You're right – there isn't. So, move. *Now.*'

As Sergeant Shödler and I walked to the commander's tent, his hoarse voice erupted in the silence.

'Do you think I'm a fool, Adler?'

Taken aback, I stumbled over my words. 'What, Sergeant?'

'You heard me. You think because the commander spoke to me in a disorderly fashion that he's now on your side, instead of mine?'

'What side? I don't know–'

'Save the bullshit for someone who is stupid enough to believe it. You and I both know how the commander feels towards me. But let me tell you this...' Sergeant Shödler's eyes moved across the landscape before us, watching the soldiers scrambling from tent to tent, guns in their hands and ready to dance with death one more day. 'I've killed more men than he ever has, and ever will. I've made them suffer. I've made them plea for me to kill them. I've done things you couldn't imagine. Don't think I won't crush you, because I will if I wish. And then I'll bury you.'

'Have I done something to offend you, Sergeant Shödler?' I asked coarsely.

He scoffed and glared at me. 'More than you could imagine.'

As we came to the commander's tent, we were stopped by the same young man as the night before.

'Oh good,' I said sarcastically. 'I missed you.'

He scowled at me. 'What is your problem, Adler?'

'I smiled at you last night, and you didn't return the courtesy.'

'*That's* your problem? Unbelievable. You are a piece of work.'

'Oh, I'm sorry. Let's start again. Hi, I'm Hans Adler. I don't want to be here.'

'Well tough, because you are. Stand up straight.' He patted me on the back of my shoulders. 'And lose the attitude. The commander didn't get a good rest last night, so he isn't in the best mood. If you step out of line, he'll rip your fucking head off.'

I swallowed the lump that was forming in my throat and walked into the tent. Like the previous night, the commander sat with Colonel Hirsch and General Koertig on either side. One would think he was incompetent at his job if he was constantly accompanied by other officers; not that I would dare say anything about it to his face.

'Private Adler,' said the commander. 'Welcome back. Sergeant Shödler told me that you were fully concentrated on the battlefield.'

I nodded in compliance, not wanting to cause anything unwanted. 'Yes, sir.'

'Good. But we have another job for you. Something that you're familiar with, I believe. You remember our little talk last night? You seem to know how to track enemy movements from atop the hill, or at least you think you can. But at this stage we're outnumbered, and if we don't do anything, we're going to be thrown in a ditch somewhere and left to rot.'

'You want me to go back up the hill?'

'That *is* what he just said, Private Adler,' hissed Colonel Hirsch, sardonically.

'Yes. And we want you to track enemy movements from above,' continued the commander. 'Obviously without being spotted. We'll send you up with someone, and then they will relay the messages to us. This is a big task, Adler. You don't tell anyone what you're doing. For this task, you don't trust anyone, except for the soldier you relay the information to. And if you feel at any point that the soldier we have chosen is not trustworthy, you will withdraw immediately. Understood?'

Nodding, I took a step backward. 'Yes, sir.'

As I was about to exit the tent, I heard General Koertig's voice.

'And Private Adler...' I turned and looked at him. 'If you make a run for it, I will hunt you down myself.'

The commander raised his eyebrows and let out a heavy breath, while looking the other way and moving awkwardly in his seat.

'Yes, sir,' I complied.

I exited the tent and followed Sergeant Shödler. He was talking to me, but above all the noise going on, I only heard mumbling.

'Sorry, sir, what was that?'

'Jesus, Adler, listen, you idiot. I'm taking you to the soldier who will be relaying your messages. He's younger than you, but trustworthy. He is a peculiar boy, very... strange. He doesn't speak much, so why they chose him for this task is beyond me. But the General isn't the smartest of men.' He quickly turned to me. 'Don't repeat that, or I'll cut out your tongue quite easily. I've done it before, and I'll do it again.'

'Your secret is safe with me, Sergeant,' I said, tittering.

'And Colonel Hirsch – the man looks like he got hit by a train... several times. Don't repeat that either.'

I thought he was joking, but his face was always serious, and when he said it, it didn't change, nor did his voice. He looked at me curiously, then continued his gaze forward.

'I'll refrain from saying anything about the commander. I can't trust you, you conniving little rat.'

'Thank you, Sergeant.'

I felt Sergeant Shödler's eyes almost cutting into my skin, trying to get into my mind, but I ignored him, and we continued walking in silence. We kept walking until we finally came to the base of the hill, where the boy was waiting. At first, I thought he was twelve. He was small, thin and never made eye contact. But when he was addressed by Sergeant Shödler, he straightened his stance and saluted. He then looked at me, up and down, and shook my hand. For a twelve-year-old, he was sophisticated – that was *if* he was twelve.

'Private Adler, this is Private Dietrich Gärtner. He's going to be your envoy, so to speak. Anything that is important, you tell him. Straight away, no delays.'

'What constitutes as important?'

'Maybe if a soldier has a gun to your head. Private Adler, I am not going to lecture you on what is important and what isn't. Use your initiative. Why do you think the commander, general and colonel chose you?'

'Is that a compliment, Sergeant?'

'Don't push it. Just do the fucking job. Understood?'

'I'll do my best,' I replied.

'You'll do *the* best, Adler. No worse. This is all on you.' His words sent shivers through my body. *No pressure*, I thought.

Dietrich and I clambered to the top of the hill and sat on the large boulder near the tree.

'So,' I began, 'how old are you? Just out of curiosity.'

'I'm seventeen,' he replied quietly.

'Seventeen? Are you joking? You're small for someone that age. I thought you were twelve.' I saw him getting uncomfortable and realised I may have been coming across rather brash. 'No offence. Sorry.'

'It's fine. I'm used to it.'

'Used to it in a bad way?' He shrugged. 'I know what that's like. Well not that, specifically. But to be victimised. When I was younger, there were these boys, and they would call me names, push me, beat me when I walked home. I was always afraid from that point on. It was as though, no matter what I did, they were somehow still there haunting me.'

He looked at me intently. 'My father used to beat me.'

Shocking as it was to me, I didn't move or show any signs of it.

'I'm sorry to hear that. You know something? I can't even bring myself to kill someone without feeling guilt; like I'm one of the bullies.'

'That's not your fault. You're just human, and a nicer one than any of them.' He moved his head in the direction of our trench lines.

I laughed humbly. 'Thanks, but you have no idea. I'm just like anyone else. We all have a dark side. Some just let it control them more than their better self.' We sat in uncomfortable silence for a few seconds before I coughed and began muttering indistinctly.

'But anyway, we should start watching the movements down there.'

Dietrich complied and sat under the tree, almost camouflaged into the bark, whilst I lay in the tall grass and watched through the binoculars at the movements on the ground. Almost an hour had passed before I spotted anything worth sending Dietrich for. Russian soldiers were moving west, toward us. They were mobilising to go around the battlefield and attack our forces from behind. I told Dietrich what was about to happen, and finished with, 'You have to hurry and tell them. Now!'

Dietrich nodded and sprinted down the hill, avoiding being seen by anyone. Waiting anxiously, I curled up and held my knees to my chest and squeezed tight. My head rested on its side on my knees, and I continuously mumbled, *Hurry up. Hurry up. Hurry up.*

I lifted my head and looked downward. They were moving slowly but would be behind our trenches within a few hours at the most. It took Dietrich almost ten minutes to run down to command, and another ten to reach the top of the hill again.

'Jesus, Dietrich, where have you been?'

'It isn't easy running up and down a steep hill, while trying not to be seen. The commander,' he puffed, 'has ordered troops to move through the hills, at ground level, and wipe out the soldiers before they reach our territory.'

'And what do we do, then?' I asked anxiously.

He held out a Karabiner 98k. I stammered as I realised the expectations on me.

'Dietrich, I'm not a sniper. I haven't been trained to use one of these! What am I supposed to do?'

'Just use it like a normal gun.'

'Then why not give me a normal gun? Why this?'

'The commander said higher ground means a prime spot for a sniper.'

My breathing fastened. 'Then send a fucking sniper!'

'Hans!' snapped Dietrich. 'Take the gun. We've been given orders.'

While staring at Dietrich, I slowly reached for the gun. My hands trembled. I looked at Dietrich, shocked that he would raise his voice at me, but understanding all the same, especially after my reaction.

'And what are you going to do?' I asked.

'The same as you.' Dietrich walked over to the edge of the hill and sat down, vanishing in the tall grass that surrounded him.

I walked over and looked around. After a long hard look, and squinting my eyes in frustration, I saw his grey coat, and then the rest of his body. He was lying still, no movement, poised with his gun aimed downward and looking through his scope. He followed the movements of the soldiers below us. Deciding it was no good to continue standing in broad daylight above a secluded hill, while enemy soldiers moved around me, I decided to lay next to Dietrich and ready my gun.

'Are you going to kill them?' Dietrich asked.

I thought for a moment, then replied, 'No. Probably not.'

'Well one of us has to. Otherwise, they will know we weren't doing our job.'

'Are you volunteering then?'

Dietrich shrugged his shoulders. 'I suppose so.'

Another hour had passed, and Dietrich was a much better sniper than I initially gave him credit for. He was good with a gun. He studied the wind, its direction and speed, and within an instant he would pull the trigger. He only ever needed one shot. He never seemed to miss. I lay next to him, watching his killing skills. Although I felt uncomfortable with the whole scenario, somehow, I didn't mind this – it seemed like an art.

Through my scope, I watched our soldiers move around the hill, about to come face to face with Russian soldiers. There were seventy of our men, and after Dietrich's shooting skills, the Russians only had fifty. Oskar was one of the soldiers sent to the base of the hill. The soldiers were about to meet the Russian soldiers, but the Russians were prepared. They were setting up tripwires that were connected to explosives. My heart raced. *They're walking into a trap*, I thought. I rummaged through my knapsack, trying to find anything that would be useful to send a signal. I found an old tin can and grabbed it.

I moved to the edge of the hill and angled it toward the sun. Moving it around, I tried desperately to flash it at our soldiers. Finally, one soldier looked up and signalled the others, pointing at the tin can. Our soldiers stopped and looked. One soldier began to climb on the rocks to get to the top of the hill. He slipped a few times, landing on his knees and cursing in pain. He didn't yell, knowing that anyone could be waiting right around the corner. Instead, he pounded the rock with his fist, cursed, muttered, and continued moving. Eventually, he had reached the top of the hill and clambered to get his foot in a better position. As he did this, he slipped, his arms flailing and his body leaning backward. Quickly, I grabbed his arms and held on for dear life. Grunting as my teeth clenched together, I held on tightly as the soldier dangled from below.

'Don't you drop me!' he screamed.

'I won't!' I snapped.

'You better not, or I'll have your guts!'

'Well, if you didn't weigh as much, I would have more luck!' I put my entire strength into pulling the soldier up, but I felt as though I would soon fall with him. Dietrich raced over and grabbed me by the waist, pulling me further from the edge.

'Quickly, Dietrich, I can feel him slipping,' I said.

The soldier's palms were excreting sweat as fear overcame him. He held on tight, and his eyes glared at me, as if to transfer his thoughts into mine that today was not the day he wanted to die. I wasn't going to let him die. Dietrich and I pulled the soldier onto solid ground, and he clambered to be there. He lay on the ground, face down, and panted loudly. Dietrich and I sat with our arms resting on the ground behind our backs, holding up our bodies. The soldier sat up and looked at us.

'Now, what the hell do you want, after all that? Why were you flashing the light at us?'

'There's a trap,' I exclaimed. 'Down there.' I got up and pointed down. 'There are tripwires connected to explosives. If you keep going, you'll set them off.'

The soldier scowled at me. 'Why should I believe you?'

I gave the soldier a questionable look.

'Are we really having this argument now? When there are men down there whose lives are in danger!'

'All right, all right. Where are the tripwires?'

'I don't know, which is why you have to get out of there now. They could be anywhere.'

Letting out a heavy sigh, the soldier nodded. 'Very well. I'll tell the captain that we need to withdraw.'

'Good,' I said while nodding. 'Good.' I turned to Dietrich. 'Well, that was surprisingly easy.'

Sweat dripped from my face, even though it was not a hot day. The adrenaline was still running through my body from it all, and I collapsed onto the ground, placing my hands over my eyes and concentrated on controlling my breathing.

Concentration Camp

Interesting indeed it is, what you find when you observe. What you see amongst what seems to be normality. Normality is the illusion created for those with power to feel that they have it – but they do not. Little do they know what is plotted behind their backs, what scheming devilish people wish them harm. But not here, surprisingly. Here, they work together to save one another.

I watched for days as a young officer, Herr Shöban, would sneak bread into the compound and give it to the labourers. Once, every week, he would go out of the compound and meet with someone on the outside. The person he met would hide in the shadows, never to be seen. Only the officer would see them. Man or woman, no one knows. But kind – yes.

Sneaking ever so quietly, he would enter the barracks where the labouring men slept. He would not announce his arrival, but rather place a delicate hand on their shoulder, and shake gently. They did not seem to mind being woken by him, for they knew what he would bring. Regaling them with stories of make-believe, their reality had seemed to disappear in an instant. Passionately, he would tell a tale, and the men, once tired and hungry, now had full bellies and cheer. They were quiet, but laughter would erupt during the officer's tales.

I admire him. I do indeed. But he hides this from other officers. When ordered to beat a labourer, he will. When ordered to humiliate a labourer, he will. He shows himself to be a man of no mercy or compassion when in front of his fellow soldiers. Only in the shadows, behind closed doors, is he this man of sympathy. He will go home to his wife and his children and love them. He will refuse to talk about his work, just as any officer does. But he refuses even to talk about what he does. Is he humble, or guilty?

It is only a matter of time before he is caught. This is not a place of kindness – there is no place for mercy or cheer. Here, the men are hardened – both prisoner and soldier. I drain whatever hint of happiness struggled to survive, and let it disappear into nothing. He may get caught, or he may not. But one thing is for certain – he will wither away with the rest of them and there will be no hope left.

CHAPTER 9

September 29, 1941

I lay on the ground for a few minutes, along with Dietrich, who sat next to me. Murmuring to myself about what might happen, Dietrich sat in complete silence. Then we heard it. An explosion that shook even the hill. Smoke began to rise, and patches of fires had started. Dietrich and I both stood immediately and moved toward the edge of the hill.

'Shit,' said Dietrich. 'The tripwires.'

'Come on, we have to help them,' I said. Before I could get my gun, I was pulled back by Dietrich.

'No,' he said firmly. 'We were given orders to stay up here. That's what we're going to do.'

'We can't just stay up here! They need our help!'

'We were given orders, Hans!'

'I don't care about our orders! Trust me, Dietrich, if you step in front of me to stop me, so help me, I *will* knock you down. Move out of my way.'

'Hans, we're staying up here, whether you like it or not.'

'What are you going to do? Knock me out? Go on, do it.' I flared with anger and Dietrich's face reddened with rage. 'Do it!' I screamed. Dietrich just stood there. 'That's what I thought.' I walked past him, deliberately knocking him from his feet.

I clambered down the hill to the base and looked around. There was too much smoke to see everything, but I could make out bodies sprawled along the grass, patches of blood and a few soldiers still alive and shooting. The smoke caused me to cough violently. My breathing became heavy and my chest ached as I sucked in the smoky air.

I crouched, walking awkwardly as I approached the dead bodies, trying to identify any of them. A few bodies were unknown to me, but a few I had known vaguely through the last few days. I continued walking, until I came across a body that had been severed from head to toe, lying in a pool of blood. The smoke impaired my vision, so as I leaned closer, the shock of the hideously deformed body hit me. I flung my head back and covered my nose with the neck of my coat. The potent stench overwhelmed even the smell of the heavy smoke that hung in the air.

I stood and examined the body. As my eyes focused on it, I had lost all concentration on the events around me, only to be brought back to reality by a bullet that had sped past my face. I dropped instantly to the ground and covered my head with my arms.

I heard yelling in a language that I couldn't understand and knew that Russian soldiers were nearby. I kept still, lying on the ground, hoping they would think I was dead. I looked around and couldn't see anyone. I looked toward the dead body next to me and thought for a moment. I sighed in contempt and shuffled towards it. I put my head back toward the sky, and mumbled, *I'm sorry*. Looking back down, I placed my hand in the pool of blood around the soldier and swirled it around. It was still warm. My face contorted as the blood ran through my fingers. I lathered it onto my face and grabbed a lump of dirt which I placed at my right temple, shaping it to look like a wound. Once I looked like I was now walking with Death, I moved a few feet back from the corpse and lay on my stomach on the soft dirt.

After a few seconds, I saw through the small gap between my eyelids the boots of soldiers, inspecting the bodies and then moving on. I could sense someone near me, but didn't dare to open my eyes, knowing they might be fixated on me. I could hear their deep voices, speaking for what seemed like forever. Then, finally, they moved on.

I waited for another few minutes before moving any muscle, then sprung up in an instant, causing my body to become giddy as I stumbled to find flat footing. The blood was drying on my face and harder to get off, with dirt stuck to it. I felt like Death itself.

As I regained my composure, I continued walking through the thick smoke, seemingly worse than what it was before. My eyes were watering, my lungs in pain and my chest was heavy.

I had walked many steps. Too many. My feet felt as though they were going to crumble at any point, and I knew I was losing control over my legs as they dragged along the ground. Walking slowly, I still managed to step into an opening in the ground that some soldiers, unknown to me, had begun digging. My footing loosened under the crumbling dirt, and I fell straight into the ditch. My head hit violently on the ground, and I grunted as my entire body collapsed onto the dirt. My back hurt from the fall, but I managed to push myself up and climb out of it. I walked aimlessly around the hazy battleground, only a small portion of where the entire battle was being fought, trying to find any sign of life.

That's when I saw it. Something I wish I hadn't seen. Something I wish I could turn back time on. It was Oskar. Lying flat on his back – lifeless. Blood that once ran warm had travelled from his mouth, down his cheek and onto the ground – now dry against his pale, ghostly skin. His eyes were colourless, staring into nothingness. I ran toward him, hoping that somehow, by some miracle, it wasn't him, or that he was alive. I knelt down next to his body and frantically shook his shoulders, tapping his face – he gave no sign of life.

'Oskar!' I cried. 'Oskar! Wake up! Oskar!'

I cried, pleading for him to come back. It wasn't fair. It wasn't fair to end like this – we were both angry. Now it seemed he would be angry with me forever.

'Please, Oskar. Please, forgive me,' I whispered huskily, tears dripping from my cheeks and onto his lifeless face. I rested my head on his chest. 'This isn't fair, Oskar. It isn't fair. I just want you to come back. Please come back. I'm sorry. *Please*.'

I continued crying, not caring about what was going on around me. As far as I was concerned, mourning was more important than fighting – it was a better healing process, anyway. I lay on the ground, my head still resting on his chest, and my arms wrapped around him.

'It's not fair, Oskar. I just want you to be here. Please.'

As I cried, I was heard by the Russian soldiers who had passed me before. They approached me and spoke in Russian. I didn't know what they were saying, but they argued for a while. I looked up at the soldiers, afraid, thinking they would put a gun to my head and pull the trigger. As I breathed faster, my chest heaved up and down violently, contemplating what to do. *There's no going back*, I thought. So, I did it – I leaped up and ran. I could hear the soldiers behind me yelling, and their voices were getting louder – they were getting closer. I looked behind momentarily, and saw a large, muscular man gaining ground on me. I looked forward and kept running through the thickness of the smoke, hoping that at some point I would stumble into our encampment and be saved by my fellow soldiers. But I didn't. The dead bodies proved to be a challenge to manoeuvre around, and the difficulty only increased as the number of bodies sprawled over the ground also increased. I continued running, until I tripped over an unexpected corpse which was hidden from view by the tall grass that surrounded it. I put my hands in front of my body, so my head wouldn't hit the ground, and quickly bounced off. I had got as far as two steps before I was tackled to the ground by the large soldier, who took no sympathy on my size. We went down with such force that a sharp pain shot through my spine as we made contact with the ground.

As we collided to the ground, my head was hit by the soldier's elbow. It spun, and I struggled to keep my eyes open, but was hauled up by the soldier. He grabbed my arms and held them behind my back, until the other soldiers caught up and handed him rope to tie them with. Then, with one swift knock to the head, I was unconscious.

I awoke with a splitting headache, and my back still ached from the fall. I blinked a few times to clear my eyesight and looked around. I was alone in a tent, my hands still tied behind my back, and an oil lamp, that illuminated the entire area, covered by a white cloth. The rest of the tent was empty.

'Where am I?' I yelled. 'Hello?'

I waited for any answer, but there was none. Then, the entrance to the tent flung open, and a tall brute stepped in. He crouched in front of me and shook his head.

'Who are you?' I asked. 'You're not the same man who took me.'

The man looked at me and smiled threateningly. Hideous facial features stuck out of his smooth skin, including a scar that travelled from the top of his left brow down to his lower lip, and the top of his left ear was missing. *Christ*, I thought. *This man is hideous – scary beyond anything. Shit.* Finally, the man leaned away from me and tilted his head.

'You are German soldier, no?' he asked in a heavy Russian accent. His German, however, was rather eloquent – better than I expected.

I looked down at my uniform. Wasn't it obvious? 'Yes,' I replied, not wanting to provoke any unnecessary actions.

The man scoffed. 'You are scum. You kill my men.'

'Your men killed us, too,' I said, defending what little integrity any of us actually had – which, at the moment, seemed slim.

'My men defend their country!' He leaned forward, only inches away from my face. 'A country *your* men invade! You think I owe an apology for this?' He moved his hand in a circle, signalling keeping me captive in the tent. 'You owe *me* an apology!'

'I don't owe you anything,' I said. 'I haven't got a choice. I don't want to be here.'

'Not for glory?' he asked condescendingly.

'Not for anything,' I began. 'I don't want to kill anyone; I don't want to hurt anyone. I hate all of this. I *hate* it.'

'But you still kill *my* men!'

'There was one, just a few days ago. It was an accident. He was coming towards me and–'

'Accident? An *accident*? How can it be an accident, kraut?'

'He leapt for me, and I flinched while holding out a knife. I just wanted to stop him from falling on me.'

The soldier let out a wispy laugh, throwing his head back.

'An accident, sure! An accident! Then I might, accidentally, cut your tongue out. No one – listen to me – *no one* kills someone else in a war and calls it an accident. You kill someone, you pay for it!'

'Will you pay for all the men you killed, then?' I snarled.

'You Germans come into *my* territory and kill *my* men. You invade *my* country and kill innocent civilians. I have already paid my debt, and more. So, listen here…' He gritted his teeth. 'We will beat your comrades in this battle, and send you either running back to Germany, or, if we get the chance, to the pits of hell.'

'Are you going to kill me?'

'Perhaps. I suppose it will depend on whether or not you tell the truth.'

'The truth of what?' I asked with a suspicious look.

'Of what I'm going to ask you, boy. I will ask you questions, and you will answer truthfully. And if you lie, I will cut off your fingers, one by one, and finally your tongue. Do you understand, or do I need to show you how serious I am?'

'No! No, I understand.'

He smiled wryly. 'Good. Then get up.'

He grabbed me from under my arm and pulled me up. Holding a tight grip, he pulled me out of the tent and into another. The sun was still out but had progressed along the sky until it was almost late noon. Soon it would darken, and I had no idea if I was ever going to get out alive.

We entered the other tent, which had a wooden table and two wooden chairs. Before we sat, the soldier brought out a knife, and I watched on, wide-eyed, as he brought it toward me. I dropped my head down and closed my eyes tightly. I sensed the soldier close to me and felt a tugging coming from my arms. Then, within moments, they were free. My hands loosened, and the rope fell to the ground. The soldier gave me a shove in the back.

'Sit,' he said.

I sat on the chair that faced the entrance, so I couldn't possibly escape without the soldiers looming over me and giving me a black eye. The soldier sat opposite. I rested my hands on the table, clasped together tightly.

'Relax,' said the soldier.

I raised an eyebrow at him. 'Relax?'

'It will make the process much easier; I promise.' He looked cynical, almost maniacal, along with his tone, and I squinted at him for a moment. I clenched my fists and gritted my teeth, horrified at what may happen next. My feet shuffled awkwardly in the dirt.

'Very well. Have it your way.'

'I will,' I said. I shut my eyes, worried that my tongue may be lost far sooner than I had anticipated. *Shut it!* I thought.

'Good. Just know that it will not do you any good, if it comes time to lose a finger.'

'I'll tell you anything. Please, just let me go.'

'That is what I like to hear. Now, question one: where are you and your comrades travelling to?'

'South,' I replied.

'Being vague will not do you any favours. I want specifics, kraut. *Where*, specifically?'

'Moscow. We were going to Moscow.'

I wasn't absolutely sure what the soldier had said next, but judging by context and violent reaction, I assumed he was cursing in his native tongue.

'You want to attack the heart of my country?' he snapped. 'The heartland?'

'I don't know, I just know that we were given orders to go south to Moscow!' I flinched as the soldier's arms flailed in the air.

'You will never get past. I swear it, kraut. I swear it!' He took a deep breath and resumed the questioning. 'Question two: why have you come from the north?'

'We were going to Leningrad, but we were told to go south to Moscow.'

'You Germans are not making any friends here. First Leningrad, then Moscow! The Russian winters are tough and are only made for the Russian people. It will destroy you,' he sneered.

'I don't doubt you,' I said. 'It's only September and I freeze almost every night.'

The soldier laughed.

'It gets worse. Never go out at night in a Russian winter – you will either get eaten to death by wild animals or taken by the cold.' He stared at me, as though searching for something inside of me; the spirit of a killer, or the soul of a lost boy wanting to know who he really was. I broke eye contact as it started to become an awkward exchanging of a staring contest. He coughed and sat upright.

'Question three: was it really an accident – the man you killed? Was it truly an accident?'

I nodded. 'Yes.'

My voice was nothing more than a whisper. I made no eye contact, instead, staring at the table until my vision became blurred. The flashes of the soldier came into my mind, as I watched him die one hundred times over, and those one hundred times over by my own hands.

'Do you truly regret it, as you seem to?'

'Yes.' Again, no eye contact.

'Why do you regret it?' I realised now that his inquisitiveness was more of a genuine sense of curiosity than a threatening session of questioning.

'Because it isn't me.' I looked at the soldier. 'I'm not that type of person, and I can never be. Trust me when I say that I never wanted this to happen. I never wanted to be a part of this, but I had no choice. I didn't want to join the army. I didn't want to invade your territory. I didn't want to kill your comrades. But I had no choice, *I swear.*' I said the last words with emphasis, and the soldier tilted his head in thought.

'Why didn't you have a choice?'

'Because they would have killed me.'

'Who? You must give me details, boy. Speak clearly and tell me everything.'

'The soldiers. German soldiers. If I didn't join the army, they would have found out and killed me.' I had said too much already. I lowered my head and watched my shoes make swirls in the dirt.

'Found out what?'

My feet stopped moving, but I continued to stare at them. 'No, I can't say.'

'Tell me, boy.'

'Please, no,' I pleaded, looking the soldier in the eye. 'I can't.'

The soldier stood abruptly and walked over to me, knife in hand. He grabbed my hand as I tried to fight him off, but he was far stronger than I was. He slammed my hand on the table and held the knife over my fingers.

'Tell me now, or you lose a finger.'

'Please!' I cried. 'Please, no! I can't! I swear, I can't! They'll kill me.'

I felt the cold steel begin to cut my skin, and I screamed. 'Please!'

'Tell me, now!'

'They would kill me because I'm Jewish!' I had said it. The first time in a long time, I had acknowledged aloud who I really was. I took a deep breath. *I'm a Jew.*

The soldier stepped back. He lowered the knife and sat in his chair, too dumbfounded to say anything. We were both silent. I sat clutching my hands together, resting closely to my chest. Then, finally, he spoke.

'How did you do it? All of this.' He gestured to my uniform.

'I ran away. And I changed my name.'

'You ran away? From whom? Your family?'

I nodded. 'Yes. My mother and my sister.'

'And what about your father? Where was he?'

'Dead. He died before the war.'

'When did he die?'

I swallowed the lump forming in my throat.

'On the night of Kristallnacht. He was killed by Sturmabteilung soldiers. They shot him.'

He raised an eyebrow and looked at me curiously.

'Effectively, he was killed by the same men that you now fight with. That is right, no?'

My blood boiled, and my face became flushed.

'You don't understand. If I didn't join, they would have killed me!'

'You didn't answer the question. Was your father killed by the same men that you now fight for? It is a simple question, and a simple answer.'

'Yes.' I spoke.

'So why would you fight for the same men that killed your father? Do you like that sort of thing?' He screwed up his face. 'Do you like joining the people that attacked your family? Perhaps you like betraying your family.'

'I didn't betray him! I was going to save him!'

'Oh, so you watched it happen? And you wouldn't save your own father? Then tell me, what stopped you? Were you frightened?' He fondled the knife, as the tip sank into the skin of his left index finger and he turned it by the handle with his right hand.

'I just watched them do it,' I said solemnly. 'I did nothing. And I regret it to this day. Every day I have to live in guilt – to see his face in my dreams and know I should have done something. To see his face in my dreams and know that's the only chance I'll get of seeing him again.'

'Your father, I'm sure, was an innocent man. And to allow an innocent man to die is a great sin. But perhaps you were unable. Not just physically, but mentally. I only say these things before because I, too, have a family. And I would do anything for them. As would you have done, I'm sure, if you were able.'

I rubbed my eyes. 'I can't forgive myself.'

'You must if you wish to move on. Your father has already forgiven you, before it even happened. He would not blame you for his death.'

'How could you possibly know? You didn't know him. You knew nothing about him.'

'I know, because no true father would accuse his own son of his death. You are young, boy, but I like you. You are a true person.' He sighed and raised his eyebrows. 'I cannot believe that I say this.'

'Thank you,' I said, pleased. 'Truly.'

'One last thing. Where did you leave your mother and sister?'

'After my father died, we moved to another village, south-west of Berlin. They were turning our communities to ghettos. I ran away soon after. When they began to take us away. I don't know where. But my mother and sister – I don't know where they are.'

'You saw them get taken?'

'No. I returned home after I ran away and found our house burned to the ground – nothing but ashes. People spoke of the women and children being taken. The men were taken separately, or killed if they couldn't fit onto the trains. Mainly the older ones, and those who couldn't work. I never saw the women and children; but I saw the men. Herded like animals – I saw them being taken by the soldiers. I wanted to run over and save them. I wanted to save my mother and sister – to hug my mother and tell my sister she was going to be all right. But I didn't. Just like I didn't when it was Father.'

I began to cry. 'I just wanted to feel their touch. To hug Mother forever. I just want them to be safe.'

I was never sure whether the soldier was sympathetic toward me, or perhaps empathic because of his own family, but he stood up and walked toward me. He signalled me to stand and placed his hands on each of my shoulders.

'Your father would be proud, that he raised such a son. We tend to group together all soldiers under the banner they fight, but there are a few that will surprise you. And you, boy, are one of them. You are rare, and rare people like you are often the ones that hide in the shadows. Don't hide in the shadows. Let people know who you are, by your ways and not your gun.'

I nodded. 'I will. Thank you.' I smiled humbly.

'Now, come. I will lead you to the edge of our encampment, and then you must go on your own from there.'

'You're letting me go?' I was in shock, stammering the words as I tried to comprehend what was happening.

'I've got everything I need. It's no good to kill the good ones and leave the bad ones alive. We have to save the good ones, so they can build a better world for people. This war...' He waved his hand in the air. 'This entire battle; it's just clearing the shit out, I suppose. Let's just hope there's less shit after all of it.'

'Thank you,' I said. 'For letting me go.'

'Like I said – we don't come across people like you. Be proud of that.'

'What's your name?' I asked curiously.

'What's in a name? You may just forget it. Just remember me as the Russian soldier who was somewhat nice to you. You know, after we got all of the nasty things out of the way.'

I chuckled. 'Somewhat? I'll agree to that.'

He patted me on the back. 'Good.'

Before we exited the tent, I picked up the rope and held it around my wrists. We walked through the encampment, toward its edge where it met the farmlands. It was evening, and the sun was almost non-existent, with the harsh cold setting in early. When we were out of sight, the soldier turned to me.

'It's time to go, comrade. Never forget what you are, because if you hide it, it can never be shared with the world, and those things are worth giving.'

'Thank you, for everything. I owe you.' I looked down at my feet and smiled, then looked back up at the soldier. 'Except for trying to cut off my fingers.'

The soldier laughed. 'You can never be too careful.'

'Never have I heard wiser words.'

We shook hands, and as we did, the soldier handed me something, and closed my hand. He smiled, turned, and walked away. I stood still and opened my hand, to find a small pendant that he had given me. It was the Star of David.

CHAPTER 10

September 29, 1941

I had run back through the farmlands, dodging through the trees, north to our encampment. Once I had finally spotted our own soldiers, I sighed with relief and sprinted. I was safe for now, at least. As I reached our encampment, I was taken by some soldiers to the medical tent. Upon examination, I was questioned by a higher-ranking soldier than myself. I was sprawled out on an uncomfortably hard table, stripped to my underwear, and told to lay still.

'It's somewhat of a miracle, to say the least, that you're still alive,' said the soldier. 'What exactly did they do to you over there?'

'I was tied up in a tent until I came to consciousness, and I was then taken to another tent,' I replied.

'*Another* tent?'

'Yes. This one had a table and two chairs, where the soldier questioned me.'

'There was only one soldier?'

'They only needed one soldier, by the size of him.'

The soldier looked down at me and scowled. 'And what did he ask you?'

'He asked what our army was doing going south, and why weren't we attacking Leningrad.'

'What did you tell him?'

I took a sharp breath inward as the cold steel of the doctor's stethoscope touched my chest and pushed down hard on my bruising.

'I told him nothing.'

I could tell the soldier didn't believe me, the way he looked down at me with a face of condescension.

'Absolutely nothing?'

'Nothing,' I lied. 'He threatened to cut my fingers off, but then he became interested in my personal life. He continued asking me questions about my family.'

'And what did you tell him?'

'Everything there is to know.'

The soldier let out a heavy breath and put down his notepad.

'Very well. Perhaps we will continue this conversation at a better time, when you have gathered all of your strength.'

He nodded at the doctor before turning and walked out of the tent.

'Sit up,' said the doctor, pushing my back. He examined my head, where I was hit. I winced as he touched the delicate bruising. 'Only light bruising,' he muttered. 'You didn't suffer any head trauma, so you'll be fine.'

Oh good, I thought, sarcastically. *No head trauma, I should live forever.*

I slid off the table and put my clothes back on. I thanked the doctor, although not extensively, and exited the tent. As I did, I passed other soldiers, who lay brutally wounded on separate tables. They moaned in agony as they were bandaged up, blood seeping from one infected wound or another. Death could not have been sweeter for these soldiers, and yet they were made to go on with life, but more importantly, the war. They would be bandaged up and rest for only a few hours before they would be given orders to go back out into the battlefield.

I went back to my tent, where I was told to rest. I looked around for Felix and Earnst, but they were nowhere to be found. I hoped they were close by and didn't succumb to the same fate as Oskar. *Why did it have to be Oskar?*

I sat inside my tent and lit an oil lamp. The ominous glow

filled the tent. I grabbed my journal and pencil and leaned in close to the light. As lead touched the paper, I began to write about all that had happened.

> They day is over, finally. Long and arduous, too many things happened to constitute my freedom from the Russian soldier. My best friend, the one that vowed to protect me – Oskar – is dead. I do not know what to do. I am afraid. So afraid of everything and everyone. Oskar and I left on terrible terms, and it feels like Father all over again. I should have taken that step. But I did not. And now, it seems, Oskar and I will always be angry with each other – but I can never be, which just leaves him.
>
> It is funny how things work out, and how the world can surprise you, even in times like these. With me, I hold a pendant that shines in the light of the oil lamp next to me. It is the Star of David and it was given to me by a Russian soldier. Of all the soldiers, he, a Jewish Russian soldier, questioned me. He was brutal at first, but once he knew of who I was, he was brutal no more.
>
> Each time I try to change the subject, the image of Oskar somehow weaves its way back into my mind. I seem to be losing everything, and I wonder next whether it will be my life. I take each day as it comes, but some days will be bad, and others worse. There are no good days, not in this war.

I put down my journal and pencil and sat, staring at the ground. I undressed awkwardly in the small space and lay down. I hid my journal in my uniform, so no prying eyes would find it, then turned out the oil lamp, immersing myself in complete darkness. Why it is that life is so cruel for some and not for others? I didn't know how to answer questions like that, only how to ask them.

I cried, thinking of Oskar. It took more energy to cry than

usual, with this war slowly eating away any strength I had. After almost an hour, I closed my eyes, and sleep finally caught up with me. Finally.

CHAPTER 11

September 30, 1941

The usual routine of waking up once the sun had appeared in the sky, eat breakfast and make our way to the trenches had asserted itself. Little did I, nor anyone who had slept that night, know that our army had made significant progress, with as many as forty-five Russian tanks destroyed, and a significant number of dead Russian soldiers decorating the space between the two encampments that was once empty.

We lost only seven tanks, and our men remained strong in number. Guns continued to fire, and men yelled – I just wanted it to be over. And soon it would be, at this rate. The Russian army was struggling, and with any luck, they would retreat within the day.

We took over from those who had fought all night. Their faces hung low and they struggled to keep their eyes open, but they had enough pride to give us a nod with a staunch face as they walked past. Blood had stained the dirt in the trenches, but the bodies had been moved the night before. From the trenches we had a clear view of the whole battlefield. Only a few Russian tanks were still standing, and the Russian soldiers, who still had enough luck to be alive, were scrambling in the trenches on the other side.

I watched them as they ran back and forth in the trenches, relaying messages and talking so erratically that I swore I saw a soldier's arms flail in the air. As I watched, I was entranced. Once they had gained structure, they began fighting once more. I was looking through the scope of my gun when a hand sternly grabbed me by the shoulder. I whipped my neck around to see Earnst grinning widely at me. I let out a relieved breath and smile.

'You know you can just say hello?' I spoke.

'I thought you'd like it better if I made you jump,' replied Earnst. 'Wake you up a bit, you lazy bastard.'

I put down my gun and hugged him and he did the same.

'Well, that's some good morning,' he said.

'I thought you were dead,' I said.

'Not quite. But I feel like I will be soon if this battle doesn't end at some point. It's only been three days and it feels like weeks.'

'I know how you feel. Where's Felix?' I asked.

'Medical. He was shot in the leg, then had a grenade explode next to him. His arm was quite badly burnt, but his face was okay. He was in quite a lot of pain when I left last night.'

'*Jesus*. Is he going to be all right?'

'I think so.' As Earnst spoke, I could hear his voice change to not just a concerned friend, but a worried brother. 'The doctor was good at mending his leg, and his arm is bandaged from his shoulder to his waist. I went to see him this morning, but he was sleeping.'

'That would be good for him. Things like that take time to heal. Everything does.'

'I just hope he will be okay. I should have been there to help him. I should have done something.'

'Earnst, you're his best friend, not his guardian. You can't always expect to be with him, especially during times like this. When there's things this big, you're bound to lose sight of each other, one way or another.'

'I know. But honestly, it doesn't matter how many times someone says that to me, I always feel guilty anyway. He's like a brother to me. He's more of a brother than any of the ones I had back at home. They weren't really my brothers, but we were all in the same orphanage.' He stopped and shook his head. 'Sorry. I should stop. Where is Oskar?'

I began to stutter. A lump began to form in my throat, and I swallowed it gruellingly.

'He's dead.'

Earnst averted his eyes, as though he was guilty somehow, and remained speechless.

'I found his body,' I said hoarsely. 'He was shot when they came around the hill.'

'Hans,' began Earnst, 'I… I'm so sorry. I know he was your best friend.'

I nodded and bit my lip, looking down.

'You know, the last words we had was an argument. The one I spoke to you about. Jesus, our last words were an argument, Earnst.' I began to cry as I tried to communicate with Earnst. He put his arms around my shoulder. 'I didn't want us to fight. I just wanted to say sorry.'

'Hans, you can't blame yourself. It isn't your fault he was killed, and I know that he would never hold something like that against you. Don't go beating yourself up. There will be a time to grieve, I promise. But right now, we have a duty, and if we're caught not doing it, it won't be pleasant. So now we have to do that duty, until we fight them off and make that time to grieve. You understand, Hans?'

I nodded and stood up. I grabbed my gun and Earnst grabbed his, and he leant on the trench wall with our guns facing outward, ready for our duty once more.

The battle had dragged on for more than two hours before we signalled something I thought I would never witness – the retreating flag. The white flag was waved on the end of a long wooden rod, and the soldier who held it wrapped two hands tightly around the wooden rod with his arms apart. Left and right, left and right, it waved until the gunfire ceased.

It seemed like low cloud cover, but in fact it was the smoke of the aftermath of the battle. It had settled close to the ground, and in some areas, it was too thick to see through to the grass. It was silent. Eerily silent. Then, we heard yelling from the opposite side, and the tanks beginning to turn around – what few tanks they had left.

Lined in the trenches, we crouched and watched what was

happening with fascination. We had never witnessed a retreat, because what few battles we had fought in, we fought the enemy until their bodies became ash.

I saw the commander walk to the trenches and stand with Colonel Hirsch and General Koertig at his sides, followed by Sergeant Shödler. They all stood facing the Russians, their backs straightened, heads held high smugly, and their hands clasped behind their backs. For a few seconds, no one moved. We all watched the commander. Then, it seemed to happen so suddenly, he turned and spoke only a few words to General Koertig. General Koertig's eyes widened, and he mumbled slightly, but then conscientiously swallowed his words and saluted.

Colonel Hirsch turned and walked toward an officer that stood with the tanks, and he gave the signal – fire. The tanks began to blast their heavy shells at the Russians. Sergeant Shödler approached the trenches.

'Continue firing at the Russians!'

We all looked worriedly at the sergeant but obeyed and turned with our guns aimed. Fingers pulled triggers and the loud sound of firing guns returned. As we were firing – our soldiers directed at the Russian soldiers and myself blindly into nowhere – we were joined by the soldiers who had spent all night in these trenches. Their faces were drained of all life, and they were no more pleased to be back in the trenches than I was to have to continue this battle. One soldier who had settled next to me was mumbling to himself, and I glanced over for only moment, but it was enough for him to glare at me and ask, 'What do you want?'

'Nothing, I just heard you mumbling,' I replied.

'Well, that's none of your business, is it?' he snapped.

'I'm sorry.'

'Yeah well, so am I,' he said with sarcasm. 'I get dragged out of bed, after fighting all night,' he paused and fired a few shots, 'and I'm told that they cannot spare any men and need all of us.'

'But I thought they were retreating?'

'Apparently they sent a group of soldiers to attempt to assassinate the commander. That's no call for retreat, is it?'

I was taken aghast.

'I didn't realise. How did they catch them? What happened?'

The soldier turned his head and looked at me.

'Do I look like I was there? No. So don't ask me. They probably caught them trying to do it, maybe? Did you think of that?'

I ignored him and continued to look down the scope of my gun. I watched as the white flag was rigorously waved, until the soldier who held it was killed in an instant. As he fell, the flag dropped to the ground. None of the Russian soldiers ran to grab the flag and wave it, but instead moved back into formation and fought for everything they had.

As I studied the Russian movements, a hand grabbed my shoulder once again. I whipped my head left, startled.

'*Shit!*' I exclaimed. 'Don't do that!'

I looked at the soldier who had startled me, up and down. He was someone I had not seen before, with slick black hair combed to one side, a slim figure that looked slender in his uniform and his face, thin. His skin was pale, and his eyes were the colour of sapphire.

'Sorry,' he said, 'but I've been ordered to get you.'

I sighed heavily. 'What now?'

'Sergeant Shödler wishes to speak to you. It's about what happened at the hill.'

I stood up and pushed my gun to the soldier, who fumbled with it against his chest before standing up straight and clearing his throat. I turned and marched to Sergeant Shödler's tent. I waited outside the tent to be summoned in. Sergeant Shödler exited and stood before me.

'Adler. Come in.' He held his arm up and signalled for me to enter the tent, and I walked in.

I sat on the chair across from the sergeant and placed my hands in my lap.

'Adler, do you know why you're here?' He placed his hands on the table, clasped together, and leaned forward.

'The soldier that you sent told me it was to do with what happened at the hill.'

He looked down to his left for a moment, then raised his eyebrows.

'I didn't have much hope that he would remember that message. Surprising.'

'I had to ask him.'

'Ah,' he said, 'that explains it.' He took a deep breath. 'Adler, you're the only one who made it out alive at the incident at the hill.'

My eyes widened, and I inhaled more air than my lungs could hold, erupting into a coughing fit. The sergeant continued.

'No soldier who was sent made it. They were ambushed, but they were expecting an ambush. So why is it that they failed, and we lost the lives of well-trained soldiers yesterday?'

'There were explosives that were connected to tripwires.'

'Tripwires? How did they set these up so quickly?'

'I don't know. But I saw them put them down, and so I signalled for our soldiers to stop.'

'And still the explosives were set off? It seems you didn't do the job you were assigned as well as we thought you would.'

'I did as much as I could. I stopped them in their tracks, and they sent a soldier to see what was wrong. After I had finished explaining to him what was happening, they had set them off.'

'So, he deliberately went against what you said, is that right?' I could feel Sergeant Shödler drilling me about the incident. 'These men, who are the best trained, decided to *risk* everything by going ahead and disregarding what you said? Tell me the truth, Adler.'

'That is the truth. One moment I had said to the soldier that there were tripwires around, and the next, Dietrich and I saw smoke rising afterward, when they set them off.'

'It's interesting you mention Dietrich.'

'Why do you say that?'

'We found his body.'

'What? He's dead?'

'When I said there were no survivors, I did mean no survivors. I didn't mean that everyone was killed, except for Dietrich.'

I sat in complete shock, silent. I stared down at Sergeant Shödler's hands, still clasped together.

'Adler.' I looked up. 'Come with me.'

I stood and followed Sergeant Shödler. He took me to the physician's tent, with deep bellows of gunfire in the distance. We entered the tent, which had a table in the centre, holding a figure that had a white sheet draped over it. Sergeant Shödler grabbed the sheet and ripped it off, revealing Dietrich's dismembered body. I covered my mouth and nose with both hands and turned. The stench was overwhelming. Sergeant Shödler pulled me by the arm, closer to the body. He held my head by the scruff of my hair, forcing me to see the distorted figure.

'Pull yourself together, Adler. Look.'

I looked at the lifeless body. It had lost all colour. The blood had dried, but as I studied it, I saw that his stomach had been opened, not by the physician, but by someone else, and barbarically.

'This was done by someone, Adler. And you were the only one to see Dietrich alive last.' He walked up to me and leaned in close, nose to nose. 'And if I find out that it was you, I will send you to the camps myself.'

'I didn't do it.'

'Then explain it!' he demanded.

'I can't! Sergeant, I lost my best friend down there. I saw his body, and all I wanted was to hold him and wish he would come back to life. I had to see his body lay there, as though he was nothing. If I could have stopped it, I would have. But I couldn't. I didn't do this to Dietrich. I would never do that to someone – especially our own. I had *nothing* to do with it.'

I hated saying it – our own. I knew I would never do it to anyone. No one, no matter who they were, deserved to go through that. But I was used to lying and exaggerating – it was who I was now.

'I don't care what happened to your friend. I've lost men, too. Good men. Don't sell me this pathetic bullshit about what it is to miss someone.' He paused and looked me in the eyes, then sighed. 'But I believe you, as much as that may be a shock. Which means it was the Russian soldiers.'

'Why would Russian soldiers do this?' As much as I was confused, somehow, I knew that this was no act done by any Russian soldiers.

'Because they are barbarians, Adler. They know how to be barbarians in war. They know how to instil fear into us – or at least attempt to.'

'I don't think this is the work of Russian soldiers, Sergeant,' I said honestly.

Sergeant Shödler flicked his head toward me and scowled.

'And why not? Is there something... odd about this? Tell me your thoughts.' He was digging – I knew he was. But he was digging for something strange, something that I couldn't put my finger on. I chose my words wisely.

'I just think that if the Russian soldiers went around the hill, and had set tripwires at the base of the hill, then why climb up it?'

'Perhaps they saw Dietrich giving covering gunfire at the top and climbed up to stop him.'

I shook my head. 'No. I don't know what it is, but it seems like it was planned.'

Sergeant Shödler scoffed. 'Planned? Of course, it was planned! The Russians planned it! It was hardly unprecedented. Adler, you better start talking.'

'Talking? What?'

'Perhaps I have my suspicions about you on this. What is there to prove that you were not, at all, involved in this?'

'Sir, with all respect, I had *nothing* to do with it! Why would I do that to Dietrich? Why would I do that at all? I called the soldier up on the hill to warn them about the tripwires. If they turned around, this would never have happened to Dietrich!'

'But that's just it, Adler. It *did* happen. They continued on, with your so-called 'warning', and they were killed. It seems like an awfully large coincidence that you claim to have warned them, but the explosives were still detonated. Then we find *this*.' He pointed to Dietrich. 'A soldier, barely out of the training grounds, slaughtered like an animal and dismembered so savagely, you would have thought the Vikings had come through here!'

'Sir, I was taken by Russian soldiers!'

'So you claim. But I also find it a coincidence that you disappear after this all happens, and somehow, you escape without injury. You're lying, Adler, and I will find out why.'

'I'm not lying, Sergeant,' I said defiantly. 'I'm telling the truth.'

Sergeant Shödler leaned in close and held his hand up, pointing his index finger at my face. He pointed a few times with a face of rage and determination, then brushed past me, exiting the tent.

I looked at Dietrich's body. His eyes were wide open, colourless. I closed his eyelids and lifted the sheet over his body. This didn't make any sense. If it wasn't Russian soldiers, who did this, then who would? I walked out of the tent and stood at its entrance for a moment, scanning the area. My eyes settled on a tent that was larger than all the others, and I decided to walk over to it, only to be stopped by Sergeant Shödler three feet away from it.

'What do you think you're doing, Adler?'

'I…' I stuttered, alarmed at his presence. 'I was going to the commander's tent.'

'Do you take me for a fool? What were you doing going to that tent?'

'Nothing. I wasn't going to go anywhere near the tent.'

'I could strangle you right here, if I wanted to.'

'Then do it,' I said, scowling at him. The challenge wasn't thought through, and for a minute I honestly thought he would do it. But he just looked at me.

'You go anywhere near that tent, and I *will* have a reason to shoot you where you stand. Don't cross me Adler. I've been kind enough to you in the past, but so far, you've proven to be a soldier with too many secrets about you. And trust me when I say that I will find out what they are. Do you understand?'

I stared at him, changing between looking at his right eye and left. 'Yes, Sergeant.'

He walked in the opposite direction, but looked over his shoulder every few steps, to make sure I wasn't going to attempt anything irrational. To set him at ease, and to take the target off my back by making sure no one was constantly looking at me every few seconds, I walked away from the tent and headed to the trenches.

As I neared the trenches, which were now a few hundred feet away, I was stopped by the same tall soldier who I had met the first time while entering the tent of the commander. While we were not on the best of terms, he was no more accusatory of me acting brash than I was of his attitude.

'Adler, I'm Josef Wärton. I met you a few nights ago at the commander's tent.'

'Yes, I remember,' I said.

'I saw you with Sergeant Shödler,' he stated.

'Yes,' I replied. 'Why do you bring it up?'

He pulled me aside, among the soldiers' tents where we were unseen by any passing officers.

'He's been acting strangely since the assassination attempt on the commander.'

'Why are you telling me this?'

'I want to know what he said to you.'

'He showed me the body of Dietrich, who was the sniper on the hilltop with me. Then he told me that he thought I did it, and that he will prove that it was me, somehow.'

'Why does he think that you did it?'

I shrugged.

'He said I was the only one with Dietrich, and no one else saw him. At first, he said it was Russian soldiers, but I said that I didn't think it was. And that's when he accused me.'

'Why would you say that it wasn't the Russian soldiers?'

'Why would they do that? His body was cut all over, and he had bruising on his limbs like he was in a struggle. Why not just shoot him?'

The soldier sighed and rubbed his eyes with his thumb and index finger.

'Why wouldn't you just agree that it was Russian soldiers and leave it at that?'

'Because I know it *wasn't*. If one of our soldiers did that, they have to be found and stopped. I'm not going to lie to him.'

'And what if it was him, Adler? What then?'

'Who? Sergeant Shödler? Why would he do something like that?'

'The sergeant has had a passionate distaste for Russians ever since his wife was killed by them almost ten years ago.'

I looked at him, aghast.

'What?'

'He was in Russia for military business, and his wife came with him. She was robbed and beaten, left on the street. It took Russian soldiers almost an hour to respond to the incident, when they found out it was his wife. She died in hospital two weeks later. He's always held every Russian accountable for that.'

'What has dismembering Dietrich's body got to do with his wife's death?'

'I think it's because he needs an excuse.'

'And excuse for what?'

'To wipe out this Russian army.'

'Wait, so what about the assassination attempt?'

He looked around nervously to make sure no one was eavesdropping.

'I think it was him. He planned it all, and made it look like it was the Russian soldiers. If he could successfully make it look like they had attempted to assassinate the commander, there would be no treaty or retreat. He would have reason to continue fighting and obliterate them.'

I stared at him in shock.

'Why are you telling me this?'

'Because he might try to pin Dietrich's death on you, and say you were working with the Russians. And to be honest, I don't want to see any fellow soldier go through something like that. That man has a taste for blood, and you ought to stay out of his way when he's hungry.'

I had given Josef far less credit than what he had deserved initially, and I felt guilty to stand and listen while he tried to help me prepare for what was expected to come.

'Thank you, Wärton. Really, thank you.' He nodded and smiled. 'So, what do we do now?'

'Somehow prove that this was all Sergeant Shödler. How we're going to do that, I don't know. But there's no need to aggravate the situation if nothing is going to happen to you.'

'But what about the men over there who innocently retreated?'

He sighed. 'When we reach Moscow, they'll be dead either way.'

Dear Oskar

Oskar,

It is hard to imagine that you are no longer here in body; that all you were is now gone. It is hard to know that I will never speak to you, nor hear you again. But what is even harder, and at this moment seems like it will never get any easier, is that what was said and done atop that hill can no longer be taken back with an apology. I missed my chance – forever.

When I first met you, you were the epitome of scary. Words cannot begin to describe the moment you stood face to face to me and stared me directly in the eyes without flinching. How frightened I was; frightened yes, but wary of who you once were. You were broken. Most people were, but you were different. You refused to show it, and even when you tried to hide behind the staunch façade, I knew that who others perceived you to be, was not who you really were. You were just like everyone else deep down – you knew how to love.

The only soldier to ever stick by me, I always remember how grateful I was that you did not decide to be positioned elsewhere. It was never about the fact that you swore to protect me, and you stood up for me; I would never ask that you stand in front of me for my own sake. No. It was the fact that you decided to stand by me, whichever my situation may be. You knew my past, and I knew yours enough to warrant feeling a sense of pride of how our friendship grew. We became family.

Each night, cliché as it may be, I look up to the sky and hope that you are there. I have trouble with the concept of heaven, and I always have, but that does not stop me from believing that maybe, just maybe, you are still looking out for me in your own way. We are only human, all of us. And that makes us susceptible to death, yet somehow, some of us cannot get enough of it, and that scares me. I like life, yet I know it will never be the same without you, ever.

I am grateful for my family, but you can never choose them, and so maybe I was one of the lucky ones. But we made each other family, and that is what makes our bond one that I never want to let go of. Maybe it is something greater than all of us trying to tell me something; maybe it is Death trying to tell me something; or maybe it is just life moving on, and somehow what we had was strong enough to last only a short time.

You will never be forgotten; I promise you that. Nor will you ever be unloved.

Thank you, Oskar.

Love always,
Hans

CHAPTER 12

September 30, 1941

For the entire afternoon, while each soldier around me was more concerned with defeating the army that had once waved the white flag of surrender, I was more concerned with the entire ordeal of Sergeant Shödler. Why would he want to frame me for something? Did he know who I really was, or had he just taken a disliking to me the moment he met me? I was nervous; oblivious to what was being said or done about the entire thing out of earshot and out of sight.

By the late afternoon, one Russian tank remained, and twenty-four men. We had won, if you could call it that. Our soldiers grabbed one another by the arms, shaking in enjoyment at the prospect of our small victory. Within half an hour, the lone tank was destroyed, and the soldiers who accompanied it had been killed. There was no more gunfire, and the only sound was the sighs of relief and cheers from the soldiers in our trenches, with stretched smiles across their faces. I managed a smile, but in the back of my mind was the ticking of each scenario that could possibly play out with Sergeant Shödler. Our officers came to the trenches and walked along, encouraging cheering from the soldiers. A temporary uplift of spirits before the long haul to

Moscow – and then that's when things would get worse. But for now, we basked in the so called 'positive' banter of their defeat, and our menial victory. Deep down, we all knew this was a minor victory, but we also knew moments like this – the smiles and the laughs – only ever came few and far between in war, so we made the most of it.

We stayed camped for the night in the same spot and, instead of the sound of gunfire which would accompany the darkness and rain, it was now men gleefully eating and conversing around campfires, though the rain had not ceased. But no one was afraid of getting wet, with the fires to keep us warm and the soldiers much happier than they had been in a long time. It was so easy to forget that we were ever in a war. It was easy to forget everything that had happened, and enjoy the present; the countryside, the fires and the company – but perhaps not the food. Nevertheless, we made it what it was.

But guilt can easily crawl its way back into minds, as it had done for me. For what we were celebrating was death, and it was death that had been orchestrated by Sergeant Shödler. He hadn't let go of the death of his wife, and not only had he never forgiven those who had done it, he held an entire nation responsible.

Had he not had his way, and had he not set up those Russian soldiers who, in this case, were innocent, we would have celebrated far earlier, and my mind, at least, would be far less guilt ridden than it currently was.

As I sat, grinning at the other soldiers who ecstatically waved their arms while discussing the details of the battle, I looked over to see Sergeant Shödler standing idle, his hands clasped behind his back and his eyes scanning over each campfire. Was he looking for me? I leaned forward and tilted my head down. I kept low for a few minutes, before peering up to see if he had moved on. He was still there, and I had stared at him long enough for his head to whip around and stare directly at me. *Shit!* I thought. I quickly ducked down, and each of the soldiers who sat with me around the campfire, which included Earnst and Felix, looked at me suspiciously.

'Hans, what the hell are you doing?' asked Felix.

'Nothing,' I exclaimed.

I could tell each eye was fixated on me, and as I answered, I had guessed that each eyebrow went up in suspicion.

'Boys.' A heavy voice sounded as my head was tucked into my jacket. It was Sergeant Shödler. 'How are we this evening?'

Each of the soldiers nodded accordingly and smiled. I felt a large hand land on my back, accompanied by, 'And what about you, Private Adler? Well, I hope?'

I looked up to see Sergeant Shödler grinning at me menacingly, his breath foul with smoke. I shrank back into my jacket, my beaded eyes watching his lips move as his tongue ran along his top teeth.

'I'm well, Sergeant Shödler,' I finally replied.

'Good,' he hissed. 'I'm glad to hear it. A shame we cannot be accompanied by all of the soldiers who started this good fight, isn't it? But that is the sacrifice of war.'

'Yes, Sergeant.' I stared at the fire, feeling his warm breath on my ear as he spoke.

'Indeed. Some people are just unlucky in war, I suppose. Don't you agree?'

'Yes, Sergeant.'

'Yes, they are.' He stood upright. 'Enjoy your night, boys. And you too, Adler. Enjoy it. Feast, for we have victory. Lives have been lost, but in the end, it is all for a very necessary cause,' he scoffed and walked away, his hands fumbling in his pockets as he pulled out a cigarette and a box of matches. Leaving a trail of smoke, he walked through the tents and disappeared.

All eyes were on me, now. Not one of them looked anywhere else. They edged forward, and the sound of Earnst's voice asked, 'What was that all about, Hans?'

I shook my head and placed my elbows on my thighs, leaning close to the fire.

'I don't know.'

One younger soldier laughed.

'Oh come on, Hans. Don't lie. He wouldn't be giving you that grimaced hiss and stare for nothing.'

'Well, maybe he just likes to taunt me. I don't know.'

The group was silent. I stood up and smiled at each of them, then said, 'I'm just a little tired, that's all,' and left.

Before I got to my tent, Earnst had followed me and tapped me on the shoulder.

'Hans, are you sure everything is okay with you and Sergeant Shödler?'

I shook my head. 'Not really. But I can't exactly say anything, that's the problem.'

'What has he done to you?' Earnst became tense.

'It's not what he's done, but I think what he is going to do.'

'And what's that?'

I took a deep breath and looked around, before making eye contact with Earnst again.

'I think he killed Dietrich.'

'You mean the soldier that was on top of the hill with you?'

I nodded.

'And I think he set up the assassination attempt on the commander. I don't know how to prove it, and I don't even know if anyone will believe me, but by the way he was talking, I think he did it. He keeps taunting me, like he's going to make it look like I killed Dietrich and I planned with the Russians to kill the commander. I have no idea what he will do, and I hate not knowing.'

I became anxious and my voice tremored. I tilted my head and shook it, my eyes doleful and breathing more heavily through my nose.

'I hate it, Earnst.'

Earnst grabbed me and hugged me, patting me on the back.

'Don't be fearful, Hans. We're all here with you, and you know that every soldier would stand up for you if it came to that.'

We let go and I sighed heavily, rubbing my eyes.

'Thanks, Earnst.'

He smiled and nodded, then headed back for the fire. I made my way to my tent and lit the lantern that was in the corner. I had no idea why Earnst was being so nice toward me, but I hoped that it would continue, especially with Oskar gone and my attitude not particularly sold to the other soldiers.

I opened my journal for the final time in this spot and grabbed my pencil. As the pencil met the paper, I began to write more and more.

We are finally moving on tomorrow. Though I wish we would go home, the inevitability of Moscow is closer and closer, and reality will soon hit me that I will be a target among surroundings of decrepit buildings and a city half destroyed.

Sergeant Shödler worries me, in a way that he is a snake. He will slither his way into any situation, silently moving around the obstacles, before he launches his attack. I appreciate a man of his intellect, but I cannot appreciate his willingness to distort it. He knows how to manipulate.

I find I grow stronger each day. The constant walking has meant an increase in stamina, and the lifting has given rise to muscles, which I thought I would never witness on me, like a growth. But I am becoming far more agile, and I feel far more able to do things that I thought my once slim and small body found impossible to achieve. Though, the constant walking and worrying also leads to a tiresome time, as though I am only strong at my weakest point.

Perhaps I am naïve in thinking that this war will end soon, but optimism is a far greater gift than pessimism – pessimism is far too easy to submit too. Though my knowledge dictates that this war will last far longer than any of us would have anticipated fighting, maybe our Führer will drop dead by pure luck. These thoughts, however, are only ever permitted to be said in my mind and written in these precious pages, for if my tongue dare lash these words in public, I dare not think what I would face. Instead, I reserve myself, with great angst and a great deal more of self-determination.

I have heard soldiers say, 'War is what it is.' What is it? It befuddles me. These soldiers never truly knew war until it preyed on their minds enough to join. Do they know why they fight? Or who they are fighting? Ignorance may sometimes be perceived as bliss, but to me, it is just stupidity wrapped in innocence. Needless to say, I think these soldiers have found ignorance to be bliss, and stupidity to be natural.

I put down my journal and chuckled to myself. I was proud, that was true. Perhaps arrogant at times, but I found there was nothing wrong with arrogance, provided the view they held was one that I agreed with. Yes... I was arrogant.

I turned out the light in the lantern and rested my head. Listening to the rain pour gently on my tent, I was at ease. Tomorrow, we would be making a move to Moscow. I would say 'Wish me luck,' but I knew I didn't deserve it.

CHAPTER 13

October 1, 1941

I awoke to the sound of an officer yelling at the top of his lungs. I struggled to get up, disorientated by the deep sleep I was having. Managing to lift my head, which felt as heavy as a tank, I rubbed my eyes and yawned widely. I felt so lethargic, and I wondered if it was due to my mind finally realising that the battle was over, and it was time to rest. I told myself the battle was over, but the war was far from it. I stood up, hunched over so my head wouldn't go through the tent, and dressed in my uniform.

As I stood outside of the tent, at this time the sun would usually be rising, and the landscape would be covered by a gentle light. This morning, however, was nothing like I had witnessed previously. The clouds were grey, almost black, rolling in from the west, and thunder rumbled as lightning struck in the distance. There was a storm coming, and it was no storm that we had encountered before. Earnst approached me.

'How did you sleep, then?' he asked boisterously with a smile.

I smiled and answered, 'I was out like I was dead.'

Earnst chuckled and put his hands on his hips.

'Well, I'm glad you're not. I sort of like having you around. At least it gives me someone to tease every now and then.'

'Oh, does it?' I asked while laughing. 'Well at least I'm useful for something then.'

Earnst laughed and slapped his hand on my arm. We turned and walked to where the food was being served.

'What do you think about Moscow?' I asked him while walking.

'I don't exactly think about Moscow. I've only ever seen it in the pictures. Why? What's wrong?'

I looked at him with a blank expression.

'What? Nothing. I was just asking.'

Earnst raised an eyebrow.

'You are a terrible liar; do you know that?'

'I think I may have been told once or twice,' I said jokingly, looking up at the sky, 'but if it comes to it, you can do the lying for me. Deal?'

'Deal,' Earnst said, laughing faintly, 'but don't let it get to you. You might not have Oskar, but you sure as hell have me and Felix.'

'I didn't realise I had *two* bodyguards.'

'Well Felix doesn't know yet. I think we should break it to him gently.'

'Should I pretend to be someone important, then? Maybe the Führer?'

'You can't even grow a beard, let alone a square moustache, Hans. You can borrow some of mine and stick it on.'

'You're too kind, sometimes.'

We both laughed and finally reached where the other soldiers were. Men were lining up, ready to receive their small, tasteless meals, yet so eager to eat something – anything. We had heard stories of cannibalism among some soldiers, possibly Russians, during the harsh winters. I was slightly concerned, although not overly, that some of the soldiers in our army would turn on one another for a temporary boost of nutrients. Some of the soldiers I had seen, and some I had interacted with, frightened me to the point of avoiding them at all costs. They would snicker and hiss, making strange remarks about some of the soldiers. They were the soldiers who would have most likely been found wandering the streets aimlessly, back in Germany – prowling on the weak and making easy money for food. I didn't trust them. No one did.

We steered clear of the table where those soldiers sat, and we also kept further away from the officers, in case Sergeant Shödler had somehow convinced them that Dietrich's death, and the assassination attempt on the commander, were somehow orchestrated by me. I spotted the table that was occupied by the soldiers accompanying us last night around the fire, and nudged Earnst while indicating with my head that we could sit over there.

We grabbed a plate of the breakfast which was being served – bread, a gelatine-like substance, and beef – and sat alongside the younger soldiers at the table. They continued talking, so Earnst and I sat eating silently while listening to the conversation.

'… and Red Square could fit thousands of people in it.'

'It's right near the Kremlin. When we march on Red Square, we will have our guns pointed at the Kremlin, and they will surrender.'

'And what if we don't get that far?'

'Shut up, Heinrich. We *will* get there. All of us. Stop being so negative about it.'

'I'm not being negative, Waldron; I'm being realistic. They're going to have soldiers on every street of that city. They know we're coming. They're not oblivious – they will have their defences up, and they will have their guns pointed, ready for us. So maybe you should stop being so stupid, Waldron.'

'What did you say?'

'Unless you're deaf, I think you heard what I just said. You're always acting so stupid; so ignorant. This is a fucking war.'

As Heinrich said those exact words, Waldron launched himself across the table and landed on him. He flung his arms behind his head, then with one swift move, knocked Heinrich in the cheek. The soldiers stood up and cheered on the fight, rather than break it up, and the two were fighting like lions. The cheers became louder as more soldiers stood around the two, barracking for one or the other.

Sergeant Shödler, accompanied by Colonel Hirsch, stepped in and grabbed Waldron and Heinrich. Colonel Hirsch grabbed Waldron by the ear and smashed his fist straight into his stomach, sending Waldron down to the ground once again. Sergeant Shödler grabbed Heinrich from under his arm and dragged him through the crowd of now silent soldiers. Colonel Hirsch grabbed Waldron by his hair and pulled him through the crowd, following Sergeant Shödler and Heinrich, as he muttered, 'You're in for it now, boy.'

Waldron squeamishly struggled as his face screwed up and he yelped in pain, his hair follicles ripping from his head.

'Let go of me!' he yelled. 'Let go!'

Before long, Waldron was in a row with Colonel Hirsch, whose face was a display of pure anger as he was kicked in the knee by Waldron's flailing legs. Colonel Hirsch, in a frightful display of anger, grabbed the back of Waldron's head and slammed it into the ground. He forced his knee into the centre of Waldron's back and leaned into his ear.

'Don't try it, boy! Now, we're going to stand up, and you're going to behave. Do you understand?' There was no answer from Waldron, as he sulked on the ground.

'Do you?' Colonel Hirsch yelled.

'Yes,' hissed Waldron.

As they stood, Waldron turned to Colonel Hirsch and head butted him. Colonel Hirsch fell back and Waldron, who stood dazed for a few seconds, finally shook his head, blinked profusely and made for the exit. Colonel Hirsch pushed away the soldiers who attempted to help him to his feet and growled through his gritted teeth, chasing after Waldron.

The soldiers were silent as we all looked at one another anxiously, waiting for someone – anyone – to break the silence. No one said a word, but simply returned to their tables and ate in silence. Over a few minutes, chatter amongst the soldiers was at normal levels, and everyone discussed the fight that had just occurred.

'Waldron is in for it,' commented Felix. 'He's going to exit Hirsch's tent battered and bruised, that's for sure.'

'It was his fault, anyway,' commented another soldier, who was younger than me and far smaller. His hair was combed from one side to the other, with a few rogue sections of it hanging down his forehead. 'He started the fight with Heinrich.'

'No, he didn't,' defended Earnst. 'Heinrich started it when he said that Waldron was stupid. If he didn't say that there would have been no need for Waldron to retaliate.'

'But Waldron is stupid. He's a moron. He thought Goebbels was the Führer. He probably thought Göring was a type of sausage. No person with a proper education would even ask a question like that.'

'Oh, come on, give the guy some credit, Luis,' said Earnst. 'He saved your life more than once, and if I'm not mistaken, you still owe him.'

'Stupidity gives no one the right to just attack another person,' I butted in. 'Regardless of whether or not you're stupid, it's no reason to attack them.'

'Who asked you?' remarked the soldier at the end of the table.

By automatic retaliation, I retorted with a snap, 'Well, you weren't giving your opinion, so I thought I'd opt in.'

Felix put his hand on my shoulder. 'Don't worry about it, Hans.'

Over the past few weeks, I had felt myself becoming increasingly irritable. Perhaps it was the lack of sleep, or perhaps it was the constant fighting, or maybe it was just because I wanted to be home – but nevertheless, I found myself growing more agitated, and willing to argue purely for the sake of it. I knew I would never beat any of the soldiers at the table in a fight – maybe, perhaps Luis – but I had my wit and when you're in a situation where physicality is not tolerated, maybe it is better to have a sharp tongue – though I knew it would someday get me into trouble.

I looked at Felix, then at Earnst, and finally at the soldier who sat at the end of the table.

'He wanted a reason; I gave it to him. And if it's such a monitored debate, then don't let me interrupt – but it isn't.'

The table was silent, and I sat staring at the soldier, who scowled at me. He continued to do so, until we were interrupted by an officer who told us to clear our plates and move on, so we could get moving as quickly as possible.

Polishing our plates from every piece of food, disgusting or not, devoured, we placed them in large steel bowls and headed outside, where the rain had begun to pour lightly. I was about to walk off and collect my things when I was stopped by Earnst and Felix. Being the more intelligent of the two, Earnst spoke rather than Felix.

'Hans, I know they can get under your skin. Believe me, I

know. But just watch what you say, all right? It isn't like you can go around and belittle whoever you like.'

'I wasn't belittling him; I was just answering him. If he's allowed to do that, to try and make people scared of him, then why should I stand for it? I know I'm not the strongest soldier, but when it comes to words, I can beat them, hands down.'

'Words won't kill a man, Hans,' said Felix. Earnst glared at him, as though he wasn't permitted to speak at all.

'Hans, if you say the wrong thing to the wrong person, you could end up hurt, or worse – dead. I'm just saying, we want to look out for you, but we can't if you keep opening your mouth to make someone feel bad.'

'Feel bad? Do you hear yourself? *He–*' I stopped myself before I went any further. I looked at Earnst and bit my lip, before saying, 'I don't need you to mother me.'

I walked back to my tent, where I stood, staring at the ground. I sighed and ran my hands up my face and through my hair, before resting them on my hips. Felix approached me from behind, completely silent.

'Hans,' he said softly.

I jumped and turned my head back to see him standing awkwardly with his hands in his pockets.

'Earnst was just trying to look out for the best. He only wants to help. I know it seems like he's trying to be a parent, but he's just trying to be a friend.'

'Did Earnst send you over here to say this to me?'

'No,' he said, shaking his head, 'he doesn't know I'm here. I told him I was going to pee. But you just seem tense, and I don't like seeing you like that.'

I sighed and shut my eyes for a moment.

'I know. But this whole thing – everything, I guess – is just so hard. And sometimes I can snap. But I don't want you to leave me.'

'Why would we leave you? You're our brother. Sure, we give you a hard time, but isn't that what brothers do? I never had a brother, mind you, but I assume that's what they do. But we also look out for each other. Do you know what I'm saying?'

I nodded. 'I know. And I'm sorry for it. I know you mean well – and Earnst. And I promise I'll try harder.'

'Don't try harder, just be happier. For me, at least. And for yourself.'

Although Felix wasn't as bright as many people, he sure did know how to make someone smile, and that's worth more than anything any education could do. I smiled and thanked him, before he forced a hug and wrapped his arms tightly around me, patting me on the back. I exchanged the hug and we smiled, before he quietly said, 'Thank you. Now, I actually have to pee.'

He walked away and somehow, that small conversation with Felix was enough to make me smile on the inside, as well as the outside.

I packed my things and tightly squeezed everything into my bag. The backpacks, which were almost as large as we were, accompanied us on our journeys, putting extra strain on our backs and feet. Today, however, the commander had ordered that each soldier was to be packed onto the trucks and tanks. He stated that it did not matter how slow we would go, he would not have his soldiers walk through the blistering storm while others were cosily inside the trucks and tanks. *Kind of him,* I thought, *for a man who is willing to send us to our deaths.*

The rain picked up and the winds howled with ferocity as the tanks gently rolled on, carrying dozens of soldiers who were packed tightly on top. I was glad to be sat in the middle, where I had no chance of falling off, unless every other soldier fell and dragged me with them. Everyone's concern was if the tanks fired, by accident of course, then it would send almost a dozen, if not more, soldiers flying through the air in numerous pieces.

There was no protection from the rain, and we were blasted with oncoming wind and cold water as the horizon offered nothing but hazy fields and grey skies. Every now and then, the soldiers inside the tank would open the small window at the top and sarcastically ask how we were doing, with a small snicker. One soldier, who was separated from me by another, had attempted to grab the collar of one of the soldiers occupying the tank as they made the remark. He was met with pain as they slammed the lid shut on his arm, clamping it between the hard steel and the cover. The soldier eventually freed his arm and nursed it as he mumbled about how he was going to get revenge on the soldiers involved.

After hours of travelling in the rain, which refused to cease, we stopped by a river which ran for miles in either direction. The icy water streamed across the rocks, and one soldier on another tank, climbed down to measure its depth. It was only a foot, and with much discussion and contemplation with the officers, who had all exited the trucks and were now chattering in a large circle, they agreed that it was possible for the vehicles to safely cross.

The trucks, which struggled to life with groans, went first, the tanks following behind. As our tank crossed, we hit a rock that was well hidden underwater, which propelled us and the vehicle into the air, crashing with a thump back down into the water again. We were all so concerned with what had happened, holding on for dear life, that we failed to notice two soldiers who had fallen from the back, into the cold water.

At first glance, we all laughed at the ordeal and watched as the two soldiers slipped on the rocks, desperate to get up and out of the water. They would stand, poised while thinking how they would make it across, step lightly and slip again as soon as their foot made contact with the icy, mossy rocks. Eventually, we helped them climb atop the tanks, where they scrambled for the middle, rather than take the risk of being on the edge again. We laughed at the whole scenario, but the soldiers who experienced it, weren't as gleeful about it as we were – then again, we weren't drenched in freezing waters with our backs aching from smashing onto the rocks as we slipped.

Although we giggled and snickered at what had happened, we comforted the two soldiers and each of the soldiers, who travelled on the same tank, offered their sincere concerns, as they shivered violently against the cold wind.

We all held on as the tank crossed the river and went uphill. On the other side of the river crossing were large open fields, separated by old, deteriorating fences, both wooden and stone. The road was nearby, and although we had kept off them for a long time, we were forced to stick to them until Moscow. They were smoother, at least, which was far more welcoming than the rough terrain we had been experiencing – all by foot, which made it harder to walk and encouraged blisters to form on our feet.

We travelled until dusk, which came unexpectedly due to the constant greyness that blanketed the sky. We came to a halt on the road, which travelled straight through a pine forest that went on for miles. The tanks and trucks pulled off the road and into the forest where they would be unseen. The soldiers all clambered down from the tanks and trucks before they were driven into the forest, and we followed, setting up camp just on the side of the road, under the cover of the forest. We emerged in darkness, with no fire to warm us, and no food to fill us. Once our tents were set up, we sought shelter in them from the continuous rain that hadn't stopped since that morning. We were cold – freezing, more like it – but we only had our blankets and coats to keep us warm, and even they couldn't protect us from the Russian cold.

CHAPTER 14

October 15, 1941

The days were getting colder, with a vicious chill about them as we made for Moscow. The travelling was truly and utterly horrible. Our feet were covered in blisters and calluses, and our legs felt immobile at times – sometimes I forgot how to walk. My mind was becoming numb to all of this, and it felt as though it was dulling all my senses.

The food supplies were getting low, and so envoys were sent to retrieve more. They were sent with several vehicles to meet with other officers travelling from the Fatherland with foodstuffs, and collecting the airdrops left for us. We would travel miles each day, and still it would feel we were going nowhere, with our army struggling to get to Moscow.

We stopped for the day and camped. We were near a Russian village – almost seven miles – and they were oblivious to the fact that we were so close. From the west, from where we travelled, hills rolled, and trees were interspersed. To the east were farmlands, along with the small village that was almost invisible among the trees, had it not been for the tall clock tower that stood tall in its centre.

The small pine forest that rested seven miles from the village provided enough cover to camp, unseen by any of its inhabitants. We set up camp and were ordered to stay in our tents, no contact with one another under any circumstances. If one sound was made, we were to go to Sergeant Shödler's tent immediately – no arguments. We were not to speak, in case any passers-by heard our whispers and ran to tell the town, at which point our cover would be blown and the Russians would know our exact location and movements. We were bound to be found out eventually. They already knew we were on our way to Moscow, but their communications on our movements had ceased when we obliterated the army that met us almost three weeks ago. For the time being, we were unknown, and it was expected to be kept that way.

So now we moved with the shadows, rather than against them. We were the shadows, rather than the Russians who hunted us down. We were unseen, and unknown for this short amount of time, and it would do us well if it was to stay that way, at least until our arrival in Moscow. I pictured our arrival in the capital as more of a jubilant display of peace and strength – the strength, if successful, would play a large part in our arrival, but not peace.

I imagined the crowds would greet us as though we were their saviours, rescuing them from the clutches of evil. That's what we were taught. When I was new to the army, we were told we were the fighters of justice, the destroyers of evil and the deliverers of peace. We were told the world would be far better under the Führer than any other leader, and our allies fought for that – though supporters of Mussolini may disagree with that cause. But all the same, we were united in strength and in determination of our own will – but that was what was wrong.

That was what was evil. Our will – the Führer's – was destruction. Complete and utter obedience to him. That was all. No peace. Peace would only come if all bent the knee, and we had more enemies than allies. Our men, good soldiers who would fight for their people, were wasted on this barbaric parade that took away my family, and many more. Sometimes I tried to fool myself into thinking that my enlistment was purely to rescue Mother and Edith, but I knew, deep down, that it was because I was a coward, and ran away from who I was. I knew I was lying to myself – the jovial display of peace in the streets of Moscow. The men I fought for were murderers, and by that standard, I was too.

The sun was setting and darkness crept in. Soon the light would be completely absent, even from our tents. No oil lamps, no torches, no fires. Nothing that would show light. If the townspeople saw one speck of light, they would investigate, and find an entire army camped at their doorstep. I was surprised the sound of the tanks weren't heard, even seven miles away.

The light was almost dead, except for the sky to the east that was illuminated by the village, and everyone was in their tents. I sat, my knees curled up to my chest and my arms wrapped tightly around my legs as I rested my head on the tops of my knees. I wanted desperately to twist the knob on my oil lamp and let the light radiate, even for a short time. But I knew if I did, even though the people in the village may not see it, the officers would. I would surely be flogged or beaten, or both, for it.

My curiosity began to peak as I wondered about the lives of the people who resided in the village, so close to our encampment. The same people we had been told countless times were the evil we were required to purge from the earth. Those same people were just a few steps away. I wanted to know them, to experience their lives and listen to their stories. I wanted to feel a sense of normality amongst this anarchy. I wanted to be me.

When it was dark, I stood up. Soldiers were on watch, but they wouldn't be able to see me in the darkness even if they wanted to. It was pitch black. I felt my way around the tent and opened it at the side, slipping out unnoticed and as silent as I could possibly be. It was so silent I could hear the grass crunch under my feet. I cringed each time I took a step, hoping no one would hear it. Maybe they were too carried away with their thoughts to hear it. That was wishful thinking, but it was a thought that seemed to be true, nonetheless, with not one curious soldier shuffling about to get out of his tent to investigate.

It was difficult to feel around for anything in the dark. I knew the ropes, which held up the tent, were sprawled out everywhere, and so each step I took was carefully felt out over a few seconds beforehand. It took almost ten minutes to walk thirty feet, as I moved so slowly as not to cause a ruckus or trip unexpectedly over a piece of rope.

Finally, after almost an hour of creeping awkwardly through the camp, I felt gravel under my feet and knew immediately that I was on the road. The moon, which was a small crescent that didn't offer any sufficient light to walk normally, provided only enough to study the outlines of the trees and hills, when squinting. I crouched and moved to the side of the road, where I kept to. There was a large ditch that followed the road downhill, used to carry the water that would wash alongside it during heavy rains. Suddenly, the outcrops of the trees and hillside disappeared, as clouds rolled in and covered the moon. *Great*, I thought.

My feet tested the ground before each step, avoiding any unexpected ditches or holes that may provide a nuisance had I stepped in them. I bit my lip each time. This became constant, leaving teeth marks on my bottom lip. I held my arms out in front, with my hands waving around stupidly in case anyone or anything bumped into me. Had I immediately been immersed in light without expecting it, I would have most likely been admitted to a clinical ward.

I continued walking until I came to a bend in the road, which turned sharply, following the hill. The road was windy as it wove down the hill and into the town. I thought about taking the risk of walking in a straight line downward but knew that if I did and something bad happened, I wouldn't be able to call for help without attracting any unwanted attention. I followed the road for the next seven miles, slowly walking, arms still outstretched and still biting my lip.

After what seemed like a lifetime, I came across a small cottage which was neatly placed on a small lot, surrounded by sheep, which I made out in the moonlight that had crept out from behind the clouds, as I approached. The lights of the town provided a far better view of everything, and as I walked closer, I could make out faces and expressions, what people wore and their lips moving.

I knew my uniform would alarm everyone, so I ducked behind a house that was fenced off by a small white picket fence. The house was made of stone, and smoke rose from the chimney as I saw through the window – a mother and her two sons sitting by the fire, talking and playing. I stood next to a tall oak tree and watched the young boys as they played with toy aeroplanes and chased each other around the living room. Their mother would occasionally laugh, holding a beautiful smile as she watched the two boys enjoying themselves. I smiled and leaned against the tree. I wanted to cry – to weep, for times with Mother, just as they were having. I didn't want to take that from them; I didn't want to take that from anyone.

I looked around for anything that may have been of use, and spotted clothes which hung from a line in the garden. Ducking through the shrubs, I crept over to the clothes and pulled them from the line, sizing them up against my uniform. They fitted around my body, but only just. I folded my uniform up and placed it by the oak tree, changing into the ordinary clothes.

Once I was in the ordinary clothes and no possible sign could give me away that I was a German soldier, I crept out of the garden and walked through the small village. I knew it was risky, and I was an idiot for doing such a thing, but I simply wanted so desperately to feel normal again – to feel loved and accepted again.

The shops were open, even at this hour, and people walked the streets with gleeful smiles and nods of greetings. Families were out, walking together as they roamed the streets and entered various stores.

What the hell are you doing? I asked myself. I shrugged off my conscience telling me I should go back – I finally felt real again as I walked through the village without any fighting erupting.

I spotted a small shop which looked to be one that sold odd bits and pieces, although I could have been completely wrong, since I didn't know how to read or speak Russian. I decided to go in and have a look, curious to see what was in there.

As I opened the door, a small bell rang and sent an elderly man, small and frail, rushing desperately towards me. He spoke something in Russian, and I simply put my hand up and shook my head politely. He smiled and went back behind the counter, where he sat comfortably in a cushioned armchair reading a thin book.

I glazed the shelves, looking at the small trinkets that were presented. There were small toys, carved from pine, which sat neatly in rows on the shelves. I recognised one, a dreidel, which I had received on Hanukkah at the age of five. I spun it, watching it as it went around and around, mesmerised and perplexed by it. It kept spinning until it reached the edge of the shelf, falling off and hitting the ground with a clap. I picked it up and made sure there were no chips in it, before placing it gently on the shelf and looking over my shoulder to see if the elderly man had heard. He still sat delightfully in his armchair, reading his book.

I hummed as I walked through the shop, inspecting each little toy that was on display, the books that sat gathering dust, some were written in Russian, some in English, and some even in German. I flicked through each of them, dust leaping into the air each time I scuffed the pages, causing me to erupt into a coughing fit or sneeze.

As I admired the pages, which were torn and battered, a gentle hand tapped me on the shoulder and startled me. I dropped the book and spun around to see a young girl, about my age, smiling at me. I smiled back and blushed as I fumbled to pick up the book I had just dropped, mumbling embarrassedly. She spoke something to me, though it was in Russian, so I couldn't understand. We were taught the basics of the Russian language, but all I managed to pick up from it was 'hello'.

I groaned awkwardly and hummed, until she cocked her head in suspicion, then began listing languages, inferring as to which one I spoke. Finally, she said, 'German?'

'Yes,' I answered with a chuckle.

'You are not Russian?' she asked with a puzzled look. 'You are German?'

I nodded, but quickly corrected myself by stating, 'But I'm not bad.'

Not the way to win a girl's heart – hold out your hands and say that exact line. I looked like an idiot, and I became even shyer than I had started out. I stuttered, trying to explain what I meant.

'I mean, I'm not going to hurt you. That sounds stupid, but I mean–'

She giggled.

'It is okay. I could tell you didn't mean any harm when you stood quietly on your own reading those books.'

She leaned in close and whispered in my ear, 'One would think if you did mean harm, you probably would have done it by now, no?'

Terribly awkward and even more so standing rigidly still, I was at a loss for words like some moron who didn't know there was a war on in their own country and had just been told. I stared at her. She was beautiful. Her hair flowed down to her shoulders – a charcoal black as it shimmered in the lamplight. Her skin was pearly white and her cheeks rosy. Her smile made dimples in her cheeks and her teeth, pure white, showed when she did. She was beauty itself. I was mesmerised by her. Already she had proven to be of quick wit and a beautiful soul, and immediately I wanted to know her more.

'I'm...' I paused for a moment, 'I'm Johan.'

It was the first time in a long time that I had told that truth, and although it may have proven, in the past, to be dangerous, here it proved nothing more than the simple truth – no danger attached.

She smiled that beautiful smile. 'I'm Alina. It is nice to meet you, Johan.'

'Trust me,' I said, grinning stupidly, 'the pleasure is mine.'

'Well, aren't you a gentleman. And what brings you to this place, Johan?'

'I was passing by.' I looked at the shelf of books and dusted it, procrastinating my words. 'I thought this village looked ideal to explore, so I'm doing just that.'

'Just passing by?' She eyed me suspiciously.

I nodded. 'That's right. Just passing by.'

'And you know that there is a war going on, don't you?'

'Is there? I hadn't noticed.'

Idiot, I thought to myself.

We stared at each other for a moment, before she softened and replied, 'Well, you won't find anything in here. This place is not exactly the nicest or prettiest. Do you want to come with me, and I can show you around our town?'

'Really? You would show me around?'

'No,' she said definitively. 'I only said that for my own amusement.'

'Oh,' I said while looking down, feeling as idiotic as ever.

As I looked at my feet, her small little black shoes came into view. She put her hand on my chest and her other hand on my chin and lifted it.

'I was joking,' she said, smiling at me. 'If I didn't want to show you around, I wouldn't have offered in the first place. So, are you ready to go exploring?'

'Yes,' I answered excitedly. Her personality was as beautiful as she was, with her wit and her, I would assume often, sarcastic humour.

She grabbed my hand and pulled me out of the building, onto the streets where people bustled with food stocked in one hand and holding their partner's in the other. Stalls were set up and sold things from food to toys. Young children had abandoned their parents to play with one another in the streets, and people smiled as we walked past them, content with the food in their stomachs and the company they had.

Alina took me to the town square where a water fountain was the main attraction, dominating the centre. It was carved from a solid stone base and moved up to a bowl, where water filled from the top and overflowed to the main basin. Above the bowl stood a smaller spout that had carvings on it. Alina tugged at my arm toward the fountain and we both sat on the stone edge, the water running behind us.

'Do you like it?' she asked.

I nodded enthusiastically. 'I do. It's beautiful.'

'I never thought I would be showing a German boy around my town,' she stated. 'But to be honest, I am glad that I am.'

I smiled and averted eye contact, giggling modestly.

'See that building over there?' Alina pointed to a tall clock tower building made of red bricks. The black clock and its numbers were outlined with gold.

I nodded.

'My grandfather built that tower. Well, not just him, but he helped. It was many years ago. Before I was born. He was a great builder, they say. But he never forgave my father for not following in his footsteps.'

'What does your father do?' I ask inquisitively.

'He is a physicist. He works away mostly. He is in Moscow at the moment, and will be until the end of the month, maybe longer.'

My stomach churned. I thought I was going to be sick, but I held it and nodded, knowing all the while that she had absolutely no idea of what was to come – and the problem was, I did.

'What about you, Johan? What does your father do?'

'He died a few years ago. He was killed by the *Sturmabteilung*. Before that he was a doctor for the army, and then he moved home and set up his own practice.'

Alina was quiet and put her hand on mine.

'I'm so sorry, Johan. I had no idea. I didn't mean–'

'There's no need to apologise. You admit yourself that you had no idea. Why would you? It's something that happened years ago, and each day, I tell myself that it gets better. I suppose I'm better at lying to myself, than accepting the truth.'

'Trust me, it can get better. I used to think the same when my mother died. I–'

'Your mother died? I'm so sorry.'

'You don't have to be sorry, you didn't do anything, Johan. We've both lost someone dear to us. Someone close. A parent. It's the worst feeling in the world.'

'What happened, if I may ask?'

'When I was nine, she was attacked on the street, left to die. Her attackers took the necklace that was her mother's, soon to be mine. She died two days later in the hospice. I remember seeing her, lying on the bed, motionless. She was fed from a cup, drinking liquids because she couldn't swallow any solids. I hated seeing her like that. She was so hopeless, and I felt I couldn't do anything. When I was sick, she would hold me, bathe me, feed me and love me. When she was sick, all I could do was love her and watch her slowly dwindle.' Alina looked up to the sky as tears pooled in her eyes.

'My father always told me that loving her was enough, but I could never believe him. He tried so hard, so desperately, to make me feel less guilty of the whole thing, but no matter what he said, I didn't believe him.'

'I thought the same about my father. I watched him die.'

'You saw it?'

I nodded solemnly.

'He was forced to the ground, and to the point when they

pulled the trigger. I remember turning my head, hoping to block everything out. And then, when it had all happened, I ran over to where he lay.' I felt Alina's hand squeeze mine, as I felt a lump forming in my throat. 'I begged him to come back, even pleaded that he wouldn't die. I didn't want him to die.'

'Of course, you didn't, but that's not your fault.'

That was the first time anyone, apart from blood relations, who told me it was not my fault, and I felt shivers run down my spine as I realised perhaps it was truth they all spoke.

'My mother,' she began, 'was the strongest person I knew. She held on for far longer than I anticipated. I could only see her until the second day she was in the hospice, and somehow, I have always thought that she held on for me – that she waited for me.'

I looked at Alina and smiled gently. 'I'm sure she did.'

She returned the smile and quickly averted her gaze shyly.

'Do you have any siblings, Johan?'

I nodded. 'One. A sister. Her name is Edith. And you?'

Alina shook her head.

'No. I am an only child. But tell me about your sister. What is she like? And where is she now? Did she come to the motherland with you?'

'No,' I said softly. 'She, and my mother, are... they were captured and put into camps back in Germany. I have not seen either of them for two years. I sometimes wonder if she would have changed so much that I would never be able to recognise her. That she would grow up into a beautiful woman, unrecognisable to me.'

Alina was silent. I knew she was at a loss of words, and I didn't blame her. She blinked away the tears, but a number travelled down her cheek, moving with the crevices. She found her voice and replied, 'No matter how our appearance changes, you can always recognise family, even if they have aged far beyond what you remember. Trust me, you would know her the moment you saw her.'

She went quiet again for a moment, as though contemplating if to ask or not, but eventually looked at me and asked, 'Why were they captured, may I ask?'

'When Father died, we were moved to a ghetto. I ran away,

afraid of everything that was happening. I was teased by many of the boys.

'On my first week, I was stripped bare by two boys and beaten until my ribs were dark purple. Then, one of them put a knife to my neck and held it tight, cutting my skin slightly. I felt the blood drip down my neck and onto the tiled floor. We were in the bathroom of the community hall, after marching for an hour. When he held the knife, he looked at me and said, "You won't last a year in this place. And if you do, we will both make sure it isn't a day over." They held my head to the cold tiles for a few seconds and pushed hard, then smacked my face, before standing up and leaving.

'I lasted two months, and I couldn't do it anymore. The boys would gather in the bathroom and wait for me to enter, before beating me again and again. Sometimes I would wait a whole day just to get home and use the toilet, I was so afraid.

'So, one day, I sat up in my bed during the night and stayed there, staring out of my window. I felt awful for leaving my mother and sister, I truly did, but I just couldn't bear the beatings anymore. If anyone touched me when my father was around, he would take them aside and say something – I have no idea what, but it worked – and they would stop.'

'Johan, I…' I could tell Alina was at a loss of words. Her voice was petite, but she managed to say, 'I am so sorry this happened to you.'

I sighed heavily. 'I packed my bags and ran far away from our house. Not for long, though. I wasn't an athlete, so I managed to get out of the gate and began panting for water.'

Alina laughed, and I followed. But it didn't last long before we were both serious again.

She looked at me quizzically. 'Why did this happen to you?'

I put my hands in my pockets, ruffling them around, desperately trying to find the pendant I was given by the Russian soldier, before I realised that I was no longer in my uniform, which had become a part of me. I took my hands out of my pockets and rested them on the stone wall of the fountain.

'Once, I never knew. I was completely oblivious. I always thought it was because I was small, and therefore an easy target.

But it was much darker than that, and much deeper.' I took a long, deep breath. 'It's because we're Jewish.'

Alina was stunned. She sat there in complete silence, looking at me. I blew it. I knew, as soon as I uttered those words, she was done with me. I frantically looked around, to the side, into Alina's eyes for any sign, before quickly averting them again to the ground. Then, I felt it. Her soft hand on mine. It was warm, and she placed it gently on top. She looked at me and I looked back at her.

'That changes nothing for me,' she said. 'Trust me when I say that I would never think, for a moment, that any of this was deserved because of that fact.'

I smiled and blinked a few times. 'Thank you.'

'I could never know what it is to be beaten mercilessly until I hurt so much, I could not walk. I... I would not even know what it is like to be mocked. I hope this doesn't make you think any different of me. I know people despise me for it. I despise myself for it.'

'No,' I replied. 'Of course not. And don't despise yourself – we all change. Some for the worse, but some for the better.'

'I was sent to a prestigious school for girls in Leningrad. My mother went there, and so did my grandmother. When I was there, I was quite popular among my peers. Everyone looked up to me, everyone would want to talk to me. The truth is, I could never tell you if I was ever mean to someone, because I forget all of those people who I never knew. If I was mean to someone, I would never – never – know, because I would never be able to tell you what the name of my closest friend was.' She looked at me, almost frightened. 'When people would say my name, I could not even remember them. The truth is, I cannot even look at you and understand what you went through.'

As she told me her story, she began to slowly cry, the tears swelling up in her eyes. Finally, they rolled down her cheeks.

'I'm sorry, Johan, I can't understand at all what you went through. What you are *going* through.'

'Alina, I'm not asking you to feel what I went through, or even understand. I just want you to know because it made me the person that I am now. Everything that happens in life makes us who we are. It doesn't matter whether you were popular or not, because that has made you a beautiful person for me to meet, and for that, I couldn't have asked for more.'

Alina blushed in the light and looked down with a smile. I knew she was unique. Everyone says they are unique, but only a few tell the truth.

CHAPTER 15

October 15, 1941

Alina and I talked further by the fountain for another hour, before deciding to walk the streets and get something to eat. Time became nothing to me, as the darkness was to be a continual phenomenon for many hours to come. I began to care less about the time and more about the mysteries of Alina – I wanted to know her more and more. People were still out, and it seemed like more than when we first walked there. People nodded and greeted Alina by her name, smiling at me afterward. We both grabbed small bits of candy that were being sold, hard boiled and decorated in all sorts of patterns and colours. We walked around, watching small performances shown in certain parts of the town; some of the local acting abilities, some of their musical nature, and others for their acrobatic skills. We finally came to a bench in a nicely manicured park, not far from all the commotion, and sat down. It was dark, with just enough light from the lamps in the town centre reaching the park, allowing us to make out the figures of trees, gardens and the few other people who were sitting together.

'What is all this?' I finally asked. 'Why the street fair and night trading?'

'Historically, this was when it started to get too cold to go out during the night, so it is the last night before people will start preparing for winter. Each year there is a street fair and night trading, which does well for the town. People buy all sorts of things, but they mainly go out for the sake of having a little fun.'

'How many people live here?'

'In the town, perhaps eight hundred. But there are thousands who live out of the town, on the farmlands, that come in all the time. They send their children to our school and buy their food from our shops. It helps us – it keeps us together as a community.'

'May I ask, why here?' Alina looked at me puzzled. 'Why this village, I mean? You said you went to a prestigious school for girls in Leningrad. So why come here? What is there?'

Alina became anxious but began talking reluctantly.

'My father's work is here. But not in town. There... there is a place just outside of the village where he works. I cannot tell anyone. But it was also the home of my family – my father's father.'

'Then why tell me?'

'Because, for some reason, I trust you. You told me about your life in Germany, and so I thought I could tell you this.'

I nodded. 'You can. I'm sorry, I shouldn't have said anything.'

'The facility is mostly underground, but there is a large building above it, too. My father is part of a team there that tests certain things for...' She looked around, whipping her head from left to right, before leaning in and whispering, 'the government.'

'What does your father do if he is a physicist?'

'He tests for weapons, I think. But he works with biologists and chemists, all of who work to develop things. At least, that's what I think it is. I never want to ask him.'

'I would,' I said bluntly. 'If my father was doing that sort of thing, I would ask him all sorts of questions. Like why he was doing it, what it was for, was he testing on animals or humans, maybe if he was–'

'Please, Johan. I don't want to think about it. Sometimes I think it is just best not knowing. I love my father, with all my heart, but I do not know if his heart has been the same since my mother died. I know I should never say this, but I know I can trust you. I think my father does round up people who are… lawbreakers, so to say. Enemies of the government.'

'Well, that isn't necessarily the same thing. Lawbreakers may not necessarily be enemies of the government.'

'Here, they are. Here, the government is the law. Whatever the government says, it is done. Without question. If they wanted all newborn children to be slaughtered, then every child would be. They are all monsters.'

'It seems all of them, everywhere, are.' There was a pause, before I continued. 'What does he do when he rounds them up?' Curiosity was no stranger, and I couldn't help but ask, inquisitive of the story and wanting to know more.

'I think he uses them. For experiments. It's like it is his way of enacting revenge for my mother's death. As though, somehow, torturing these people will make it all better. I would never accuse my father, but when he comes home with stains of blood on his shirt, and no desire to speak to me, I have to wonder what is going on.'

'Sometimes we assume too much. We think we know all answers; we think we know exactly what is happening, what has happened and what will happen, sometimes we think we know how to fix it, and the truth is, we haven't a clue. That's called life. People are still trying to figure it out. Some people are still searching. The fact that I met you, I would never have known would happen. Sometimes we don't know, and it's for the best.'

'That's what I want. I know that maybe, only maybe, my father is doing what I suspect. But I'm not ready to know. I just want this to be over, so I can have my father back; to sit and talk to him about my life and not his. Not about how tired he is or how stressful his day was, but about what I want to do, where I want to go.'

I felt my stomach churn as the thought of her father in Moscow brought with it the sickening feeling of death, again. All she wanted was her father back, and she had no idea what was to come. But I knew, and I could not bring myself to look at her the more I thought about it. If her father survived, it would be a miracle, and if he died, it would just be another death in the war – but it would be a death that I foresaw.

I thought about telling her but cowered at the thought and remained quiet. I attempted to think of another conversation point, but the image of her sitting by her father's grave dominated my thoughts and refused to go away. As I thought frantically about what to say, I felt her arm wrap around mine. I looked at her.

'Come with me,' she said. 'I want to show you something.'

She took us to a hill which, thankfully, was on the opposite side to where our army was camped. We walked to the top and sat on the grass, which was cold but not wet. I outstretched my legs and lay on my back, looking up at the stars. There were no clouds, just the moon and stars. Alina lay next to me.

'Whenever I look up at the stars, I always wonder just how small I am,' I said.

'My father always told me that we are tiny. We are not even a speck in the universe. We are invisible. He always said that too many people think they are something important in this world, and that they have more of a right than anyone else, but that all they had to do was look up at the night sky and know how truly small they were.'

'I know a few people who could do that,' I said.

Alina laughed.

'Me too, Johan. There are too many people that need to do that.'

'When I was young, I had a teacher that would never look at the boy who sat at the back. She said that the boy was filthy, and until he cleaned and presented himself well, she would refuse to teach him. Everyone called him Odie. We found out his parents had died, and he had nowhere to live. All he wanted was to learn. I made friends with him one day, and he was so grateful that he offered me a piece of his apple, which was his only piece of food for the day.'

'That was nice of you, Johan.'

'After that, the teacher sent me for a caning. She said I had disobeyed her and should be punished. The day after, I found a letter that was from Odie, written in terrible handwriting and he could not spell. But he tried, and I managed to read it. It said:

Johan, I am sorry for getting you into trouble. Please forgive me. You are a good person. God bless you. I ran away because it was the best thing to do. Thank you for your kindness.

Odie

'I never saw him after that. The teacher was pleased, and so were many of the students in my class. But I wasn't. I missed him. Maybe that teacher should look up and realise that everything she ever said won't matter soon. It will all be forgotten by everyone, except for Odie.'

'My teacher hated one girl who was in my class for Literature. One day, she pulled the girl out of the class and hit her across the face. Do you know why she did it?'

'Why?'

'Because the girl was from Poland. She said she did not deserve to be in such a prestigious Russian school, and that she should have gone back to her homeland. The girl was in tears. That teacher is now the leading lecturer of Literature at the Lomonosov Moscow State University. That was where my father studied.'

I sighed. 'Sometimes life is unfair. Most times, I think.'

'I agree. And it does not go well.'

'But sometimes it is. If it isn't fair once in a while, I would never have met you.'

Alina blushed.

'You are the kindest, and yet the most clichéd person I think I have ever met.' We both giggled. 'But I am glad I met you too, Johan. Sometimes it is nice to know that there are people out there like you.'

I laughed shyly.

'Trust me, if the whole world were people like me, it would be a disaster.'

'Which is exactly why you are unique, and I am lucky.'

Alina sat up and motioned me to do the same. She pointed and whispered, 'Look there.'

She pointed to the village, which gave off a gentle glow amidst the forest and hills. The tower was clearly visible. The village was circular, with only a few buildings scattered around the outside of it. When we were silent, the noise from the chatter was faintly heard from the hill, as people were still about.

'When does it all end?' I asked.

'Are you joking with me? This is only the start. It goes until the early hours of the morning. Most people begin the drinking at around this hour.'

'Drinking? Of what?'

'It is mostly drinking competitions, especially of vodka, which is the favourite. Do you want to try, do you?' she giggled.

'Actually,' I began, 'I really should be going soon. But I don't want to leave.'

'Where do you have to go to?'

I paused for a moment. 'Back to where we are camped.'

'You are with people?'

'There is a group of us. We were only passing by. But none of them came down to the village.'

'Where are you camped?'

I started to become anxious. I didn't know how to answer Alina's questions, nor could I respond in time before it began to look suspicious.

'Far away,' I finally said, 'on the other side of the village, quite a distance.'

'You are welcome to stay with me, Johan. Come, and I can take you to my home for the night if you wish. I don't mind, truly. The housemaid will make you comfortable in the spare bedroom.'

'I can't,' I said apologetically. I stood up, and Alina followed shortly after. 'I'm sorry, but I really *have to* go back tonight.'

Alina was upset and disappointed, and so I approached her and put my hands on her upper arms.

'But not before we have a little longer. Maybe I can see one competition.'

Her smile was from cheek to cheek as she quickly grabbed my hand and led me back into the village, where we gathered with the rest of the people from the village. We arrived where the fountain was, all encircling a small wooden table with two chairs. Placed on the table was a bottle of vodka and two small glasses.

Two men emerged from the crowd and sat at the table. One of the men was largely rounded, with a grey beard that flowed down to his stomach, and a stare that could kill a man if he looked long enough. The other looked younger, and in far better shape than his opponent. He was clean shaven, and his muscles bulged from his clothing as he flexed them to the crowd.

Both men sat down as they wrapped their fingers around the glass in front of them. A woman walked to the table and announced something in Russian, before pouring the vodka into the two glasses. Both men sculled it within seconds and the woman poured another glass.

This continued until both men were onto their thirteenth glass, holding onto the table for dear life as they swayed from side to side. The larger man grabbed the glass with his thick fingers and brought it up to his mouth, before collapsing to the ground and smashing the glass with him on the cold stone. The younger man played with his glass, moving his finger up and down it before tipping it over and slamming his head on the table.

I wasn't sure who had won, let alone if anyone actually did win, but the crowd cheered and I was bumped left to right as the people next to me jumped up and down in a frenzy. I felt Alina's hand on my shoulder as she pulled me back and out of the crowd. She looked at me, saddened as she knew that we would now part. But although I was saddened at the thought of never seeing her again, this night was the one time in my life that I had felt I truly belonged in a long time. It was the first time that I had opened up to a person like that, and I hoped she felt the same. She looked me in the eyes.

'I don't want you to go,' she said. 'I know you have to, but to me, I wish you could stay forever.'

I smiled. 'And you said I was the cliché one.'

We both laughed, which managed to suppress the poignancy that we both knew was inevitable.

'You know, coming here is one of the best decisions I have ever made, and I wouldn't trade it for anything.'

'It will be hard to watch you go, Johan. Tonight is the first time I truly realised that there are good people in the world, not just bad ones. Especially some of you Germans,' she giggled.

We sighed with a smile in the corner of our mouths, before the tears began to show. We looked at each other for a moment. I looked into her eyes as she looked into mine. She approached me and pecked me on the lips with hers. She pulled her head away just enough so our eyes met again, before she said, 'Maybe someday life will be kind to us again and let us meet.'

'I will always look forward to that day, Alina. Every day, until it happens.'

'So will I, Johan. Stay safe. And never forget that you are better than what you let people say you are. Just do not let it make you someone you dislike. If ever you need, look up at the stars and know who you are, and how small you are. Just to keep you on course.'

Smiling, I nodded and looked down as I squeezed my eyes shut tight, trying to make the tears go away. But they didn't. They kept coming. I looked up as the tears trickled down my cheeks. Alina smiled, her eyes filled with tears too, and turned. I turned, my hands in my pockets, and looked down, sniffing as I cried. With one last gesture, Alina kissed me on the cheek.

'Remember,' she began, 'when we look up to the night sky, we both look at the same stars.'

I wiped the tears from my face and smiled.

'Always,' I replied. 'Always.'

I went to the house where I had left my clothes and changed into my uniform. I hung the clothes I had worn all night, back where they were and headed back to the camp. I crept through our campsite and crawled back into my tent. As I lay there, I kept thinking of the night which I had just experienced. Something I thought I would never see in this war. Human kindness, love, affection and beauty. Alina taught me that life may be cruel, but it's what you do with it that matters. And I chose to go into that village. I made the decision, and it rewarded me with everything that followed.

I lay with my hands resting on my stomach, smiling as I thought of what had occurred. It was like magic, but it was better – it was real.

Concentration Camp

Humans are odd creatures. They claim to feel empathy, even sympathy at times, and yet they are the coldest species on earth. They are capable of killing, of torture, of hate, and yet they expect to be loved in return. The fiery ball of flames that hangs in the sky will, with any mercy, engulf them as they continue to murder.

But there are those that love, and in return, they expect nothing more. They want to love for those who are not loved, and they want to let them know that, perhaps, the entire species is not as guilty as the ones who have power are.

Each day I see men, the same, sometimes different, who come and go. They hate, and they hate mercilessly. They will not tolerate anyone who shows a glimmer of hope. I watch on as they beat the men who are already beaten, torture the men who have been tortured one hundred times over, and spit in the faces of hope. A sign of hope is a threat, and the sign of a threat must be eliminated.

I remember the faces of the men when I was young, and they were new. My walls had no marks on them, and my steel would glisten in the sunlight. The men would look up in awe or horror – it depended on why they were looking. Some looked on because they built me, others looked because they were to keep charge of me, and the unlucky ones were those who had to endure me.

They were frightened, I could tell. And I was not going to show mercy. I was in my prime. I was new, pristine, a statement to an empire. I was to keep control of them. But as time goes on, I become weakened by nature and by man. My walls are decorated with carvings from the labourers, my steel is now rusted. I have seen all too well where these men go – hell is a holiday for them.

They neither sleep nor eat well. They are forced to work, every bit of energy and will being sucked from them like the last drops of water from a cloth, until they are worked dry. They lay on their wooden beds, barely breathing, crying, praying and hoping that their time will end.

Clickity clack, clickity clack, the sounds of Death's footsteps approach. He sits and watches, as they plead for the end. Death is not as merciless as some may think. Death comes at the right time, whether people are ready or not. Death will watch, observing everything that occurs. And sometimes, Death will weep for those who wish to die, for no one should wish it. But out of that dark place of desperation, they cry for it.

CHAPTER 16

November 18, 1941

The landscape was pure white, snow trickling down with no intention of stopping. We continued to head for Moscow, but the weather had begun to slow us down rapidly, with little progress some days, and none on others. But today we slowly moved towards the capital of the motherland, inch by inch. The tanks and trucks were slowing down, and we stopped multiple times to refuel and fix the engines. The cold had meant that each morning, the vehicles were started up an hour before we continued moving, so the engines were running properly. They struggled in the cold, just as we did – their gears grinding slowly in the sharp frost.

I walked with Earnst and Felix for most of the trip, carrying our heavy backpacks and guns, trudging through the thick snow. We wrapped our coats high above our chins to escape the cold from our mouths, which muffled our voices as we spoke. I pulled down my coat so my mouth was exposed, chilling my lips. Frost flowed from my mouth as I breathed heavily.

'This weather is too cold,' I complained. 'It isn't half as bad back in the Fatherland. Where I grew up, we didn't get much snow. Mainly rain, but a bit of snow every few years.'

'Same with us,' replied Earnst. 'It used to be the same where I grew up. We would get a bit of snow, and then too much rain. In the morning, the snow would be brown and slushy, and we would run out and jump in it in our boots.'

'I did the same with Edith and Father. Though Mother never liked it. She always said that we would catch a cold, and that it was terribly silly behaviour. Then I remember when Father pulled her out of the house and into the puddles,' I laughed. 'She was in a terrible mess, but couldn't stop laughing with Edith and me.'

'I remember when I was very young at school, I threw a large chunk of this disgusting brown slush at one of the older boys.' Earnst shaped his hands in a ball, showing the size of the snowball he was describing. He motioned a throwing action. 'I threw it as hard as I could, and it landed straight on one of the boys' faces. His name was George – he was from England. He was visiting for a short while, and it hit him straight on the cheek. He was knocked backward and then I remember the whole group chasing after me. So, I ran as fast as I could through the school hallways and out of the front doors. I ran into the nearby forest and sat under a large tree that was near a hollow. Ever since then, I would always go to that tree after school and sit, think, sometimes I would bring a friend. I had my first kiss there.'

'With the brown sludge?' I grinned.

Earnst laughed and punched me lightly in the arm. 'No. A girl. I can't even remember her name. But I remember what she looked like. Long, blonde hair. Bright, green eyes. She was beautiful. But I know I'll never see her again after this. She's long gone.'

'She might not be, you know. Just say, theoretically, this war ended once we get to Moscow. You could go straight back home, and she could be there, waiting for you.'

Earnst shook his head.

'No. She went to study at university overseas somewhere. I doubt she would go back to where we were.'

'The world is a funny place. Anything can happen.'

'Like what?'

'We have a man with a moustache like Charlie Chaplin giving us orders. Trust me when I say that *anything* can happen.'

We both laughed at the sentiment.

'I met a girl,' I continued.

'Oh, yeah? Where did you meet her?'

'Do you promise not to tell?'

'Hans, we talk about everything together and I haven't said one word.'

Not everything, I thought. *Not everything.*

I glanced over at Felix to see if he was listening, but he was long gone from this planet, wandering awkwardly off to one side. He wasn't paying the slightest attention. I looked back at Earnst, then forward again.

'When we were camped outside of that village, when we weren't allowed to speak or even light a candle. Do you remember that?'

'Hans, that was weeks ago.'

'I know, but do you remember it?'

'Of course, I do.'

'Well, that night, when it was completely dark, I snuck out of my tent and went down to the village, where I met a girl.'

'You snuck out of your tent? Are you crazy?'

I nodded and smiled, widening my eyes.

'Of course, I am. Someone has to be. Anyway, when I went down there, I borrowed some clothes and–'

'From whom?'

'Well, I don't know who it was. But they were hanging outside. So, I changed into them and hid my uniform. And I went into the village.'

'Into a village that spoke a language you didn't understand?'

'Well, that's when I met Alina. I was in a small shop, reading through some dusty old books, when she tapped me on the shoulder. It took a while before she realised that I spoke German, but she was fluent in it. She went to some prestigious school in Leningrad, and they had to learn fluent German, English and French.'

'She can speak four languages fluently?'

I nodded.

'Poor Felix has enough trouble with our own,' Earnst joked.

I laughed with him.

'She was really sweet. And so beautiful. She showed me around the village, and we talked for a long time, almost everywhere. I told her about myself, and she told me about herself. We both opened up to each other, like we had known each other already for such a long time before.'

'What did you do?'

'She showed me around – there was a local fair on that night. I stayed until the drinking games started and watched one before I left.'

'You mean, there were drinking games and you didn't invite me? Or at least bring me some when you got back?'

'Knowing you, you would've finished the bottle and stumbled into camp asking Sergeant Shödler if you looked like his wife.'

Earnst laughed heavily.

'You're in love,' he said smugly.

I grinned.

'I think I might me. She was so beautiful.' I paused for a moment. 'But I'm never going to see her again.' The thought hit me. *I would never see her again.*

'You said yourself, the world is a funny place. Anything can happen.'

I nodded. 'I hope so.'

'Have you heard anything from Sergeant Shödler lately?' Earnst asked.

'What do you mean?'

'Well, has he threatened you or talked to you at all since the battle a month ago?'

'He mentions it here and there. I still think he framed the Russian soldiers. But it's too late to prove any of that. No one will believe me, and if I say it too loud, Shödler will probably gag me during the night and beat me.'

'You can't keep quiet forever.'

'I have about a lot of things. It isn't that hard. We can't exactly change what happened.'

'I never thought I would hear you say that.'

'Say what?'

'That we can't change what happened. Hans, you are one of the only people I know who is willing to stand up and do the right thing. You keep saying that we should be trying to find peace, and you always look for the good in people.'

'What luck that's done me,' I mumbled.

'Don't be like that. We all have our qualities, and I would bet anyone that yours are far greater than a lot of men in this army.'

'Thanks, Earnst. Do you know something? You are one of the only soldiers who still looks out for me. Like Oskar did.' I went quiet for a moment, swallowing as my voice became hoarse. 'I miss him every day. I think about it every day. It used to just be my mother, my father and my sister, and now it's him too. Sometimes I just wish he was here to tell me what to do. To help me, like a big brother.'

'Oskar was a great man. He would have done anything to protect you. And you know he would have taken a bullet for you. And maybe he did, but you just don't know it. We don't know what happened at the bottom of that hill. A soldier may have been about to pull the trigger on you, and Oskar jumped in. But we know that he died fighting, and we both know that's the way he would have wanted it.'

I raised my eyebrows in contemplation, then bit my lip to one side.

'I suppose. It does make me feel better knowing that, even though it was too soon for me, I knew he wanted to die in battle. It may not have been this one, and at that age, but he did anyway. But I still want him back. I don't want anyone to die. Especially not him.' My voice trembled. 'I want him back, Earnst.'

I felt Earnst's hand on my back.

'You're not alone. That's just being human.'

Being human means a lot of things. It means to love, to hate, to have empathy, to misunderstand, to cry, to laugh, and all of that can sometimes be good, and it can also be poison. I knew that I had felt all of these at one point, and I intended to feel them again in the future, but when and where was a mystery.

Being human also means you can be an angel – you can love and be loved. But it also means you can be a demon. The choice is yours alone, and that is both a beautiful thing, and something to be feared.

We continued walking until it was dark, which had become earlier and earlier as the winter set in, far quicker than we had expected. We camped the night on open farmlands which were now covered in snow. We knew camping out in the open was far too risky as an alternative to travelling further a few more miles for cover, but all around us were open lands. One lone pine tree stood a few feet from our camp, and a clump of about ten were further east, but they wouldn't provide the cover we needed. Our commanders decided that it wasn't worth it, and we set up our camp. Our tents were becoming damaged, and so it was three men to a tent, to preserve what we had for as long as we needed. Naturally, I was sharing a tent with Earnst and Felix, which wasn't as bad as I had expected – although Felix's wriggling during his sleep turned into a violent escapade of kicking the space around him, which was now occupied by two other people.

Sleep was difficult in this weather. The cold draughts would come in slowly, and then develop into large gusts that would almost knock us from our feet, more than just a few times. The nights were the worst, however. They provided no comfort, and even bodily warmth was at a minimum. Wrapped in our uniforms and greatcoats, along with blankets and shelter from the wind, the chill would still seep in, and we would shiver in the night. I would tuck my head beneath all layers that I was cocooned in, and let my warm breath try to keep my body warm, but it never seemed to work – and when I would take my head out of the layers, it would freeze, and my face would feel numb.

We sat around our own small fire that warmed eight sets of hands. There was nothing to sit on, so the cold, wet ground had to suffice. It was not all bad once we were used to it, it was the initial point of forcing ourselves to sit in it, and the emotional build-up beforehand that bothered us. But as we sat and held our hands out, wrestling each other for more warmth, we talked as much as anyone could talk, about anything and everything. Some men at other campfires were silent, too silent – but we, as young boys who craved life, kept each other alive. I sat and listened to the conversations like usual, putting in my points every few moments, just to let people know I was there, and alive.

'... and he rushed up to me, with his fist clenched like this, and took a swing. But I managed to duck in time and push him over, and he landed straight in the mud,' exclaimed a boy named Roderick.

He was seventeen, one of the youngest. He had lied about his age to be accepted into the army, and we all had our suspicions that he was lying about this story too.

'Absolutely shit, Roderick,' said Felix. 'You're lying straight from your teeth. You wouldn't push him just after he threatened to split you in two!'

'I did!' snapped Roderick. 'If you were there, you would know.'

'Of course, because we were going to be at your school when you were fifteen,' Earnst said sarcastically.

'You should have seen me at school,' said Heinrich. 'Everyone feared me. Even the teachers.'

'They probably avoided you because of the smell,' I said.

All of the soldiers laughed, though it was at Heinrich's expense. Heinrich managed a small smile in the corner of his mouth.

'I'm only joking, Heinrich,' I said, just to calm the waters between us.

He smiled and nodded, then looked down at his feet.

'What about you, Hans? What were you like at school?' Waldron asked.

'I... I wasn't exactly the tough one,' I explained. 'I was more the one who was beaten up.'

The group was silent.

'But I bet I could take them now. If not, I'll just introduce them to Sergeant Shödler. I'm sure that bastard could clean them up.'

I felt uncomfortable saying it, especially when it was criticising people directly, but it made the group laugh and for once I felt as though all positive attention was on me.

'Heinrich was pretty bruised from the beating he got from Sergeant Shödler, weren't you Heinrich?' said Waldron.

'You weren't much better,' retorted Heinrich. 'Colonel Hirsch left you with a cut on your ear and bruises all on your stomach.'

'You were both extremely messed up by those two,' said Roderick. 'Though I could probably do a better job.'

The whole group sighed in unison and rolled our eyes, knowing Roderick was just playing on his strength again, as though he was Hercules.

'Shall we put you in a tent with those two after we've got you into trouble and see who comes out looking better then?' said Felix.

Roderick raised his eyebrows, then picked up a stone and threw it into the fire.

Waldron leaned in close to the fire, and whispered, 'I heard that the Russians didn't really try to assassinate the commander.'

'Where did you hear that from?' I asked anxiously.

'Some soldiers were saying it. They said Shödler was just trying to get revenge for something. Was he?'

'How are we supposed to know?' said Earnst. 'The man is a psychopath. He may have, he may not have. We can't expect to keep on his trail all day, every day and know his exact movements, can we?'

Waldron bowed his head, then turned to Earnst.

'No, I guess not. Sorry, I was just wondering.'

'It's fine, Waldron. Just don't ask questions that no one can answer, or that will get us into trouble. It's hard enough trying to do right by Sergeant Shödler without accusing him of wanting to destroy a surrendering army.'

I looked at Earnst and mouthed, *Thank you*. He smiled and nodded. At least Earnst knew how to keep a secret, and what the difference between life and death was, especially when it concerned our own soldiers.

Our chatter continued into the night, as we shared stories, laughter, silence, even a few tears. Felix was in the middle of a story about how, when he was very young, he fell into a river and was swept upstream. The story was intriguing, and as I was entranced, I was startled by the presence of someone standing behind me. I could see out of the corner of my eye, as Felix stopped almost immediately, and everyone looked up. I turned around to see Sergeant Shödler glaring down at me.

'Adler, a moment. *Now*.'

I heard Earnst whisper, '*Shit*.'

I nodded and stood up, swallowing nervously. I followed him into his tent, and he signalled for me to sit. He sat with his legs crossed and his hands clasped in front of his chin, his elbows resting on the arms of his seat.

'Are you happy, Hans?' he asked.

I gave him a confused look, and asked, 'What do you mean, Sergeant?'

'I mean, are you happy? You don't look happy. I thought perhaps I could help cheer you up.'

Was this some kind of twisted joke? Of course, I wasn't happy. None of us were in this mess. He looked at me, waiting for an answer.

'I suppose not,' I said.

'You suppose not? Disappointing answer, but it will have to do. Do you know why you are unhappy, Adler?'

I shrugged. 'I guess.'

'Why, then, are you unhappy?'

'I suppose I don't like the war.'

'You don't like fighting for the empire you love? You don't like defending your homeland? You don't like fulfilling the Führer's dreams and hopes for our empire?'

'I don't like being here.'

'Being here, as in Russian territory, or being here as in being here with me?'

'Both,' I snarled.

Sergeant Shödler snickered. He leaned forward and pointed at me.

'I think the reason you are unhappy is because you have been spreading naughty little stories about me, haven't you?'

'What? No, I haven't.'

'Oh, but you have. And I don't like soldiers who spread deceiving little messages about me.'

'You never liked me in the first place.'

'On the contrary, I tried at one point, very early on. I thought I would give you a chance, but you have proven to be nothing more than a lying scoundrel. You wish to bring this army to its knees, I know it. And I am here to tell you that that will not happen. The commander enquired if these allegations were true or not – the little lies you've been spreading.'

'I haven't said anything.'

'Don't speak!' He stood up and leaned over the table, his hands placed firmly on the wooden board and his face close to mine. He gritted his teeth and continued, 'I will do whatever I need to, in order to protect myself. I have seen more war than you, Adler, and I know how to kill. So, take the hint when I tell you to leave it, and never speak of it again. Do you understand?'

I nodded quickly. 'Yes, Sergeant.'

Sergeant Shödler smiled wryly.

'There's a good boy.' His face then changed to a contorted wreck of anger. 'Now get out, before I cut you in two.'

I stood up and walked, almost jogging, out of the tent, and headed straight for the campfire. As I sat down, the soldiers leaned in and asked what he wanted. I remained silent and shook my head, staring into the flames that licked up into the night sky. I had never been so scared in my life than at that moment. Sergeant Shödler had complete power over me, and I felt as vulnerable as I would if I stood in the middle of a battle with a thousand guns all pointed at me. He had that effect, and he knew how to use it. He knew how to make someone tremble in their boots with just a look, and he would use it if it meant getting his way.

That was the end of mentioning anything about Shödler and his suspected antics, though I couldn't speak for any of the other soldiers. Earnst looked at me and tilted his head away from the group, signalling to walk over with him. I stood up and followed when Felix shouted, 'Where are you two going?'

'We won't be long, Felix. Just wait there, we'll be back soon.'

Felix nodded, and the group resumed chatting while Earnst and I walked to the tents where there were only a few soldiers. He stopped and turned to me.

'What happened?'

My breathing became heavier as I recalled Sergeant Shödler's temper, and the way he had acted in his tent.

'Shödler, he... he threatened me. He told me he was going to kill me if I said anything about what happened with the army a few months back.'

'He threatened to kill you? Hans, you have to go and tell the commander!'

'No!' I said exasperatedly. 'I can't say anything. I shouldn't even be talking to you about it. If he finds out and the commander does question him, he will know it was me and come after me. I can't risk it.'

'The commander can keep you safe, Hans.'

'He couldn't even tell Shödler was lying when he was told about an assassination attempt on him. No one knows what Shödler is truly like, and he keeps it that way. He manipulates their thoughts and makes sure no one would suspect him.'

Earnst studied my face, which was already worried, even just talking about it.

'Well, if we can't tell anyone, what are you going to do?'

'Keep quiet. If I don't do anything, nothing will happen, and it will be the end of it.'

Earnst sighed. 'All right, but if *anything* happens again like that, and I mean anything, I'm the first one you come to, got it?'

I nodded. 'Fine. But please, don't tell Felix, or anyone for that matter.'

Earnst raised an eyebrow. 'Do I look stupid?'

'Don't make me answer that,' I joked.

Earnst laughed and motioned an uppercut punch into my stomach a dozen times quickly, then turned and began to walk off.

'Come on,' he said. 'The boys are waiting.'

'What will we tell them it was about, if they ask?'

Earnst looked at me with an expression of determination.

'Shödler is a sour man, who likes to torment people for the sake of it. We'll tell them exactly that, and that he was just in one of his moods.'

I nodded and walked with Earnst back to the campfire. For some time, I felt that Felix was beginning to become jealous of Earnst and I, talking almost all day, every day. I could see it in his face. Every time Earnst and I laughed together, he would be close by, scowling at us. But anger was not a part of Felix, and he mostly hung his head low and talked quieter whenever feeling upset.

Just before Earnst came back to the tent, Felix entered and lay next to me. His breathing was heavy, and I knew he was nervous. He finally turned to me and asked, 'Do you think Earnst doesn't want to be my friend anymore?' His voice quivered.

'What? Of course, he does. Why do you ask that?'

'It just seems he enjoys talking to you more often than he does to me. We used to be close, and now he only ever says good morning to me.'

'Well maybe you could find something he enjoys talking about,' I suggested. 'Then you can bring it up and have a conversation with him.'

'It never works. He knows I'm not interested in the stuff he is. I try, but nothing works.'

'Don't get yourself anxious over nothing, Felix. Earnst still considers you his best friend. He would never think of deserting you. Trust me. The things we talk about, Felix, are to do with me. They're my problems, and he's just concerned. He only helps me where he can – offers me advice when I need it.'

'Then why not help me if I'm his best friend? Why shrug me off, just as a past memory? And why don't you accept my help when I offer?'

'I shrug off most advice I'm given. Believe me, I'm saving you a great deal of time and energy trying to counsel me. I don't listen to Earnst all that often; I know I should, but I don't. And Felix, Earnst would never think of deserting you. You're his brother.'

'He already has,' said Felix quietly.

He rolled over to the edge of the tent, with his back turned to me. I didn't know what to say, and just when I was about to speak, Earnst entered. He lay between Felix and me and ruffled Felix's hair.

'Going to sleep already?'

No answer. Felix remained still. Earnst turned to me with a look of confusion. He mouthed, *What's wrong with him?* I closed my eyes and shook my head. Earnst turned back to Felix and put his hand on his shoulder.

'Felix, what's wrong?' asked Earnst.

As he spoke those words, Felix stood up and mumbled, 'Fuck off, Earnst,' before storming out of the tent. He covered his face, which I assumed was full of tears, and ran. Earnst stood up and went to chase after him.

'Felix!'

I poked my head out of the tent to see Earnst desperately chasing after Felix, who was eager to avoid him for the time being. I waited in the tent for one of the two to return. I rolled my eyes, knowing it may have just been hormones between best friends. They reminded me of a married couple at times, and I chuckled. Felix never held a grudge for long – that I knew.

Earnst arrived back almost an hour later, worried and out of breath.

'We can't find Felix,' he exclaimed. 'We looked everywhere.'

'Wait, wait, who's we?' I asked. 'Who was looking?'

'Heinrich and me. We looked everywhere.'

'He's probably just tactfully avoiding you. Don't worry too much, he can't have left the camp. He's probably spending the night in another tent.'

'But why?'

I sighed. 'Before you came into the tent, Felix was upset that you were going to abandon him.'

'Wait, what? Abandon him? Why did he think that?'

'He sees us talking all the time, and he never knows what to talk about with you. He said he's tried, but that you know he isn't interested.'

'That's because he isn't.'

'But he's still trying. He makes the effort, and you fob him off like he doesn't know anything. He sits by himself and watches us laugh and talk, and not once do you invite him into the conversation. He was your best friend before you and I even knew each other. Don't lose him, Earnst. You helped him to read. You teach him things that none of us could. You've been his best friend, his bigger brother, so to speak.'

'So, what if I've done all of that? He doesn't thank me; he doesn't show any gratitude for it.'

'Earnst,' I said softly, 'he shows it to you every day. You may not see it, but everything he does for you is his way of saying thank you. Do you realise you both seem like hormonal teenage girls fighting over nothing?'

Earnst sighed. 'Well, what am I supposed to do?'

'Let him spend the night elsewhere. He needs space, and he needs time to think.'

'But what if he's gone away?'

'He won't get past the soldiers on watch, don't worry.'

'You did.'

He was right, I did. I didn't know how to approach the comment, and remained silent for a short while before answering,

'That's because it was dark.'

'I know you're just trying to make me feel better. That's a shit answer.'

'Anything I say will not solve the problem. Just leave it until the morning.'

'Fine,' he moaned. 'Good night.'

'Good night. And make sure you sleep, not stay up all night worrying.'

'Yes, Mother.'

I snickered. 'Good boy.'

The truth was that I was worried for Felix. Though I didn't show it, and tried to act more mature in the situation, had I displayed how I truly felt, I would have been frantically searching for Felix as well. He was in such a mess when he left, that I was worried for his safety – from himself. Out there, he was his own enemy. We weren't being attacked by Russian soldiers; we weren't being bombarded by Russian tanks. We were quietly camped. And if no one out here is an enemy, that's when you turn on yourself.

CHAPTER 17

November 19, 1941

Once I awoke, I turned straight to Earnst and shook his shoulder. Startled, he sat upright almost immediately and looked around.

'Where's Felix?' he asked anxiously.

'I don't know,' I replied. 'I only just woke up.'

Earnst groaned and dressed quickly, then exited the tent. I stood up and dressed, though not as fast or panicked as Earnst, and wandered out. It was early still, almost dark, and soldiers wandered out of their tents slowly, half asleep and wishing they were still able to sleep. Officers began to walk around and awaken anyone who was still sleeping, to which we would hear disgruntled moaning and groaning. I looked around for Earnst, and spotted him yards away, talking to soldiers, which my guess was the whereabouts of Felix. I jogged over to him and put my hand on his shoulder.

'Any luck?'

'Well, if you were here earlier you would know,' he snapped.

I closed my eyes and took a deep breath. This was not the time to be arguing, nor the subject to be arguing about. I bit my tongue, though I yearned to retaliate, and said politely, 'Earnst, I know you're worried. But it's no good taking it out on those who are trying to help. We'll find him. He's going to be around here somewhere.'

Earnst nodded and hung his head low. 'I know, I'm sorry.'

'It's fine. Let's just work on finding Felix.'

We walked around the campsite, asking soldiers if they had seen him, but none did. We were worried, I knew we were. Neither of us showed it, but I knew Earnst was worried, and he knew I was, too. I became doubtful that Felix was even in the camp and resorted to standing with my hands on the back of my head and breathing heavily. I tilted my head back and closed my eyes. *Where are you, Felix?* I thought.

We were beginning to move again, and there was no sign of Felix, from anyone. No one that had sat around our fire last night had seen him, which made both Earnst and I even more worried. I felt partially guilty for putting Earnst in this state of paranoia and anxiousness. Though it wasn't intentional, nor was there any malice, I still somehow knew that had I refrained from saying anything at all, he may have been far more reserved than he was. But perhaps this was better. He was concerned for Felix and wanted to find him for good reason – to apologise and make amends. The conflict in my head of whether I had done the right thing was always fighting, every moment of every day, and it seemed to intensify when things become bleaker.

Our camp was now packed up, and we were moving again. I desperately wanted to sit back on the tanks, to rest my feet which had blistered so badly that my feet were raw, and my skin constantly flaked. They burned, and each time I stepped, I would cringe as the pain grew. But I pushed on, as I knew every other soldier was doing.

It had been almost half an hour that we had been moving, when we came to a sudden stop. The truck that Colonel Hirsch travelled on stopped next to us. Colonel Hirsch stepped out, squinting with his mouth open in befuddlement.

'What is this? Why have we stopped?' asked a number of soldiers.

He walked off into the distance. He was gone for only ten minutes before he returned and sat in the truck. He looked at us all.

'We will be moving soon. Get ready.'

Then I heard it. He turned to the driver of the truck and the other officers who accompanied him, and said, 'They found a soldier, almost dead. One of ours. He's lucky we got to him in time. Had he been there any longer, he would be dead. Idiots, thinking they can wander about in this weather.' He shook his head and breathed heavily.

Felix.

I looked at Earnst, and he looked at me, his eyes wide and his breathing faster. As we began to march again, Earnst quickened his pace. He began to jog lightly, then broke into a run as he sprinted further forward in fear. He stopped soldiers as he frantically asked where the injured soldier was, but they continued to march on, giving cold looks at Earnst as though he was one of the soldiers who had finally cracked.

I walked faster, but didn't run, knowing I would trip on my aching feet and collapse in the snow, while the soldiers would laugh, and I would be in agony. So, I limped on as fast as my body would allow me and began to gradually catch up to Earnst. Panicked and out of breath, Earnst approached me.

'It's Felix. He's in one of the trucks.'

'Which one?' I asked.

'I don't know, but when we camp, we have to find out.'

'Of course, we will. But you can't panic. It isn't going to do either of us a favour.'

Earnst nodded. 'I know. But they said he's in a bad way. I want to see him now.'

'We won't be able to see him now. We will have to wait until we camp. Earnst, he's going to be all right. Just don't worry yourself. They found him, that's the main thing.'

I knew Earnst would panic for the rest of the day, and as would I in all honesty, but it was the best I could do in a situation like this. Earnst nodded dutifully, then hung his head low and sighed.

'We will be in Moscow, soon,' I said, trying desperately to change the subject to anything other than the recent discovery of Felix's wounded body.

'What do you think it will be like there?' asked Earnst. 'I mean, do you think there will be many people?'

'There might be. I know it's a big city, but they may have

evacuated all the residents by the time we get there. With any hope, anyway.'

'You don't want any residents in the city? They could watch us march in, waving the flag of our empire. We could show off a bit.'

I smiled lightly.

'You just want to show off to all the pretty Russian girls. Somehow, I don't think they would like it if you marched in and invaded their city, though,' I joked.

Earnst smiled with a little giggle, which was better to see than a perpetual look of worrying.

'The girls at home are better, anyway. But not to you, maybe. Do you still think about that girl you met a few weeks ago?'

I nodded.

'What was her name, again?'

'Alina. Every day, I think of her. It gets easier, I suppose, but at the same time it gets harder. I only knew her for one night and we went together so well. I could tell her almost everything about me and–'

'Almost everything?'

'Well, yes,' I stuttered.

'When you're with someone you truly love, you should be able to tell them everything.'

'Well, I meant everything. How do I know it was even love? It's stupid to think that. Even by my standards. It was one night.'

'One night which changed something for you. You didn't tell her everything, did you? There's something you didn't tell her.'

Earnst studied me for a moment, squinting his eyes and moving his lips from side to side as he thought. Then his eyes widened.

'Did she know you were a German soldier?'

I hung my head low and avoided eye contact.

'No,' I replied quietly.

'How do you expect to start a relationship – if that's what you were going to do anyway – with someone who doesn't know that they're supposed to be fighting against people like you?'

'It wasn't like that. She knew I was German, which was a start.'

'Possibly because you couldn't speak Russian and replied to her in German.'

'Yes, but she accepted me for it. She knew I wasn't a bad person and didn't hold it against me that I was German. I'm just lucky that she could speak fluent German.'

'What would happen if she didn't? She would realise you weren't from around here, assume you were a German soldier and tell the rest of the town, who would have hanged you for being a German.'

'Don't be ridiculous. That wouldn't happen.'

'But it *could* have happened.'

'But it *didn't*. You don't need to worry about me. She and I knew that we were both different to the others, and that we had some sort of connection.'

Earnst rolled his eyes.

'Spare me the love story. What comes next? You proposed to her, had one of the quickest weddings in history, and galloped off into the sunset majestically?'

My face dropped and my eye lids were closed halfway. Earnst could sense I was irritated.

'I was only joking. But really, what was she like? What did her parents do?'

'Her mother died when she was young, and her father was – is – a physicist. She was so kind – so understanding – which is why, I guess, I opened up to her as much as I did.'

Earnst was looking down at his feet. I knew that he was back to thinking of Felix, and how he was so determined to mend their friendship. Talking about being so open with Alina had reminded him of how close he was to Felix, and we were back to square one.

'Earnst,' I said softly, 'you can't stay angry at yourself forever.'

'Oh, trust me, you can. For a long time, I've been angry at myself, for a lot of things. We never realise what some actions can do. Did you know, I made a joke of one boy at school, and he killed himself? He had had enough. He drowned himself in the river near the town. I didn't even know he was going through what he had been through. His father used to beat him and his mother. The students at school would never sit next to him, or even talk to him. And when that happened, I thought about doing the same. But I didn't. I vowed to be a better person, which is why I always try to look for the good in people. And this whole thing with Felix has these memories flooding back like it has happened all over again.

'That boy wanted to be a painter. All of the boys at the school made fun of him. They said he was a girl, and that he belonged with the girls. So, he took them up on that offer, and approached the girls at lunchtime, asking if he could sit with them. And then, without even thinking, one of the girls threw her lunch at him, and everyone laughed. They laughed like it was nothing – like he was nothing. But every one of those nothings added up to a something. And then, when he finally did it, to us it was an instant shock, but to him it was a growing reality.'

I was at a loss for words. I wondered whether I should have offered some consoling words or advice, but the fact was this whole revelation was so new to me, I couldn't even begin to think what to say.

'Earnst, sometimes we do things that we later regret,' I began, hoping the words I chose wouldn't hurt him. 'Sometimes we make mistakes, and sometimes we were a different person to who we are now. It doesn't get easier when we never forgive ourselves, and when we–'

'How can I forgive myself? After what I did? Nothing I do will take away the reality that I drove him to death.'

'Earnst, I really don't know how to convince you. Sometimes, you have to let go and accept it. Accept what you cannot change, and then use it to better yourself. It seems to me you've already done the second part. Look at you now. Look at how you treat others, with compassion and the wanting to help.'

'But I always think if I hadn't done that, and that boy didn't take his own life, then I would have never become this person that I am now. And that scares me, Hans.' His voice quivered. 'Who am I? Am I really the kind person everyone sees? What about when Felix and I did the same to you?'

'That's just what this war does – it makes it seem normal to give each other a hard time. But that's what friends do, it's part of growing old together, just never growing up.'

Earnst let out a faint laugh.

'You're more than just the kind person. You're a friend to so many, and you're a brother to Felix and me. And I wouldn't change that, ever.' I took a deep breath. 'Look, you can never change what happened – that's reality. But you can use it to change you – that's an option. And you've taken that option. There is no point in blaming yourself every day for it, and when you finally take that step, and you really forgive yourself, things will change. I know that what happened would weigh terribly on your conscience, and you've done the first step to get past it – acknowledge it. Now forgive yourself. It wasn't only you. *You* are not the singular factor.'

I could tell he wasn't entirely convinced, but there was no other way to present it. I took a deep breath and put my hand on his shoulder.

'There's no other way to convince you, Earnst. Just think about it. Please.'

I slid my hand off his shoulder and dropped back into the pack of soldiers behind us. Earnst looked behind, searching for me, but he had no luck. I walked behind two soldiers, one larger and one of average build, and could see Earnst through the gap in the middle of the two. He hung his head low, kicking the snow as he trudged along.

Not everyone is perfect, and those that boast that they are, are usually the most imperfect of us all. When we make a mistake, we are being human. And when we forgive ourselves, that's called being human, too.

Dear Edith

Edith,

My little sister. The one who makes me smile, who makes me forget my worries and transgress all evil in this world. The thought of where you are, what is happening, I cannot bear it. You were always on my shoulder, asking to accompany me when we were young. You would follow me around like you were stuck to me, and to me that was the most wonderful thing in the world.

A day in November, when it was cold, I was beaten to the bone. I remember limping home, crying in agony. All I wanted to do was to sit in front of the warm fire and be held by Mother. But Mother was not home, and that was when you answered the door. Your face was one of horror, as I limped into the sitting room and curled up next to the fire, unable to move. And then I felt it. Your small, gentle hand on my shoulder.

'Johan,' you said, 'please don't be frightened. What happened to you?'

You grabbed me a glass of milk and helped to pour it into my mouth. And since that day, I have known that whenever I am in pain, you would be there for me. So why am I not there for you? Why did I leave you?

I think about your sweet face each day. Your perfect smile, the dimples in your cheeks. I hope, each night, that you are safe. I can never bear to think of what pain you are in, what is happening and what might happen.

I remember the day we walked into the forest together. You held my hand tight as you walked carefully, frightened but excited. And that moment you turned to me and said, 'I wish this day would never end.'

I wish for that day, every day. I wish for us to hold hands one last time and roam through the forest, pretending to be in another world. I remember when we pretended to be soldiers, and how different it was to now. I would never wish that upon you – to be a soldier. To be a soldier is to be something you are not. You are not a killer, and neither am I.

I never think it is fair that this has happened to us. And I always question whether it is just something of a greater plan, or whether this is the plan. Either way, I wish for its end. Even if it is for just one last time, all I want to hear is your voice say, 'I love you, Johan, more than all of the stars in the sky.'

I love you Edith, with all my heart. Take care, my little angel, wherever you may be.

Love always,
Johan

CHAPTER 18

November 20, 1941

Earnst and I didn't speak for the rest of the day, and I knew that it was not the time to approach him. He was in a deep, contemplative state, and to take him away from that could possibly push back everything I said. Even in the tent, we didn't speak. He remained quiet, and only managed, 'Good night, Hans,' before drifting off into a deep sleep.

When the morning came, he was more willing to speak, though he kept it to a minimum. We both dressed and exited the tent. I stretched widely, then turned to Earnst.

'We can see Felix today, if you want,' I said.

Earnst nodded. 'I'd like that.'

I managed a small smile. 'Good. Then let's go and see him.'

'What, now?'

'What's wrong? If we don't see him now, we won't get a chance later.'

'I know, but I–'

'Don't make excuses, Earnst. We're going to see him, and we're doing it now.'

'Yes, my Führer,' he joked and saluted a small salute.

I quickly grabbed his arm and pushed it down, and said in a serious tone while smiling,

'Jesus, Earnst, don't do that. If someone saw, we'd get into trouble.'

Earnst chuckled. 'Just have a little bit of fun.'

'Save that for when we see Felix, then. Come on, let's go.'

We walked to the medical tent where Felix was and entered. We were stopped by the army doctor, who held his hand up and glared down at his paper. He then looked up at Earnst and me, peering over his glasses.

'What are you doing here, boys?'

'We're here to see Felix,' I replied. 'The soldier who was found on the side of the road.'

The doctor rolled his eyes and sighed.

'Very well. Make it quick. We have to move him soon when we continue our travel.'

I nodded. 'Thank you.'

'Yes, yes,' the doctor said, annoyed.

We walked to Felix's bed and stood awkwardly, watching his chest heave up and down. His eyes were shut, but he managed to open them when he heard us near his bed.

'Felix,' Earnst said.

I tapped Earnst's hand to get his attention and widened my eyes while shaking my head just enough as to not grab Felix's attention. Earnst shot a confused look my way, then proceeded to talk to Felix. I rolled my eyes and breathed heavily.

'Felix, I am so sorry for what I did,' began Earnst, 'I didn't mean—'

'Please, don't,' Felix said. 'I look like an idiot for what I did and how I acted. I'm so embarrassed. I just wasn't myself.'

'Felix, you had every right to be annoyed and upset at me. I pushed you off to the side and made you feel left out. You're a brother to me, and I don't want you to go.' Earnst began to sob. Felix looked over at me, and I shrugged while giving an estranged look.

'Earnst,' Felix said, 'I don't want to put you through this. I don't want to make you upset.'

Earnst took a deep breath and wiped his face.

'I just feel terrible for how I treated you, Felix. And when they found your body, I thought it was the end.'

'For me too, actually. I thought I was going to die.'

'I just want us to be the way we were, before. Please.'

Felix nodded. 'Of course, we are.'

Earnst smiled humbly, then looked at me and down at his shoes.

'I should probably go and pack up,' he said shyly.

He walked out and left me at the bed of Felix. I sat on the end of the bed and sighed.

'You know, he was worried about you when you left.'

Felix gave a guilty look. 'Really?'

I nodded. 'He would have ripped the camp apart to find you. And he didn't sleep well. I know you were upset, but you put him through hell. And here he was blubbering like a baby. I've never seen him like that.'

'Neither have I,' said Felix. 'I feel awful for what I did. I didn't know I was going to put him through that. I was just upset and angry, I had to get away.'

'I know what that's like. But you could have been killed, Felix.'

'And I said I'm sorry.' Felix's voice raised. 'What more do you want me to say?'

'Nothing, Felix. I just want you to realise that people care about you more than you think. And when you do something like that, people who are close to you, especially people like Earnst, they go mental and start blaming themselves. We're in a foreign country, with soldiers all around that want us dead.'

Felix was silent and bowed his head. I stood up and put my hand on his shoulder.

'Don't do anything like that again, please. For all of us.'

I turned and exited the tent without looking back, but somehow, I had a feeling that Felix still stayed in the same position.

Once we had packed up, we began moving straight away. We were almost at Moscow, and it was beginning to feel surreal. I sat on one of the tanks as it rolled through the snow. It was slow, and we had been having trouble with the vehicles in the extreme temperatures. My coat folded over my mouth as I breathed in my uniform, attempting to warm up my body. It didn't seem to work, but it didn't stop me from continuing to do it. If I uncovered my face, the chilled wind would blast onto my lips and freeze. Each day, we had moved slower and slower, hoping we could reach Moscow before the tanks ceased to move at all. That hope was slowly fading, but we knew we only had a few more miles to travel before we would be standing in Red Square, our guns pointed at the Kremlin as we ordered their immediate surrender.

We continued on-route slowly, and I sat next to a soldier who I had only ever passed, but never spoken to. He turned to me.

'I hate this fucking weather.'

I nodded. 'Sometimes I just want to be back home, in front of the hearth.'

'I think about that every day. And every day, I freeze my bones, just so the leaders back home can sleep well at night, knowing they're safe.'

I leaned in close, and said quietly, 'You might want to watch what you say to certain people. Some may think you're a traitor.'

'Do you think that?' He glared at me.

'Not at all. Everyone would rather be back home, in front of a fire in this weather. But some will take it as an insult to their loyalty to the Reich. Just... just be careful.'

He nodded compliantly.

'I'm Richter, by the way.'

'I'm Hans. It's nice to finally meet you. I've passed you a few times, but thought not to say anything, in case I held you up.'

He shrugged and smiled.

'There's no need to think that. I would have been glad to meet someone else and get away from the soldiers I'm stuck with.'

'Why? What do they do?'

'They're the type that don't stop talking about the Reich, and how they're a hero for freedom and for our people. It was fine to start with, but once you hear it, night after night, day after day, all you want to do is hope they fall off a tank and get left behind.'

I chuckled. 'Be careful what you wish for, someday it might just come true.'

'Well could it hurry? I want it to happen sometime soon.'

'And then what happens when you miss them?'

'Well, there will be that. They are good men, honestly. But it doesn't fix the problem that they're a broken record. Have you been in the panzer army since the start?'

I nodded.

'I was there at the invasion of France.'

Richter quietened.

'So was I. It wasn't what I expected it to be. I didn't think it would be as bad as it was.'

'Why was it bad for you?'

'I always imagined that we would be shooting soldiers and finally, at some early point, they would give up. But I never imagined killing a civilian.'

'Mistakes can happen, I know all too well. Especially in war, you're always going to make a mistake – even if it's fighting in the war in the first place.'

'It's not so much fighting in the war. We're fighting for our homeland. But when I was made to kill those civilians, something in me was lost that day.'

'You were made to? By whom?'

Richter fell silent, fiddling with his hands as he breathed heavily.

'Richter, who was it?' I asked, almost demanding.

'Sergeant Shödler,' he whispered. 'But please, you can't tell anyone I told you.'

'Don't worry, I won't,' I said while staring down at the snow as the tank kept rolling onward. 'But why did he make you do that?'

'He said that if we didn't, they would feed information to the French army and have our positions uncovered. I asked him why we couldn't take them as prisoners instead, and he hit me with the barrel of his gun and knocked me down to the ground. Then he said that prisoners can escape, but no one can escape from the grave. If we didn't shoot them, then he would have shot us on the spot.'

'Who's we?'

'Me and two other soldiers. One died in France, and the other died in the last battle. I try to avoid him if I can, but sometimes he's just there. I've seen him try to intimidate you at times, too. What did you do?'

'I heard something I shouldn't have, and now he thinks that

I'm trying to get everyone to turn against him. I think he's had a vendetta against me for a long time. Sometimes he acts as though we're old friends, and then others he acts as though he would want to see my head on a pike.' I sighed and shook my head. 'I can never get what he's thinking, or what he wants. He's so mysterious and is always changing what he thinks. One moment he's smiling – rather creepily, but still smiling – and the next, he's screaming at the top of his lungs in the face of a soldier.'

'Someone told me he wants revenge for his wife, who died some years ago.'

'Revenge? The guy is a psychotic sergeant that would see the whole world dead if he knew he was the last one on it.'

I was at a loss for words, but nodded anyway, trying to stay in the conversation.

'He…' I stopped and swallowed, then continued, 'he is a man of… strange convictions. But we shouldn't talk too loud about him, someone may hear us.'

'You're right. Who knows how many soldiers are working for him.' He looked around to make sure no one was listening in on the conversation. All of the soldiers hung their heads low, bouncing lightly as the tank rolled over the bumpy road.

'Why don't you like fighting in the war?' asked Richter.

I stammered.

'What? Who told you that?'

'Relax, Hans. I'm not going to oust you out to anyone. I don't even care if you do or don't, I was just curious as to why. You seem like a peaceful person. Is that why you don't like it?'

'I… uh…' I was unable to say what I wanted but was determined to push through. 'I don't see taking a life as any different from what they do to us. I mean, I just don't see the point.'

'Well, if we don't do it first, then they would do it to us.'

'But don't you see? By that logic, war will never end. I'm not a supporter of war, but–'

'Then why fight?' Richter was curious, but his curiosity became more so of an annoyed tone mixed with judgement.

'Because I had to,' I said, blatantly.

'You *had* to? So, you didn't want to. Is that it?'

'What's it to you?' I asked defensively.

Richter settled down and shrugged. 'I was just wondering.'

'Sorry, it's just some people who are "just wondering" want to know so they can hassle me. It's nothing against you.'

Richter nodded.

'Sorry. I just wonder why half of these men fight – what their stories are.'

I shook my head.

'It's nothing. I was given a hard time for it... for not wanting to kill anyone, or even being a soldier.'

'You don't want to be a soldier? At all?'

'No, not really. But I thought I should because it was my duty to protect my country,' I lied. 'So, I joined up in the army, and now I wish I hadn't. I knew many people that wanted to be in the army from the Hitler Youth.'

'I used to be in that. When I was younger, and the war wasn't happening. We would do drills and games, and everyone would get along.'

'Well, at least it was fun for you. I wasn't well liked by the people in the Hitler Youth, where I was.'

'Oh, I'm sorry. I didn't realise. Now that I look back, I only realise now that they were training us for the army. With the drills and the so-called games. They were all war drills. I must admit, they were fun.'

'Well, only if you liked that sort of thing.'

'What do you mean?'

'I was one of those children who would prefer to sit under a tree and read a book of good literature, or to go and help my father at his practice. That's probably why I wasn't liked very much.'

I knew exactly why no one liked me or took to being my friend during my years at school, but one hint to my identity, to who I truly was, and Richter, as nice as he was, could not be trusted to keep a secret. He was new to me, and therefore untrustworthy. But everyone was considered untrustworthy with a secret like that.

'What did you read?' asked Richter.

'I always liked Tolstoy. I can't exactly say that now, but I would read his books and be entranced every time.'

'I didn't read much when I was at school. The teacher always told me that I should read more, but I would dismiss it and go out into the streets and play with the other boys.'

I chuckled.

'Sounds like most of my bullies.'

Richter remained deathly silent.

'Not that I'm saying you were a bully,' I corrected. 'I didn't mean it like that.'

'It's fine. I know what you meant.' Richter took a deep breath and exhaled loudly, frost emerging from his mouth. 'I never thought it could get this cold, anywhere on earth.'

I knew he was desperate to change the subject, and I was happy to play along.

'Antarctica is even colder than here.'

'Colder?'

I nodded.

'This isn't even the worst of it yet. When it's the middle of winter, we will, no doubt, cry for a fire to be built because we are shivering too much and our fingers feeling like they will drop off at any point.'

Richter's face dropped, and he stared airily at me.

'Do you mean that?'

I shrugged.

'That's what I heard. It isn't even winter here. It's still autumn. So, winter has to be colder than this. But hopefully, with any luck, we will march into Moscow, and they will surrender to us. And then, finally, we can go home.'

'I wouldn't mind just going home now. Stepping off this tank and walking back.'

'Walk back? You would make it three miles, and then come running back, begging to sit back on the tank.'

Richter laughed.

'In all honesty, I probably would.'

It was getting dark early, and the tanks stopped suddenly. We were doubtful as to whether the tanks, and even the trucks, would start again in the morning, but kept hopeful, knowing the capital of the lands we were marching in was just above the horizon. We were to camp for the night.

The officers went around each fire and congratulated the

soldiers on making it this far, and assured them that, with all certainty, the Soviet Union would realise the strength of our army and immediately surrender. But they soon added that if no such thing was to occur, we would show them the might of our forces, and they would soon surrender afterward.

Richter was seated around a different fire with other soldiers, and had invited me to sit with them, but I kindly declined, knowing the other soldiers were the type that would find it easy enough to pick out my flaws. I sat with Earnst, who was still anxious about the whole ordeal with Felix. I rolled my eyes in annoyance, hoping the conflict between the two would end that morning, but instead, it made Earnst far warier of how he was acting toward Felix.

'I don't know what to do, Hans,' said Earnst.

'Earnst, please,' I sighed, 'just let it go. Honestly, he said it was fine.'

'But I could tell he was still upset.'

I was growing more frustrated with Earnst and snapped without realising.

'Well, say sorry. Do whatever you want, but just stop worrying about it.' I lowered my voice. 'I'm sorry, Earnst, but we are this close to walking into Moscow. Your anxiety about whether Felix is still upset, which he isn't by the way, isn't helping the situation. This time tomorrow, we will be in Moscow, hopefully. And this time in a month, Felix will be fine, you and Felix will still be best friends, and we will be at home.'

'That's wishful thinking.'

'What, you and Felix?' I snapped.

'No,' Earnst snapped back, 'being back home. We won't be home in a month.'

'Well, that's put a dampener on that, then.'

Earnst raised his eyebrows.

'Keeping hope alive, I see.'

'You can't do much else.'

'I suppose not. What are you thinking about Moscow?'

'What do you mean?'

'I mean, are you scared? Or excited?'

'To be completely honest, whenever I think about it, I don't become scared or excited. I just always have different scenarios play out in my head, and then I lose all form of concentration and drift off somewhere else.'

'What type of scenarios?'

'The good ones: we march in, they surrender, and we stand, cheering in Red Square. Allowing them a peaceful surrender – no fighting. And then the bad ones: we march into the city, and they have already prepared enough to know how many there are of us, and they completely obliterate us.'

Earnst looked shocked, staring coldly at the ground.

'What do you think will happen?'

'I don't doubt that we will have to fight, and I may have to overcome my hatred of killing someone in order to save myself, but at the same time, I think we have a chance.'

'They won't give up, you know. They fight to the end, and they would never just surrender to us. When I saw them surrender at that battle, I couldn't believe my eyes. I never thought they would. I thought they would fight to the death.'

'You can't expect all of them to fight to the death, or their whole people would die out.'

'Trust me, they would.'

Earnst and I went quiet and listened to the other soldiers talk about what Moscow would be like, but soon grew tiresome of the boring banter. Instead, I decided it was better to get some rest for the next day. I announced my departure by standing and grabbing Earnst by his shoulder.

'I'm going to go and get some sleep.'

Earnst nodded. 'I won't be far behind.'

I made my way to my tent and curled up, hoping the cold sensation would soon go away, but it never did. I breathed heavily as I watched the frost blow from my mouth in the small light that shone from the campfires nearby. It was hard to get to sleep, but soon I drifted off, leaving everything behind.

Concentration Camp

Young boys, no older than fifteen, are sent to me. Their faces are stricken with fear, and a sombre mood is carried with them. Some meet their fathers and embrace them tightly. Others are alone, with no one to love. Instead, they sit on their lonesome, and they hang their heads low, hoping this is not their final destination. There is one particular boy, Aurik, who sits, shaking as he mumbles to himself.

'I just want to see my mother. I just want to see her. Please let me see her. I just want to see her, my mother. Please.'

His voice quivers each time he speaks, and his body rocks to and fro, nervously. His feet patter the ground without hesitation, over and over.

It was at that moment that an older man, in his thirties and well built, approached Aurik. He looked up at the man, then back down at his shaking feet. The man placed a gentle hand on Aurik's shoulder. This man in particular, is known around these walls as a leader. Often, he would comfort those in need, and offer sound wisdom to those who wish to see their world end. He would throw himself in front of anyone who was abused by the officers, and would often take blame for something he was no participant in. To these men, he was their leader. But to the officers, he was nothing more than a rebellious prisoner who was to be tortured and beaten mercilessly. And even then, he would still persist.

There is an odd sense of longing for these men. Even when the candle is snuffed out, they still relight it each time. And each time, the wax gets smaller and smaller, they still find a way to prolong it. Strange, but admirable.

I have watched on for years now, as men come and go from this place. They are disposable, like any household item. There is no chance for them. They cannot leave, and they cannot earn anything. They work, and if they work well, they are given more work. And if they do not work, they face Death. That is the reality.

Young Aurik, a boy of thirteen, was well built for his age, which is why they chose him. He was comforted temporarily, before being forced into the tiresome labour. He was yelled at more than once by the officers and was reduced to tears even more times. But that did not stop him. He persisted. He persisted until the point that he forced it beyond what he could compete, and eventually he became ill.

His illness lasted a week, and he was back on his feet. But he could no longer work. His body would shake far too much for any man to be able to work sufficiently, and his steps were small and fragile. His hope had ended.

Almost as soon as he came, he was gone. Taken elsewhere, to my sibling. Perhaps he is looking down now, or perhaps he is just in the ground. Either way, his candle had gone.

CHAPTER 19

November 22, 1941

We were closing in on Moscow. Our destination was finally near. We were only thirty miles from the city, when we finally met with Russian resistance. Our tanks were met with the heavy force of Russian tanks, and our soldiers were under fire from out of nowhere. The terrain was not flat, but small hills that carried on to the horizon, which provided enough cover to keep moving and push forward.

Trudging through the snow, we mounted our guns on the higher upward slopes and lay on our stomachs as we watched the enemy in our sights. Our soldiers were sprawled along a three-mile line, facing east. The Russian soldiers had scattered too, and were now spreading themselves along the terrain, facing us. We faced each other – looking into the eyes of the beholder of Death.

I watched down my scopes at the Russian soldiers moving through the terrain. They were far better prepared for the harsh winter, living with it their whole lives. They wore *ushankas* that covered their ears, and thick fur coats that draped down to their large boots. Their faces were hardened with determination; to defend, to kill. Flanked toward the north, our men were soon under fire by seven Russian soldiers. A small group, but well trained, the snipers unleashed a torrent of gunfire.

'Snipers to the north!' one of the soldiers screamed. 'There's snipers at the–'

With one quick shot, his voice was silenced, and he dropped to the ground. The bullet pierced through his skull with such force, his head seemed to split in two for an instant. I watched in horror as his body spiralled to the ground, rolling down the hill toward my feet. Immediately, we ducked for cover as the sound of sniper rifles repeated, shooting down two more soldiers five feet away from where I was positioned.

'Where the hell are they shooting from?' yelled another soldier.

I looked around and saw a young soldier shakily point north, where higher hills rolled, and more scattered trees stood.

'In between those trees,' he yelled. 'The snipers are over there.'

'If we can't get rid of those snipers, we're going to be trapped,' said the other soldier.

'Can we move back south?' I asked.

'There's too much gunfire. And we can't go west either. The tanks are there.'

'Then how are we going to get past those snipers?'

'I don't know, yet.'

'Well think!' demanded the younger soldier.

'Listen boy, if you've got any suggestions, then speak up!' yelled the other soldier. 'Otherwise, shut your mouth.'

The young soldier quietened down and looked toward me.

'What about a diversion?' I suggested.

'A diversion?' asked the older soldier. 'They wouldn't pay much attention to a diversion with all of the gunfire going on. They have their sights set on us.'

'Well, if they have their sights set on us, they won't be expecting anyone to move toward them.'

The two soldiers looked at me quizzically. I sighed and ruffled the snow near our feet, so that a map could be drawn. I drew dots in the snow and a line that represented we three soldiers and the hill line. I drew several crosses to the left, representing the snipers.

'If one of us goes westward, between the trees,' I drew a line that went from the dots to the crosses, 'the other two can provide covering fire, drawing their line of sights here. When the other soldier, whichever one of us decides to do it, gets behind the snipers, they open fire. Then we give the signal, and we can move to higher ground and push forward by going around the long way, which will prove quicker.'

'I'm not running up there,' stated the young soldier.

'You're the smallest of us three,' I said. 'No one will see you.'

The young soldier sighed and looked at me anxiously.

'You planned this all along – for me to be the one to go! You bastard – I don't want to die.'

'If you don't do this, we all die. Me and...' I looked at the older soldier and signalled to him, rolling my hand in the air, trying to get him to announce his name.

'Jürgen Siegfried,' he said. 'But just call me Siegfried.'

'Hans Adler,' I replied. 'Siegfried and I will draw their fire away from you. They won't even know you're coming.'

'But what if they see me?' he asked anxiously.

'Look boy, what's your name?' asked Siegfried.

'Oskar.'

'Okay, listen.'

'No, wait,' I interjected. 'What did you just say?'

He stared at me and squinted. 'Lars.'

I stammered. 'Wh-what?'

'Listen Lars,' began Siegfried, 'we need you to do this.'

Siegfried continued to talk to Lars, while I was still baffled at what I heard. There was a loud ringing in my ear as I looked up to the sky, my mouth open and my mind elsewhere. I had begun to think that I was able to move on from Oskar – not forget about him, but to finish grieving. But deep down, somehow, I knew I would never stop grieving. He was everything I had ever wanted in a friend, and he never ceased to amaze. My mind had made me hear his name, as though a constant pain that caught me unaware – one that I thought I was rid of.

But I soon realised that this battle was reality, and what was happening was reality. The unresolved sombre feelings I had for Oskar's death could continue later, or cease forever right here, but they had to stop, nonetheless.

'Hans and I will keep an eye out for you. If anything goes wrong, we will come and get you, if we can. Isn't that right, Hans?'

Siegfried shot me a glance, and widened his eyes momentarily, signalling for me to agree. I nodded and looked down at Lars.

'You're going to be fine. Just head up the hill and around, until you're behind them. And remember, keep low. Don't give away your position for anything. That's when things can go astray. You'll do well. I know you will.'

Lars nodded and took a deep breath. He turned and held his gun tightly to his chest. He nodded at Siegfried and me, turned while crouched low, and moved along the ground. Crawling up the hill, he looked back and smiled, then continued. Siegfried grabbed my shoulder.

'Let's give him some covering fire, then,' he said.

I nodded and grabbed my gun. We mounted ourselves on the hill that faced north and hid in the tall grass, which provided enough cover to avoid being detected for a time. Was I any better than my generals, sending someone to die for my own purposes?

I watched through my scope as Lars crept up slowly on the hillside, doing well enough to keep hidden while the Russian snipers were still firing on us.

'How is he going?' asked Siegfried.

'He's doing well,' I replied, my sights still set on Lars and his movements. 'He's avoiding enemy fire rather well, actually.'

'That's because they keep fucking firing at us.'

'Well, that's what the plan was, wasn't it?'

Siegfried remained quiet but mumbled something derogatory under his breath. I shook off anything negative that came from his mouth and continued watching Lars like a hawk, hoping for the best.

When it came to war, and the necessities of what needed to happen, I wasn't oblivious to what was done. I opposed killing, and with it, death, but I was cornered – literally. If Lars didn't do this, we would die.

I breathed in heavily and focused my scope on the snipers in the hills. I closed my eyes.

Forgive me, I thought. My finger tightened on the trigger, and I pulled.

The sound was deafening, and as I looked toward where I shot, the body of one of the snipers collapsed to the ground. My eyes squeezed shut and my breathing more rapid. I killed him. I looked to Siegfried, who was still focused on the snipers. He didn't even acknowledge, as though it was just some everyday task – and it was, for every soldier. Yet I found the act so deplorable, I was forced to shut my eyes when doing it. But this time, when I saw the body fall, I knew I had to do it. This was for my life.

I took aim again and opened fire. Missing, but only by inches, the snipers dodged each bullet and clambered to the ground, trying to gain better sight of our position.

'They're moving left,' said Siegfried, worriedly. 'Why the hell are they moving left?'

'I don't know,' I replied. 'But we have to stop them. If they keep moving left, they will see Lars. Fire left off their position and try to draw them right again.'

'Where is Lars?'

'Shit, I can't see him.'

'Neither can I. He can't be atop the hill already.'

'No, but I can't see him on the hillside.'

Where are you, Lars? I thought.

'There!' exclaimed Siegfried. 'He's to the left of that large rock, ten o'clock.'

I looked around until I saw Lars's small body moving through the dead grass, slowly and steadily. If he moved any further to his right, the Russian snipers would spot him immediately, and within an instant, he would be dead.

'He has to stop moving,' I said. 'Otherwise, he will be spotted.'

'He needs to retreat back down the hillside a few feet,' said Siegfried. 'If he stays there, he's going to be shot.'

Siegfried and I opened fire to the left of the Russian snipers, drawing them from where they were headed, and instead pushed them right. They crawled through the grass and finally returned to the tree they had positioned themselves near in the beginning.

'We have to go right,' said Siegfried. 'Then it will take the focus from Lars's position.'

'If we do that, they will be forced to move left again, and Lars won't be able to move behind them.'

'We can't stay here forever, Hans!' Siegfried snapped.

'We won't have to stay here for much longer, if we keep providing cover fire for Lars. *Jesus*. We had a plan, so follow it. If we had it figured out then, then we keep going through with it.'

'You mean *you* had it figured out then. It isn't exactly foolproof.'

'*Foolproof?* Lars is depending on us up there,' I said while pointing to the hillside. 'And if we fail, it's because you were too busy criticising the plan, instead of doing what we decided.'

Siegfried bit his lip and glared at me.

'We proved the plan isn't foolproof by sitting here arguing, instead of helping him,' I added. 'If you don't want to help, be my guest to climb up the rocky hillside and get shot at by the Russian snipers who have the high ground. But I'm going to stay here and do what we said we would.'

'I've seen more war than you, boy. This is going to get us killed.'

'Sitting here will get us killed. You didn't suggest anything beforehand, so we're going with this.'

I turned and pointed my gun back to the snipers' position, and opened fire. The adrenaline coursed through my body from the argument so much, that I had no quarrel to pull the trigger, and hold it down.

Lars was halfway up the hill, grabbing the rocky edges and hauling his body over them as he tried to remain out of the enemy's lines of sight. I glanced over and saw his right foot slip, with the lower half of his body dangling on a steeply sloped section of the hillside. If he fell, he would drop ten feet down onto a small incline of sharply pointed rocks – daggers that would pierce his skin and kill him in an instant.

He managed to pull his body forward and to safety, where if he did fall, apart from alerting the snipers, he would slowly roll down the rough hill which had a smaller gradient than the immediate drop beforehand.

I looked behind the small contour that we were trapped in, and saw fellow soldiers lying on their stomachs, shooting eastward, while we fired north-north-east. I, and even Siegfried, knew that once the snipers were eliminated, it gave us a greater advantage to move forward. But while they were there, they not only trapped us, but the soldiers behind us, who would be shot down almost instantly.

'He's almost there,' said Siegfried. 'Let's just hope he can get behind them without alerting them.' He stopped for a moment, thought, and then asked, 'What if he doesn't successfully eliminate them?'

'He has an effective assault rifle. He should be able to eliminate them with one pull of the trigger. There's six up there.'

'But what if there's more?'

'What do you mean?'

'We can only see six, but there could be more up there.'

My stomach churned. '*Shit*. What are we going to do?'

Siegfried thought for a moment, then said, 'We're going to have go up there.'

'What? How are we supposed to get up there?'

'I don't know yet, but we have to think of something.'

'*We?* No – *you!* This is you're brilliant idea!' I flailed my arms in the air. 'You think of an idea of how to get there!'

'Oh brilliant, Hans! You're a great fucking help!'

'I don't know what to do, Siegfried! If you think it's such a good idea, then you think of a way!'

We were both at breaking point. I sat with my arms rested on my knees, and my head resting on my arms, breathing heavily. I looked up towards Siegfried and watched as he threw his head back and planted his hands on the back of his head, sighing greatly.

'Look,' I began, 'I know we have to get up there. And we have to figure out how. So, let's just both get our heads together and stop worrying about who's going to think of it.'

Siegfried lowered his arms and rested them on his knees which were level with his chest. His rough hands hung over in front, and his gun was placed next to him. I could hear his heavy breath inward, then exhaling even louder. He nodded.

'Well, we have to think of something quickly,' he said. 'Lars is still scrambling up that hill.'

I nodded. 'Yes. But what?'

'Grenades. How many do you have?'

I felt around my waist for the band that held my grenades.

'Two,' I replied.

'So do I. We could lob them over onto the hill and give enough cover to sprint up part of it, then crawl up without them seeing us.'

'I can't throw that far.'

'We don't need it to go that far. Throw it as far as you can, and it will explode on the hill.'

I looked at him, puzzled. 'What will that do?'

'The dirt and rock that's upheaved by it will create enough dust to move quickly to the base of the hill. That's when we make for it and use the remainder of our grenades when we're on the hillside to distract them.'

'What if they spot us?' I asked anxiously.

Siegfried thought for a bit, then said with utter conviction, 'Then we're going to be killed.'

I gulped.

We had no idea how many Russian soldiers were atop the hill. Whether it was only the six that we could see, or whether there were more hiding behind, we didn't know, but it was better to be safer than not.

I nodded. 'Let's do it, then,' I said.

Siegfried nodded and managed a small smile, as though a gesture of thanks for me agreeing to follow his intuition. We lay on our stomachs against the mound of dirt that gave us enough cover, our guns in hand.

'On the count of three, I'm going to throw my grenade. As soon as you hear it explode, you run. Got it?'

'What will you do?' I asked.

'I'm going to be right behind you. Are you ready?'

I nodded. 'Yes.'

'One. Two. Three.'

Immediately after three, Siegfried twisted the handle of his grenade and threw it against the hillside. I poked my head over the mound and watched it bounce on the rocks, running down the hill, before it finally exploded about three quarters of the way down.

'Go!' yelled Siegfried, giving me a little shove.

I leapt up on my two feet and held onto my gun with both hands. My feet awkwardly stepped on the rocky surface, which also happened to be covered with icy remains from the previous night, making it more difficult to keep my balance. I continued running, until my right foot slipped on a large rock that was concealed by grass. My leg plummeted downward, in the space between two rocks. I screamed as my leg crunched downward and became stuck.

'*Fuck!* Help me! Siegfried!'

The pain darted up my leg and into the rest of my body, as I continued to yelp. *Please, somebody help me. Anybody.* I tried desperately to wriggle my leg free, but it was clamped between the two rocks, and they weren't about to miraculously move at any moment. My right foot was twisted as it bent with the awkward shape of the crevice, and put more pressure on my leg, crushing it in the painful position for what seemed like a lifetime.

As I continued to attempt to release it, I felt a strong hand on my shoulder and turned to see Siegfried staring down at me, mortified.

'What happened?' he asked.

'I slipped. My leg is caught in the gap,' I replied in agony.

'The dust is going to settle soon, and they're going to see you. We have to get you out.'

'I can't move my leg,' I insisted.

Siegfried grabbed my leg and pulled it, only to have me scream in pain in his ear at the movement.

'I don't know what to do,' I said.

'We're going to need more time to get you out.'

Siegfried examined the area my leg was caught in and frowned while thinking for a solution. He turned around to see the dust settling and the image of the snipers atop the hill beginning to reappear. He turned to me and took off his coat.

'Put this on you.' He draped his coat over me, then turned and tore the dead grass out from the ground and layered them on top. 'Hold still until I tell you. I'm going to keep moving and try to get to the top and help Lars.'

'Wait, you're leaving me here?'

He nodded.

'I'm sorry, Hans, but there's nothing we can do. They're going to be able to see us if we both stay here. Just keep your head down and don't move.'

'Won't you be too cold without your coat?'

'It won't be for long. I just have to get to the top of the hill and clear them out. Then I'll come back for you.'

I sighed heavily but nodded. 'Fine.'

But what I was uttering in my head was, *Shit, why are you leaving me here, you bastard?*

Siegfried turned and ran for the hillside before the snipers could see well again. I lay on my back, uncomfortably resting on the rock, and grunted in pain as my knee bent with the rock and shuffled my leg slightly. I focused on my breathing, hoping to keep the cold at bay while I lay completely immobile. Then I heard it.

A sniper shot. *Crack.*

CHAPTER 20

November 22, 1941

I pulled the coat off my face and sat up cautiously, looking around for Siegfried. I scanned the hillside but saw no sign of him. The Russian snipers had their sights still set on where we were previously trapped. The plan must have worked. They had no idea that we had moved. I felt a warm sensation on my right leg and looked down, witnessing blood trickling down. The more blood that continued to drip, the more my leg slid in the crevice and started to become loose.

I moved it around, hoping to free it. I had no idea as to where the blood was coming from or where the wound was, with a sharp pain radiating throughout my whole leg. This made it near impossible to pinpoint the exact spot. Wriggling it a little more, I cried in pain as it slipped downward again and slammed onto the rock. *Someone help me*, I muttered.

I looked down at my leg, then up to scan the hills. My eyes fell upon three Russian soldiers who ran across the rocks, coming directly toward me. Adrenaline surged through my body, my heart beating faster with every step they took. *Shit! Where is Siegfried?*

I lay back down and put the coat over me, trying to calm

my breathing. But my body shook violently as I worried about what they would do if they found me. The rocks pressed hard into my back, and I gritted my teeth as I failed to move into a more comfortable position, lest they see me and shoot me down immediately. I was restrained by a back-wrenching position for what seemed like an hour, though in reality it was only a few minutes. I heard nothing. No footsteps – just gunfire. I poked my head from out of Siegfried's coat which still covered me and looked around. The Russian soldiers had made their way to the base of the hill and were now moving south, closer to our soldiers. If they successfully snuck through and opened fire, too many of our men would lose their lives unexpectedly – and it would all be to just three soldiers.

I looked up to the hillside, and saw a figure jump up from the tall grass and rocks, running behind the Russian snipers. *Siegfried!* I closed my eyes and hoped he wouldn't be met with any more soldiers than expected.

I heard continuing gunfire, witnessing two bodies drop from the top of the hill, down to the base. My stomach churned as I immediately thought it was Lars and Siegfried. In a panic, I wriggled my leg with immense pain, and managed to get it free from the crevice. I swore as my flesh tore from the bone.

I limped down the hill, each time the weight transferring to my right leg with agonising shots of pain being released. I grunted each time, but determined, nonetheless, to keep going. I kept my head down to avoid any gunfire and limped over to the two bodies.

I stopped and stood staring at them both, confused. *That's not our uniform.* One body lay face up, while the other was face down. I approached the one facing down and rolled it over, stepping back on my right foot and then hopping as the weight invited more pain.

After a small dance on my left foot, I went back over to the body and crouched beside it, examining the face. It wasn't recognisable, and I let out a sigh of relief as I realised, they had succeeded. I looked up toward the hill and saw Siegfried standing with his hands outstretched and a confused look, mixed with horror, staring directly at me.

Both Lars and Siegfried made their way to the base of the hill and approached me worriedly.

'Hans, what happened? Are you alright?' asked Lars, who ran over and knelt beside me. He placed a hand on my shoulder.

'My leg got caught in a crevice. I haven't seen where the wound is yet. I can't see it with all this blood.'

Siegfried knelt down near my leg and looked at me.

'It doesn't look good, Hans,' he said gloomily. 'I'm going to need to have a look at it.'

'You know medical stuff?' I asked.

He cocked his head to one side. 'A little. My father taught me the basics. But I've done these sorts of things before, don't worry.'

Siegfried attempted to lift my leg, but soon let it down gently as I screamed out in pain.

'*Jesus*, Siegfried!'

'Hans, I have to know where it's damaged. Just let me do it.' Siegfried's voice was firm and partly annoyed, and I decided rather than irritate him to the point that he would be willing to leave me there with no aid, I would let him do what he needed.

He lifted my leg again, and this time I tried desperately to muffle my cries of discomfort. I breathed heavily as his fingers dug into my leg. I tilted my head back and breathed faster.

'You're doing fine, Hans,' said Lars. 'Just keep breathing.'

My eyes were shut tightly, and I clenched my fists. Siegfried finally let my leg down gently and rested it on the ground.

'You've taken all of the flesh off your upper shin, near your knee.'

'We need to get him to a medic tent,' said Lars.

I shook my head. 'No. We have to keep going.'

'We will keep going,' said Siegfried, 'but you have to go to a medic. Otherwise, it will get infected. It's beginning to stick to the inside of your trousers.'

I shut my eyes and bit my lip.

'No, I can keep going. I have to get to the top of the hill.'

'Hans,' Siegfried said firmly, 'you're not going to the top of the hill. I know you want to help, and you have. But now, we have to get you to a medic before your leg becomes infected. If it gets worse, which it will, if you leave it any longer, you may lose it.'

They didn't understand. I finally pulled the trigger and aimed it at a soldier. I no longer flinched, and I no longer shot into the distance. If I backed down now, I would be at square one. It was becoming natural for me; the demon had awakened, but I knew that demon would get me through this war, and that's what I was afraid of.

'Please, Siegfried, I'm begging you,' I pleaded. 'I have to get to the top of that hill.'

He shook his head and looked down.

'It's not going to happen, Hans. If you get it fixed now, you may just make it in time to march through into Moscow.'

Siegfried stood up and signalled Lars to stand. Siegfried approached me, and I shuffled back.

'Please don't,' I begged.

Siegfried became more determined and picked me up. He tossed me over his shoulder with brute strength but was careful enough not to knock my leg at any point. I hit his back as he dragged me off and Lars followed.

'Put me down!' I demanded. 'Fucking hell, Siegfried! Put me down! I have to get to the hill! Please! Siegfried! Lars, do something.'

Lars shrugged his shoulders and whispered, 'I'm sorry, Hans. I can't do anything.'

Siegfried stopped and threw me to the ground. My right leg crashed to the ground, and I held it tightly in agony. I screamed in pain, and as Siegfried approached me, I whimpered. He knelt down and pointed directly to my face.

'Listen here. I am taking you to the medic. I am doing it for your own health. You are *not* going to the top of that goddamn hill. And if you hit me one more time, I will grab your leg, and I will twist it.' Siegfried gritted his teeth. 'Understood?'

I nodded full of embarrassment and slumped my head. Siegfried stood up and picked me up again, resting me on his shoulder as he walked slowly southward to where we were positioned.

I realised Siegfried wasn't under any obligation to carry me to the medical tent, nor was he obliged to even help me on the hill and stay under cover. I owed a lot to him, and instead of thanking him and following his word, I outwardly cursed him for helping me.

As we arrived at the medical tent, we were greeted by the same man who I had met with Earnst when we saw Felix. He looked at me and ordered Siegfried to lay me on the bed.

Siegfried lowered me slowly, and the doctor looked through his spectacles at my bloodied leg, which was still covered by my trousers. Glaring at it for some time, he turned to Siegfried.

'I will send one of the nurses in. Do you know what happened?'

'He tore the skin below his knee,' replied Siegfried. 'All of it is gone.'

'When did this happen?'

'Only within the last hour.'

'Good. We may be able to sanitise it in time.'

Both nodded to each other, and the doctor walked toward another soldier laying two beds down, who was clearly in more pain than I. His cries made me tilt my head forward to see what had happened. Upon first glance, I became sick as I saw his stomach open, with his organs visible to everyone. The doctor scrambled with three other nurses to attend to the soldier, and they carried him out to another tent to perform emergency surgery.

I looked up at Siegfried, who gave me a concerned looked, then said, 'You're going to be fine. Just let the nurses do what they have to.'

'I will,' I replied.

'And don't hit them like you did to me.'

'Don't worry, I won't. Look, Siegfried, I owe you an apology. I know you only did what was best for me, and if it wasn't for you, I probably would have been dead almost instantly on that hill. And I haven't said thank you yet, so thank you.'

Siegfried bowed his head and smiled.

'I just did what any other soldier would have done. And your leg; it will heal quickly enough. They're going to look after you better in here, than if you were out there in the cold.'

'I know. Thank you, Siegfried. Really.'

'It's fine, Hans.' Siegfried looked around. 'Well, I should go.'

'Make sure you look out for Lars, out there.'

'I will, don't you worry.'

I smiled, then looked around for Lars, but he was nowhere

in sight. Siegfried turned and walked away, and I was left lying on the bed with no one near me. I attempted to move into a more comfortable position, but my trousers rubbed against the raw skin, and I breathed in quickly through my teeth. I rested my head back and placed my hands on my chest, looking up. I waited for almost thirty minutes before any nurse came to my bedside.

'Private Hans Adler?' she asked.

I lifted my head and looked at her. My eyes widened, and I nodded. Her emerald eyes were staring at me, and dimples in her cheeks showed as she smiled. Her hair was tied up behind her hat, but the few rogue strands which stuck out showed strings of gold.

'Are you in any pain?'

I nodded again, finding no words to say other than how beautiful she was. I was an awkward schoolboy again, and I realised how stupid I must have looked.

'Do you speak at all, Private Adler?'

I blinked a few times, then nodded.

'Ye-yes,' I stuttered. 'Sorry. And you can just call me Hans if you like.'

She smiled. 'That's quite a gesture, Hans,' she said jokingly.

'What's your name?'

'Klaudia. Klaudia Schuster.'

'That's a pretty name,' I said, 'for a pretty face.'

I felt like an idiot, having no idea where that statement came from. Klaudia, however, enjoyed it enough to giggle shyly and look down at her feet.

'You're quite the gentleman.'

She took her eyes from mine and looked at my leg. She bent over and examined it carefully, then turned her head and stood upright again.

'I'm going to have to take your trousers off,' she stated.

'What? Why?'

She laughed. 'Don't worry, it's not that bad. But if we're to fix it up and dress it, we will need to take them off.'

I gave her a worried look, but she just smiled.

'Hans, it's fine.'

'Fine,' I sighed. 'Will it hurt?'

She bent over again and took my boots off. She then looked up my leg through the foot hole of my trousers and screwed her nose. She looked toward me and nodded.

'You're going to need to bite on something.'

'Why? What's happened? Is it bad?'

'You skin is beginning to fuse to the trouser leg. And there's also a lot of blood.'

I felt I was going to be sick and flung my head backward onto the bed. I raised my hands to rest on my forehead. I felt a hand on my arm and looked to see Klaudia standing right beside me.

'Hans, the sooner we do this, the sooner it will all be over. I'm going to look after you.'

Her voice immediately calmed me down, and her reassurance that she was going to look after me, only her, gave me enough satisfaction to nod. She smiled and turned, heading for the table that held the medical equipment. I shifted my head left and right, trying to see what she was going to use, but her body was in the way and I couldn't see anything. She walked over briskly and handed me a thick piece of white cloth.

'Here, use this to put in your mouth.'

She then went back over to the table, shuffled around a little more, before wheeling over a frail-looking table that was simply a few bits of metal welded together and four wheels attached at the bottom, with a plate on top that allowed the tools to rest on.

'When I say, I want you to bite down hard on that cloth. Understand?'

I nodded, shooting a worried look at her.

'Okay. Start biting down now. Don't fully bite down. When the pain increases, bite down harder. You can't move, however. Under any circumstances.'

My breathing became faster, and my hands shook violently as I worried about the pain which was to come. Klaudia grabbed a pair of scissors from the metal tray and began to cut my uniform trousers around the wound. Once the trousers were disconnected, she wriggled my pants down, holding one hand above the wound so that it wouldn't be knocked by the trousers, and pulled them off my legs. Once my pants were off, she looked at me.

'Bite hard.'

My teeth sank into the cloth as she began to cut the piece of uniform that was beginning to fuse with my wound. As she cut, the tugging became harder whenever she got closer to the wound, and I jolted in pain.

'Keep still, Hans,' she demanded.

She continued to cut until she could no longer get any closer without cutting skin. That's when I became even more worried. On the tray was a bottle of clear liquid, which I assumed to be water, but was something far worse. Vodka.

She grabbed the bottle and opened the cap. She examined the bottle's contents, then sniffed it, and finally looked at me. I could see in her eyes that she knew what was going to come, and she quickly rallied two other nurses to assist her. The nurses rushed over and stood either side of me, and put one hand on my arms, and the other on my stomach.

Klaudia nodded at both of them, then looked down at my legs and poured the vodka over my wound. I screeched and tried to fight off the two nurses, but they pushed down hard on my body. I was exhausted, and they easily held me down while my wound burned. My leg felt as though it was on fire, the burning sensation reducing me to tears.

'Now that it's soft, I'm going to remove the clothing stuck to it,' Klaudia said to the two nurses. 'Make sure he doesn't move at all. Once it's done, I'm going to need one of you to use the vodka to wash it while I put enough pressure on it to slow the blood flow. Then we can bandage it up. The other one is going to need to hold him steady.'

The two nurses agreed and held me down tightly.

'Hans, make sure you're biting down for me.'

I clamped my teeth down as hard as I could without straining my jaw and waited for it.

Klaudia grabbed the clothing still stuck, and began to pull it, inch by inch, while I wailed for mercy.

'It's too deep,' she exclaimed. 'We're going to need to stitch him up.'

'We can't stitch him up. We don't have enough resources, Klaudia,' said one of the nurses.

'Heidi, if we don't stitch it up, he's going to bleed out. We underestimated the wound. We have to stitch it up. Get me the supplies, *now.*'

Heidi obliged and rushed over to the table that Klaudia had been to earlier, frantically searching through the supplies for a needle and thread.

'I can't find it,' said Heidi.

'Look harder,' snapped Klaudia. 'The bleeding is getting worse.'

I could feel the warm blood dripping over my leg and onto the bed as Klaudia applied pressure on to it. My body still shook, and my left foot swayed quickly from side to side, as though it somehow compensated for the lack of movement in my right foot.

Heidi ran back over to the bed and presented Klaudia with a needle and thread. Klaudia looked at them and nodded.

'Hold here,' she commanded. 'Make sure you apply pressure. I'm going to attempt to close the wound.'

'How deep is it?' I asked.

'Nothing you have to worry about,' replied Klaudia, although I knew she was lying. 'Just lay still, and don't move.'

She reached over and poured a small amount of vodka into a metal tin and placed the needle in the vodka. She stirred it around and shook the metal tin in a few circles before picking the needle out and shaking it. She then carefully put the thread through the needle and tied it at the tip.

Grabbing the metal tin of vodka, she poured half of it over the wound as Heidi moved her hands and clamped the skin together. I clenched my fists and squeezed my eyes shut. That's when I felt it – the needle pierced the flesh and pulled with it the thread. I tried to move my leg, but Heidi put her weight on top of it, and pushed the lower part of her arm even harder downward, making sure my leg was immobile. Each time the needle stabbed my skin, I grunted in pain and felt the thread pulling its way through afterward.

Klaudia was about halfway done when she poured a little more vodka over the wound and continued to stitch up the gaping laceration. What felt like an arduous task was soon finished, and Klaudia washed the gash and wrapped it in soft cloths and bandages. I hesitantly thanked the two nurses for their help before they left, and lay exhausted, attempting to give Klaudia a smile.

'You really know how to fix people up,' I said.

'It's my job to know, otherwise I wouldn't be here,' she replied, rather softly.

'Do you ever want to stop?'

Klaudia sat on the edge of my bed and looked around the tent at the other soldiers on the beds, before concluding that she could speak for a little while before her duty would call again.

'Sometimes it gets hard,' she began, 'but it soon becomes all that we know. Those other two nurses are only new. They don't really know what real work is like. But they will soon learn.'

'How long have you been doing this for, then?'

'Two years. It doesn't seem much, but even just a year is enough before you know what horrors await you in this tent. I was eighteen when they signed me up.'

'You're twenty?'

Klaudia nodded. 'How old are you, Private Hans Adler?'

'Nineteen,' I replied.

'Nineteen? I thought you much older than that. You seem far too mature for your age.'

'Older? Not too much older, I hope.'

She giggled. 'No, not at all. Only a little bit.'

'Was I braver than the other soldiers in here?'

This time she laughed. 'Absolutely not.'

'No?' I raised an eyebrow.

'You were louder than a baby crying.'

'So, I'm worse than a baby?'

'I think you're just a big baby, yourself. But I never said that's a bad thing. Just harder to fix up, then. At least you show emotion. Some men come in here as though they were already dead.'

'Well, I'll try and be better behaved next time.'

'Let's hope there isn't a next time. We don't want you hurting yourself all the time.'

I shrugged. 'I suppose not, but then I would get to see you more.'

'If you think like that, Matron will come and teach you a thing or two,' she giggled.

She stood up and spread a blanket over the top of my legs.

'Now, keep warm. I have to go and attend to the other soldiers. I'll come and check up on you later if no other nurse has.'

'Can you still do it if they already have?'

She smiled. 'We'll see, Hans Adler.'

She turned and walked over to another soldier who was obviously in more pain than me, due to his constant moaning and wailing, while clutching his stomach in agony. His hands were covered in blood, and I realised he had been shot in the stomach. Four nurses were already attending to him, but Klaudia pushed her way through and started bellowing instructions to each of them, all of whom were relatively new to it all.

I lay back on the bed and rested my head sideways, to the right, watching Klaudia at work. She always stayed calm, no matter what was happening. She would be patient with the nurses and make sure they comprehended what was to be done, before demonstrating it.

The soldier screamed in pain as they washed the wound and attempted to remove the bullet. The nurses stood back with shocked expressions as they watched Klaudia carefully manoeuvre the tools around and remove the bullet from his stomach. Their stunned expressions soon disappeared when Klaudia ordered them to stop standing around and do something useful. One nurse began to clean the wound, while the other attempted to stop the bleeding, but to no avail.

I continued watching, curious as to what was going to be done next, when I heard a voice speak from my left. I turned and looked at the young soldier next to me. I squinted and shook my head, signalling that I didn't hear him the first time.

'Sorry, what?' I asked.

'What happened to you?' he asked again.

'Oh.' I looked down at my leg. 'I tore the flesh from just below my knee. I fell into a crevice and became trapped for a while. They had to attend to it before it became infected.'

'Sounds bad.'

I nodded. 'It is. But not as bad as some other wounds in here. What happened to you?'

'I was shot in the foot,' he said annoyed.

'That must have hurt. How did it happen?'

Expecting a story of some heroic act that incorporated the soldier leaping up and unfortunately getting shot by a Russian soldier, I was disappointed to hear the results.

'One of the new soldiers doesn't do well under pressure. When we were ordered to get into position, we were lying on our stomachs on a small incline. I went to move to a different position, and he grabbed me, but swung his gun around and accidentally pulled the trigger. Well, so he says. I don't really know if it was an accident. I mean, how stupid can someone be, to shoot another person in the foot? And one who fights *with* them, no less.'

'Oh, you would be surprised. Some people do stupid things, but they're not really stupid. They're just under a lot of pressure. Maybe he was trying to help you.'

'By shooting me in the foot? Yes, because that will help.'

I chuckled. 'No, I mean maybe when you were moving, you were vulnerable, and he was looking out for your best interest.' The soldier gave me a hardened stare. 'Or, that explanation was bullshit, and he was just clumsy enough to shoot you in the foot,' I retracted.

We both laughed, and the soldier nodded.

'How long have you been in the army for?' he asked me.

'I've been in this army since the Battle of France,' I sighed. 'Yes. I was there when we marched straight through into Paris. When we fought our way to get there. What about you?'

The soldier nodded in agreement.

'I was there, too. It was scary at first, I remember. I had never fired a gun at anything, and then we were thrust into battle and told our target was Paris.'

'Did they tell you to just fire at anything, too?'

'Oh, yes. I remember that. It must have been the new recruits they told that to. "Fire at the enemy." How were we supposed to know who the enemy was from that far away?'

'At least it wasn't as cold, like it is here. It seems to just get worse – never better. I swear my fingers felt like they were going to fall off out there.'

'We're almost there, though. A few more days, and we can sweep through into Moscow.'

'And then we can finally–'

As I spoke, I was cut off by a nurse who made her way to the end of my bed, then shuffled beside me. I stopped and looked at her.

'Private Hans Adler?' she replied.

I nodded. 'Yes.'

'You are the one that had the stitches? Flesh removed from below the knee?'

'Yes, that's right.'

'I am to inform you that you can only rest here for a short time, and then you are ordered to go back out to the battlefield.'

'What? But why?'

'Sergeant Shödler saw you and asked about your wounds. When we told him, he said you will be well enough to fight. With increasing casualties and low supplies, minor injuries are only permitted to stay for a short time after treatment.'

I boiled with anger as I sat up and swung my legs out of the bed. 'This is bullshit!'

'You don't have to leave right now,' said the nurse, 'but in a short while.'

I bent over and put my trousers on, struggling to move them over the wound. I put my boots on, tied the laces, and began limping for the exit. My uniform was creased and ragged, and my undershirt wasn't tucked in, hanging lower than my jacket and visibly flapping about. I determinedly walked awkwardly to the exit, my right leg completely straight and stiffened. The nurse tried to stop me, putting her hands on my shoulder, but I brushed her off and made way for Sergeant Shödler's tent.

Once I had reached the tent, I saw no one was waiting outside, and decided upon arrival that waiting would do no good. I marched in and threw back the tent flap, angrily limping to his desk, where he sat. I slammed my hands on the table, and he looked up at me slowly. He then smiled wryly, and I knew he suspected why I was here.

'Something wrong, Private Adler?' he asked cunningly.

'What did you say to those nurses?' I demanded. My arms shook, with the adrenaline coursing through my body.

'I think you know what I said, otherwise you wouldn't be here. Ask me what you really want to know.'

'Why did you tell them to release me after a short time, then?'

'Because I had to. It's nothing against you, I can assure you.'

'You're lying. You have everything against me. Everything!' I was losing control, but I kept my hands glued firmly on the table.

'Trust me, if I was going to lie, it wouldn't be to you. I would gladly tell you the truth if you wanted to hear it. And the truth is I had no choice. Our supplies are rapidly deteriorating, and with soldiers being wounded left, right and centre, I have no choice but to dismiss the minor injuries. Our medical tents are becoming increasingly full, and the only way to keep things moving is to keep our soldiers moving. If every soldier is in a medical tent, who are fighting the Russians? No one.'

I stood upright and took a step back from Sergeant Shödler.

'I know you would very much like to accuse me of intimidation against you, but that's how these things work. There is a pecking order, and you are at the bottom. There is *nothing* you can do about it.'

I went to walk away, when Sergeant Shödler snapped.

'Adler!'

I turned. He stood up from his chair and walked past the table toward me. He stopped and leaned in close.

'Who the fuck do you think you are? You come in here, demanding things from me. You order me as though I am a common soldier.'

He lifted his left foot and knocked my wounded leg, which sent me crashing to the ground in agony. I gritted my teeth and cried loudly, clutching my leg. My leg burned, the feeling of thousands of knives tearing the flesh, cutting to the bone. Sergeant Shödler leaned down.

'Now, you listen here. I am *your* superior. You listen to *me*. And if you ever cross me again, I will make sure you are in so much pain, you will wish you were dead. Do you understand?'

I nodded and grunted, trying not to cry. *Don't let him see you cry*, I thought to myself.

He placed his foot on my leg, placing pressure on my leg. He was enjoying this. My heart raced as he applied pressure to the wound.

'Good.' He placed his foot back to the ground. 'Now, get up.'

I struggled to get up, but eventually managed to push my body from the ground and walk to the exit. I was only two feet outside the tent when Sergeant Shödler called me again.

'And Adler,' he began, 'don't ever come into my tent unannounced.'

'Yes Sergeant,' I muttered.

I turned and limped back to the medical tent and rested back on my bed. I pulled my trousers off, and saw the bandages now covered in blood again. When Sergeant Shödler kicked the wound, he broke the stitching. *Bastard.* I still believed he did it to spite me – I knew it.

The nurse who tried to stop me from leaving came back over and examined the wound.

'I told you to stay,' she said. 'Now look what happened.'

She frowned at the blood-soaked bandages, unwrapped them gently, and then looked at me.

'We're going to need to restitch them. And it isn't going to be comfortable.'

I looked over to the bed to my left, witnessing it now empty.

'Where's the soldier that was there before? When I left?'

'He was dismissed. He was considered only a minor medical attentive, and like I said before, my orders were to dismiss those that are classed well enough to fight.'

Shit. Shödler wasn't lying. That was a change.

'Now,' continued the nurse, 'get ready to bite down on this cloth, and pray it's over and done with quickly.'

Not again.

Concentration Camp

Laugh in the face of Death, sing in the face of fear. Or sing in the face of Death and laugh in the face of fear. Either way, they will both come at one point, and one of them will succeed.

Never let it smell your fear,
It grows darker, near and near.
Death, upon which you will see,
Never let it sup with glee.

Interesting, Death is. No one knows what is on the other side, and it is with all observing eyes and ears that I know, no one wants to know. When Death is concerned, they shriek. They cry and mutter and hope it not to be true, but in the end, it comes on swift wings. And yet, after all is said and done, they lust for it.

There is a young man, who does just this. His name, well, I do not know. His name has not been uttered, and he makes it so. He sits, he mutters, he moans, and he cries, and yet there is nothing for him. He wails for his family, and he wails for his own life. Like a child, he cries for his mother, and like a child he curls up in his bed and rocks gently.

Fear is just the beginning,
Then it turns to longing.
Soon they wish it was something,
Other than Death.

Oh, the young boy will not cease his crying. He cries in the night, and when day comes, he cries some more.

'Please let me out,' he pleads. 'Please, I will do anything.'

Anything?

Often said, but never sure. One would not do anything to be let free. Anything is far too willing, and none of them are willing. They are more hopeful, more wanting than willing. And that can be dangerous. Their tongues will lead them to trouble, and when that time comes, they will regret it.

The officers wait for this false sense of willingness, and like a tiger, they pounce. They rip from the man everything he has left, and they crush what remains. Now, he is a lifeless corpse that roams the halls, labours during the day, and little by little, he dies at night. Soon he will wish for Death, and when he does, that will be his wanting, and he will be willing.

CHAPTER 21

November 22, 1941

After a few hours in the medical tent, I was sent back onto the field. Klaudia snuck me a small bottle that contained some whiskey, and I took it gladly to help relieve the pain at certain times. At first, I refused, worried it would make me unconscionable on the field and my mind would be elsewhere, but she assured me it wouldn't be so.

When I was dismissed, I was met at the exit by two soldiers, one whose skin peeled from his face, blood dripping to the ground, and the other who had been shot in the arm, squeezing it tightly. Our soldiers were being slaughtered, and the medical tents were becoming fuller each hour. I worried that it may come to utter chaos if this continued. The two soldiers looked miserable, their faces drooping low and their eyes looking down at their boots. Their eyes showed almost no sign of life.

I limped toward the frontline, looking for Siegfried and Lars. My hand rested on my upper right thigh as I limped on when I was caught up by another soldier.

'Alder! Private Adler.'

I turned to see a soldier running toward me with my gun.

'Your gun,' he said, 'you can't go on the front line without it.'

'Oh, yes,' I said, rather dazedly. 'I didn't... uh... I didn't know where it was.'

He handed me the gun, which seemed heavier than last time I held it.

'Well, if you're ever in the medical tent again, though we both don't want that to happen, all weapons are minded by two soldiers in the adjacent tent: whichever medical tent you're in.'

I nodded and smiled. 'Yes, of course. Thank you.'

The soldier returned the smile and nod, and walked back toward the medical tent. I continued to the frontline, slowly walking with my right leg outstretched and my left leg struggling to take the weight.

Once I had reached the frontline, I ducked for cover and, with great difficulty, shuffled around the dirt mounds to try and find Siegfried and Lars. I decided to move to where we were caught out before, but cautious this time as to make sure I had enough cover to escape if needed.

I crawled over to the opening and looked around. I rested against a large dirt mound, with the base having been dug a small portion since I had left, acting as a small trench. I looked around, and then turned my attention to the hill. Scanning the hillside, I saw no movement amongst the rocky outcrops. I looked up at the hilltop and saw no sign of life there either.

After considerable thought, I made my way to the hill's base and crouched down, looking upward and scanning left and right for any movement. There was none.

Finding it difficult to climb up the hill, I managed to persevere in the task for only a few short minutes before my leg ached and I no longer had the strength to use solely my arms to heave my body upward. I was conscious of the icy rocks, knowing if I slipped again, the pain would be unbearable, and my cries would not be held in.

I sat on a small, plateaued piece of the hillside, leaning against a large rock. I rested my gun on the uneven surface and peered through the scope, hoping for any sign of the two. Forward – nothing. Right – nothing. Left and up – a small glint, but what I assumed to be nothing. Nevertheless, I decided to follow it anyway.

Perfect, I thought. *This is going to prove more than just difficult. It's going to be impossible.* As I looked up at the hill, it seemed more like a mountain. Its sides were grazed with large boulders and rocks, and from the gaps in between, sprouted long, dead grass, blowing in the wind.

Leaning on my gun, I used it to heave myself up and began crawling for the top. The incline wasn't too steep, but it was steep enough to force those wanting to climb it to zigzag upward rather than climb straight up. I followed the path that Siegfried and Lars used earlier, keeping fully aware of the crevice that had my leg in agony.

Almost halfway up the rocky hill, I struggled to keep a grip on the large boulder that I had to get over before I was safely on a plateaued bit of ground. I attempted to heave my body up, but to no avail. My legs were sprawled behind me, half on a small edge and half dangling off in mid-air. Grunting, I gave it one last pull, my fingers aching as they cut on the sharp rock and bled. My body moved inch by inch, and with the final pull, I felt my body moving over the boulder.

Eventually, my entire body had lifted onto the flat piece of earth, allowing me to rest for a moment. I sat with my right leg rigid, with the pain of the wound getting worse. I rested against the inclined ground and placed my hands on my chest, breathing heavily. My eyes were closed, and I listened to the distant gunfire, accompanied by the yelling of soldiers.

'Hans! Hans! Is that you?'

I slowly opened my eyes and saw a figure crouching atop the hill, slightly to my left.

'Hans!'

I sat up. My eyes slowly adjusted, and I squinted into the distance, seeing Lars resting on his stomach and leaning over the edge.

'Lars?'

'What the hell are you doing?'

'I was trying to find you and Siegfried.'

'What? Why?'

'I wanted to know if you were both all right. Are you?'

'We're fine. Are *you*?'

'I'm fine. My leg is aching, though.'

'Wait there, I'll come down to you. Keep your head low.'

I waited for a few minutes before Lars climbed down and sat beside me.

'Why are you up here, Hans?'

'Like I said, I was looking for you and Siegfried.'

'How's your leg?'

'It hurts like hell.'

'Then why are you out here? Shouldn't you be in the medical tent, getting some rest?'

I shook my head.

'They ordered me to get back out in the field. The medical tents are becoming too full, and the nurses are under enough pressure. Those with minor injuries aren't permitted to stay in the tents for too long.'

'Who told you to go back out to the field?'

I looked at Lars and tilted my head. 'Sergeant Shödler.'

Lars tilted his head back. '*Jesus*. What happened this time?'

'What do you mean "this time"?'

'Hans, everyone knows about the arguments you and Sergeant Shödler have. It's obvious you hate each other, and you're not exactly quiet during them. He's a bastard of a man, I know, but you have to stay away from him.'

'It wasn't my fault. I was told he gave the order for me to go back out to the field after a few hours of rest, and I thought it was a personal vendetta against me. You can't blame me for getting angry when you're not told the whole story.'

'So, who told you initially?'

'One of the nurses. Then I went to Sergeant Shödler's tent with so much rage. He told me what the actual story was, and I thought he was going to let me off. He threatened me, and he came up close to my face, with that look he has. Every time he does that, I retreat like a child. He kicked my wound, then stood on it while I was on the ground. I was in agony.'

'*Shit*. Trust me, if he couldn't scare anyone like that, I don't think he would have made it to sergeant. And what about your leg? What did they do?'

'The wound was fusing with my uniform, so they cut it and

cleaned it up. Then wrapped it and sent me on my merry way,' I said sarcastically.

'Are you going to be able to make it up the hill?'

I looked up the hillside. 'I was hoping so. I got this far…'

'And then you collapsed and rested for too long. You're exhausted. Look at you.'

'There's nothing I can do about that. It's either fight in the pits with every other soldier or get up there and think of a better plan.'

'All right then, let's get you up.'

Lars put his left arm under my right, and interlocked it, then held my chest with his right hand.

'Okay, it's going to be difficult to get up with the both of us, so just listen and do what I say.'

'All right, Commander.'

'I may be younger than you, but you have a wounded leg, and I don't. Don't make me leave you here,' he joked.

'Well, let's do this.'

Lars struggled to keep my weight up, and I could feel his arms trembling as he desperately tried to help me up the hillside. He planted his right foot firmly behind and looped my right leg over his left. Each time we faced a hard step upward, he would make sure my wounded leg was supported enough so I could get my left leg up and pull us up together.

It was a slow and arduous process, and I thought that at any moment Russian soldiers would spot us and shoot us down.

'What if we get spotted?' I asked.

Lars grunted, pushing his body against mine as I pulled up.

'We won't. Just keep moving, we'll be fine.'

'Lars, down there!'

'Fuck! They're going to see us. Hans, we have to drop.'

'Drop? Are you insane?'

'Look, just beneath us. There's a small bit we can land on. But we have to be smart about it.'

'We're not both going to fit on there, Lars. There's nothing smart about it!'

'We have no choice, Hans! They're going to see us if we don't drop. I'll drop first, and when I land, you then drop. I'll try and catch you.'

'What if you don't succeed? That's a steep drop if I miss.'

'Then don't miss.'

My breathing became faster, as did Lars'. I could feel his heartbeat get faster as he pushed up against me. I looked down to where the Russians were moving. They were encroaching on our embankments, where we were trapped earlier. If they got there, they would have a clear view of both of us slowly working our way up the hill and have no hesitation in shooting us down.

'Do you promise you won't let me fall down that slope?'

Lars nodded. 'I'll try.'

I sighed heavily. 'That's good enough for me. Let's go.'

I dug my hand in the earth and with the other, gripped onto a thick root that was partially sticking out of the ground. Lars dropped and slipped slightly as he landed, but gained his balance. There was only enough room for a small child to be beside Lars on that edge, but I couldn't stay where I was, my stomach resting awkwardly on a rocky surface that was too steep to let go of anything. I shut my eyes tightly, and hoped for the best, but expected the worst.

I let go.

I slid down the hill, the rocks hitting my back and my legs up in the air, flailing about. I gritted my teeth as I tried to block out all the pain but couldn't bring myself to open my eyes.

'Hans! Get ready! Open your eyes!'

For what seemed like forever, sliding down the hill as thousands of pieces of earth were disturbed by my body, I opened my eyes. There, oncoming, was Lars with his arms outstretched ready to grab onto me.

I slammed my left foot down, which made me go off balance. With a deep breath, I slammed my right foot down and yelled in pain as I felt the force push against my wound. Both of my feet dug into the ground, and I slowed down enough to allow Lars to grab hold of my arms tightly and prevent me from falling again.

'It's all right, Hans. I've got you,' said Lars.

'We are never doing that again,' I stated. 'Ever.'

'Agreed. I thought you were going to go over that edge.'

'If I did, you would have come with me.'

'Well, we're here, so let's lay low.'

Lars and I lay low for a few hours as the Russian soldiers fought their way into our front line. We provided covering fire for the men, but with no sniper rifles, it was like shooting ducks miles away. We made sure we weren't detected, firing only when they were under enough pressure so they didn't know where our gunfire was coming from.

We watched as the Russians attempted to cross the contours that outlined our army's position, laying on their stomachs with their guns pointed at the ready, and pulling the trigger, unleashing a fury of flying bullets upon them. I shot one soldier in the leg, and after watching him stagger to the ground and attempt to stand and run a number of times, I pulled the trigger once more, this time with the sights set on his head. It felt like putting down an animal that had been injured and struggling to maintain its independence, but it had to be done. If one of our soldiers captured him, they would show no mercy in his interrogation, and the only noise coming from his mouth would be screams of pain.

I've seen the interrogations before and vomited twice while watching two. When we had becoming newly signed-up soldiers, they liked to make us watch them and get a taste for it. One was a French soldier. He sat on a small wooden chair and faced an officer that I had never come across before. The soldier was of a small build, with a moustache that ran across his upper lip. His cheekbones were sharp, and his dark green eyes followed the interrogating officer's footsteps, each single step. The German officer, who was so large, it wouldn't have come as a shock to me if it was true that he was a body building champion before his days as a brutal officer, leaned to the French soldier and ordered, 'Look at me. Look me in the eye.'

The French soldier lifted his eyes, and once they made contact with the German's, he was struck by a strong hit to the face.

'Your filthy French eyes are not worthy enough to look upon me,' the German officer said. 'Why do you look at my shoes?'

The French soldier averted his gaze. The German officer approached him and lifted his chin.

'I asked you a fucking question. Answer it.'

The German officer's voice was calm but intimidating at the same time. Whenever he spoke, I could hear the ripples in his croaky voice.

'I cannot look at your eyes,' said the French soldier in broken German.

'So, you think you can look at my shoes?'

The French soldier shook his head.

When the German officer proceeded to ask questions about the French army's plans, the French soldier would seal his lips and not make a sound. Each time, he was struck harder and harder. Then, he started with the fingernails. One by one. When he got to the third, and the screaming was so loud, I exited the room and vomited. I couldn't watch any more of it. I don't know why I stayed for as long as I did. Perhaps, it was the admirable courage the French soldier had, or perhaps it was because I was so intrigued by the process, which made me think I was worse than some other soldiers.

The next soldier was a British soldier. After the invasion of the French borders, and successfully capturing Paris, five soldiers, including myself, were transferred back to Berlin for a brief two weeks. Our instructions were that we were under strict orders to carry out a mission, though we never found out what it was. But while we were there, we were to witness the interrogation of a British soldier who had fought in the French resistance. The man was tall, well built, with hazelnut hair and sapphire-blue eyes.

I sat with the four other soldiers, all who were around the same age as me, behind a rusted metal cage in what seemed to be an old warehouse, with lights dangling down by rusted steel. The walls of the room they were in, were only small, about four feet higher than I was, and then the warehouse roof stood a further twenty feet over the top. We were all nervous, but I was more so. I knew what was coming, and I knew what this soldier was about to become. The other soldiers were anxiously waiting.

'What are they going to do?' one of the soldiers asked.

I shook my head.

'They ask him questions, and if he doesn't answer, they beat him like an animal. I saw one once.'

'Do we have to watch this?' asked another.

'It's part of our training, apparently,' spoke another soldier, 'to make us learn what to do to the enemy out on the battlefield.'

'Why us?' asked the first soldier.

The other shrugged.

'Maybe we're easily swayed – or the worst of the soldiers. Maybe we're to be the monsters on the battlefield.'

My stomach twisted. *No, I'm not*, I thought.

'I'm not,' said the first soldier, as though he was agreeing with my thoughts.

'Neither am I,' added the second.

It was then that I realised – I wasn't alone. I wasn't the only one who thought these practices were barbaric. I wasn't the only one who didn't like this at all. My Jewish heritage wasn't the singular factor that made me think that – it was our inner morality.

I turned to the soldier and solemnly shook my head.

'Just turn away and think of someone else. Don't let them see you, though.'

The British soldier was questioned, with a translator present. The German soldier, who stood directly in front of the British soldier seated on the chair would ask the question, and the translator would repeat it in English.

'How many soldiers is Britain lending in aid to the French?'

The British soldier shook his head. 'I don't know.'

A blow to the head.

'Where is the main base of operations of the French resistance?'

Another shake of his head, and another swift hit to the face, this time drawing blood from his temple.

'Why are the British trying to stop our advances in North Africa?'

The British soldier stopped and thought for a moment, then looked directly at the interrogator.

'To protect the colonies.'

The interrogator laughed. He hit the British soldier in the face, sending him crashing to the ground, then kicked him repeatedly. He began to bleed at the mouth, and his face turned crimson as he gasped for air. Two German soldiers approached him and sat his chair upright. The British soldier hung his head low, breathing heavily.

The interrogator summoned for a screwdriver. One of the soldiers fetched it on the metal tray in the room and handed it to him. The interrogator grabbed it and launched at the British soldier, stabbing him in the crevice between his thumb and forefinger. He screamed in pain, while pleading in English. The interrogator laughed maniacally and proceeded to slide the screwdriver's steel along the soldier's face, wiping the blood along his cheek.

'Tell me, what is the next move of the British?'

The translator repeated it in English. The British soldier gave a worrisome look and shook his head.

'Tell me!' yelled the interrogator.

The British soldier moved his head back. The interrogator grabbed his cheeks and stretched them, until finally the soldier yelled in pain. The interrogator grabbed a knife that was on the metal tray and began to slice the soldier's fingers, until he reached the bone. The screams echoed throughout the warehouse, and I shut my eyes.

'I can't watch this,' said one of the soldiers.

'Neither can I,' said another. 'I have to get out of here.'

'Why are they doing this?' asked the first. 'That man, he's in agony.'

'Because they're animals,' I said quietly. 'All of them.'

Once the interrogator sliced into the British soldier's thumb, I turned and ran for the exit, barely making it before I vomited on the dirt. Coughing and choking, I stood hunched over, then straightened up and tilted my head back. I breathed deeply.

The other soldiers followed soon after. One of the soldiers also vomited, and the other sat against the wall of the warehouse, breathing heavily. The third walked out, no emotion on his face. He watched us, sat on the ground, and burst into tears.

I looked down at where the Russians were crouched. I watched as one attempted to go over the hilly ground and move to where our soldiers were positioned, but I knew if they could, they would take him prisoner. Whether they interrogated him here or in Berlin, no mercy would be given either way. My gun was perched on a rock, ready to fire. I wrapped my finger around the trigger, and when the sights moved over and rested on the soldier's head, I pulled it.

Forgive me.

Dear Alina

Alina,

How funny it is, the world. From a strange scenario, it can create the perfect opportunity. But that opportunity is missed, now. Each night, I lay and look up at the stars before sleeping. The cold wind would blast on my face, but I would never notice it as I gazed up at the starry sky, each time thinking about what you were doing.

When I first glanced at you, standing there with that beautiful smile, I almost fell to my knees. I felt them shaking as I wondered what such a beautiful person wanted with someone like me. You trusted me, even though I was from the other side. You still smiled as we spoke, and when we walked, it was like it could last forever. But that was the trouble – it didn't last forever. Each night I think about it; I ache for that time.

I told you things I would never tell anyone close to me. I told you about my true identity, and in return, you told me about you. That's all I could ask for. In this life, people want temporary pleasures and thrills, but all I wanted was someone to be honest with – and I found you. It wasn't long before I felt comfortable around you. Almost immediately, in fact, I felt comfortable around you. No judgement was reserved, nor any malcontent toward me. You were just beautiful, inside and out. You proved to me that people are still beautiful, amongst all this chaos.

I felt like a young child again. Instantly I wanted to marry you; we would go away from all of this and settle down with a family. That's always how I've imagined it to be. When we fall in love, we don't usually know it until after. But I knew. I knew the moment I saw you in that little store, and I knew all along as we laughed, cried, and talked together.

The thing about love is that it never dies. I can look to the stars and know that you look at the same sky, and that for me is enough for now.

We breathe the same air, we witness the same rising sun, and we touch the same earth. Somehow, we are connected, and I know you will always have a place in my heart. Always.

Until we meet again. One day.

Love always,
Johan

CHAPTER 22

November 26, 1941

We had fought our way through the defences of the outer lands of Moscow and were slowly making our way towards the city. We were twenty miles away, and I could almost smell it from where we stood.

The tanks were slowing down due to the weather, and a heavy blizzard of pure white snow swept in, almost burying us. The wind howled and blasted against us as our feet sank low in the snow. We were still fighting. No amount of snow could deter us from what we set out to do – although it sounded more appealing to me to feel the warmth of a fire, with a drink to warm my stomach, rather than guns firing as we ran through the snow for dear life.

Nevertheless, I was stuck in a white world with nothing more than rolling hills covered in snow, and the odd tree that stood protruding to the sky. The Russian soldiers were used to this and they were trained for this. They knew this land and they knew how dangerous it was. Stay in the same spot and you would be engulfed in feet of snow.

'Come on, you bastard,' mumbled Earnst as he looked down the sights of his gun and fired into the distance. 'I've got you now.'

I glanced over from the sights of my gun to Earnst, who was smiling wryly.

'Have you got him?' I asked.

'Almost,' he replied, staggering out the words for a time before finishing it. 'He's just about to... almost there... come on, move out.'

Earnst, Felix and I were reunited after days apart. Felix had moved south-east with another group of soldiers, cutting off the Russian soldiers' advances from the south and trying to sneak past to attack from behind. Earnst was on the frontline, holding off any Russian advances and defending our position. Our army had seemed to stagger over the days, and our supplies dwindled to a non-existent hope that all of us held in our minds.

Our tanks were breaking down, struggling through the snow and blizzards that blasted us, their tracks taking a lifetime to indent the snow and move on. Time was against us, and more importantly, so was the weather. Everything in this place was against us, and they had every right to be. Willing to stop us at anything, it wouldn't be long before we would be trapped, struggling and praying for a way out, when our obliteration would come.

I didn't know how much longer it would take for our impending doom to finally kick in, and I wasn't entirely sure we would reach Moscow at this point, which made me even more wary of everything that was going on. If something was going to happen, now would be the time, and I was ready for anything.

Earnst, Felix and I made our way to the higher ground. We had advanced just four miles in four days, and it was only getting slower. Houses that were once homes to families on small farms provided good shelter from the oncoming bombardments. Scrambling across the abandoned farmlands, small contingents of our soldiers ran across the fields. We were accompanied by Waldron and Heinrich. The two had resolved any issues before accompanying us, knowing well that if they started a fight in the middle of the battle, one of us would be sure to end it. Surprisingly, they got along enough to work together and keep the group solid.

The gunfire had not ceased for one moment since the battle

started. The other groups that moved forward on the fields were providing enough covering fire for us to run across to where a small farmhouse was situated.

When we got there, Earnst kicked down the door and we all entered. Dust had settled on everything. Not one spot in the house was clean. The spiders had made it their home, cobwebs hanging in the furthest corners of the rooms, attaching itself on the chairs and tables, and along the fireplace.

'This has been abandoned for a while,' said Waldron. 'Do you think they knew all along that we were coming?'

Earnst shook his head.

'No. They can't have. They might have abandoned it for the bad weather. Look at this place.'

'We can't stay here for long,' I interjected. 'We have to keep moving.'

'Surely we can stay here for a small while,' said Felix. 'Just to get out of the blizzard and rest.'

'I agree with Felix,' said Heinrich. 'We need to get as much rest as we can. I haven't slept for four days, and I don't think anyone else has either.'

'Not for too long,' said Earnst. 'But I do agree, just a small time. We need it, Hans.'

I grew increasingly frustrated with all of them. Once you stop, you want to stay there. This war wasn't going to be easy – no one said that as a reassurance, ever. In fact, most soldiers knew what they were in for. It was the few naïve soldiers that thought it was going to be a walk in the park, so to speak.

'We can't stay here,' I said desperately. 'We have to keep moving.'

'Relax, Hans,' said Earnst. 'It won't be for long. Just sit down and relax for a bit.'

'If you tell me to relax one more time,' I began, 'I swear I will…'

'You will what?' asked Heinrich. 'If you want to leave, then leave. But don't drag the rest of us out with you when we're exhausted and need just a little bit of time to rest. That's all we're asking for, just a little bit of time. Jesus, Hans.'

I sighed and tilted my chin up, keeping an eye on Heinrich.

'Fine,' I said. 'But only for a small time.'

'Yes,' said Heinrich indignantly. 'We did all agree on a small time, didn't we?'

I nodded in agreement, and we all found a place to sit. Earnst and Waldron cleaned the cobwebs from the chairs that were placed in front of the fireplace, while Felix, Heinrich and I sat at opposite ends of the room on the floor.

We all rested our guns on our laps, in case of an emergency that required them. I sat rigidly against the thick stone walls; my hands clasped tightly around my gun. I tapped my foot incessantly on the ground, hoping the time would pass quickly and we wouldn't be caught in any oncoming fire. The wind howled, battering the windows of the cottage.

We were all silent, until Waldron spoke.

'It would be nice if we could light that fireplace.'

'Don't even think about it,' snapped Heinrich. 'They would see the smoke from a mile away, and before you know it, they would bombard this place in a second.'

'I wasn't going to, you moron,' whined Waldron. 'I just said it would be nice.'

'Both of you, don't start,' said Earnst. 'Please.'

The more I knew about Earnst, and the more I was in his presence, the more I admired him for his wisdom and kindness. When I first met him, I compared both he and Felix to the same character – stupid and callous. But the more I knew him, and the more he knew me, the more he showed that he was intelligent, a leader, and had a kindness that not many people I knew possessed.

As for Felix, although not the brightest spark, he still had the kindest heart of them all. Before they knew me, and I them, it was important for soldiers to display a certain domineering charisma, to prove a point. But as we grew to know one another, so too did our friendship. The soldiers I knew weren't bad people – they were just lost young men fighting for a cause they were told was right; at least, that's how I saw it. I couldn't forgive for what was done to my people, that was something which I knew deep down, but I could forgive the soldiers that I fought with, for what we did. Perhaps I kidded myself, thinking I was somehow ethically better than those who threw my people in the ghettos; that I could somehow come out of this feeling more righteous than them. But maybe I was right, too. And that's what confused me. We were young men, thrown into a war we didn't understand, only to be told that those who opposed us were evil – were we evil for believing it?

I started to hum quietly, until it grew into a louder melody. When I stopped, Heinrich turned to me and asked, 'Why did you stop? Don't stop.'

'This isn't a time for joyful songs. This isn't a time for joyful anything.' I replied.

'It doesn't have to be joyful,' said Felix. 'Just keep humming. Please. It was soothing.'

I hummed for a few minutes, then stopped and sat in silence. My knees were tucked up to my chest and my head tilted onto my left shoulder, as I stared at the ground. We listened to the distant gunfire and shouting from the soldiers who made their way through the fields.

The Russian army had pulled back a few miles to refuel and resupply, which was foolishly taken as an advantage to us by our superiors. It wasn't, however. Once we went forward, it would be far more difficult to go back, and with our deteriorating state of supplies, fuel and most of all, morale, it would mean too close for comfort.

'What's that in the distance?' asked Earnst. He perked up and peered out of the window.

Heinrich stood up and walked over to where Earnst was standing and looked out. Both of their faces dropped as Heinrich hissed, '*Shit*. Russian tanks are moving.'

'What?' screeched Waldron. 'I thought they were refuelling!'

'That's what we all thought!' snapped Heinrich. 'It was a trick to lure us in. *Fuck!*'

Heinrich began to panic, and his breathing became far more abrupt.

'We have to move, now!' said Earnst. 'Get your guns and whatever else you brought. We're leaving, right now. No excuses.'

'I knew this would happen,' I said.

'Oh, shut up, Hans!' yelled Waldron. 'No one knew this was going to happen.'

'I told you not to stay here. I told you all to keep moving!'

'If we kept moving, we would have met up with those tanks far sooner, you idiot!'

'Sooner? We would have crossed the river and walked straight past them without even knowing it, and Heinrich over there wouldn't be having a panic attack!'

'Both of you, shut it!' demanded Earnst. 'This is no time to argue. Let's just admit we all made a mistake and move on. We have to get out of here.'

I picked up my gun and walked over to the door, while mumbling,

'I didn't make the mistake.'

Waldron heard me and grabbed me by the collar.

'If I hear you say that you knew, or that you didn't make the mistake, I will throw you to those tanks. *Everyone* makes mistakes.'

'And you were just the product of your parents' mistake, then?' I sneered.

Waldron's face reddened, and his grip tightened before throwing me across the room. Crashing into the table that held a small lamp, it smashed as my weight crashed down on top of it. I stood up and wiped my face, but before I could react, Waldron had launched himself at me. I fell straight to the ground, where Waldron climbed on top of me and began to mercilessly beat my face until it was raw and bleeding. My wounded leg had smashed to the ground, and I grunted in agony as the burning sensation returned.

Earnst jumped on top of Waldron and dragged him off, throwing him across the room. I was left lying on the ground in agony, as I placed my hands inches from my face and shook in fear. Though I didn't feel any fear of Waldron in particular, I feared my face was dismembered, and the fear of the possibility that it could have been a lot worse if it was just the two of us also frightened me.

Earnst came over to where I was and knelt down beside me. He grabbed my hands and gently placed them down on my lap, and then further examined my face.

'How much does it hurt?' he asked.

I shook my head and averted any eye contact. 'It doesn't hurt.'

'Don't try and be a hero, Hans. He gave you a large beating; we all saw it. Where does it hurt?'

'My cheeks and part of my nose.'

He put his fingers on my nose and wriggled it slightly. 'Does that hurt?'

'No, not really.'

He touched my left cheek. 'What about that?'

I winced in pain. '*Jesus!* Yes, that hurts.'

'And the other cheek?' He tapped my right cheek.

I squinted and bit my lip, nodding fast.

'I don't think he broke anything, but it will become swollen and cause you a bit of pain for a while.' He leaned in closer. 'Hans, why did you have to do that?'

'What? Do what?'

'Provoke him. You could have kept your mouth shut, at least while we were stuck in this house. Now look what happened.'

'Why are you blaming me?' I asked, short of breath. 'I wasn't the one who decided to throw someone across the room and start beating them to death.'

'He wasn't beating you to death, Hans. Besides–'

'If he was given the chance, and you weren't here to intervene, Earnst, he would have easily beaten me to death. I can't fight him off, so who would have?'

'That's not the point. You provoked him, and you knew it. You try to say these things that may seem witty, but they just get you into trouble.'

'I don't need a lecture from you, Earnst. That's how I survive. I don't have a large-built physique, I can't fight; I can't do anything. We had this discussion before, and you know all of it.'

'And you still didn't listen!' Earnst yelled, his face close to mine and his eyes staring directly at me, while Felix, Waldron and Heinrich were now at the opposite end of the room, crouching down and watching the events unfold between us.

'Christ, Hans! That's your problem. You don't listen! You never have. You think you have it figured out – that everything can bend to your will – but you don't!'

'I have never thought that!' I began to yell, with tears streaming down my eyes. 'If I did, I wouldn't be in the mess I am now!

My father would still be alive, and my mother and sister. And I wouldn't have to get by on nothing but what I say. Trust me, if I could bend everything to my will, I would, because I hate who I am! I hate it! I hate this place. I hate this whole fucking war! Everything!'

I began to cry, fighting for too long to hold back the tears. They came naturally, and it was a time to unleash it. Earnst still knelt beside me, but had moved back away from my face, and stared with a stunned look on his face. He covered his mouth with part of his arm, then dropped it to his side.

'I don't particularly like this place either, Hans, but it doesn't mean I don't have to do my duty.' Earnst's voice had softened, but still had a stony edge to it. 'We have a job to do. Everyone has experienced heartache and sadness, but we put it behind us until this is finished, and then we can revisit it to properly mourn.'

'I didn't mean you, Earnst,' I said quietly. 'None of it. I meant *him*.' My eyes darted across the room to Waldron, who crouched quietly. His eyes widened.

'What?' he asked indignantly. 'What the fuck are you saying?'

I shook my head, deciding it wasn't worth the trouble. I rested my head on the cold wooden floor and sobbed quietly. Earnst placed his hand on my shoulder.

I kept an eye on Waldron, and saw him shuffle strangely, as though he was contemplating something. Then, in a short moment, he jumped up and headed straight for Earnst and me. As he marched over, his shoulders hunched to his neck and his fists clenched, the wall adjacent to where we lay was destroyed. Splinters of wood rained across the room, and Waldron was flung to the ground a few feet away.

The noise caused a ringing in my ears as dust carried up in the air and the wood finally smashed to the ground. I could hear the coughs of the other soldiers, and I too started coughing. I moved around and lifted my head, looking around to see if anyone was injured.

'Is anyone hurt?' yelled Heinrich from across the room.

I looked up at where the destruction happened, and saw the inner wall completely demolished and the roof partially collapsed. *A tank*. They were closer than we thought.

'Are any of you hurt?' he repeated.

'We have to get out of here!' I yelled.

'We need to know if there is anyone who is injured,' said Heinrich.

I looked at Earnst, who was hauling himself up from off the ground.

'We're fine,' I said.

'What about Waldron?'

Earnst made his way over to where Waldron was thrown. I stood up and followed. I stood behind Earnst as he crouched down beside Waldron.

'He's unconscious,' he said, 'and... his leg is caught under one of the wooden beams.'

'There's tanks coming!' exclaimed Felix. 'We have to go.'

'What about Waldron?' asked Heinrich.

'We're going to have to leave him,' replied Earnst.

Earnst stood up and was about to walk past me, but I stopped him in his tracks.

'We can't leave him,' I said.

Earnst gave me an odd look.

'We can't take him with us. It will take too long, and we have to get out of here.'

'So, you're just going to leave him here to die?'

'We have no choice,' he said firmly. 'I thought you, of all people, would be glad about that.'

He brushed past me and went over to Felix and Heinrich, carefully stepping over the collapsed beams. I crouched beside Waldron, examining the extent of the damage, and hearing the muffled tones of the others across the room.

'Hans! Let's go,' said Earnst.

'I'm staying here,' I replied. 'I'm not a fucking monster. Not yet anyway.'

'Don't be stupid, Hans. We have to go. Now.'

'Go on ahead. I'll be there soon. Just keep moving.'

'Hans, we're not leaving without you.'

'And I'm not leaving without Waldron.'

'The man almost gave you a broken nose, Hans! Leave him be!' said Heinrich.

I stood up and looked at the others, who were signalling me to get out. I turned back to Waldron.

'No,' I said. 'He's not going to die like this.'

I crouched down and attempted to lift the large wooden beam that had trapped Waldron's leg but couldn't move it enough to free it. I glanced over and saw Heinrich, Earnst and Felix leaving the house. Earnst looked back and gave a worrisome look before turning and exiting.

'Come on,' I muttered as my hands slipped under the beam and hauled it.

I counted to three. One… two… three. Every bit of energy left in my body was exerted to force the beam off Waldron's leg. Waldron groaned and tilted his head left and then right.

'Waldron,' I said, exacerbated. 'Waldron, I need you to shuffle your leg out from under this beam when I lift it. Do you hear me? Waldron.'

He groaned again, then squinted up at me. 'Ha… Hans?'

'Waldron, you have to listen to me. We're running out of time. I'm going to lift this beam that's crushing your leg, and I need you to move it out. I can't move the beam over enough, so you're going to need to move it quickly. Do you understand?'

Waldron nodded vaguely and blinked slowly.

'On the count of three. Are you ready?'

Waldron nodded.

'One… two… three… go!'

I lifted the beam, grunting as the weight pulled down on my small arms. Waldron pulled his leg out from under the beam and clutched it tightly. I breathed in heavily and moaned in pain. I dropped the beam and grabbed Waldron from under his left arm. He yelped in pain as the weight pressed on his left leg.

'I can't walk on it,' he said as he shot me a worried look. 'You're going to have to go without me.'

'I'm not doing that,' I said defiantly. 'I said I would get you out, and I'm going to. I can't pick you up, so you're going to have to help me out here. I want you to put your weight on your right leg and hop on it. I'm going to hold your left side and help support your left leg. Don't put any weight on it, otherwise if it's as painful as you showed before, you'll drop like a fly and slow us down. Understand?'

I looked at him directly in the eye, and he exchanged a more sombre look to me, as he saw the effects of his previous brutality on my face.

'Waldron, do you understand?'

He quickly nodded and wrapped his left arm around my shoulder and hopped on his right foot. We turned and headed for the door but were stopped by the beams of destroyed wood that had fallen onto the ground and made a mound to obstacle around.

'Damn,' I cursed. 'You're going to have to climb up and roll over it.'

'Roll over it?'

'Just sit on it as high as you can and work your way over it. I can't help you over it.'

Waldron hastily climbed over the mound of beams, pushing up with his right foot and both hands. He was finally over and sat on the ground waiting for me. As I went to step on the beam, Waldron said, 'What about your gun?'

I looked behind me and quickly grabbed my gun before climbing over. I easily made my way over the top, almost slipping as one beam came loose and slid down. I regained my balance and climbed over to Waldron. I grabbed his right hand and hauled him up, placing his arm around me.

'Once we go through that door, we have to move quickly. Are you ready?'

He nodded.

'Okay, let's go. Now!'

Waldron hobbled along as I pulled him with me, trying to move as quickly as possible. Once we were out of the house, I stepped into the snow and felt my foot sinking into the soft white ground. *This will be more difficult than I thought*, I thought.

Waldron was struggling to keep his balance as every step we took, we sank a few inches into the snow. Waldron, however, only had one leg to keep him stable, and hopping out of a few inches of thick snow proved more difficult than I had anticipated.

Nevertheless, we both pushed on, knowing that once we stopped, we were an easy target for a tank shell.

'Keep going,' I said. 'We need to go into those trees over there. Not as much snow gets through the top, so it will be easier for us to get back to our tanks.'

'But we're heading east, right into the enemy lines,' said Waldron.

'We have to sneak past the tanks before we go west. If we go west, there's no cover for us. If we go east, we can cut through the northern forest and get back to our soldiers. Look, over there. We're only a few yards away.'

We hurried along, with every hop resulting in a grunt from Waldron. Once we had made it to the firmer ground, we turned west and continued through the trees.

'Keep low,' I said. 'There may still be some Russian soldiers that travelled further than the main number of soldiers and the tanks.'

As we moved along, a large crash sounded from behind us. We stopped and turned to see the house we were in collapse completely as two tank shells obliterated it. Waldron and I exhaled loudly, then turned and continued on.

We emerged from the forest and continued south-west until we saw our soldiers moving in the opposite direction to us.

'Hold your fire,' I heard one soldier bellow. 'Friendly soldiers to the north-east.'

Two soldiers approached us.

'He needs to get to the medical tent,' I said. 'His leg is wounded.'

The two soldiers grabbed Waldron from each side, his arms resting on either soldier's shoulder.

'What about your face, soldier?'

I put my hand up. 'I'm fine. I have urgent news for command. I need to speak with them.'

The soldier studied me for a moment, then nodded. 'Very well.'

They carried him off and I was left to find my own way. I stood for a few minutes looking around and watching various groups of soldiers making their way eastward. I jogged back west and made my way to the officers' and command tents.

'Soldier, what are you doing here?'

I turned around and saw Colonel Hirsch staring at me, his hand behind his back.

'I know you,' he said. 'I've seen you before. Then again, I've seen many soldiers. Your name, soldier, what is it?'

'Private Hans Adler,' I replied.

'Yes. Hans Alder. You shouldn't be here. Why are you back here? Tell me your reasons, Adler.'

'I just came from where the Russian tanks were. There were five of us, and we were trapped in a small farmhouse.'

'You were trapped? Why?'

I sighed. 'They wanted to stop in the house. I told them we shouldn't, but they went ahead anyway. And then a tank bombarded the house and caused the roof to collapse, before the whole house collapsed after we escaped.' I could hear myself talking without any breath.

'Russian tanks?'

'That's why I've come back here. I had to tell command. The Russian tanks are closer than we thought and caught us by surprise. We were one of the first soldiers to go east.'

'Come with me,' he said.

He turned and walked briskly to the commander's tent, and I followed closely behind. I was stopped at the entrance by the colonel, who turned and put his hand on my chest.

'Stay here for a moment,' he said staunchly. 'You will be summoned shortly.'

I nodded and waited outside. I could hear the murmurs from outside, but couldn't make out any distinct conversation, though I knew what it was about. I looked to the sky, small flakes of snow falling on my face. For a moment, I forgot what state my face was in, and let the gentle cold touch of the flakes warm and melt onto my skin.

After a few minutes of hopping around to try and keep my blood flowing, I was called by Colonel Hirsch who had poked his head out of the tent flap. I turned and entered, where a large wooden table dominated the centre of the tent, with seats placed around it. The commander, Colonel Hirsch, General Koertig, and two other men I had not seen before, were gathered before me.

'Private Hans Adler,' said the commander.

I nodded.

'Take a seat.' He signalled for me to sit on the chair I stood in front of.

The commander was seated directly in front of me, with Colonel Hirsch to my left. General Koertig was to the left of the commander, with one of the soldiers to my right and the other on the commander's right.

'This is Major General Müller,' he said, signalling the man to his right.

Major General Müller was a well-built man in his forties, with thinned hair that was transitioning from charcoal black to grey. His face was still young, however, and his blue eyes met mine while he nodded.

'And this is Lieutenant General Jung.' He signalled to the man that sat to my right.

Lieutenant Jung was a muscular man with most of his body looking as though it was about to explode from his uniform. He had a thick brown moustache that travelled down the sides of his mouth, but his head was spotless, with no strands of hair showing. We exchanged nods and then focused on the commander.

'Your face – what happened?' asked the commander.

'Another soldier and I got into a fight,' I replied, embarrassed. He scoffed.

'Boys will be boys – men will be men. Colonel Hirsch tells me that you saw Russian tanks only a few miles from here.'

'Yes,' I said, while nodding. 'That's correct.'

'Tell us exactly what happened. Don't miss out any details.'

'There were five of us who had gone ahead. We were one of the first to go eastward. Some of the soldiers were tired and wanted to rest, and we came across a farmhouse that had been abandoned and decided to enter it. We stayed there for a time–'

'You *stayed* in there? Why the hell would you stay in there?'

'The other soldiers wanted to,' I said cautiously. 'I told them not to, but I was outvoted.'

'How long were you in there?'

I began to stutter.

'Uh… about… about an hour, I think. Maybe more. Or less. I'm not particularly sure, to be honest.'

'Never mind about the small details, boy,' said Major General Müller. 'Just tell us what you saw. Surely we can spare the whole storytelling?'

'Major General Müller, we have to know what happened, so we understand the boy's story,' said General Koertig.

'Hardly,' said Lieutenant General Jung. 'Every moment we are here listening to this boy tell every single detail, the closer those tanks get. And soon enough, we won't need to know the story or how to approach the situation, because they will be here.'

'Very well,' said the commander. 'Skip this and tell us where the tanks were.'

While the officers were squabbling about everything, I had absorbed what they said, but found my mind drifting off and thinking of Earnst, Felix and Heinrich, and if they were out of any danger.

'Private Adler, tell us about the tanks that you saw,' said the commander.

I looked up from the table and blinked a few times.

'It wasn't far from where we were, and it fired on the farmhouse, causing the roof to collapse and fall on Private Waldron...' I stared at Colonel Hirsch, not knowing what Waldron's last name was.

'Krämer, sir,' said Colonel Hirsch.

The commander raised his eyebrows, then dismissed the name as but another soldier, and a private, nonetheless. To him, it wasn't worth worrying about.

'And what happened to this Private Krämer?'

'His leg was caught under the roof beams. He couldn't walk, so I helped him to get back here.'

'You walked him all the way back here?' asked General Koertig.

I nodded.

'That's some accomplishment, especially for someone as small as you.'

'I don't care about his heroic antics, I want to know about the tanks that are on their way here, right now! We cannot waste time.' Lieutenant General Jung became agitated. The commander shot him a menacing glare, then looked at me.

'Private Adler, let's hurry this along. How many tanks?'

'There was one in the beginning, but I think another two were behind. I'm not completely sure. But I'm worried for the other soldiers. They may walk into a trap.'

'We must assume the worst,' said General Koertig. 'We must pull our soldiers back.'

'We're not going to pull them back,' said the commander. 'We are so close to Moscow and I'm not going to back away from it now. The Führer would be furious.'

'*You* are not the one in the battlefield, and *you* do not have full authority. We have the charge of making sure our soldiers are out of danger.'

'War is danger, General Koertig. And you do not question me in front of a soldier.'

The tension in the tent immediately rose, and everyone averted their eyes from General Koertig and the commander.

'If you cannot do what you are charged with doing properly, then I would not just question it, I would challenge it. We will pull our soldiers back. If we go with what you want, we would have no soldiers to bring back.'

'And where will we go, then? Where are we supposed to go, with our dwindling supplies?'

'Stalingrad.'

CHAPTER 23

November 28, 1941

We had moved forward only a few miles east, now fourteen miles from the city. The tanks that attacked the farmhouse were taken by surprise and defeated within the night. Luckily, it wasn't accompanied by any Russian army, and just three rogue tanks that had moved westward on their own. But they took the lives of sixty-seven of our men before they were defeated.

We were given the order to pull back, with our supplies deteriorating, and even more so, our morale. The soldiers were becoming hungry and tired, exhausted from walking miles without rest. Russian soldiers, most of whom had run ahead of the main army, hid in the forest and lurked in the shadows, and when the time came, they killed our men without warning. They were gunned down almost immediately, but not before they took the lives of seven soldiers.

Earnst, Felix and Heinrich were not spotted by any other group, and I was beginning to think the worst. Their absence meant the great pit of unknowingness grew larger, and it became another worry that sat on my shoulders, weighing me down each day as I trudged along.

At no point did I regret what I had done, however. Although

Waldron was, to me, the greatest idiot that ever walked this earth, and possibly of all to come, and a brutal one at that, saving a life means more than taking one. It takes more to save a life than to take it, and life is so much more beautiful than death. He should not have succumbed to that fate because of the selfish act of another.

I had spoken to him only the night before. He was dismissed within two hours of entering the medical tent, most of which became overrun with soldiers whose blood secreted more on their external body than internally. Battered and bruised, injured, and disorientated, soldiers piled into the medical tents seeking help. Most, if not all, were attended to, though the timing was slower than usual. Once you were fixed up, you were allowed to rest for an hour before being sent back out to the battlefield.

Waldron apologised for his behaviour, though I think it was more out of obligatory circumstances that he and I just happened to bump into each other. He was awkward, terribly awkward. He acted like an embarrassed child trying to find the right words, mumbling and stuttering. His feet twitched and moved in the snow, and he kept touching his ear, pulling at it and twisting it. After the arduous apology, I nodded and smiled at him, and then walked away. I wasn't going tell him that I'm fine. I wasn't fine. In fact, my cheek had swollen just hours after the violent ordeal and was far too tender to even touch.

Tanks could be seen on the horizon as we retreated, following us and hoping something could slow us down enough to destroy us all.

'Keep moving!' yelled one of the commanding officers in the field. 'Don't slow down! If they catch you, they kill you! We are pulling out!'

A few of the younger soldiers giggled quietly or managed a smirk at the sentiment, making sexual jokes about the remark. They were quickly silenced when the commanding officer walked up to one, held him by the back of his neck and threw him to the ground. He crouched beside the soldier, held the strands of his hair and spoke directly in his ear.

'This is not a game, and it is not a joke! I don't find it funny, and it won't be funny if those Russians catch up to us, so keep your mouth shut and your legs moving!'

The soldier nodded fearfully and shot up, walking off briskly with his other giggling friends. I walked alone, hoping no one would approach me or say anything. The bruising on my cheeks was still evidently clear, with shades of purple covering my face and under my eyes. I wanted to be alone, where only I could be inside my head.

I looked ahead and saw a large hill that we were to climb. *Fantastic*, I thought. I became weary at the thought of having to walk up it but looked back to see mobilising Russian tanks in the distance, and quickly moved forward.

I thought of Mother and Edith, hoping they would still be alive. I began to think about life and death, and what happens when you die. Growing up, I was always taught we were God's children, and that he designed us just as we should be. But as I grew older, those stories became just that – stories. I was told that when we die, we go to a new place that is better than this one, and that's the only thing that I could cling on to, purely out of fear. It was fear that kept me curious, rather than believing, and it was fear that made me tighten my grip on the hope that there was such a place. But fear can grip the minds of the vulnerable, and that belief slowly dwindled over time.

After Father's death, I immediately encouraged the belief that he was somewhere better; somewhere more beautiful. I had wondered whether he looked down on me everywhere I went, or whether it was just some petty desire that I wanted to be true. I had never liked this world. Sometimes it could surprise you, with a picturesque view, or even the people you meet. But the underlying feeling was that it was just a poison, and that poison was always infecting us until we finally died. We ceased to be.

Mother would tell me that God loved us all; that he knew each of us. But I always doubted that from the beginning. If he knew me, he would know how much I suffered. Each day was a struggle to survive, with each day being one step closer to death. Beaten and bullied, that's what I wished for every day – death.

When Oskar died, I felt that I could no longer be here. He was, at the time, my only source of comfort and sanity, where I had none. At one time, I had truly thought he was my saviour, though that belief quickly shunned itself and I saw him more as a guide. But as he opened up to me, and I to him, I realised we both guided each other. No one ever guides another, without the other studying what their counterpart does. To guide someone, you have to know them, and when you teach them your ways, you're guiding them into your life.

Death is instant, and it can happen so suddenly. Sometimes it's longer and sometimes it isn't, but the one universal thing about death is no one desires to encounter it; but we have a fetish to condemn others to it. Life is beautiful, and it took me a long time to figure that out. I used to think that life was just as poisonous. I enjoyed life, but not the world. I enjoyed life, but not the people. There are beautiful people, but they are too quiet. The people that are known are the ones that seek adoration from everyone, and will do anything to get it. But those who are quiet, they are usually the ones that fight the hardest battles.

If I ever meet Death, whether he or she, I would shake its hand and concede defeat. Because as I have grown stronger, the only thing that can take me is Death, and Death is everywhere.

We were back where command was, miles from the battlefield, safe in their tents and guarded by a number of our tanks. They were comfortable, not having to worry about the incumbent attack on their troops while they rested enough for most of us. The common argument was they had fought enough of their battles in the past not to have to lower themselves to a common soldier, and that's what angered most of the soldiers. While they sipped their secret stashes of whiskey and wine, in the company of a warm fire, we endured the cold blizzards that would see many to their deaths. Frostbite was becoming more and more common, and the onset of only more blizzards meant more soldiers would suffer from it. My feet were frozen, and the more I walked, hoping to keep the blood flowing in them enough until we had officially pulled back, the more pain it caused.

The previous night, a soldier who was in his mid-thirties pulled off his boots. We urged him not to, but he said the pain was too great to have to go through any longer. As he pulled his socks off and over-foot garments, layers and layers, it revealed feet blacker than anything I had ever seen. His toes had rotted, and the sight made most of us sick to the stomach, with a few even vomiting. He gasped as he touched them.

'I can't feel them,' he said anxiously. 'I can't fucking feel them! What the hell is this?'

He became hysterical and began to shake his foot, hoping for the feeling to return. But it didn't. And the more he shook, the more frightened he became, until he shook it so much that his large toe snapped off. He screamed, not out of pain, but of shock. I sat there quietly along with the others, as we stared in amazement at what we had just witnessed. None of us were entirely sure what to say, or how to comfort him. Leaning over and saying, 'It will be fine. It's only a toe,' didn't seem to register as the greatest advice to give. So instead, we sat in silence and watched this terrified man scream and cry as he tried desperately to regain the feeling in his feet.

Once we arrived back, we were ordered to collect anything we may have left behind and told that the long march ahead was going to be arduous.

'The Russians will kill us all if given the chance! We must move hastily,' bellowed our commanding officer.

I ran around, looking to see if Earnst, Felix and Heinrich had returned. I asked some of the soldiers that I knew, and who knew them, but none had seen them. After a time of frantically wondering if they were safe, one soldier nodded at my question.

'You *have?* Where?' I asked excitedly.

'They were found by some of the soldiers that were in front of the rest, scouting out the Russians' movements,' the soldier replied. 'I think they may have been admitted to the medical unit.'

'Are you sure? I have to find them. It's important.'

'I'm dead sure of it. Go to the medical tent south, I think that's the one they were taken to.'

I nodded and thanked him, as a bounce in my step returned, the little glimmer of hope that they were well and alive. I walked to the medical tent that was south and stepped in, only to be stopped by a nurse who looked at me and raised an eyebrow.

'You don't seem to be in any need of medical assistance,' she stated. 'Why are you here?'

'There were three soldiers who were admitted here, I think.

Earnst, Felix and Heinrich. Are they here?' My eyes darted around the tent.

She looked at me and squinted in thought, then nodded.

'They're over there, at the far end. Make it quick, soldier.'

'Of course,' I replied, nodding in compliance.

I approached the end of the tent where the three of them were, laying on their beds. Their heads turned, and they shot up immediately once they saw me.

'Hans!' said Earnst. 'You're all right!'

'Me? I thought you were gone,' I said. 'Are you all well?'

'We're fine,' said Felix with a smile. 'Did... Waldron make it?' He strained himself to ask, as they all looked at me curiously, with a hint of fear.

I nodded.

'He's fine. He went off with some others, but he'll be glad to know you're all fine.'

I smiled at them all, pleased that they were alive.

'Where did you all go?'

Earnst chuckled.

'We went east for a while, until we realised, we were lost. All the landscape looks the same with so much snow. And then we came across a river that ran north to south, so we followed it north for a small time. We ended up spotting the Russian tanks rolling out westward, and so we figured they were headed to our soldiers. We followed them, keeping low and moving through the trees and bits of forest before we were finally picked up by some of our own.' He paused for a moment. 'What I want to know is how the hell you got out alive with Waldron?'

'It wasn't difficult. He helped most of the way, so it wasn't a struggle.'

'Don't be modest, Hans,' said Earnst. 'How did you really do it?'

'We helped each other most of the way.'

'You mean, *you* helped him? Not that he would have helped you.'

'Well, we both had each other's arms interlocked, and I helped him walk back.'

'Jesus, Hans, for someone your size I'm surprised you did that.'

'You're not the first person to say that to me. But I did what I had to.' I took a deep breath and nodded. 'It's what I had to do.'

'Is he angry with us?' asked Felix quietly.

I shook my head.

'No, Felix. Don't worry yourself about it.'

'But we left him there.'

'Honestly, he hasn't mentioned anything about it, so don't worry yourself.'

'If he hasn't mentioned anything about it, then he's most likely upset about it,' said Heinrich. 'I know I would be too, but I would also know that we had no choice.'

I rubbed my eyes with my thumb and index finger, sighing.

'I've got to go. I need to help get ready, and the nurse said not to be in here for too long. How long until you're dismissed?'

'An hour I think,' replied Earnst. 'I'll catch up to you later, then. We can talk.'

'Deal,' I said.

We smiled at each other, and then I turned to Felix and Heinrich. Felix managed a large smile, like a small child, while Heinrich only had enough in him to show a half grin.

I turned and walked out of the tent, thanking the nurse as I walked past her.

'We march south!' yelled one officer to the soldiers surrounding him. 'We cannot go west to the Fatherland yet, men. We still have a job to do, and once it is done, then we can go back. Be prepared to push through the limits like you have never done before!'

Some soldiers cheered while others sighed in contempt, secretly hoping that we would retreat from this land and go back home.

Once we had left no trace of what was once the command centre for this battlefield, with no tents standing, nor any tanks at our defence, we left for the south. None of the soldiers at this point knew where we were headed, but I knew. We were going to Stalingrad, and I knew that I may die there. We hadn't even begun to experience the brutality of this war.

I was ready for it. I was ready for Death, but Death may not have been so ready when it met me.

CHAPTER 24

February 14, 1942

I looked in the reflection of the water and ran my fingers over my chin – I had grown a small beard. No shaving for months had resulted in small hairs sprouting and attempting to grow on my face, though they didn't do so well as many of the other soldiers. Some had grown beards so large, they resembled Neanderthals. Others looked like the Greek scholars of the ancient past. But I still looked like a frightened teenage boy.

We were bitter about Moscow – fifteen miles from the city, almost at what we had set out to do, the heart of the enemy, and we were defeated too early. We had fought off the Russian soldiers' counter offensive for months, though I could hardly bring myself to call it that; we ran more than we fought.

I can't speak for all soldiers, I know, for I was the first to dodge any incoming assault and hide elsewhere until it receded for what remained a day or so. The Russian army was mobilising their tanks and their soldiers, with determination in their eyes and a fire that burned within. My candle had almost gone out, but theirs had grown to a furnace ablaze. Not one Russian soldier would be prepared to let us go, and not one of us was prepared to leave. Though some wanted to, and I was surely at the top of that list. We were not going to leave, especially when our brothers in arms needed us the most.

We were headed south, toward Stalingrad, when we were cut off by Russian soldiers and tanks. Every soldier that was on foot dropped into the grass, and our artillery began to fire.

'Enemy to the south!' screamed an officer, who jumped out of the armoured vehicle and began bellowing orders to each soldier.

'Get into position! Do not let them flank us! Do you hear me? Do not let them flank us under any circumstances!'

As we crawled, our armoured trucks began to turn around while the soldiers led the way as the first line of aggression. The armoured trucks that held the resources – food, ammunition, and medical supplies – were sent to stay miles behind the fighting so nothing was lost. At a time of desperation, those trucks and the soldiers that drove them were treated like royalty, knowing they oversaw everything that kept us alive and pushing forward.

I was grabbed on the shoulder by a soldier who didn't look me in the eye, but had his sights set straight ahead.

'You're coming with us,' he said. 'We need a few more soldiers.'

'What?' I asked, confused. 'Where are we going?'

'South-west. We're going to cut them off on the west side, so they won't flank us.'

He continued crawling through the grass and I followed.

'If all goes to plan, we can attack from behind.'

'But we don't have the numbers for that.'

'That's why you're coming. There's twenty of us. That's all we need. If we take too many, we would be easily spotted and shot down.'

'Where are the others?'

'Up ahead. Just keep following.'

'Why did you choose me?'

'Don't think that highly of yourself. I chose you because you were there. Congratulations. You were in the right place at the right time... or wrong time, depending on how you would look at it. But either way, you were chosen only because you were there, so you better prove yourself.'

'You have high expectations,' I said with a hint of disdain.

'You wouldn't believe what I've seen, what I went through in the Great War. So, when I say that you'd better prove yourself, don't take it lightly.' His eyes locked onto mine, burying deep into my mind as though he began to relieve his pain. He ran his fingers through his greying hair, showing hints of what was once an array of auburn locks.

I remained quiet, rather stunned, and annoyed at his bluntness, but also, dare I admit, thankful that he stopped it from getting to my head.

We had moved half a mile before we met up with the rest of the soldiers we were to accompany. A contour that rose just over a foot off the ground shielded us from any enemy view, as we crouched in the snow. The soldier, whose name I still hadn't learnt, began to draw in the snow with his finger.

'We're here,' he said to the group, who were all crowded around him, including me. 'We collected as many soldiers as we could without raising an alarm. Only one officer knows what we are doing – me. The rest are oblivious. If they knew, they wouldn't let us do this. It's dangerous, and it could cost lives, but if we do it right and exactly to the plan, we may just help to take the Russians by surprise and win this battle. It involves a certain amount of espionage if we make it behind their artillery and soldiers' front line.

'We go south-west, where we will be met with considerable force, no doubt. If we make it through, which we're obviously hoping to do, it will mean their attempts to flank us from the west will be stopped. And that's when the espionage starts. We have a number of explosives that we snuck out of the artillery truck. We didn't manage to get as many as we would have ideally liked, but they will be enough if we don't waste any of them.' He continued to move his finger in the snow, making lines and markings of our targets and path. 'But I'll hold out on sorting the voluntary soldiers who wish to plant the explosives and wreak havoc until we make it further south. Time is of the essence, men, and we need to move now.

'And for those who are yet unacquainted with me, for whatever reason as to be dragged off suddenly...' He looked toward me, and my eyes widened as I didn't know where to look. 'My name is Colonel Eldrich Böhler.'

My heart skipped a beat for a moment as I heard the name –

Colonel Eldrich Böhler. I had heard of him, and his stories seemed unreal when I first heard them, but they had been confirmed by so many others. In the Great War, he escaped the capture of British soldiers, ten of them. He had convinced one of them to get close enough so he could grab their gun and shoot him straight through the head. For days, he had rubbed the rope that tied his hands on a piece of splintered wood. He took the rest of the men by surprise, shooting them all one by one, or using the bayonet to pierce their necks. He was on foot for weeks with little food and water, running from the lands of France back to Germany. His uniform had been confiscated, and so he travelled for hundreds of miles with nothing but briefs and a ripped shirt.

Being a sceptic, I had always raised an eyebrow at this, thinking he couldn't have possibly walked for so long with such little clothing and rations. But he had stopped in a small village only a few miles from where he was held captive and found some clothes and food. Other rumours also stated he killed a French soldier on the road and dragged him into the forest, where he ate the body because of lack of any nutrients. Whether I believe that, I'm not sure, but I sure as hell wouldn't want to find out.

When he stood, I realised just how tall he was. He stood six feet and five inches, and he was well built for a man in his fifties, though he didn't look it. The only thing that gave it away was the small number of grey hairs that had sprouted at the side of his head, and the few wrinkles beginning to develop around his eyes. He had a look of menace and determination rolled into one, and I thought for a moment that maybe he *was* capable of eating another man.

We began to move south-west. We ran for the small bits of land that allowed us to, with our backs hunched over enough to hide behind the mounds of snow and contours that seemed to easily flow in the direction we were headed. But they would end and start in a different area, so we were forced to crawl to the next mound and the process would start over again.

I could have sworn we had travelled over two miles south-west, though I knew it was an exaggeration. Our tactics were simple, and each soldier knew what to do from our intense training of open field warfare. Four men would run ahead and crouch low, scouting the area for any sign of Russian soldiers. If the area was clear, another four men would run to where the first four were situated. They would then go only a few yards ahead to a different location with a different view of things. If it was clear, the rest would follow. Another four would then start the process again. Each group went first, rotating the perspectives so that not one group was left to make a mistake.

'Fresh eyes for each run,' Colonel Böhler would say.

When it was my turn, I followed the other three men. I knew relatively what to do, but in order to make it look like I knew what I was doing, rather than mistaking one location for another, I stuck to the back so I could follow. We ran to a small ditch, where we slid down and cocked our guns. Each of us looked down our sights in each direction, scanning the pristine white landscape for anything. Nothing – north, south, east and west. We gave the signal for the second group to move to their location. They scanned for any life – nothing, again. The signal for the rest of the group to move was given.

The sheer length of time it took for these tactics, made it stretch out our movement when we finally came across the enemy. The group that was sent in first spotted Russian soldiers pacing back and forth in a trench dug behind a long stretch of mounded dirt and snow. They waved down the rest of us to stay put, until Colonel Böhler ran toward them.

They crouched low and spoke for a few minutes, with the colonel's hands moving about to motion what was going to happen. Once they had finished, Colonel Böhler ran back to the rest of us and huddled in.

'There were more than we expected. But there is a way to take out a large number of them. There are two supply trucks behind the mound, though the tops can be seen from where our men are positioned just up ahead. The supply trucks have fuel barrels in each of them. I need two skilled snipers to take them out.'

He looked around. Every soldier avoided eye contact and looked to the ground.

'*Any* snipers?'

Two soldiers anxiously raised their hands slowly.

'Then you two are the ones that will do it.'

'But what if they see us?' asked one of the assigned snipers.

'That's what I'm getting to. The rest of us need to attract their gunfire westward. If we can lure them west, it gives the two snipers enough coverage to take out the supply trucks.'

He turned to the two snipers.

'You need to make sure you hit them right.'

'Hit them, *right?*'

'The tyres. Once the trucks are immobile, it gives us a chance to set the explosives to them. All you have to do is fire a shot into each tyre, and one into each of the fuel barrels. Do you understand?'

The two soldiers looked worried but nodded in agreement.

'On three, we run to the mound up ahead. One… two… three!'

Every soldier sprinted for the mound up ahead that would provide the cover. Our legs sank into the deep snow and each step was more of a struggle than the last. Our guns were held to our chest as we pushed harder with each stride. I looked up and focused on my destination, when bullets rained down on us. The sound as they struck past stung my ears. Soldiers dropped to the ground and the once white snow had soaked to a rich red, as blood flowed from their wounds.

'Keep going!' yelled Colonel Böhler. 'Do not yield to the enemy!'

A large ringing sound came to my ears as the bullets pelted the other soldiers around me. My vision had blurred. *Don't die, Hans, don't die. I'm not ready to die just yet.* I continued running until I felt the safety of the snowy mound on my hands. Launching myself at it, I landed with a thud and readied my gun. Colonel Böhler was only a few feet away. More soldiers than I had thought made it, but when I looked back, there were still too many bodies that lay lifeless in the snow.

'Get ready to drag them west, men. Let's give our snipers enough cover and destroy those supply trucks.'

The Russian soldiers had quickly dug trenches that lined east to west, and they faced north as they directed their fire at us.

'Fuck!' yelled a soldier who was beside me. He collapsed in a heap on the ground and held his arm tightly. I crouched down beside him.

'It's my arm,' he said. 'I'm shot in the arm. It burns!'

'I need something to tie around it and put pressure on it,' I exclaimed.

The soldier's hands shook as he fiddled around his pockets, looking desperately for anything. Finally, he pulled free a long cloth. He stood up, grunting with his eyes closed tightly shut.

'No!' I screamed. 'Get down!'

But before I could pull him back to the ground, behind the safe cover of the raised earth, a bullet soared through the air and splintered into his skull. Instantly, he dropped dead at my feet. I looked at his body, his eyes still wide open. His blood seeped from the bullet hole in the side of his head. *Fuck*, I thought. *I can't deal with this for much longer.*

Our men had pushed the Russians westward in their trenches, enough to allow the snipers to fire at the supply trucks. They took more than what was expected by the colonel, but we all knew deep down the colonel didn't expect them to succeed at all. This was a suicide mission at best, and we weren't supposed to know until it was too late. But most of us knew before we set foot into our mission, secretly hoping for it to be the last resort as a way out of this war.

Once the supply trucks had been successfully immobilised, the snipers, along with six other men, attempted to plant an explosive on one truck, hoping it would cause a large enough explosion to the next. They were right, and the explosion could be seen from miles away. The sound was almost deafening, as the large bang reverberated through our bones. Black smoke plumes rose into the sky as we looked back and witnessed it stretching to the sky.

The remaining Russian soldiers in the trenches, being pushed westward, retreated south. The colonel called us in. Small fires had been lit in the wood that held the trenches up, set alight by our soldiers.

'Those soldiers aren't going south,' he said bluntly. 'They're going to go south and then move north-east to the main trench line. If they get there, we're going to be caught out.'

'I think we've already been caught out with the explosion that went more than twenty feet in the air,' said one soldier, who was in his mid-twenties, breathing heavily.

The colonel sighed.

'That may be the case, but I never said anyone would get out alive.'

The brutal truth seemed to take everyone by surprise, even though we knew it to be true. To hear it from the leader's mouth was a definite stab in the heart.

'We have to take them out from the south. If we can take them by surprise, then we may just win this battle. Our men are counting on us.'

'Our men don't even know we set out to do this,' replied the soldier. 'Our men think we've either died, or we were cowards and run off.'

'They don't think we're cowards. No soldier I know thinks of another as a coward. We're all in this together; all of us. From here, to over there.' The colonel signalled with his hand to where our army fought, north-east of our position. 'And if you think there is anyone here who is a coward, speak up now. Because I will prove you wrong.'

My stomach heaved as I thought that someone would point me out. Surprisingly, no one did. We cut across the trenches to try and intercept those soldiers that had retreated south. Heading south-east, we continued until we were almost where the main Russian army was positioned.

Sneaking past the officers, I thought we were surely going to get caught. My heart raced as I watched the officers pace back and forth, while we crawled through the snow at the base of the small hill. The ridge was only three feet high, but it was enough to give complete cover to our movements. We reached the narrow temporary road that led into the camp.

Colonel Böhler held his hand up, then signalled for the first four men to run across to the opposite side. The next four went, so there were eight on each side of the road. At the command of Colonel Böhler, we crawled up to the road and stood up, with our knees bent and our backs hunched over. We ran into the camp and stopped behind one of the trucks. The other eight men followed and positioned themselves behind another truck.

In total, ten supply trucks were parked, and there were officers that would occasionally pace back and forth to guard them, though none were present. Their weakness was their misunderstanding that any soldiers would come from the south and therefore believed it to be safe enough to only pay attention there occasionally.

Colonel Böhler gave the orders to plant the explosives, and once they were in place, we had thirty seconds to make a run for it. Each truck had one explosive planted in it, and then a further five explosives were placed beside the tents closest south, ready for chaos to erupt. Every soldier ran for dear life, knowing that if we weren't far enough away when the explosives finally went off, we were to be incinerated with the rest of the trucks.

My heart raced as I sprinted away from the area. I wasn't worried about getting spotted, but rather I was worried the explosion would knock me from my feet, and then we would be discovered.

The explosion sounded. The reaction was enormous, as though one thousand bombs went off at once. Wind struck past us as it pushed us slightly forward, but not enough to knock us down completely. We all simultaneously looked back, as smaller explosions still went off, catching fuel or other highly flammable substances. The fire spread wildly as the tents disintegrated within seconds. Soldiers flocked from the northern trenches to see what had occurred, struck with embarrassment and confusion as their befuddlement led them to stand there motionlessly. Debris flung from the air and landed in the snow only feet away from us.

The Russian soldiers finally spotted our large bodies, cloaked in grey, running through the pristine white snow, and their bullets began to spray us. Only feet behind Colonel Böhler, a bullet scraped past my leg and sent me sprawling to the ground. It had broken the skin, the upper thigh of my right leg burning with pain as I held onto it tightly with my hands, wailing as I did so.

'Come on, soldier!' yelled Colonel Böhler.

He grabbed me by my left arm and heaved me to my feet, then pulled me along with his steps.

'You've made it this far, boy. You're not going to go down now. Where were you hit?'

'My right leg,' I replied. 'Upper thigh.'

'Into the thick flesh,' he said. 'The nurses will have a field day.'

'That's if we get back and see a nurse. It cut through the skin.'

He turned to me with a determined look while we kept moving.

'We're getting there, boy. Like I said, we've come too far to fall behind. It will heal quick enough. Keep moving, I've got you.'

We had run miles north to where our soldiers were when we had left, to find they had used the opportunity of the explosion to launch a full-scale assault on the Russian defence line. German soldiers flooded the trenches that ran from east to west and pushed forward through the thick defences and snow.

Blood had transformed most of the snow into a red landscape as bodies were scattered en masse. The Russian forces had pulled back as much as they could but found themselves losing ground as their supplies dwindled and their soldiers were unable to comprehend what to do.

This was going to be a long battle, and we had the upper hand. I just hoped we could keep it, long enough to see Stalingrad. The sooner it was over, the sooner I could see an end to this hell.

We held our defensive position, knowing our supplies were low, and the only way forward was to hold the ground we already had. If we held this ground, we were to be reinforced and reimbursed with supplies and soldiers, and our march to the city in the south would begin again. We couldn't let them win. Like the colonel said, we came this far, and we didn't intend to be pushed back any further.

But lurking in the back of my mind was the knowledge of how much death surrounded each one of us, and the lust for more. More death meant more victory; but for me, it meant more guilt that I would face for the rest of my life.

Concentration Camp

Strange how the word of one man can change in the mind of another. How the information given can be twisted and ultimately used to destroy the previous sole holder. In these walls, I am privy to such entertainment. The officers often pass on information about the overall war, although the only war I am concerned about is that of my complete and utter care. I accept only the utmost diligence when it comes to my care, and often I find myself singing to the music, that is, conversations privy only to those who speak it.

The officers are planning a mass execution and are secretly testing the labourers in order to know which ones will be made… redundant. Their work ethic will either determine whether they stay to do yet more work, or whether they are to face the firing squad. But they are all bound to meet Death eventually, are they not? Most beg for it to come soon, crying for it all to end.

Too many firing squads have smoke rising from their guns of late. The sound of a bang, and within an instant, Death is standing at my gates once more, waiting. The labourers wait inside, sitting on the edges of their beds as they wait for the noise, and once it sounds, their heads hang low. They hope that a miracle will happen, like always, but none ever does.

But to these officers, it is a game. You see, the privy information I speak of is that of placing bets. One officer will place a bet that a certain labourer will face the firing squad, and another officer will bet on a different one. On certain times, if the stakes are high enough, more officers may bet on the same labourer, although the winnings are then less. It is a game of chance and is determined by the superior officer – the overseer – who is not privy to this gambling of lives.

The labourers continue to work under the threat of death, for they know if they do not follow orders, their deaths become slow, painful. Their screams can be heard, echoing through my halls; others cringing at the sound, and possessing the knowledge that they face the same fate if they cross the line – the line of defiance. They gamble with their lives each day without knowing – some days working hard, while others seem arduous and tough, and so their work begins to decrease, leading to their demise.

The gambling of these lives is but a game to the officers. They will bet on one life to lose, but in the end, every life loses. It is a shame they never bet on their own.

CHAPTER 25

May 16, 1942

I often find myself wondering what I am perceived like in the eyes of another; namely, my fellow soldiers. In just the past year, I have grown from a boy who was afraid to pull the trigger, to a man fighting for his life. That's what I tell myself, anyway.

While my morals have never swayed, I've always known deep down it's hard to take the life of another human being. The frightening thing is that each time it feels more natural than the last. As though murder is natural. Death is natural, and inevitable – though no person likes to think it is, especially those I find myself fighting with, or against, for that matter.

The gun I hold is still the same gun that I held when I braved the winter almost a year ago, and yet it feels to have grown on me. The curve of the trigger feels natural as my finger wraps around it, and the scope seems to have become a second sight. It's almost a growth, its weight constantly pulling me down as its grip tightens, suffocating me.

But there is no denying that I'm frightened. I'm not just frightened of what is to come – the impending battle we arduously journeyed south for – nor am I frightened of the prospect of death, though it can make me quiver at times. I'm frightened of who I may have become. I'm frightened that some time ago, I lost who I once was and have now simply blended into the rest far too easily, because I allowed it to.

I can kill without hesitation. I once thought that to be a good thing, and now all I want to feel is the same feeling I had before I became like this. But I know it will only get worse before it can get any better, with the looming prospect of a bloody battle up ahead. Stalingrad will not be inviting to us, and nor do I blame the Russians for it. But this is life and death, and I don't think I'm ready to die just yet.

Each time these thoughts swamped my mind, I couldn't help thinking of what Mother and Father would make of it all. They would be more disappointed than angry, and I feared that more than anything else. I could handle when they were angry – anger is something I could deal with. But the disappointment – it was a mixture of sadness and confusion, wondering who their son had become. It made me sick, knowing I disappointed the two people in my life who taught me that all lives are valuable; that there is good in everyone. Sometimes, you just have to dig a little deeper.

We were within fifty miles of the city, and it would take days before we would reach it. I overheard that the Luftwaffe were to fly over the city before we reached it, and bombard it enough for us, along with the Sixth Panzer Army, to sweep over the city. Officers would often talk at decibels above what they thought was quiet, and so the soldiers who were standing near them overheard most of what the invasion involved.

We were to approach the city from the south, and the Sixth Panzer Army was to approach it from the west. We would obliterate what was left and meet in the city. As we marched, Earnst and Felix caught up beside me. I hadn't seen them in days, and their faces were a reassuring sight before the dread that was to come.

'Are you new here, stranger?' Earnst asked with a grin.

'I haven't seen you in days,' I replied.

'Far too long to be without friends, I would imagine.'

'I did all right. It just might have been better. You never know.'

'Oh, come now, do you really expect me to believe that? You can't survive without us, it's just near impossible.'

'I think you're right. Though it has been quieter.'

'Not anymore, it won't be,' said Felix.

'Just think, within a few days, we will be in Stalingrad,' said Earnst.

'I can't believe it's so near,' I said. 'When we turned back from Moscow, it felt like an eternity would pass before we would get to Stalingrad. Now I can't help but think it's too soon.'

'Too soon? How can it be too soon? Look how far we've come, Hans. We're so close, and you're suggesting we stop and have a little rest before the Russians decide to come and wipe us out?'

'I'm not suggesting any of that,' I said. 'I'm just saying that in the last year, this whole war has changed me, and I don't know if I'm ready to go beyond the barrier, so to speak.'

'What barrier?'

'The barrier that keeps me from becoming something I never wanted to be in the first place.'

'I know you have a hard time with the whole killing situation, but–'

'It's not that I have a problem with it anymore, it's that it has become somewhat natural, and I'm scared what that might lead to.'

'Don't let it bother you, Hans. We defend ourselves, that's all. You have a few more days with Felix and me before we make it there, so we might as well spend it doing what we do best.'

'What's that?'

'Laughing like friends do, no matter the circumstances. The day will come when you look back and realise that you defended your life, and it was something you had to do. It may not be now, but one day it will come.'

I couldn't agree with them, so I simply sighed. The wind picked up as we marched south, and it reminded me of the harsh winter that we endured only last year. It was an icy cold wind. There was no snow, however, which meant we were able to tread easier than in the winter.

When it was dark, we camped with extra soldiers on guard in case of any imminent attacks against us. I was ordered to keep watch along the east. The soldiers were sprawled along the edge of our encampment, and we paced back and forth, watching in the distant black abyss for any light or life.

I watched but saw nothing for a long time. That was until a

small glimpse of light caught my attention. We had cut across farmlands, through the fields and destroying any plantation that may have been attempting to grow. Cautious of making something small and insignificant into a large mess of blazing guns and soldiers running into nothingness, I crouched low, out of sight of anyone, and looked to the east. The light flashed, but only dimly, and then died again. I squinted to see if I could make out anything in the darkness, but nothing could be seen.

As per the usual orders, any lights were to be out before nightfall. No fires were to be lit. The officers told the soldiers that it was not winter yet, and to let our bodies slowly get accustomed to the chill, before the deathly winter sets in. I knew I was out of sight as I crouched. My silhouette against the starry sky would vanish, and I would become invisible in the night.

I began to slowly move toward where the light had flashed, trying not to make any noise as my body rustled through the tall grass. My arms pulled the rest of my body, rather than flaying my legs about trying to push my body, and I soon became tired enough to warrant a small rest.

I turned onto my back and looked up at the stars. There was no light to dim their brightness, and I looked up in awe at the sight of such magnificence. Each time I looked up, the thought of Mother and Edith would jump into my head and block out any other thoughts. I wondered if they were well, if it was as bad as some had said. I was nervous for what they were going through, and tears began to caress my skin as they trickled down my cheek. *Shit*, I thought. *Keep it together.*

We were almost at Stalingrad. They said that this would be the determining battle of the war. If we captured this, the south of Russia would be ours – and then we would hit the heart. But I don't know if I want to go to the heart. The heart is something that keeps the rest of the body alive. If we destroy the heart, we destroy the entire body; it's an entire body that people live on. Who am I to be so cruel? Who have I become?

I've become someone who no longer cares about the prospect of death for others, and that in itself is something far more frightening than this war. I once thought that to kill someone was such a barbaric act, no matter the person. That belief evolved into one that you can kill a person if they are bad. That stemmed to the belief that you can kill a person if they are on the opposing side to you. I'm scared for what the next step will be.

Change is something I often wonder about. If I can change so drastically within such a short time, then how will others change? Will the world change in such a short time? And if it does, will it change for the better, or for the worse?

I can never believe that a person's life is worth less than mine, but the demon that makes it come true is the belief that death is an absolute for everyone else, apart from yourself. No one person is better than another, and yet, why am I then fighting this war? I like to think I'm tricking myself into thinking it's for my mother and sister, but I know that it isn't that. Mother would never tell me to take another person's life, even if that person is willing to take yours. She would always tell me every life is worth living, and if you live it right, then perhaps death isn't such a terrible prospect as people think it is. And those willing to kill – perhaps their life is worth living, so they can embrace the change we so strive for.

After a few minutes had passed, I turned onto my stomach and began to crawl again, this time using my legs. I was far enough from our encampment to make a small sound without alerting any attention, and the use of my legs proved far easier and faster.

As I got closer to where the light had flashed, I made out a small figure in the distance. I stopped and waited for a moment, before deciding that it was necessary to see where the light source was coming from… or from whom.

A young boy, no older than four, sat hunched over, sobbing quietly with a lantern beside him. I stood and placed my gun on the ground, slowly walking toward him. He looked up at me and froze. I placed my hands in the air, showing him I was no threat. He continued to stare at me, then looked down at the ground and sobbed.

Next to him was a body that lay face down in the ground, with a gunshot to the head. In the body's hand was a small pistol, and I immediately dropped to the ground. The young boy wept as he held his head in his crossed arms. I gently placed my hand on his back, and his head slowly crept out from the cover of his arms. He looked at me, his face dirtied with the earth from where his tears had fallen, and his eyes staring sorrowfully into mine. I wiped the dirt from his face and combed his golden locks of hair.

I had assumed he spoke no German, and so I remained quiet as he looked up at me.

'*Otets*,' the young boy said. '*On ushel.*' He rubbed his eyes and sniffled.

I looked at him quizzically.

Otets, I thought. *Father?* The boy sniffed and rubbed his eyes. It was his father. And by the sight of what had happened, his father had taken his own life. I pointed to my chest.

'Johan,' I said.

The boy tilted his head slightly, then raised an eyebrow.

'Johan?' he asked slowly.

I nodded. 'Johan.' I pointed to him and shrugged my shoulders. He pointed to his chest and replied, 'Nikolai.'

I smiled and nodded at him, and he returned the favour, with tears still fillings his eyes. With the language barrier an obtrusive difficulty that impeded on us speaking at all, apart from our names, we sat there for a few minutes in complete silence. I looked around, trying to avoid the sight of the corpse of Nikolai's father, and spotted a small mound of fur in the dirt. I looked at it and pointed. Nikolai turned and grabbed it, then smiled and passed it to me.

He had passed me a small bear. It was old and tatty, but I guessed it was well treasured by him. I examined it, flipping it over and looking at it for some time. As I went to give it back into Nikolai's hands, he stopped me and shook his head, then pointed to me. I pointed to my chest and tilted my head, and he nodded. He had just given me a gift.

I had nothing to give Nikolai, unless he wanted a gun, which would be out of the question. I stood up, signalled for Nikolai to stand up, and shrugged my shoulders.

'Home?' I asked.

He looked at me cautiously, having no understanding of what I was saying. I crouched back down and drew a house in the dirt, and his eyes brightened a bit. He nodded and grabbed my arm, then the lantern. Before he started walking, he looked at his father. As he stared, his breathing became heavier. I grabbed him and hugged him close, holding his head to my chest. Once we hugged for a few moments, he looked up at me, his eyes glazed with tears, and smiled, nuzzling his face back into my chest. He then began to walk me even further from our encampment.

We reached a small house among a few trees, and he pointed to it. He let go of my hand and ran to the door of the house and opened it. I ran after him, hoping there was no trap that lay waiting for him in the dark. He held up the lantern in the house, and waved his hand at me to come in. The floorboards creaked and groaned as I slowly walked around, hoping no one else was present. As I looked around, I saw pictures of Nikolai and his family in frames on the table which sat against the wall near the front door.

In all the photos, he sat smiling. In some, his family smiled. In others, they remained staunch. I didn't often see photos of families smiling; they were normally expressionless, their eyes seeming to be an empty void; an abyss of nothingness. But there was a photo of Nikolai with his mother and father. Nikolai sat on his mother's knee, and his father stood behind, his large hands resting on both of their shoulders. Their smiles showed a glint of hope — a picture of love for history. They will always know the power of it.

I took the heavy wooden frame down gently from the mantle and slid the photo out. I crouched down to Nikolai and folded the photo, putting it in his jacket pocket. For him, he should know the love of family that he once had, and that photo would always serve as a reminder to him.

There was no sign of his mother in the house, and I wondered what had become of her. He mentioned nothing of her, not even in his native Russian tongue, and so I decided to keep it without being mentioned.

There was a large fireplace, accompanied by two chairs and a radio on the mantle. A large dark oak dining table with six chairs was placed adjacent to the fireplace, with a large candlestick holder that hung from the ceiling. Nikolai grabbed my hand, and I looked down at him.

'Johan,' he said and pointed to a hallway.

I followed as he pulled my arm, and led me to a room, which

I figured was his in the light. A small bed was placed against the furthest corner, and beside it was a small bedside table with a candle on it. There was a chest directly under the window, which was opposite the door as we walked in, and a cupboard beside it.

Nikolai sat on his bed and tapped for me to sit on it. I sat beside him and looked around. He gently touched me on the shoulder and looked at me. Waiting for him to signal to something, he simply smiled at me, and rested his head on my arm. I wrapped my arm around him and held his head close, all the while wondering what I was going to do.

If I left him here, he would die from lack of survival skills, but I couldn't take him back to our camp either. I breathed heavily as I shut my eyes tight. A few tears streamed down my face as I contemplated the worst possible solution. Nikolai lifted his head from my arm and shook my leg. I looked down at him, his small blue eyes full of wonder and sorrow. He brought his hand up to my cheek and wiped the tear from it, and immediately I broke into tears again. I held him tight, weeping as I knew I didn't want to do this. I couldn't. But I didn't know what else to do. As I held him, his arms wrapped around me and he sobbed quietly. His warm tears dripped onto my shirt, as his small body heaved up and down with each breath.

Over the sound of Nikolai's sniffling, I heard distant voices from outside. I stood up and looked out of the window, to see lights flashing around and soldiers approaching the house. My heart raced. I knew I could show Nikolai mercy, but they wouldn't. I turned and grabbed Nikolai from the bed and moved him to the cupboard. I opened it and grabbed the coat that hung, and boots to replace his inefficiently thin shoes. I draped the thick fur coat over his small body and fitted the boots onto his feet. I ran to the kitchen where I dug around for any food that I could find. A few tins of food and odd vegetables were all that was available, and I put them in the pockets of his coat.

Racing through the house, I took Nikolai to the door that led out the back of the house. We made our way past the trees and crouched low in the darkness. I buttoned up his coat and crouched in front of him, our eyes level.

I pointed to his chest and flexed my muscles, to which he

smiled and flexed his. I nodded and began to draw in the sand. I drew the best drawing of a town as I could, which was not the greatest illustration, but it worked. Nikolai nodded and pointed east. I nodded anxiously and pointed to him, then eastward. He understood and nodded but dropped his head. I picked his chin up and hugged him, and he held me tight, his face nuzzled into my shoulder.

I grabbed the bear he gave me from my pocket and danced it up to his face, kissing his cheek with its nose. He smiled and tilted his head down, then grabbed the bear and placed it to my chest. I put one hand on it and the other where my heart was and nodded.

The sounds of the soldiers were getting closer, and I looked around, then to Nikolai and nudged him to go. He held my hand, tears beginning to form. *Be safe*, I thought. *Keep safe, Nikolai.* I smiled as we both wept, though he remained stronger than I, it seemed. As we released our grip, we gave each other one last smile, one I wished lasted a lifetime. Once moments past, I nudged him forward, and he ran through the trees and disappeared in the dark.

A light flashed into my eyes, and I covered them with my arms.

'Identify yourself!' the man spoke. He was a German soldier.

'Private Hans Adler,' I replied.

'What the hell are you doing out here?' the man asked.

'I…' I hesitated for a moment. 'I thought I had seen something and came to investigate.'

'You are hundreds of yards from the encampment, private. You are not supposed to leave the encampment under any circumstances.'

'I was on watch.'

'That is even worse! You cannot risk the lives of these soldiers simply because you claim to have seen something in the distance. You report it.'

'But what if it was a Russian offensive army?'

'Are you trying to be smart with me?'

'No, sir. What if what I saw was something like Russian soldiers?'

'Then you alert the other soldiers on guard, and your commanding officer! You are coming back to the encampment with me, and you will explain yourself to Sergeant Shödler.'

'No! Please, don't make me see him. I beg you. Please, anyone but him.'

The soldier smiled wryly, then replied, 'You know what he is capable of, then? Well you are going to have fun when we get back.'

He signalled the two other soldiers to grab me and escort me back to camp, where I was to face Sergeant Shödler.

As I was escorted away from the house, I looked back into the distance. I saw a small figure standing amongst the trees, and a small hand wave in the air. I knew it was Nikolai, and smiled, knowing he had a chance. And he had a chance because I gave it to him as soon as I knelt down next to him. Part of my old self was reasserting itself, and it felt more than good. I felt over the moon.

CHAPTER 26

May 16, 1942

'Well, well, well. If it isn't Private Hans Adler,' sneered Sergeant Shödler. 'And what 'heroic' deed were you doing this time? Carrying another wounded soldier across the fields to look at the stars? Perhaps the Russian tanks wanted to decimate *that* farmhouse too? So, what pathetic story have you to tell me, to convince me that you were out there for no other reason but your duty?' He inhaled a large puff of smoke from his cigarette and leaned in close, blowing it on my face. My eyes fluttered, and I waved the air around me.

'I was on guard,' I said to him after coughing mildly. 'And I thought I had seen something in the distance.'

'Something in the distance? Was it the Russian tanks? Is that what it was? And you felt compelled to save another officer?' Sergeant Shödler's voice dripped with disdain as he stared into my eyes, waiting for any answer, just so he could slap it back down again. I could tell he was enjoying this.

'There was a light in the distance,' I said exacerbated. 'And so, I went to see what it was, in case it *was* a group of Russian soldiers.'

'And was it what you expected it to be?'

'No,' I said. 'It wasn't.'

'Then what was it?'

'It was a lantern. It was near a dead body. The man had shot himself.'

'What a pity,' he said sarcastically. 'And what of your other friend?'

'Other friend, Sergeant?'

'You're a smart boy, Adler, and you don't play the stupidity card extremely well, especially under pressure. There were two people there. The soldiers that escorted you told me there were marks in the dirt next to the dead body.'

'They must have been made by the man, before he killed himself.'

'Tell me the truth, Adler!' Shödler screamed. 'Who else was there?'

'I was there,' I said calmly. 'Next to the dead body. No one else.'

Sergeant Shödler stood in front of where I sat and crouched down. 'I have ways of making people speak.'

He pulled a knife from his belt and waved it around in the air. He then leaned forward and reached for my jacket. I looked down, afraid of what he was going to do. He reached in my jacket and pulled out the bear that Nikolai had given me.

'And what is this? I can't imagine that it would be yours, Adler. Though, perhaps it is. You're just a child inside, waiting for your mother to tuck you in at night, her soft lips to kiss your forehead.'

I gritted my teeth and stared at Shödler menacingly, trying to control my anger. My breathing became deeper. Shödler smiled and looked at the bear, then ripped its head from its body.

'Whoops. It's a shame that had to happen. Now, tell me who else was with you.'

I remained silent and closed my eyes, hoping someone of higher authority would walk in.

'Pull down your pants,' demanded Shödler.

I looked at him wide-eyed. 'What?'

'You heard me. Pull down your pants.'

Hesitantly, I pulled down my pants and slid off my boots, standing in my briefs and a jacket.

'And your briefs,' he demanded.

'Why?'

'Because I told you so.'

'Why? What are you going to do?'

'You're going to start answering questions, or I'm going to cut it off slowly, until you tell me. So, take off your briefs. If you start talking, I won't have any reason to cut it off.'

I shook my head. 'No.'

'Take them off, Adler!'

He launched at me and tackled me to the ground. I fought back, kicking at his lower abdomen, but he managed to get a hold of my briefs and rip them off. He stood back in shock as I backed away and covered my privates.

'You are circumcised?' he asked.

I stared at him, not saying a word.

'I knew you were different, somehow. I knew you weren't who you made out to be! You filthy little Jew! What did you do? Did you watch as your mother and father were taken to the camps, only to run like a coward and join the very people who did this to you?' He cackled insanely and then stared at me. 'You're a fool. A complete and utter idiot!'

He moved closer to me; the knife still gripped firmly in his hand. I backed away, but each time I moved, he moved with me. I decided the only thing to do was to run. I pulled my briefs up quickly, stumbling as I did, and waited for the right time to dodge him. He snarled as he moved closer and launched himself at me. I moved to the side, dodging his attack. As he stumbled, I grabbed his arm and twisted it in the hope of forcing him to drop the knife. He dropped it, but turned with his other hand, fist closed, and knocked me in the cheek. I crashed to the ground. The adrenaline rushed through me, and I could see in the corner of my eye that he was coming at me. I lay on my back and kicked my leg upward with all my strength, thrusting my foot into his crotch. He dropped to the ground and screamed in pain. I stood up and grabbed my pants and boots, and headed for the exit, before going back for the bear. I curled it up in my pants and rushed outside.

I was stopped by Colonel Hirsch, who held his hand up and stopped me from rushing past as he pushed on my chest.

'What is going on here, soldier?'

I looked at Colonel Hirsch and then back at the tent. He saw where I looked and entered, where he discovered Sergeant Shödler moaning in pain on the ground.

'What the hell happened?'

Colonel Hirsch shot me an anxious look, then moved his gaze down to Sergeant Shödler. Sergeant Shödler heaved himself from the ground with great difficulty, his legs shaking, and his right hand still firmly grasped on the area I had kicked.

'This little shit is what happened!' screamed Sergeant Shödler. 'Sir, I discovered that he is–'

'He tried to attack me!' I interrupted, making sure Sergeant Shödler couldn't get a word in. 'I spotted a light not far off the campsite and went to investigate what it was, but it was merely the reflection of a piece of metal from the moon. And that's when Sergeant Shödler came.' Colonel Hirsch raised his eyebrow. 'He ordered two soldiers to escort me back to his tent, where he pulled my pants down and sat me on the chair.'

I dropped my head and fell silent, hoping the story would work.

'Is this true Sergeant Shödler?'

'He's lying! I brought him back for questioning, and you will never believe what I discovered. The boy is a Jew!'

'What?' I looked up to see Colonel Hirsch's eyes widen in shock. 'Is this true, Private Adler?'

'No, he's lying, sir!'

'The boy is circumcised. I saw it with my own eyes.'

'That doesn't mean I'm Jewish!' I snapped.

I nervously looked at Colonel Hirsch, who was now staring at the ground and entranced in deep thought. He finally looked up and set his sights on Sergeant Shödler.

'While we often associate the circumcision of a boy with his hereditary Jewish roots, the boy is right. It does not, at all, mean he is Jewish. You're making a very large accusation, Shödler, and if it turns out you're wrong, you will have sentenced an innocent man of our army to death.'

'It's only one soldier less,' replied Sergeant Shödler.

'And if you were to do it to every soldier who was circumcised in this army, we wouldn't have enough to fight the Russians with.

Now, I don't want to hear anything out of you, or I'll be forced to rip out your tongue, and leave you stranded, awaiting the cold winter alone. Do you understand?'

'Yes sir,' he said, standing to attention.

'And you,' Colonel Hirsch turned to me, 'keep your privates to yourself from now on. I don't want this sort of thing to happen again.'

I nodded. 'Yes, sir.'

'Good,' said the colonel loudly. He turned and exited the tent, leaving me facing Sergeant Shödler alone.

Sergeant Shödler walked up to me and put his face close to mine.

'I'm going to make sure you know the real meaning of pain, Adler. You might be able to fool Colonel Hirsch, but you can't fool me. I know what you are, you filthy little rat.'

'I may not be able to fool you, but you're right, I can fool Colonel Hirsch,' I began. 'And remember, he's ranked higher than you, so I wouldn't have a problem with it. Don't ever touch me, or he and the other officers will know of it.'

Sergeant Shödler's face boiled with anger as he stood upright.

'Get out,' he ordered.

'Yes, Sergeant,' I replied. I exited the tent and smirked as I walked out.

Sergeant Shödler and I avoided each other for a while after that, and the feeling of knowing that he no longer had any power through manipulation or force was one that, although I enjoyed, knew wouldn't last forever. I made the most of it, striding with a confident step and smiling to myself each day. We were at war, but it had only felt like I was ever at war with him, and it had ceased, just for now.

He knew I was Jewish, but somehow it felt liberating. He couldn't prove it, and I knew if anyone else found out, I would be dead. But I could lie to the other officers and manipulate Sergeant Shödler, and I intended to do just that.

CHAPTER 27

June 28, 1942

It seemed like a lifetime, but we had finally reached the gap between the parallel courses of the flowing Donets and Don rivers. This meant we were only weeks away from Stalingrad, and we all knew it. The soldiers had changed from the slumped-over, dull-eyed, dreary wrecks to boisterous, alert, ready men who stood tall and proud. They wanted to show off their power to the Russian civilians, and it was only a matter of time before they knew what would hit them.

I was cautious about how I acted, even in private. I never did feel comfortable lying about myself or how I usually acted, and so I tried desperately to fit into the cheers of the soldiers and the yells of triumph, even though we hadn't even reached the city. But it felt awkward. I threw my arms up with them, but there was no jump in my step and no resounding spirit in my voice. We were about to kill thousands of innocent people, and when we did, I knew I would never be able to forgive myself this time.

God forgive me for what will happen, and if there is no god, then may the innocent shed my blood as they do so theirs.

The sixth army had split from us, leading the attack on Stalingrad from the north as we headed south. We were to follow the Don River as it led us south, then bending south-east toward the city. Earnst walked beside me as we marched closely behind a tank.

'The boys are talking about you, again.' He spoke to me bluntly.

'That's nothing new. What are they saying this time?'

'They're saying that you got it on with Sergeant Shödler a few weeks ago, and Colonel Hirsch caught you in the act. I'm not saying I believe them, but why would they say something like that?'

'It's all stupid nonsense. And it was over a month ago. I thought it had left my thoughts entirely. They've been saying things like that since it happened.'

'But you haven't said anything about it.'

'Why should I? I don't have to prove anything to them.'

'Right. So, what happened then?'

I turned to Earnst and looked at him earnestly.

'Do you give your word you will say this to no one? Not one single person?'

'Hans, I know how to keep my mouth shut. Besides, you're one of my closest friends. I would never say anything that can get you into trouble.'

'If only you knew,' I mumbled under my breath.

'What?' asked Earnst, his ears pricking up as he leaned in closely.

'When I was on watch weeks ago, I saw a small light that illuminated in the field not far from our camp. So, naturally, I went to see what it was. And when I got closer, I saw a small boy crying over his father's dead body. It was the lantern he was holding, giving light to the darkness around him.'

'A Russian boy? What happened to him?'

'He took me back to his farmhouse, and we were only there for a few minutes before two soldiers came looking for me. He pointed to the direction of the nearest village, and I sent him there with as much food and clothing as he could carry.'

'That's it? Nothing else happened? Did they find him?'

I shook my head.

'No.' I smiled and looked down. 'He even gave me his teddy bear.'

Earnst put his hand on my shoulder. 'You're a good person, Hans.'

'I just don't know why they would begin to talk about it now. It was weeks ago.'

'Some boys overheard Sergeant Shödler and Colonel Hirsch talking about it. They only got wind of what was said, but your name was mentioned and how Colonel Hirsch found you coming out of his tent.'

I cocked my head back.

'Oh, that. That was when the two soldiers brought me back. Shödler threatened me with a knife, and I kicked him in crotch. He dropped to the ground like a sack of potatoes.'

Earnst threw his head back in laughter.

'We wondered why he was limping around the next day. Whenever we stared at him long enough, he would come over and slap us on the head and scream for us to get back to whatever it was we were doing.'

'He hasn't approached me since. And I think Colonel Hirsch has kept him under close watch, which is a good thing for me. One moment alone with him and I'd be cut up and served as the next lot of food for the soldiers.'

'We have your back. Not just me, but the others, too. You're well-liked by all of these soldiers. They may give you a mouthful sometimes, but it's just their way of expressing friendship.'

'It's a weird way to express anything.'

'I know, but we're all from different parts of life. Some of these soldiers are from the higher end of society, their parents well respected and they went to posh schools. And some are from the lower end of society, having to work since they were young and unable to go to school. And then there's the middle ones, like you and me.'

'The world is odd enough as it is without having to give labels to people for the sake of it.'

'You're a man of the world, aren't you? Sometimes I wish I had the same mind as you.'

'Trust me, if you did, you would go insane within the first day. Thinking too much can get you into trouble – it's probably why the stupid ones are always the most popular.'

Earnst laughed.

'There's nothing wrong with thinking, it's just what you choose to say, instead, that can get you into trouble.'

'That is… very true,' I chuckled.

Our conversation was cut off immediately as soldiers in front of us screamed, 'Russian tanks! Get to cover!'

Within seconds, enemy tank shells rained on us. We dropped immediately at the deafening sound as the shells collided with the solid metal of our own tanks.

'Formation!' yelled our commanding officer. 'Into formation!'

We crawled along the dry ground, the hot sun beating on our backs. The Russian summers were just as extreme as the winters, and it seemed there was no middle ground. Just as there was no middle ground in war – you choose one of the two extremes.

Earnst grabbed my right arm and pulled me forward.

'Stay with me,' he said, panting violently. 'Just keep next me.'

I nodded and crawled with him. We crawled until we were only a few feet from one of our own tanks, and jumped up, crouching behind the metal beast. Earnst peered around the side of it, and then turned to me.

'There looks to be more than twenty Russian tanks, and more soldiers. We follow our soldiers. We're going to have to weave behind our tanks. Just follow them.'

'They're going to attack them from behind.'

Earnst nodded. 'Like every other time. Let's go.'

We ran behind our line of tanks, and I turned to my left, watching the Russian soldiers run down the hill to the south, along with their tanks. We thought this would be easy enough, that the battle would cease within two days and the hill would be sprawled with the bodies of Russian soldiers. But our will to fight and our physicality were lower than we expected of ourselves, and it almost immediately began as a disaster, followed by more disrepute. The lack of sleep that each soldier suffered soon became evident as they fired their guns into nothing but dirt.

The Russian soldiers seemed to pour down the hill like a flowing river, following their tanks and diving for cover in the small contours at the base. Our tanks fired ferociously, their shells contacting with the opposing side and sounding large bangs.

As our tanks continued to bombard the hill, a number of our soldiers made their way for the top, moving westward, and then south. Earnst looked behind him every few hundred feet that he ran, to make sure I followed close behind.

'We are so close to the city, men,' yelled our officer. 'Do not let this small number of Russians deter us! We strike them from the back, and we do it quickly! Let's beat them at their own fucking game.'

We came to a line of trees that continued on as a large forest spreading further west. Our commanding officer held up a hand, and we came to a halt.

'We have sixty soldiers here, another two hundred and forty will follow behind, and a further six hundred will go eastward and attack from behind. The rest will provide assault from the north as we head south. Show these Russians no mercy. They are here to stop us from reaching Stalingrad, and by God, we will persist!'

The soldiers saluted.

'We will take them. Heil Hitler!'

'Heil Hitler,' replied the soldiers.

'We move, now!'

We began to move southward, the earth slowly inclining as it merged with the hill. The soldiers kept in the forest, moving between the trees so that at least, if we were to be seen and attacked, we would have enough cover to push forward.

'We're going to surround them soon enough,' said one soldier who shuffled next to me. 'Hopefully by nightfall.'

'You're optimistic,' I replied.

'Have you even been present in any other battle?' asked another soldier to him.

The soldier looked puzzled.

'Our soldiers will get to the top of the hill and surround them.'

'See that hill?' I asked, pointing south. 'That's miles away, at the least. It would take us at least a couple of hours to reach the top of it without Russian soldiers in the way. But if you hadn't noticed, there are Russian tanks and soldiers everywhere, and they will see us when we reach the very base of the hill, emerging from this forest. They're going to press us, and they will press us hard.'

I saw a smirk on Earnst's face.

'It will take us a day, perhaps two at most, to get to the top of that hill, and when we do, you'll be too tired to want to push any further. Trust me when I say, get your rest now and save your strength for when the time is truly needed.'

'Spoken like a true commander,' said Earnst.

The young soldier nodded.

'I was only sent to accompany the army two weeks ago. I don't know much of it, sorry.'

I shook my head.

'Don't be sorry. If I sounded too pessimistic or self-appointed, you may want to get used to it. It's been a long week… in fact, this war has been long. We're all dreary, and the trek uphill won't be any easier. So, where did they recruit you from?'

'Just north of Berlin. My father was killed in the Battle of France. He was a commanding officer. Shot in the stomach and died three days later.' He looked at his boots. 'My mother, I'm not sure what happened to her. She left two weeks after she learned of what happened to my father, and I haven't seen her since. She left no note, or anything to let me know of her whereabouts. I had nothing.'

'So, you joined the army?' I asked.

He nodded. 'Yes, shortly after.'

'You're very well spoken.'

'Thank you. My mother taught me literature when I was younger, and my father would always make sure I was well spoken. He wanted me to become an academic, like he was, and his father.'

'Why not in the army?'

'My father was once a professor. He taught advanced mathematics. When Hitler…' he turned around to make sure no one could hear his voice. 'When Hitler came to power, my father joined the army. He said he knew what was going to take place, and he wanted to be a part of history. He rose through the ranks and eventually became the commanding officer. He saw the things that happened, and even before he was in the army, he knew it all. He never wanted me to lose my life fighting for someone else's dream.'

'Sounds like an interesting reason. Then why did he join?'

'I don't know. I've never known, and I've always been curious as to why he did it. He was such a placid man, so gentle and quiet. He would sit in his study and keep to himself. I would peer through the door, and he would summon me in with a smile on his face, sit me on his knee and tell me a story. Nothing about war. It was all peaceful.

'Then when he joined the army, he started to become angrier. He would lash out toward me and my mother in anger, and unexpectedly throw something. But every time he would get angry, I could never stop thinking of him as the father he was before.'

'My father was everything to me, too.'

'What did he think of you joining the army?'

Shit. I paused for a moment as I swallowed hard, trying to fight away any hint of emotion.

'He died before I did. But somehow, even though he would say that he was proud of me, no matter what, I don't think he would be proud of me for this. He...'

I was cut off as gunfire erupted for the hill toward the forest. We scattered and dropped to the ground. I fumbled for my gun and looked back at the soldier.

'Stay with me,' I yelled.

He nodded and shuffled to my position. I aimed down and attempted to focus my vision on the hill but couldn't make out anything.

'Keep moving to position!' yelled our officer. 'They're in the hills! Aim for the hills and shoot, and hope it hits one of them!'

We continued to move through the forest, weaving in and out of the trees to avoid any gunshots. I looked east and saw two tanks turning to face us. Another soldier must have seen it, too, before screaming, 'Shit! Tanks to the east! Get to cover!'

Almost immediately after, the tanks opened fire and obliterated a group of trees that stood clumped together. Crashing to the ground and sounding a boom, louder than the tanks, twigs broke off and dust was swept to life.

'Keep moving south-west! Keep moving!' yelled the officer.

If he says, 'Keep moving,' one more time, I'll shoot myself, I thought.

I ran in a short spurt, and making sure the young soldier was behind me, took cover behind a large pine tree. I crouched low next to the trunk and aimed my gun. I fired random shots into the distance, hoping that if I did hit any soldier, it would only be in the limb.

And then, as if by a stroke of universal justice, a bullet pierced the lower part of my left leg. I screamed in pain as the bullet shredded my skin and shot through the other side. The shower of blood soaked my trousers red. I dropped my gun and held my leg, sitting awkwardly on the ground as the pain shot up. I began to feel slightly dizzy as the noises around me became merged as one, the voices faint. My vision became blurred. Each time my eyes moved over, it was slow and seemed to stretch out as a haze. My heart seemed to beat out of my chest, faster and faster as I became more panicked, until finally, everything became black.

CHAPTER 28

June 30, 1942

'Where the fuck am I?' I yelled, sitting up in the hard bed.

I looked around, realising I was in the medical tent. A nurse came over, this one old and unable to walk well. A few rogue strands of grey hair had loosened from her bun, and the dark rings under her eyes suggested little to no sleep.

'What is all this commotion?' she demanded.

'Sorry, I didn't realise where I was for a moment.'

'Well, keep your mouth shut and let the others rest,' she hissed. 'You suffered a large amount of blood loss. You were unconscious for over twenty-four hours. Lay down and rest, and no more of that incessant yelling.'

'Yes, ma'am,' I said quietly.

She nodded staunchly and walked away, and I lay down again. I looked to my right, witnessing a soldier sleeping with bloody bandages wrapped around his head, and his left leg levied up on a metal frame, also covered in bandages.

To my left was a soldier that had bandages wrapped around his stomach, a small red patch growing around his lower right abdomen. I looked to the tent roof and placed my hands on my stomach. I attempted to wriggle my left foot, but the pain was too much. I tried not to scream, but instead made muffled grunts and cries.

Violent coughing erupted from the soldier to my left, and I turned to see him clutching his stomach and gasping for air. The bloodstain had increased to cover his entire bandages and transferred to his hands as he clutched his stomach tightly. He attempted to yell for help, but his breath had gone, and he struggled to breathe the air around him. I yelled for help.

'Nurse! Someone help! Anyone!'

The old nurse burst in the tent and marched up to my bed. 'What did I say about keeping your mouth shut?'

'It's not me, it's him!' I pointed to the struggling soldier. 'He can't breathe!'

The nurse gasped and went to the soldier.

'I need help in here!'

Two nurses entered the tent and went over to the soldier's bed.

'He can't breathe,' said the older nurse. 'His wound has opened up again. We need to stop the bleeding. Get me a breathing apparatus.'

'Matron, there are none,' said one of the nurses. 'We're too low on supplies.'

'What the hell happened to the supplies that were delivered only last week?'

'They're all being used. There are too many wounded soldiers.'

'Well, we need to stop the bleeding, at least. Quickly, get me a sterilised needle and thread. We have to stop the bleeding and sew it up again.'

The two nurses looked solemnly at the matron, and then the first one shook her head. The matron sighed and rubbed her eyes, then leaned on the metal railing of the bed. The soldier was still coughing, but they didn't seem to care. The matron looked at the nurses and nodded.

'Take him. But do it quietly.'

The second nurse started to whimper, with small specks of tears forming in the corners of her eyes. She began to shake her head and held her hands to her mouth. The matron stepped forward and grabbed her by the shoulders.

'You are to do this, now. No excuses. Stop wasting time with your tears. Go.'

'Wait,' I interjected. 'Where are they taking him? What are you doing?'

The matron turned.

'I said for you to remain quiet. You would be wise to do so, young soldier. You speak of this to no one, or I will make sure you have the same fate.'

I lay on my bed looking at matron, wide eyed and shaking. I gritted my teeth and shook my head.

'You can't do this,' I said. 'You can't do that.'

'We do not have the resources!' snapped Matron. 'We cannot save him. It is best to do it quick, so there is no misery. Now shut your mouth and keep it that way.'

She glared at me ominously, then turned and walked the opposite way of the two nurses carrying the stretcher bed with the soldier.

I felt despondent and punched the side of the bed, grunting. They were going to end his life because they didn't have enough resources. At that moment, I would have gladly taken his place, to see one less person suffer. I squeezed my eyes shut and rested my hands on my forehead. My breathing was loud and broke in a few places as I tried desperately not to cry in frustration.

'He'll be going to a better place,' said a voice to my right.

I turned to see the soldier who was previously asleep, now resting on his side and facing me. His emerald eyes blinked a few times.

'Anywhere is better than here,' I mumbled, looking up at the roof. 'Any place.'

'Soon he'll be at peace. I can only hope that I will be there soon enough.'

'Stay here while you can.'

The soldier gave me a quizzical look. 'Why?'

'You don't know what happens when you die. You think you know, but you don't. No one does until they're dead. My mother used to say that we would go to heaven, but somehow, I knew she was lying. She didn't believe it. She just said it so I would feel better. As far as I'm concerned, you rot with the earth, and if you're lucky, people might remember you.'

The soldier was shocked and lay with his eyes glaring at me.

'You're just one of those people who want to rain on the parade of others.'

'No, I just want you to be around for that little bit longer so you can witness life now, not pretending to after death.'

'And what if there is a god, and you're wrong? Then what?'

I paused for a moment, staring at the roof, and then turned to the soldier.

'Then he has a lot to answer for.'

Dear Nikolai

Nikolai,

I find it amusing how life can throw in unexpected pleasures in the midst of chaos. You were that rose among thorns, the unexpected gift which I received and humbly accepted. For that small moment, a blink in the eye of life, it was a sight, nonetheless, and I know I will not be able to let it go.

The soft-hearted nature of a child; you were saddened by your father taking his own life. And as fate would have it, I walked into it after seeing your small flash of light from a distance. I, too, lost my father, and instantly felt your pain. Nothing can replace a father, I know. But as your small, glimmering eyes met mine with curiosity, you smiled. As though we knew each other, we became comfortable in each other's presence. Your golden locks of hair tousled under my fingers willingly, and we instantly shared something special.

The small bear you insisted on handing me, I kept. I kept it as a reminder that there can still be hope in a world torn by evil, as clichéd as that may be. But I still hold it true. I hold true that there is always good in people, though we may not see it to begin with. I hold true that not everyone wants this, but they do it for the ones they love. And I hold true that the world can be one of awe and inspiration, among man's bidding to do evil.

You invited me into your home, and you showed me your life within but a few short minutes, and somehow it is as if I have known you for a time beyond this war. Rushed as it may have been, I can only hope you found refuge. I hope that you did, I truly do. I could never forgive myself knowing that I sent you to the void beyond life.

I looked among your memories – the pictures that adorned your home. Your family was one, and this war tore it apart. I looked at your moments you shared with your mother and father – moments of happiness, caught forever within a picture.

As time goes on, you will forget about me. You will forget about our encounter and the gift you gave me – not just the bear, but you, yourself. And as time goes on, you will grow up and I will grow on, and age will come about. But as it does, I know I will not forget you, nor the moment we shared. It bound us, and it taught me many things that I thought were dead. You were the hope in the field of shadows – the light that illuminated.

Take care of yourself, always.

Love,
Johan

CHAPTER 29

With heavy feet, we marched through the small villages that stood just miles out of Stalingrad. The sixth army was to attack Stalingrad from the west, and our army was to attack from the south. We had followed the Don River west as we moved closer to the city. We were to follow the Don River south and go through the village of Kotelnikovo. We would fight our way through until we finally reunited with the sixth army in the city.

We had received word that the Sixth Panzer Army had obliterated the villages of Aksai and Abganerovo. Word spread quickly of the brutality, but we could never tell if they were just rumours, or reality.

'Some of the men in the sixth army are cannibals,' one soldier had said. 'I hear they ate most of the civilians and soldiers before they moved on.'

'That's a load of lies,' another soldier replied. 'But they didn't leave any survivors.'

'Apparently they didn't leave any bodies, either.'

'Oh, fuck off, you idiot.'

The soldiers talked about the prospect of taking the great southern city of the Soviet empire. They spoke of how we would sweep in and control it within days, giving us an advantage over the south of the Soviet Union and then north to Moscow. They were determined. But I wasn't. I was too tired. It wasn't laziness, but I lacked the sheer will to continue, remaining apathetic while we walked. The resounding feeling of regret would soon come.

The civilians had set tank traps along ours and the sixth army's routes to deter us from marching onward, with our tanks getting stuck and ultimately slowing us down. But we pushed on, and did it with brutality. We left no survivors, with every wounded person, civilian or soldier being shot dead. I had only hoped I could single myself out of this misery, but I was a part of this whole thing, and until it was over, it was still going to be 'we'.

The Russians weren't going to give up so easily. Our soldiers had often wondered why they would throw themselves at us, risking their lives as they didn't care so much about death as they did about the life of their nation. We could never comprehend the sheer brutishness that was instilled in everyone down here, both the Russians and us. This battle was not going to be easy – we knew it, and they knew it.

I looked over the horizon, north-east, and saw a collective of houses. Smoke was rising from the chimneys, families still residing in them. I was hoping no one else saw them, but I knew that was only wishful thinking. The officers sighted them almost immediately as they came into view and bellowed commands to the soldiers.

'Over there! Take the village and leave no survivors! They're only useful if they have information.'

We were given our order. We marched across the fields, the dry grass crushing under our boots. As we neared the houses, we realised it wasn't a village, but a small communal farm with few families, just like we lived on back at home.

Instantly, I wanted to turn around and leave. I paused for a moment as my heart seemed to beat out of my chest. A large hand hit me on the back and pushed me forward, as a soldier said, 'We can't stop now, soldier. We're almost there.'

We made it to the houses; small cottages that were built almost touching. They were made of smooth stone, their pointed rooftops covered in neatly patterned tiles. The soldiers transformed into something I had never seen – they were like wild animals.

Running with their guns in hand, they kicked down the doors of the houses and raided them.

Soldiers poured into each house, coming out with civilians in headlocks, or holding them by the hair. The civilians screamed and cried as they mumbled in Russian, what I perceived to be begging for mercy. One woman, who was held by her hair, clasped her hands and shook them at the soldier, wailing words no one could understand. The soldier slapped her across the face, and instantly I felt sick. *What the fuck am I doing here?*

The children were crying, their hands flailing towards the women as they, too, cried for their children. The children they had promised to protect, to nurture; they now felt impotent to the whole situation. One of the commanding officers stepped forward and shot his gun in the air.

'Silence!'

The civilians stopped, deadly silent, and stared in horror. They shook vigorously, trying to hold back the many tears they wished to shed – even some of our soldiers attempted to do the same.

'Our orders were no survivors. So let us show them – no survivors!' The officer pounded a fist in the air, and the mass of soldiers roared with cheers.

Some, like me, stood at the back of the pack and remained silent. The civilians squirmed as they were held tight. One woman cried for a small boy, who I guessed was her son.

'Dmitri! Dmitri!'

I looked over to her struggling for a young boy, who was held by his shoulders by a brutish soldier, his own shoulders broad and his face harbouring a sickly grin. The boy struggled and cried for his mother, but the soldier held on tight.

The soldier brought forth the young boy and held a gun to his head. The woman screamed, my ears ringing from the sheer sound. She cried and grabbed the soldier's arm that held her hair. The soldier hit her hard, sending her crashing to the ground. As she looked up, the boy was staring wide-eyed at her, tears streaming down his face.

And with one pull of the trigger, the soldier had taken his life. The shot echoed on the walls of the houses. The boy dropped to the ground and the mother screamed again, wailing as she became weakened by the sight of her son's dead body, all life now gone. She rested her head on the ground and continued to cry. We all stood around, remaining silent as we watched a mother mourn her son's death. Not one soldier said a word, but instead all remained deathly silent. The boy's blood filled the cracks of the already disintegrating pavement, weaving its way through each crevice.

One of the officers grabbed the woman by the hair and heaved her from the ground. She remained limp, having given up all hope once her son had gone. The officer smiled that same sickly smile, rubbing his face against hers. I looked away, feeling sick to my stomach. He had no mercy. And within seconds, the trigger was pulled again, and a thump sounded as the body hit the ground.

I looked around at the soldiers, who made no eye contact, but instead looked down at their feet. Whether it was shame, or perhaps empathic agony, I do not know. But nevertheless, not one soldier dared to look up. The officer raised his hands in the air and cheered, letting loose a victorious roar, but to no response. His face turned red with anger as every soldier remained silent.

'And what the fuck is wrong with all of you depressed bastards?' he said menacingly. 'Never seen a dead body before? Answer me!'

He flung his arms through the air, his feet dancing around the centre of the circle that surrounded him. He grabbed one of the soldiers and held him by the collar, drawing a knife from his back pocket. He held it to the soldier's neck and hissed through his teeth.

'I should cut your neck right now, son. What are you going to do about it?'

The soldier stared at him worriedly.

'*What are you going to do about it?*' screamed the officer.

He pushed the soldier to the ground, who scurried back to the group and stood up, adjusting his uniform. Every soldier still held their tongues, staring at the officer, who had apparently gone mad.

One soldier stepped forward and faced the officer. He stood well over six feet tall, his bulky body accompanying his muscular arms, which could easily be bodies of their own. His charcoal hair was combed to one side and his face was staunch, glowering at the insane officer.

'What are you going to do, big man?'

The officer walked up to the soldier and spat in his face. He laughed and pirouetted on his foot, ready to turn and walk away, when the soldier grabbed him by his uniform collar and threw him to the ground.

'What the hell do you think you're doing?' screamed the officer.

The soldier approached him and picked him up, which was no large feat, and threw the officer again onto the hard ground. The officer glanced up nervously as he scuffled along the pavement, trying to get away from the soldier. But the soldier now reached for his gun and pointed it at the officer's head.

'This... this is treason!' exclaimed the officer.

'No, it isn't,' said the soldier, and pulled the trigger.

CHAPTER 30

August 23, 1942

The Luftwaffe came in full force. Mercilessly, they carried out a devastating raid on the city. They were ordered to destroy the city before we soldiers were to enter Stalingrad. By the afternoon, when the sun was settling in the west, we could see the smoke rising just miles off. The evening rays seemed to almost glimmer through the smoke.

Yesterday, the men were talking about how they were determined it was only a long, hard day's drive from the city, and we would be there. They were no longer as adamant about this fantasy. The victory and spoils withered away – they were scared and I was just glad that I was no longer the only one.

The plumes of smoke rose steadily, the constant flow amounting to a thick, black mass in the sky. With it so heavy, the sun was finally blocked out and darkness ensued over the horizon. It was eerie, with everything suddenly going dark, but not so dark that it was difficult to see. Everything was shaded, and the sky seemed to glow red as the fired burned. It looked like a pit of lava swirling in the sky.

'See that, boys? We're heading straight for it,' said our commanding officer. 'Remember, these Russians won't hesitate, and neither should we. Keep your gun close and shoot at anything that wears that red star.'

The Führer had spoken to his field marshals back in March about what this battle would entail, and it was then sent via letter to our commanding officers. The Führer knew more than we did, even so far away, and I didn't like it. I was tasked with taking it to the next officer, as I was apparently one of the few trustworthy soldiers who would do it without opening it and reading it – they were wrong. On my way through the camp, during the darkness of night, I was carrying it to another officer, by immediate request of my commanding officer. He urged me to take it quickly, and without reading it. Curiosity had got the better of me and I opened it, only to catch a short glimpse at what it had contained. I remember reading the quote the Führer had apparently said in one of the meetings. It read:

> *The Fuhrer was expressly clear as to the details outlining what is to happen. He is quoted as stating in the Fatherland:*
> *'The war against the Russians cannot be conducted in knightly fashion. The struggle is one of ideologies and racial differences and will have to be waged with unprecedented, unmerciful, and unrelenting harshness. All officers will have to get rid of any old-fashioned ideas they may have. I realise the necessity for conducting such warfare is beyond the comprehension of you generals, but I must insist that my orders be followed without complaint. The commissars hold views directly opposed to those of National Socialism. Hence, these commissars must be eliminated. Any German soldier who breaks international law will be pardoned. Russia did not take part in the Hague Convention and, therefore, has no rights under it.'*
> *By this decree, may their blood be shed with no mercy.*

When I had read it, my stomach twisted inside, and I felt physically sick. I ran to the officer's quarters and delivered it, without saying a word, and left immediately after.

No choice was given when it came to the brutality against the Russians, and no justification for our brutality was needed, other than it was by order of the Führer. I had mentioned it to Earnst, who looked horrified to begin with, and then sighed as he simply replied, 'We have orders.'

The war had drained everything from us – our minds, our dignity, our life. I didn't even know how much more we could endure. Soldiers quarrelled far more frequently; they cried more, though it was always in secret – we were all breaking. We all wanted it to be over.

Up until now, I never imagined what the city looked like. It was simply a name with no image, a city without people. But as we saw the smoke rising high above the horizon, for the first time I began to think about what it was like.

I imagined it to be like Berlin, with the old architecture still intact and standing storeys tall, boasting beautiful craftsmanship throughout history. I imagined a large central fountain that was surrounded by thousands of bricks neatly placed along the ground, with trees that surrounded it and children playing nearby. I imagined it all, and with one quick blink of reality, the realisation that imagining it now was futile, had hit.

My chance to dream of the city had long gone, with it amassed in ruins miles away as the Luftwaffe continued their ferocious assault. I was supposed to be happy, rejoicing. I was supposed to be glad that our mighty force in the skies had gone ahead of us to clear the way that we may be safe. I was supposed to feel a lot of things in this war, but I felt none of them. Nothing had ever felt true.

The first time I had killed a man, I didn't feel like more of a man myself, as I was supposed to. It was supposed to be the true time I would be a man, and yet it was the true time I felt like a monster. And even though I felt heinous after the ordeal, the trigger on my gun was pulled from then on, with the scope aiming at a human being, not the clear air. I was everything I despised, and since then, I've never stopped hating myself.

'Up ahead!' yelled our officer. 'Russian soldiers up ahead. Formation!'

I blinked and watched other soldiers rushing past me, clutching their guns as they found their positions. I stood there, dazed for a moment, before finally shaking my head, blinked a few times and then quickly moved to position.

We crouched low behind a mound. It was silent. The only noise was miles off, and even that seemed like a faint whisper. I looked around and saw every soldier poised, resting with their backs against the mound, or lying on their stomachs in the dirt.

After a few minutes of silence, a gunshot sounded, and a piece of the earth shot up only a few feet away from us. The rain of gunfire ensued as a sea of men poured out and headed toward us.

'Hold your position!' yelled the officer. 'Do not let them push us back. Hold your ground!'

We began to fire on the Russians as they found positions which were low enough to avoid the oncoming bullets from our end. I glanced to my right and saw the officer yelling at some of the soldiers, barking orders and waving his hands northward. They nodded and moved further east, behind the shrubs and trees until they were out of sight. I squinted in curiosity, wondering what they were going to do, but dismissed it and turned to face the Russians' defensive line.

After almost an hour of fighting, with our men only advancing a few feet, some of the soldiers, including myself, spotted a group of our men rearing behind the Russians' defensive strip. There seemed to be more than what I had seen disappear.

The Russians turned in surprise and yelled, shooting aimlessly into the distance. They were surrounded, and one by one, their soldiers fell. Some sprinted to the east and others to the west, but those that chose the east were cordoned off and slaughtered. Blood sprayed as the bullets perforated their skin – for a moment, a red curtain of pure blood covered the air.

Only a small number still stood, with what I assumed to be one of the commanding officers, yelling to his soldiers, snapping his head rigorously left and right in a panic.

'Move up!' yelled our officer. 'Move up!'

Our soldiers stood and moved over the mound, following the

road that continued to lead up to the city. We moved slowly, dropping to the ground and crawling while trying to aim and shoot at the same time.

Within the next hour, the small group of Russians was all but defeated. Their dead bodies, smeared with blood and dirt, sprawled across the land. Their eyes seemed to follow us as we marched – watching us destroy their homes. We had reached where they had planted themselves and witnessed an elaborate set of trenches that moved fluently with the earth. Wooden beams were planted across the walls to prevent the dirt from collapsing, and small tunnels had been built to attach each segment of the branched-out trenches together.

'Clear out the trenches,' commanded our officer. 'Some Russian soldiers may still be hiding in there. We don't want any calamities in the event they escaped and decided to bring back more soldiers with them.'

Every soldier nodded, and we made our way into the trenches with our guns poised. I crept slowly into one of the tunnels, my back arched over as I tipped my head down to avoid hitting it on the beams above. A small doorway was dug to my right, and I stopped for a moment. I placed my ear to the grated tin that ran along the wall and listened. Nothing. Cautiously stepping, I made my way around the corner and walked through the doorway into a small room. It contained two rickety beds, a table with papers on it, a lantern and a wooden box filled with food and ammunition.

A small noise came from underneath the furthest bed, in the left corner of the room. I turned quickly and held my gun up, aiming directly beneath it. I walked toward the bed and crouched down slowly, seeing a young soldier hiding. He held his hands up to the base of the bed. I stood back and he crawled out from beneath the bed.

His face was covered in black soot, and his uniform was dirty and ripped beyond repair. He would have been no older than me, and he had seen far worse than I had. His blue eyes stared at me, and his body, well built, shook.

He closed his eyes and turned his head to his side, expecting me to fire. I walked over to the wooden box and looked through it, seeing a small tin can of food. I grabbed it and put it in the soldier's hand. He stared at me with a blank expression. I pointed him to the bed and ushered him to crawl back underneath. Once he was under, I grabbed the thin blanket from the other bed and took it to the soldier, awkwardly putting it over him to hide as much as I could.

He looked at me, and I gave him a nod, to which he then did the same. I held my index finger to my mouth, making sure he remained silent while he was in hiding. He nodded.

I stood up and walked back through the doorway and out of the tunnel. I was walking through the trench when I saw Sergeant Shödler standing in the middle, blocking anyone from getting past. He looked at me and gave a cold smile.

'Hans Adler,' he exclaimed, 'Well, well, well. Isn't it a shame that we haven't seen each other in months?'

'I liked it like that,' I hissed.

'There's no need to be like that. It is our reunion after so many months without each other's company. It was my fault, however, I must admit. I was sent for back in Berlin. Only a week, but it was still better than this shit show. It was so good to be home, away from all of this. But I feel at ease, knowing that you're still alive and we can enjoy what time we have together left.' His voice was sarcastic, and every word he spoke felt like Death had personally chosen not to take him; to torment me for a little while longer.

'Now, did you find anything in that little tunnel?'

'No,' I said, defiantly. 'There was nothing.'

He smiled wryly and cocked his head to one side. 'And I don't believe one word that comes from your fucking mouth.'

He put his hand on my shoulder, and I quickly smacked it off. 'Don't touch me.'

'I did miss our times together. But you know what I think was the best thing? I visited a concentration camp when I was back in the Fatherland. And all I was able to think of, was the fact that you should have been in there. I can imagine your family in there – all of them. Your father, mother, and whatever siblings you may have. You belong there with them, you filthy little rat.'

'My father's dead.'

'Dead? Already? Was he sent to the extermination camp? That must have been a terrible thing to have to go through.'

'He was never in a camp,' I said angrily. 'He died before the war. *None* of my family are in any camps.'

Sergeant Shödler leaned in closely.

'Listen here, you pathetic piece of filth. You may be able to fool the officers and the soldiers you fight alongside, but you cannot fool me. I know who you are. I know *what* you are. And when I have my way, and believe me, I will soon enough, you're going to wish you were never born.'

'And I hope that if anyone is going to die in this upcoming battle, it will be you. Bloody and gruesome.'

Sergeant Shödler's eyes widened, and he flung his hand up, slapping me across the cheek.

'Don't tempt me, Adler. I *will* kill you and make it look like it was a Russian soldier.'

Shödler was about to continue speaking, but was cut off by a soldier who stood above the trenches, on solid ground.

'Let's get moving!'

Shödler turned to the soldier.

'Speak like that again to me, and it will not be the Russians that you will have to worry about.'

'Sergeant Shödler,' exclaimed the soldier, 'I apologise, Sergeant. I didn't see that it was you.'

'What do you think this is, a fucking private uniform?'

The soldier stood there in stupid silence, and Sergeant Shödler turned back to face me.

'It looks like it's time to go.'

He smiled again at me, the same macabre smile that he gave every time, and then turned and walked away.

I was left in shock. After months of not having to see him, I had attempted to forget about him completely, and succeeded for a small while. He had no longer occupied my mind and I had felt a little safe, in the broadest context of this war, that is. I had no idea where he went, and to be perfectly honest, I didn't care. And yet, as soon as I saw him, my heart sank, and my stomach churned. Every memory of him flooded back into my mind, and I felt if anything was to destroy me, it would be him.

I made my way out of the trenches and regrouped with our army. I was shaking, but I tried not to let any of the soldiers see. I wanted to find Earnst and tell him about it, but I hadn't seen him at all for the rest of the day. I breathed heavily and began moving with the soldiers and tanks, trying to think of anything but Sergeant Shödler. I thought of Mother, Edith, Father, Oskar, Nikolai, Alina, and yet despite all the heartache they induced, Sergeant Shödler was still lurking in the background.

Concentration Camp

I laugh because the soldiers that walk these corridors are becoming far more insane than those that are stuck here. I laugh because they are becoming far more homesick than the prisoners here. I laugh because, in a turn of sweet poetic justice, the soldiers are breaking down, crumbling as they yearn to be free – and the prisoners push on.

I find it ironic, nay, bittersweet that such an occurrence has come to light. The savagery of these beasts that lurk around the corners is never ending. I was built for the very purpose that I serve today. But I was not only to hold the prisoners, labourers, or other names they may be called – I was to break them. But as time goes on, I rust and I crumble, and they, dare I say it, soldier on.

Perhaps I am getting less perpetually aggressive as I was meant to be – as I was. Perhaps, with the deterioration of my walls, I am becoming far more promising to exhibit sympathy. This, I do not oppose, yet nor do I show it boisterously. My exterior is still hardening to the eye, and my interior will still show nothing but the stone walls that enclose hundreds of men to be tightly compacted together. But as the soldiers become agitated, weary, and angry, I become more amused at the sight of it, for they now feel the pain of those they have kept locked away in here.

Some soldiers speak of the war outside of these walls. They want to join; they want to fight and gain more honour than they would walking backwards and forwards in these dreary corridors. They exchange information between one another of what they have heard from the outside world. Speaking of the soldiers that they know, fighting in a foreign land, and the troubles they find themselves in. And yet, despite this information of death and chaos, they still yearn to be in it.

Odd creatures, humans are. They destroy one another because of an indifference, and yet they still cry out for love and mercy from one another. What next, I ask?

Time is running out, I must admit. They may condemn so many to death, but Death will come for them soon enough. And what then? Everything they had hoped will be lost. Death comes for everyone, sooner or later, and the inevitability of its arrival is imminent. The man who wished the destruction of another is blind, for he thinks he can outmanoeuvre Death, but he is not immune.

And so, I watch upon with a growing tiredness that I cannot fight. Perhaps Death is on my own doorstep? Or closer than I think. Whichever it may be, perhaps my own demise is one of beauty in the eyes of a human, though it means I will no longer be. But for this, I am growing to be ready.

CHAPTER 31

August 28, 1942

My blood pumped furiously, and my bones ached and cracked. Exhaustion was getting the better of me – all of us – and the Russian soldiers seemed to be coming from everywhere. We were still miles from the city, fighting through wave after wave of Russian soldiers. They flooded the plains like a swarm, determined to their last breath. Civilians attacked us, too. The tank traps they had set spiked a sense of urgency in our army, with the officers sending forth soldiers to scout out the grounds before the tanks rolled on.

Just two days prior, we had been trapped, cordoned off by two separate groups of Russians. They came from the north and the east. To the west were farmlands, the openness being too much of an advantage for the Russians, and we couldn't retreat south – the Führer would be furious had we even thought of retreating.

Our advantage was our tactics. The Russians sent in swarms of people, anyone – soldier or civilian – and they would be shot the moment they stood to run. Our tactics were what we had used throughout our whole time in Russian territory. We used what surroundings we could get to cover. While our soldiers at the front held off the oncoming Russians, separate groups were sent to attack from behind. Never did the Russians expect it, even though it was a crucial part of our offensive. Instead, they were surprised by the sudden appearance of German soldiers behind them, strenuously shooting rounds of bullets that cut through the air, some hitting our men and others travelling in the opposite direction.

Once we had gained the upper hand, it took only a short time to finally defeat them and move on. But our journey was still slow, and we had to get to the city quickly.

Each step I took, it felt as though I stood on razors, with the skin peeling from my feet and my soles raw. I gritted my teeth and tried not to show any pain. I kept walking and pretended that everything was fine – that's what I had been doing this whole time, anyway. The tips of my toes had worn away, the once rough skin now delicate and painful.

'Hans!'

I whipped around to see Earnst smiling. He hugged me and patted my back hard.

'Earnst!' I exclaimed. 'Where the hell have you been?'

'I thought you were dead, to be honest. I kept asking around, but no one had seen you.' He sighed. 'Shit, Hans. I really thought you were dead.'

I tilted my head back.

'Says a lot about the soldiers here, then. Well, I'm still alive. I think, anyway.'

He chuckled.

'I was sent to scout out anything ahead. We were gone for two days, sending messages back and forth to command. Where's Felix?'

'I thought he might have been with you,' I said.

Earnst looked troubled.

'You don't think…?'

I shook my head.

'No. Not at all. It would've been mentioned by someone in our group. But if you keep thinking like that, it won't do you any better. I'm sure he's fine. Ask around. They would probably know where he is – he's better known by the soldiers than me.'

'I don't know about that. You've made quite a name for yourself among the men.'

'Not a good one, I would imagine.'

Earnst cocked his head to one side and pouted his lips.

'Some think your wit is something to be admired at. Some don't. The ones that don't are probably the ones that are on the receiving end of it. I wouldn't worry too much. Everyone's liked by some and disliked by others. It's the way of life.'

'I'm not worried. We're all bound to each other by this uniform. It's not like they can pull out their gun and shoot me dead in front of everyone.'

'Throw you in the middle of the gunfire, perhaps, but not shoot you. Oh, no. We couldn't have that now, could we?'

I looked at him, and a small smile showed in the corner of his mouth. I tried not to smile, but it came out anyway.

'I suppose that's true. But if I go, you're coming with me,' I joked.

'It's a deal then. So, how's your leg, anyway?'

'It hurts like hell,' I replied, 'My feet have begun to peel and they're raw, and my leg aches each time I have to get down on the ground and then get back up again – which seems to be every second hour these past few days.'

'Have they sent you to the nurses?'

I shook my head.

'They said that supplies are too low to even consider sending me to the nurses. One of the officers said we need all the medical supplies we can get for what's up ahead. They bandaged my leg and sent me away.'

'They think it's going to be that bad?'

'Worse. And to top it off...' I paused for a moment. 'Sergeant Shödler is back.'

Earnst widened his eyes.

'I thought the guy was dead, or gone for good, at least.'

'He caught me when I was clearing out the trenches a few days ago. As soon as I saw him, my heart dropped. He tormented me, just standing in the trenches.'

'What did he say to you?'

'He threatened that he would kill me and make it look like a Russian had done the job. I saw him yesterday and avoided him, but it's getting ridiculous to have to dodge *him*, rather than the oncoming bullets from the Russians. It's like a living nightmare with him around. And what's worse, he can tell me what to do if no commanding officer is around.'

'I bet he hasn't even seen a battle up close against these Russians. He would be hiding in his tent, cowering.'

'Regardless of what he does, I don't want to be anywhere near him. I...you know how I had the trouble of killing those soldiers?'

Earnst nodded.

'And it's nothing to be ashamed of.'

'No, it isn't that. I had so much trouble trying to shoot any of them, because I was afraid of taking their life, and a life away from their loved ones. But Sergeant Shödler... Earnst, if I could, I would put a gun to his head and pull the fucking trigger.'

Earnst looked around to make sure no one had heard and put his hand on my shoulder.

'Just don't say it aloud, Hans. We don't want any soldier getting the wrong idea, and having you face the officers for saying that. But I think we're safe in assuming that thought goes through every soldier's head.'

'I don't even care. I want him to know it. I want him to know how easy it would be for me. The hell he has put me through, and the constant humiliation. I'm nothing to him, except for a means of entertainment.'

'Hans, I know he makes you angry. He makes me angry just at how he treats you, and so I can't even imagine what you feel towards him. But please, don't say this to anyone, and especially not aloud. I don't want you to end up killed for being a loudmouth. Please?'

I broke my stare from ahead.

'I won't. It's fine.'

'Good,' replied Earnst, nodding. 'Good.'

We continued walking, mostly in silence, but a few words were spoken that broke it up. When you've said everything there is to be said about your family and life back home, there's nothing but talk of the war. And even that had died amongst the soldiers. They were quiet; deathly silent. We had walked alongside the tank for a time when I took a step and fell to the ground. I pushed my face up from the dirt and groaned, then looked at my foot. I had stepped in a large hole, and a large wire had trapped it down.

Earnst and another soldier rushed to my aid.

'Hans, are you all right?' asked Earnst.

I nodded but closed my eyes tightly as the pain began to release up my left leg where the bullet wound was still healing.

'It looks like it was supposed to be a tank trap, but they abandoned it,' said the other soldier.

'They abandoned it fairly early then, by the size of the hole,' replied Earnst. 'His foot can only just fit in there. He may not be able to walk on it.'

'Well, he will have to find a way,' came a voice from behind Earnst. It was our commanding officer. 'We do not have time to care and nurture him. Get his damned foot out of the hole, get the wire off it and get moving.'

'How is he supposed to move?' asked Earnst.

'Help him. Or sit him on the tank. But remember, he's vulnerable up there. One look at someone who is sitting eight feet tall, and one bullet is all it takes.'

I thought for a moment, then looked at Earnst. 'Will it be safe?'

Earnst nodded. 'Of course, it will. There are scouts up ahead.'

I nodded.

'I'll go on the tank, then. I don't want you to have to help me the whole way.'

'I wouldn't mind, Hans.'

I gave him a glance and then looked at the ground.

'Don't be so noble. Just help me up on the tank, please.'

Earnst shrugged his shoulders.

'Fine, if that's what you want.'

Earnst and the other soldier heaved me up from the ground and launched me onto the tank, where I sat uncomfortably on the side. My legs dangled over the edge, and once we were moving again, I watched the tank's tracks move in a never-ending circular motion.

I refrained from talking to anyone for a while, embarrassed about the whole ordeal and wanting nothing more than to curl up and not have to face the world. I felt like that often – more often than not. It felt as though all eyes were on me, and so I kept mine averted from anyone's stare.

Two hours had passed, and we had moved slowly, still only on the outskirts of the city. The ground was rough, and every soldier was unsure of what was to be expected ahead. My backside ached from the constant thumping against the tank, its cold metal slapping my bones. The men in the tanks were constantly yelling out to keep checking the roads that no mines nor any traps had been set.

Paranoia had set in, and no soldier was immune. Heads whipped left and right at any sound that was made in the trees and shrubs. Any glint of light, however far away, was immediately spotted and groups of soldiers were sent to track it and search it out, armed and ready for any conflict. Half the time, it was nothing. Just a piece of metal reflecting from the sun. But sometimes those reflections led to our soldiers finding bunches of cottages behind the trees, with Russian civilians hiding in the cellars. No mercy was to be given, and none ever was. I was just glad I didn't have to see it. But my conscience burned every time I thought of what happened. I knew what happened. We all did, but we uttered not a single word.

The smoke coming from the city still blocked out the sun. The lands were dark, but the sky was a mixture of red and grey. As I watched the sprawled-out trees slowly go by, my thoughts begun to multiply, with everything running through my mind.

What is less prudent? The man who is willing to kill others in the name of war, or the man who is willing to kill his own people in the name of war? What is more humble? The man who preaches peace, or the man who acts on it?

What I found truly alarming is all these young men, some younger than me, acting in sheer excitement at the possibility of death – even their own. Once it was just the prospect of war – glory, as they thought – that excited them, and then it was the battlefield. And even after Death had swept in, had brushed so close to them, almost kissing them on the lips, they still thrive on it. The mind is a funny thing, but the heart is stranger.

CHAPTER 32

September 13, 1942

Some of the soldiers, including myself, had overhead the officers arguing. We had cleared out a number of trenches, and made ourselves comfortable for the night, awaiting any attacks that may arise in the darkness. We had captured a number of soldiers that benefited us with intelligence, and were being questioned in another room, almost in the centre of the maze of trenches. We could hear the screams, even from so far away – it brought me back to the Fatherland, when I had witnessed the interrogation of the soldiers. I knew what they were doing, and what the soldiers were going through.

But near where we sat, huddled in a bunker that was no more than ten feet wide, we were all crammed inside, fighting for space. The officers were arguing over the Führer's decision to bring in new top commanders, and the old ones would step down. Their voices were muffled, but one soldier who sat next to the door had heard bits in between. One argued that they liked it the way it was, because he was often given perks by one particular commander who he had become well known to. The other disagreed, saying they were useless when it came to the strategies of battle. They argued for a few minutes – ten at least – and then it finally ceased.

Our front line was thirty miles long in the offensive against the Russians. Our soldiers fought bitterly, pushing further and further into the city. But the Russians fought even more fiercely with every breath they took. Their determination meant many of our soldiers were pushed back a number of times before they could finally push forward.

Today we were to launch a two-phased attack. The morning sun was rising, and yet it was still dark. The constant smoke was from burning oil that had been spilled and set alight just four days prior, and it continued to burn. Trees and plants burned, houses burned, everything that had the possibility of attracting fire, did. Buildings collapsed as the wooden structures were reduced to ash, leaving remnants of a once glowing city to nothing. And it was about to get worse.

Our first phase was going to be a day-long bombardment of the southern part of the city. It was not going to cease until the day was over. Once the bombardment had stopped, the soldiers would race against time to claim the key areas that were needed to gain the advantage. The first was the hilltop of Mamayev Kurgan. It provided an overview of the whole city. From the factory area of the north to the Volga River, which ran parallel south with the city, and the civilian housing to the south – the panorama view was the ultimate advantage.

Another two divisions were to attack from the west, diagonally from Gumrak, toward the central landing stage. And, like a steel nail, another two divisions were to drive through the southern suburbs of Stalingrad, heading north-east towards the same finish point on the riverside.

It was going to be a bloody battle. We had not reached the city, and we already had more blood on our hands than any other battle we had fought.

I was in the division tasked with driving through the southern suburbs. My heart was beating fast for the entire day as the bombardment occurred, knowing that this was going to be the hardest thing I had to do. Civilians would look you in the eye, would hide from you or they would attack you – and either way, I didn't want to be there. Some soldiers wanted to be there, but the number of soldiers that had a lust for battle had now lost it. They saw what true war was and they didn't like it. I was no longer alone.

The sun had set, and the bombardments continued. Heavy artillery fire sounded constantly. At first, the sound was a sheer thrill. Loud and striking, the moment you heard it, it had a sense of power that it carried. It made your bones vibrate, and the crack that separated the air was striking. But as time wore on, so did the noise. After the first few minutes, it was no longer a sense of power, but a sense of wonder. That wonder soon turned to reality, when the realisation that those shots fired were aimed at weeding out the people still left. Civilians – too many to count – had sacrificed their own lives so we would be pushed back, perhaps a few yards. We knew they were desperate to keep their city from falling into our hands, and that made us more eager to pry it from them. These soldiers I fought with were merciless, and I was expected to be the same. I had done it before, but I didn't want to do it again.

By midnight, the artillery bombing had stopped. Soldiers were put on watch throughout the night to guard the tanks and trenches. I don't think any soldier slept easy. No one was strong enough to sleep with both eyes closed and yet they acted like heroes when it became daylight. The irony of war or, perhaps, it's the irony of ego.

Lying in the small bunker, one soldier whispered quietly out in the dark.

'Is anyone awake?'

Several soldiers answered, and I followed suit.

'You boys should be asleep,' said one voice.

'So should you, Jürgen,' said another.

Jürgen was a twenty-five-year-old man, but many of the younger soldiers admired him. He was quiet, but spoke when needed to and especially when giving advice. He was kinder than the usual soldier I would come across, but like every other soldier, I treated him with as much suspicion as the enemy.

'I'm trying to, but I can't if everyone begins to speak at the same time,' spoke Jürgen's voice.

'Sorry,' said the first voice who called out. 'I'm just... to be honest, I don't know what to expect of tomorrow.'

'You're scared?' asked Jürgen.

The soldier stuttered.

'Most of the soldiers in this bunker would be scared, I would imagine. Hell, I'm scared. We don't know what tomorrow will bring, but we all have to help each other. When you think you don't need anyone, the time will come when you truly do need someone's help, and you find you're all alone.'

'We've just got to be strong, men,' said another voice. 'Stick together.'

'That's right,' said another.

'I'm with you,' sounded yet another.

Before we knew it, each soldier sounded triumphant agreements that we were to stick together and look after each other. It was the first time, since I knew, that I felt part of a larger group, with more soldiers willing to look out for me than just Earnst, Felix and perhaps a few others.

'Now, get some rest,' said Jürgen. 'All of you. As much as you can. Tomorrow is going to push all of us, and we need to be as ready as we can.'

Various 'Yes, Jürgen' sentiments were muttered and then there was silence. I couldn't imagine any soldier being able to sleep that night, and I imagined every soldier in that bunker lying on their backs, staring into a sea of black, their eyes wide open and their minds constantly replaying the possibilities of what the next day would bring.

I awoke in the morning with a surge of adrenalin, along with fear that had seeped into my mind through the night. It was endless speculation of what today would bring, but most of the soldiers were confident we would pull through.

We all slowly woke, after having orders barked at us to get up and ready. Our faces sank low and we shuffled our feet slowly, but once the artillery bombardments had started up again in the distance, we began to realise we had little time to feel sorry for ourselves.

Once we were ready, our guns cocked and prepared to fire, we all exited the bunkers. Many other soldiers that stayed in the neighbouring bunkers were also piling out into the trenches and heading for higher ground. I felt slightly claustrophobic as we were pushed in the small, narrow trenches, but it was no sooner that we found higher ground and stood in formation.

Our officer addressed our division.

'You are tasked with piercing the southern suburbs. You are to drive every Russian, whether it be civilian or soldier, not out, but into the ground. They will become ash, and we will march forward.'

My stomach churned at the brutish speech.

'You will not leave any survivors. If we are to ensure a victory, if we are to ensure that this city is captured, then we are to ensure that no Russian blood runs in the veins of men, but on the ground.'

If there was to be blood running on the ground, in the drains and to the infested underground world as corpses rotted, I hoped it would be ours – and in particular, mine. I tried to talk myself up, to tell myself I could do it, that I had done it before, but that self was fading. I once found it impossible to kill, be it animal or human. And then, as if this foreign land had turned me into a monster, one eager to spill blood, I had a taste for it. It started out as a must – I had to do it to survive. But soon it became a lust, like some kind of sport. I was a demon that cloaked myself in the lie of desperation. I was surrounded by demons who were willing to take away the home of the innocent in exchange for a short time of glory. The history books wouldn't remember them – they would only remember the people that were thousands of miles away, in the comfort of their own home, behind a desk. Someone like the Führer. We fought this war for his glory, not our own. And I positioned myself in the middle of it all by convincing myself I could help Mother and Edith this way. That feigned hope washed away soon after, and I knew it was going to be a hard journey. It was going to be hell.

I blinked a few times and realised the officer had only just finished speaking. We saluted him and then stood at attention.

'God be with you,' he said finally. 'Long live the Führer. Heil Hitler!'

'Heil Hitler!' chanted the soldiers.

If there was going to be anyone, or anything, with us today, God would surely not. I no longer believed God existed, that everything I was taught was a lie. And at this present moment, I still believed that. No one was going to be with us, except one another – and even that in itself was a worry.

CHAPTER 33

September 14, 1942

We began marching toward the southern suburbs of the city. As we neared the edge of the suburbs, shots rang out. I whipped around but saw nothing. Just as I sought to dismiss it, soldiers to the east screamed out, 'Enemy spotted! North in the second storey!'

I scanned the buildings and spotted soldiers perched behind a wall that had a hole blown in it. The buildings were badly damaged, with debris from the bombardment scattered across the once elegantly paved paths. Walls were missing large sections, while some buildings only stood within an inch of collapse. The roads were covered in debris, mounds of rubble providing hiding spots for some.

We moved forward and crouched low behind a small cottage that was still intact. I peered around the corner but flinched back as gun shots pierced the wall beside me.

'Careful, Hans!' yelled Earnst.

I looked to see Earnst and Felix behind me.

'How did you get here?'

'We were with the tank in the second group. Stick with me.'

There was no time to talk, so I nodded in compliance. We kept to the wall, crouching low as bullets spun past. Soldiers were yelling from every direction, both Russian and German, and the sound of gunfire was deafening. This was different than what we were used to. And this was only the start.

'We have to take out the soldiers directly ahead of the cottage,' said Earnst, 'but there are soldiers in the second storeys of the buildings that have a greater advantage than us. If we make one step out, we're dead. We have to take them out first.'

'How are we supposed to do that?' I asked. 'You said it yourself, if we get out of the cover of the building, we're dead.'

'Wait here. We need artillery reinforcement to collapse the buildings. Hold them off as long as you can, but don't go anywhere.'

'Where are you going?' I asked frantically.

'Just stay here,' he demanded. 'I won't be long.'

Earnst ran back southward. I had four soldiers with me, all of whom were crouching low and avoiding any gunfire.

'We have to hold them off until Earnst has artillery reinforcement. Ready your guns!'

They all stared, dumbfounded, and said nothing.

'Don't just stand there! You've been given an order!'

'Who the hell are you to give us orders?' asked one of the soldiers.

'Listen, you can either sit there and whimper about being shot at, or you can help every other soldier that is actually fighting by holding them off!'

'We're not whimpering!'

'Then get up and fire!' I screamed the order and realised just how quickly I assumed the role of an officer. I was surprised, but a little proud as well, the sense of giving orders like a commander.

'You heard him!' yelled Felix. 'Do what you're fucking told.'

I returned the gesture to Felix and smiled. I mouthed the words, *Thank you*, and resumed position. The men looked at each other and then stood up. I nodded at them awkwardly, turned and rested my back on the wall. I held my gun around the corner and shot a few rounds into the open before taking cover back behind the wall.

Almost twenty minutes had passed before Earnst ran back and sat on the ground, resting against the wall as he panted. I quickly moved and crouched beside him.

'Are you all right? What's happening?'

He nodded, then put his hand up before breathing heavily for a few seconds, catching his breath.

'We have five minutes to get into defensive position.'

'What?'

'The tanks are going to roll in. We have five minutes to slowly back out before they come in and fire. They're going to try and take out the buildings' structures on the bottom.'

I nodded.

'Then we need to pull all of our men out.'

'The other groups are being taken care of. We just need to get everyone here, out.'

He stood up and dusted himself down.

'Let's get moving, now. Felix, with me.'

We had gathered the nearby soldiers and told them to go back. The bullets were soaring through the air like wind, so we could do nothing but yell it across the open spaces between each building to the others. After yelling at the top of our lungs, exhausting our breathing capacity, they finally got the message and began to move back.

We only had a minute left before the tanks were to come in. We quickly headed south and took cover behind the contours. We watched as the tanks rolled past into position, only a few hundred yards from the buildings. They started firing, their deafening shells crashing into the buildings. One building's structure had been broken on the left side and began to slide to the ground. The walls crumbled and the wooden posts that graced the outside snapped and sent the whole building plunging to the ground in one great momentum.

As if it were a pack of dominoes, the rest of the buildings followed suit. The Russian soldiers attempted to escape, some luckier than others. Those that escaped jumped onto the ground and ran northward, behind the blockades that had been built on the roads. Those soldiers that escaped, however, were few. The rest had been caught under the collapsing buildings and were now lying under masses of rubble – either dead or barely alive.

Once the tanks had stopped firing, our soldiers moved forward again, this time targeting the blockades. The blockades were made of wooden pylons that had shaved tips into sharpened points, crossing over one another, with barbed wire rolled along the ground. Wooden barrels and crates were piled atop one another, and bags filled with sand were stacked up high to create makeshift walls. Russian soldiers lined the stockade, with turret guns mounted behind the sandbags.

Surrounding them were buildings in ruins. Almost no building was unharmed, and the debris and rubble had amassed on the streets to create enough cover for some of our men to use. Others wove in and out of the ruined buildings, trying to find well-placed positions in order to move forward.

I ran with several other soldiers and then took a sharp right into a two-storey building. I ran up the stairs and lay on the ground, aiming my gun at the first stockade. Earnst, Felix and the four other soldiers that were adamant they weren't whimpering behind the building, had followed.

'How could the stockades have survived the bombing, yesterday?' asked Felix.

'They didn't. These were most likely built last night, while we were too busy sleeping,' replied Earnst with a hint of annoyance.

'You say that like it's a bad thing,' I interjected.

Earnst turned and looked at me.

'Of course, it is. Why sleep when it's wasting time for the Russians to set up stockades like this?'

'People need to sleep, believe it or not,' I said, while looking down the scope of my gun.

I saw Earnst lay down next to me in the corner of my eye, aiming his gun at the blockade.

'Let's not do this now, Hans.'

'Please, let's not,' I hissed. 'We have more important things to worry about. Keep your sights sharp, Felix.'

'Already on it,' he replied.

We watched as the Russian soldiers moved in and out of the buildings, behind the stockade and using their surroundings to easily cause havoc for our soldiers. The stockade was a few hundred yards from where we positioned ourselves. Our snipers had found other buildings to position themselves in and so we stayed where we were. Our guns didn't have the range to hit a target dead from the distance we were at, but it was no use running at them with no clue as to where we were going, without watching their movements first.

We fired into the distance at a group of Russian soldiers who mounted themselves on a pile of rubble, lying low to avoid the oncoming gunfire. The turret guns began to fire at our soldiers. We focused our fire on the Russians at the turrets, exhaustively trying to stop the flood of bullets that rained on our soldiers, who were pushing the offensive on the ground. Shots were fired at us as we dived for cover. Bits of wood seemed to shatter like glass, spraying as the bullets hit the beams above. Our snipers, crouched low in the windows and some even climbing to the rooftops of the two-storey buildings, began to open fire.

We were under fire for almost an hour before we finally decided we wouldn't be able to get past the stockade by pushing forward – we had to go around. We crawled on the floor until we were out of the open space of the second storey and in the doorway. Running down the stairs, our footsteps were loud, but they were overshadowed by the sounds of gunfire from outside.

I followed Earnst as he took a sharp right, running through the lower part of the building and through to the next. The buildings still had wooden chairs and tables that were sprawled along the floor, and some photographs still graced the walls. *People like Nikolai used to live here*, I thought, holding back the tears that tried to forcibly show. Running through the rooms of strangers, it seemed all the eyes in the photographs watched us trudge through their homes. It was as though Nikolai watched me. We wove through the buildings, until we were behind the stockade. Another group of soldiers had followed us through, and more had thought of the same strategy on the other side of the road. Crouching low, below the windows that overlooked the paved brick road, we waited for a few minutes. Earnst looked at me.

'Grenades?' he asked.

I nodded. 'Throw it out and aim for the stockade,' I replied. 'Try and aim for something that can explode with debris. It will put them off for a few moments.'

The five other soldiers, including Felix, nodded.

'One... two... three... go!' I ordered.

Earnst and I stood, and each threw a grenade out of a window. Twisting the handle and quickly tossing it, I threw hard enough to reach more yards than I thought I could. Airborne for a few moments, it finally fell, clinking on the hard ground near a semi-wall of wooden barrels. Earnst's landed near the wooden poles that created the first section of the stockade.

Splitting the air with a large crack, the grenades exploded. Wooden pallets flew in the air, splintering and causing chaos for the Russian soldiers. Most fell from shock, stunned as they lay on the ground in wonder at what had happened. Yelling followed as they spotted us and the other soldiers in the nearby windows behind them, and began firing frivolously. Bullets pelted the building as we tried to hold them off, allowing the soldiers further south to advance forward. The air was pungent with a mixture of diesel and gunpowder. The smell of decaying bodies had not set in yet, but it would lie dormant in the air for a long time after this battle was done. Of that, I was sure.

The Russians were pressing on us hard. Our men further south had not pushed forward, leaving us vulnerable to be slaughtered like animals. I watched through a small gap in the wall as the Russians advanced on our position. They would wait until they were close enough for absolute accuracy, and with one move of their arms, they threw grenades into the buildings.

'Shit!' cried out Earnst. 'Everyone, find cover!'

Leaping to the corner of the room, the grenade went off, sending a shock wave coursing through the building. The blast blew a large portion of the rear wall out, which allowed us to move through to the back. Earnst turned to all of us, who lay on the ground, still stunned after the grenade's explosion.

'Let's move! Quickly! Out the back!'

Moving almost instantly, we jumped up and ran through the newly created opening and out to the back of the building. We were in a large area surrounded by a low wooden fence. A small bench sat under a large weeping willow, and a fountain had stopped running in the centre. We moved to the weeping willow and crouched low.

'Grenades ready!' Earnst yelled. 'Throw!'

Earnst and two other soldiers twisted the handle on their

grenades and threw them into the opening. Screams sounded from the building as the grenades exploded.

'Let's move!' commanded Earnst.

I had never seen him like this. He was not our superior, and yet he knew exactly what to do in a time when we needed it most.

'Where are we going?' asked one of the soldiers with us.

'We're going to double back around,' replied Earnst. 'We need to get back to where our men are. We're leading the Russians away from the stockade, which is better than letting them hold us off and eventually trap us in.' Earnst looked to the building as yelling sounded from its direction. 'We have to move quickly! Stay together. Go!'

We began moving northward, where we reached the small wooden fence. Earnst kicked it down and took a sharp right turn, veering back around to the next building. I looked back to see the Russian soldiers emerging from the building, now yards away from us. Two of the soldiers with us fired randomly in their general direction, making them dive for cover while we anxiously made our way into the neighbouring building.

We entered a large room that had a wooden staircase in the left corner and a doorway into another room straight ahead. It was dark in the room, the windows covered in once flowing elegant curtains, now reduced to ragged cloth, blocking any possibility of light coming through. It felt eerie, like an unnatural presence lingered somewhere close. The floorboards creaked and groaned beneath us as we moved quickly into the next room.

The next room was lighter and had three elegant, cushioned chairs that surrounded a fireplace, a table that held an assortment of bottles, and a glass decanter that sat gracefully on a patterned tray. As one of the soldiers ran past the table, he reached out and grabbed a bottle of whiskey, tucking it into his jacket.

Earnst stopped at the door.

'They're still out there. Quickly, move back. Through into the other room and up the stairs.'

He brushed past us and made for the staircase in the first room, and we followed after him. We got upstairs to see most of the wall, adjacent to the stairs, had collapsed. The wall that faced the main road was still sealed off, which gave us an advantageous amount of cover. We moved to the opening, which led into the next building and had also been hit, possibly by the same bomb. Leaping over the small gap, rubble fell to the ground as it chipped off the edge once our feet had made the jump.

Before Felix jumped, he stopped and fumbled for a grenade. As he gripped it, his leg splintered, a shower of blood spraying in our direction. Felix collapsed to the ground and screamed, writhing in pain. A Russian soldier had managed to catch up and shoot Felix before he jumped. A group of soldiers ran up the stairs and I looked to Felix. I clutched Earnst's arm as we both watched on, struck with horror. As the Russians reached the second floor, Felix looked at us and smiled. He twisted the handle of the grenade that he gripped tightly, gritting his teeth.

'Felix, no!' Earnst screamed.

He attempted to leap forward, but I hitched him back toward me, and plunged our bodies for cover. With one large explosion, the entire second floor was blown to a piled heap of splintered wood. The second storey began to collapse, the supporting walls crumbling. Earnst sobbed; his head nuzzled into my shoulder. I tried to keep myself composed, but the tears couldn't be defeated. They wouldn't be. My eyes flooded as I wailed.

After a few moments, I turned my head to Earnst.

'Earnst,' I said croakily, 'Earnst, we have to keep moving. We have to keep moving. Please, Earnst. Please.'

The four accompanying soldiers grabbed Earnst from beneath his arms and hauled him up. Earnst screamed.

'No! Felix, no! Please, no!'

The soldiers pulled Earnst toward the back of the room.

'Earnst,' I said softly. 'Remember what you taught me – there will be a time to mourn, I promise. But right now, we have to keep going. Please. I can't lose you, too.'

'Why did it have to be him? Why him? Why couldn't it be one of these fucking men?' Earnst's voice raised bitterly. '*Why him?*'

I hugged him tightly.

'I don't know, Earnst. I don't know.'

After a few seconds, I looked at the other soldiers who stared awkwardly. I held Earnst by his shoulders and looked him in his eyes. They were reddened, pools of tears still welling.

'We will get back to this, I promise. But right now, we have to go.'

In Oskar's case, I knew what had happened when I found his body, and I wasn't going to let it be Earnst's reality, too.

He nodded.

'Let's kill these bastards.'

I nodded, but deep down I didn't want to agree with him.

Rushing down the next flight of stairs, we checked the entranceway to see if any soldiers were nearby. I assumed the lead of the group as Earnst remained silent, still accepting the reality of Felix's passing. I tried to come to terms with it, but each time I did, my mind would reduce me to tears, and now wasn't the time. There were groups of them at the front, holding off at the stockade while our soldiers pressed them.

'We go out the east door and back out around southward,' I said.

As we made for the door at the back of the building, the front wall exploded, taking the front part of the second storey to the ground. We all flinched as we looked back to see dust rising up and blocking our view of any useful sights.

Deciding it wasn't useful to simply stand around and watch the rubble stay immobile, I ushered them out of the building and into the daylight once again. Looking at our surroundings, small yards with quaint wooden fences around them and once elegant gardens, we saw no Russian soldiers around and continued moving.

We reached our south position the soldiers had held and were still attempting to push the Russians back so we were able to move past the blockade. We approached a group of our own soldiers lying behind a mound of rubble, beside a small building that had most of its front façade missing.

'What's the situation, soldier?' asked one of them, lying on his stomach.

'The Russians attacked us as we were trying to cut them off from the east,' I replied. 'We were meant to cut them off so they would have nowhere to go and too many places to fend off.'

'What about the group that is attacking from the west?'

I shook my head.

'I don't know. We didn't see.'

The soldier looked down and frowned in thought.

'The tanks need a clearing to get through. I'll give the order to push them at full strength. Let's hope those soldiers attempting to attack from the west position can pull it off. What about the Russians who attacked you?'

'They were cut off at one of the buildings close to the blockade.' I looked down. 'We lost one of our own.'

The soldier put up his hand.

'That's war, son, if you hadn't noticed.'

His words were like daggers. He was all too familiar with this. He soon dismissed our woes and changed the subject.

'There may have been more soldiers following. What direction did you come from?'

I turned and pointed to the group of buildings a few yards away.

'We need to defend those buildings at all costs. If they get through, they can take out our men from behind and damage us severely.'

He shook the arms of the other soldiers that were lying next to him and ran to the buildings. We all followed and got into position. Crouching low, we waited for any sign of Russian soldiers. None. We waited for a few more minutes. Still nothing. Then we heard it – screaming and yelling from our soldiers as they dived for cover, shielding themselves with their arms.

The Russians had moved to the second storeys of the buildings that ran parallel with the main road, on our side of the blockade. The soldier who commanded us, turned and yelled at one of his soldiers crouched beside a tank. The soldier knocked on the tank and yelled, then moved to the next one and gave more orders.

The two tanks began to roll forward, and soon the mass of tanks that lined the south of the suburbs began to roll in. The large gun moved upward and pointed at the buildings, then fired. Stone and wood rained down on the ground, and the Russian soldiers moved quickly out of the buildings if they had not already been obliterated.

Firing large shells and collapsing numerous buildings, the tanks rolled onto the main road and toward the blockade. The first tank exploded as it hit a mine placed strategically on the road, and the second immediately stopped. Trapped in the middle of the road, the tank sat idle until our soldiers poured in.

After two long hours, fighting with every core of our body, our soldiers broke the line and poured over the stockade. The tanks followed after, and soon we were flooding the streets of the once busy suburbia.

Soldiers moved through buildings and tried to keep from the roads unless accompanying a tank. No other blockades had been built for hundreds of yards, allowing us to easily push our way through the streets without any chaos erupting.

The Russians fought with the ferocity of beasts, emerging from cellars underneath the buildings or the sewer pipes, catching us by surprise. They would wait until we were in close proximity before throwing grenades and forcing us to move back, lest we wanted an early call with Death.

The last stockade was large, with walls of sandbags stretching as far as the eye could see. The road that ran northwards was blocked off, and along the road that ran from east to west, a line of barbed wire and sandbags had been placed in front of the buildings, with guns facing southward. These buildings were tall – four storeys that overlooked from where we had emerged. The Russians were ready.

Concentration Camp

The air is potent. The air is dangerous, intoxicated. Potent with the smell of death, it lingers around and refuses to leave. Too much death, everywhere. Even from afar I can smell it – the world is ripe with it.

News travels from the east, where soldiers fight a bloody battle. Is it their death I can smell? The guards are jealous, wanting to fight for glory rather than to guard already dead men. They snicker and hiss amongst one another; they want nothing more than to be already dead men, for a few moments of glory.

I hear of the bloody battle that is underway in the place they call Stalingrad. They do not suspect that perhaps it is a foolish errand; a quest that will soon show itself for nothing more than wishful attainment. A desirable observation from the men who do nothing but sit behind a desk, their eyes widened, and their hands clenched tightly as they look on in angst. I laugh at them. For they do not see it yet, but when they are on their death bed, they will.

Death is a natural step in the order of things, but it can come unnaturally, and at an unnatural time. These men are meeting Death unnaturally, at the hands of another man. It will never do if each man turned against the other, for no one would be left. And yet, here I am, a tool for their propaganda, a weapon for their cause. And all I have to do is stay here.

I can hear the screams from miles away; they are the screams of the world. They are the screams of the innocent, the screams of the once hopeful. And soon, when their screams die, so too does their cause. Men fight wars because they see it as duty. But what one's true duty is the fellowship of each man to another – for their children, and their children's children.

It is sheer stupidity that one would seek glory in war, for all one will ever get is death and destruction – only the glory of a sadist.

And it is sheer selfishness that would allow the wanting of the demise of another – that was what I was built for. But as the world around me tickles my ear, as the elements begin to break me, I no longer feel the just need for it. Soon, I will be of no use and I will be pulled down. The horrors of my walls will forever be remembered but will no longer scar the surface of the world.

I am the voice of the stony cold walls that house the prisoners. I am the voice that was meant to break them. I was built to do my duty, not to speak of the horrors. I was built to withstand time. I was built to last forever. But forever is no more.

CHAPTER 34

September 15, 1942

The buildings were lined at the bottom with one, long, singular stockade. Barbed wire was rolled from east to west, following the wooden poles that crossed one another; the sharpened ends facing our direction. Russian soldiers crouched behind a line of sandbags, with their guns mounted over the top. Snipers were positioned in the buildings' second and third storeys, and past the buildings were more blockades in the event that we broke through the first.

'This is going to be hell,' remarked Earnst. 'I can't do this.'

'*Shit*,' exclaimed one soldier who stood to my left. 'How are we supposed to get through that?'

'I think the idea is that we don't,' I replied. I turned to Earnst. 'You can do this. You and I, together.'

He nodded.

'Tanks at the ready!' yelled one of the officers that stood a few yards behind. His voice echoed through the city, splitting the silence that had settled over as we looked on in awe and angst.

'Guns up! We're going to break through that stockade, soldiers!' He held his right hand in the air, and within a quick second, threw it down. 'Send them to hell! Let's go!'

Our soldiers must have looked like ants as we spilled out and into the buildings opposite the stockade. Getting to cover, we used the windows and doorways to peer from inside the buildings and shot at wherever there seemed to be something moving. Bullets rained down as the Russians began to fire. The turret guns were mounted on the stockade and the heavy bullets broke through the thick walls with debris flying through the air.

Our tanks opened fire at the tall buildings. Their thick shells blasted through the walls but didn't do enough to bring them down. They continued to fire, providing enough cover for some of the soldiers to move into safer positions. Russian soldiers in the multiple storeys scrambled, and shortly after, through the windows, emerged rocket launchers.

'*Jesus Christ*,' exclaimed one of the soldiers. 'We have to move! They have bazookas!'

I heard orders bellowed in the distance from one of our commanding officers.

'Pull the tanks back! Get them back!'

But it was too late. The Russians pulled the triggers on their rocket launchers, aiming directly for the tanks, and sent waves of rockets soaring to the ground. Multiple rockets hit several tanks at once, the metal monsters exploding on impact. Four of our tanks were taken out, and the Russians began to reload.

The commanding officer screamed again. 'Take out those bazookas!'

The remaining tanks aimed for the second and third storeys and opened fire. As the shells impacted the stone walls, they were reduced to rubble as holes began to appear behind the smoke. The tanks fired again. All soldiers focused their fire on the second and third storeys.

'How the hell did they get their hands on bazookas?' screamed the commanding officer, yet again. 'This better be the last of them.'

We remained positioned in the building, assisting efforts to repel anymore bazooka attacks. I was accompanied by Earnst and three other soldiers, two of whom were with us beforehand. The other soldier was young, with thick, curly hair the colour of gold. He sat in the corner of the room with his knees bent to his chest as he clutched his gun tight. I ran over and grabbed him by the shoulder.

'If you stay in the same place for long enough, eventually those bullets will hit you,' I said. 'You have to move.'

He looked up at me, his eyes watery with fear.

'I can't do it. It's too much.'

'Listen to me. What's your name?'

'Oskar.'

I paused for a moment as my heart seemed to drop.

'What?' I stuttered.

'Ritter,' he replied.

I stared at the ground for a few moments, shaking as I breathed heavily. *This war is killing me,* I thought. *I'm going insane. Don't do this again. Not now.* I shook my head and tried to focus.

'Ritter, we all have to stay together. I'm not going to leave you. Do you understand? Stay close to me and keep moving.'

'Please, I can't do this. I don't want to be here.'

I pointed to Earnst.

'See him over there? He lost a brother yesterday. He's in no condition to fight. We haven't mourned. We haven't had time. We have to fight. I don't want to be here, either, but I am. I got myself into this storm, and now I have to fight my way out of it to stay alive. These are your brothers now, whether you like it or not. They're mine, too. We have to stick together, do you understand? We're in this together, now.'

He nodded with a heavy breath and I helped him to his feet. His legs shook with so much ferocity that I thought he would collapse again. I helped him by his arm as I watched his legs, until he took a few steps and regained his composure.

'Let's go,' I said.

We moved back to where Earnst and the two other soldiers were, crouching under the windows that faced north, looking at the great face of the Russian stockade. They moved up and down, shooting as they tried to avoid the unwanted bullets that constantly battered the building.

I crouched low under the window that was directly in the centre of the room. The moment I attempted to peer over the window ledge, the Russians' guns all seemed to turn on me. I shot down to the ground immediately and looked over at Earnst.

'We're not going to get out of this,' I yelled over the gunfire.

Earnst half stood to look out of the window, fired his gun numerous times and then crouched back down again. He turned to me.

'I'm not dying here, Hans,' he replied, 'and neither are you, or anyone else in this building. I won't let it happen, again. We'll get out of it, somehow. The Russians will run out of ammunition soon enough.'

'What if we run out first?'

He stood over the ledge and fired again, then returned to crouching beside the wall.

'Then we find another way to beat them.'

He sounded angry, and I knew he was using the anger from Felix's death against the Russians. The feeling of guilt washed over me as he said those words – *another way to beat them*. It was evident we were not leaving here until we had won; until every Russian, whether a soldier or civilian, was dead and this city was brought to ashes. The number of lives I alone, had taken, was unknown to me, but I knew I had sent too many to the dark abyss beyond life.

As I leaned against the wall, I shut my eyes and breathed heavily. Everything around me transcended reality, and I was soon in a world of my own. Oskar appeared before me, smiling, and calling my name.

'Hans! At whatever cost, I will protect you. I'm not going to let you die, understand me?'

I nodded and smiled at him, crying as I saw his face fade away into darkness.

Mother came forth, holding Edith's hand who stood shyly, suckling her thumb.

'Johan, my dear boy. You're doing this for us, I know. But are the other lives worth it for ours alone? I love you, sweet boy. Father would have been proud.'

Felix stood behind her, smiling at me.

'Thank you for everything, brother.'

'Mother!' I exclaimed. 'Felix. Please, no! Don't leave me.' I sobbed, stating quietly, 'Don't leave me.'

They both vanished.

I opened my eyes to Earnst's hands locked on to my shoulders, shaking me.

'Hans! Hans!'

I blinked a few times, then squinted at him.

'Earnst? I don't want them to go.'

'Who?'

I looked at him and began to sob.

'It's my fault Felix is dead. It's mine.'

Earnst hugged me tightly.

'No, it isn't, Hans. It's no one's fault. No one. You gave me strength to push on, so now use it for yourself. Don't let yourself down. Come, look outside.'

He pointed out the window. I stood up and looked out to see one of the three-storey buildings had completely collapsed, allowing a section of the stockade to be breached. Russian soldiers climbed out slowly from under the rubble as our soldiers opened fire. Like liquid, our soldiers moved across the wide brick road and broke through the blockade, over the collapsed building. The nearby building to the left groaned heavily as the supports began to bend and rip apart. The wood cracked immediately as the beams that stood next to the collapsed building, fell under the weight of the rest of the building. The old structure fell to the pile of rubble already there from the other building and crashed to the ground. Its walls crumbled and the roof, which was dome shaped, made of metal and glass, shattered as it hit the ground with a blinding force. Russian soldiers ran in the opposite direction, trying desperately not to get caught under the building, screaming orders and yelling for their comrades to get out of the way.

'This is it,' said Earnst. 'For Felix.'

I looked at Ritter, who gave me an anxious stare.

'It will be fine,' I said. 'Stay with me, and stay low. We'll both be fine.'

He nodded, but I could tell he was still frightened. He witnessed me break down, crying into Earnst's arms. I knew I lied to him, telling him that we put aside all fear for this war. We had all weakened. The demons inside were breaking me apart, disintegrating my soul. I didn't know who I was now, and I was trying to convince a young boy that he had no right to be frightened. Who was I? No amount of soothing talk would let anyone, that was as frightened as him, think his was going to be fine. But he persisted and held his gun at the ready as he stood next to me. We waited for Earnst, who was watching out of the doorway to see when it was safe to go.

'Get ready. Okay, now!'

We sprinted out of the building and across the road. Hundreds of our soldiers moved across the opening, piling out from the south buildings. I made sure Ritter was with me and we made our way to the rubble, where the dust lingered in the air. The stench of gunpowder, burning wood and metal was heavy in the air, and one whiff caught me off guard as I erupted into a coughing fit, covering my mouth from the dust.

'Hans, what's wrong?' asked Ritter.

'Nothing, just don't breathe in too heavily. The air is toxic, I swear.'

'Oh,' he said surprised. He shook his head. 'I won't.'

I looked around to find Earnst and the other two, but he was nowhere around.

'Did you see where Earnst went?' I asked.

Ritter shook his head. I looked around but couldn't find him.

'Let's keep moving.'

I covered my mouth and nose as smoke rose around us, and hot embers glowed amongst the cracked cement and broken bricks. Ritter followed, making our way north and finally catching up with some of our own soldiers. I looked over to see a familiar face in the distance. As I squinted, the face became clearer. *Felix.* I blinked hard and he was gone. I desperately wanted to yell out, to see him and hug him. Felix's innocence, when it came to anything intelligible, was somewhat comforting at times; he was just like a child willing to help in any way he could. And that's what I needed. I needed sanity disguised as innocence – I just wanted it to be normal. But that was soon waning into dead hope.

Ritter and I moved quickly over the rubble and to the rest of the soldiers. We took a sharp left turn into a row of buildings that were only one storey. Moving through the rooms, a number of our soldiers had entered the building ahead of us. As we walked into a large room, I quickly turned to see guns pointed directly at me to my right. They lowered as we realised they were German, and we nodded at each other. They ushered us to keep moving as they held their defensive position.

One of the officers stopped us at the door, holding his hand up as he looked behind us to where we came from. Several other soldiers had followed in, and now waited with us.

'We attack from the west side,' he said, while peering out of the doorway into the distance.

He cocked his head to the side. In an instant, he dived in the air and took us all down to the ground with him as his arms hooked around us. The wall was blown to pieces and bits had surged through the air and landed heavily on us. The dust was like a volcano, spewing ash as the room darkened.

Coughing and spluttering, we got up slowly; some limping and others clutching wounds. The officer looked to us, then looked back to the large hole that was now present in the wall.

'Let's get moving!'

The dust that kicked up now blocked our view of anyone outside the building. The officer pushed past and backtracked through the building. We followed. He looked around frantically, desperately trying to find an opening of some sort that could be used as an escape.

'Shit!' he screamed as he flung his arms in the air and then threw them to his sides. 'Find an exit! All of you! Go!'

Scrambling around the building to find any door or window that was easy enough to get through, shouts came from where the explosion had gone off.

'Russians! They're moving in!'

Their tactics were brutal. Waiting to get close to our soldiers, luring them in and, when we were finally within a short range from each other, they would twist the handles of their grenades and throw them our way. We would dive for cover as they landed nearby and set off, deafening us for a few moments. We knew what was coming.

They pushed us through the building, throwing grenades in the rooms and leaving us with nowhere to go but back from where we came. It was difficult to navigate our way back through the long halls of the building, the connecting rooms, and the similar layout, without feeling lost for most of the time.

But two of the soldiers had volunteered to guide us as we fought off the oncoming ruthless Russians – and I think they were the lucky ones. Bullets flew past, and many a time I had thought that perhaps I was ready to die, but as luck would have it, I was still kicking and determined to get out of this.

We eventually made our way to where we had first entered, and I felt a sudden sense of relief as we ran out into the open space – but that was short lived as the Russians were still in pursuit. Another explosion sounded and we dropped to the ground, but it was nowhere near us. It had come from the building and no Russians were emerging from it. A large crack in the air and a bullet shot directly next to my leg.

'Sniper!' screamed the officer.

Another crack, this time hitting one of the soldiers, killing him instantly.

'Get to cover!'

Where were we supposed to go? The building north was full of Russians, and the buildings everywhere around us were now just rubble. Smoke rose around us and blocked the afternoon sun, with a cold darkness setting over the city.

The sniper continued to fire. I shot up, looked around for Ritter, who was lying low on the ground. I grabbed his arm and pulled him along as I ran for cover. A large cement slab that stood upright from the building's collapse, provided enough cover from the sniper. Crouching low, I turned to Ritter.

As I was about to speak, the officer called from the building, 'The building is clear!'

I raised an eyebrow.

'How did that happen?' asked Ritter.

I shook my head. 'I don't know, but we have to get there from out of the sniper's sight. We're going to have to run.'

Ritter's eyes widened.

'I can't do it,' he said shakily. 'I can't.'

'Ritter, if we don't get to that building, we're going to be stuck here. We have to get there. I'll make sure you're not going to be harmed. I promise.'

Ritter's breathing was heavy. He didn't trust a word I said. But he eventually nodded reluctantly.

'When I count to three, we run. Both of us, together. Are you ready?'

Another nod, but this time he was more determined.

'On the count of three. One… two… three… go!'

I grabbed Ritter's arm to make sure he followed behind. We ran as quickly as we could to the building, as the sniper shot at us over and over. Cracks sounded each time, and then a slight pause as he reloaded his rifle before firing again. We were feet away from the door when another shot was fired, but this time it was followed by a scream. I turned to see Ritter, who pulled away from me and clutched his arm, falling to the ground. Blood poured down his hand and dripped through his fingers. He looked up at me, tears filling his eyes, as though it was a silent plea to help him.

I leapt to where he lay and heaved him up by his torso. Half carrying him to the door, I hoped that the sniper wouldn't have enough time to shoot one last time. Taking a leap, I pulled Ritter through the doorway and into the building, safely out of sight of the gunman. Gently I sat Ritter down against the far wall and crouched beside him.

'It hurts so much,' said Ritter. 'The pain is too much.'

'Let me look at it,' I replied.

Gently, I lifted his hand from the wound to much pain and aggravation. I looked over the gunshot wound, which was on his upper right arm. It was still bleeding, with the red patch getting larger on his uniform. He hissed in pain as I tried to move his uniform.

'Sorry. We have to stop the bleeding.'

'He needs medical attention!' said a soldier who had come up behind me.

'There is none,' I snapped back.

'Apply pressure to the wound, and then send him to a medical tent. Now!'

'And who are you to order me to do that?'

'Sergeant Korden, soldier!'

I fell silent and nodded. 'Yes, sir. Sorry.'

'You will not address me like that, again. Understood?'

'Yes, Sergeant.' I hung my head low, pretending to examine the wound, but doing it more out of shame.

'Now, go.' He waved his hand at Ritter to leave. I stood up to accompany him, but the sergeant stopped me. 'Not you. He can go on his own.'

'Someone needs to help him get back,' I argued.

'I said, you are to stay *here*. We need every able soldier to push our offensive. He was shot in the arm, not the leg. He can move as well as anyone else. He goes alone.'

The sergeant turned and walked away, and I was left to address Ritter.

'I'm sorry,' I started. 'If I could go with you…'

'It's fine, Hans,' replied Ritter. 'If it wasn't for you, I think I'd be dead. Don't be sorry, there's no need to be. You made sure I pulled through like every other soldier.'

Ritter put his hand out. I grabbed it and shook it passionately.

'Thank you,' he said gently. 'Thank you.'

I smiled and nodded.

'You're very welcome, Ritter. Look after yourself.'

He turned, clutching his arm, and made for the doorway. Glancing either way out of the door, he took a deep breath and began to sprint. I watched until he was out of sight, behind the rubble. I smiled a little, and sighed. Within seconds of reaching the rubble, however, a gunshot went off – the crack of a sniper rifle. My smile had gone.

Dear Felix

Dear Felix,

I don't know what I'm going to do. I don't know what I'm supposed to do. And to be honest, I don't know if I can keep going. Your smile, your innocent curiosity – they are no longer. Earnst is tearing apart inside. He needs you now more than ever. I need you now more than ever. You saved us – you took your own life so that we may continue our own. I can never repay you and knowing that it is now impossible; that kills me even more.

Each night, the tears persist. I can't stop, knowing I will never hear your voice again. We started rough, pretending to be brutes who hated everyone. You did it better than I. But somehow, we stood by each other. You were there when Earnst and I fought, as though you were afraid we would never reconcile. You comforted me in my darkest hours and reminded me in my happiest – you were my brother.

As the years go on, I will never forget you. I promise you this. I will never forget your calming voice and your childish heart – a heart of love that was worth loving in return. I will never forget the love of a brother you gave, reminding me that love endures greater than anything – including this war. You loved me like a brother, and I will forever love you like mine. Wherever you are, you will never be forgotten.

Although we didn't see eye to eye, I forgive you. I haven't forgiven myself yet, but I hope you can forgive me. Your view may have been deceived, but I hope you weren't deceived in our friendship. My people are just like yours – we are one. We're all human, and that's all you knew – you did what you were told was right, and I can live with that. I can live with it, because we became far more than comrades, we became family.

And as I look to the night sky, the stars glowing in their millions, you will join Father as my family. They will remind me. You're part of our family now, and no matter what happens, they forgive you, as they have forgiven everyone.

I love you forever, brother.

Love,
Hans

CHAPTER 35

September 16, 1942

The grain elevator stood just beyond the suburban area. A solid, concrete building, the large structure stood tall, stretching to the sky. Our army was to attack from the south, and the men who stormed from the west would attack from there. Our artillery had been positioned far from the elevator, with our leFH Howitzers lined up and ready to fire four-inch shells onto the building. When we first reached the elevator, we couldn't see many Russian soldiers holding it. There were forty, at least, but no more than seventy, perhaps. Our confidence had grown, but it was at a cost. As we underestimated the desperate fight the Russians would throw back, we were forced into a world that we didn't understand – our forces, everything we threw at them, they defended the grain elevator every second and every bit of will they had left.

Two days after our first attack on the grain elevator, we were still pushing the Russians, and still getting nowhere. That day, we launched ten attacks on the elevator, all of which failed. I felt my will to keep going fail, day after day, as the miserable battles stretched out. I watched soldiers who I knew, die; I had sat with them, ate with them, talked with them, and marched with them. And within only days, most had lost their lives. But Felix and Ritter lingered in the back of my mind, joining the memory of Oskar.

Each day, I would awake from a sleep that only lasted a few minutes, not wanting to face the world – or what was going to be left of it. This war had drained whatever I had left. It was impossible to smile, even in our victories. It was impossible to feel anything but life slowly trickling away, my will to live dwindling as death seamed more and more opportune.

After another two days, we launched our most ferocious attack yet. At noon, twelve of our tanks approached from the south, and the Russians had already depleted their stockpile of antitank rifles and grenades.

Approaching from two sides, our tanks began to fire on the grain elevator. The Russians fired their machine guns at the infantry to stop us from entering the elevator. From our position, we could see the Russian soldiers ducking as concrete rained down on them, our tanks blasting the strong structure to oblivion.

One of the tanks hit a maxim, blowing it up along with its gunner, and a second was hit by shrapnel, bending the metal to make it unusable – there was only one light machine gun left. Our soldiers were to move forward, in front of the tanks, and assault the elevator.

There were over two hundred of us, with machine guns in hand, approaching the elevator. Cautiously moving, we threw grenades in front of us and then ran forward, trying to distract the Russian soldiers so we had a clean run before approaching the concrete giant. Flames licked through the holes blasted in the elevator, as the grain caught on fire. Some of the Russian soldiers caught our grenades and threw them back, forcing us to dive in different directions as they bombarded the earth. They gritted their teeth as they seemed to clasp our grenades in their hands, fighting to their last breath.

After pushing through, with the tanks continuing to fire on the building as we moved forward, we entered the building from the left side. The smoke was thick, and the only indicator that the enemy was near was the noise of their breathing as we got closer.

Firing at anything that made a sound, we had no idea whether we were firing at our own or at the enemy. I stayed low, hoping they would pass over and we would finally be finished.

While lying low, I almost screamed out as a hand grabbed me by the wrist. But as my face got closer to theirs, I noticed it was all too familiar – Earnst.

'Stay close,' he whispered. 'Don't make any loud noises. The Russians are moving to the south of the building. If we move north and to the west, near the edge, we can avoid them. It's too dangerous to fight in this darkness.'

I nodded, though I was sure he couldn't see me do so, and so I replied, 'I'm right behind you.'

Earnst and I moved to the north and then westward, trying to move near an exit, knowing our tanks were there to protect us if needed. The building was surrounded by tanks only a hundred yards away, as our soldiers moved through, wiping out any Russian soldiers that were left. That night, we took the elevator as the Russians broke out to the south, our tanks moving back and forth to the north and east of it. Corpses sprawled across the ground throughout the elevator, stained with blood and dirt. Their eyes had lost colour, but they still seemed as though they were alive, cursing us each step we took; almost watching us. We had finally taken it. But at a cost.

During the days, dogfights in the sky could be seen, as smoke trails followed planes that had been hit and plummeted to the ground. The Russians had taken areas we took only two days ago and the battles started over again as we struggled to maintain our grip on the city. Our soldiers were dying, not just in the front line, but from the rear, too. The Russians had moved around us and now threatened our soldiers as they moved through the ruins, unbeknownst to us, and began to fire.

Through the thickness of the smoke, we could make out a few figures as it cleared, though the smoke was constant, with fires burning throughout the city – or what was left of it.

We were caught unaware at one point when the Russian

soldiers had remained hidden in the cellars and the second storeys of multiple buildings, launching attacks against us as we marched through. The fights were far fiercer than to begin with, in short range of each other. A number of times it came down to knife fights and bayonets. We could see the other soldier's eyes, we looked at each other before we knew it was over for one of us; we felt the warm breath of the other on our cheeks, and we touched their hardened skin before plunging the sharpened bayonet into their stomach.

Each time we did so, I felt ever guiltier. It was a far different game now. From a distance, they are just figures – they are unknown to you, and it stays that way. After a time of grumbling to myself that it was for my own safety, I found the courage – or the evil – inside of me, enough to pull the trigger from afar. Now, it was reduced to looking them straight in the eye and taking their life. You could not cower; you could not whimper; for if you did, you would be the one that waited as Death took you to the darkness.

To look at a soldier in the eye, to see them, touch them, and think of what life they may have, or would have, it took every piece of self-worth away to kill them. They may have had children, they may have had a wife, they may have been a gentle person, and yet, on the battlefield, in the ruins of a once great city, within moments, you had the choice of life or death – and you would choose anything to live.

I would flirt with Death often, hoping we would soon unite, and I would be spared anymore of this wretched war. When given the chance, I would cower at the thought and do what I had to do – as though I looked Death in the eye and could not look any longer.

The fighting was intense, and as time went on, every soldier, whether German or Russian, became far more desperate to end this, doing what needed to be done.

I was caught in a small building, backing into the corner as a Russian soldier held his bayonet up, scowling at me. I walked backwards until I felt the stony wall on my fingertips, knowing I had nowhere to go. I looked at him, hoping he would change his mind for some miraculous reason, but he continued to walk towards me. With one lunge of his bayonet, the sharp steel hurled towards my stomach. I grabbed the end of the bayonet where it was still rounded and diverted it to the left. Grabbing the bayonet with one hand, I thrust my right leg into the air, making contact with the soldier's stomach and winding him. As he dropped to the ground, his grip on the bayonet loosened, and with a quick heave, I relieved it from him completely. Hurling the back end of the bayonet in the air, I then swung it back around, sharply hitting the soldier in the cheek with a large crack.

Slowly, he looked up anxiously. His eyes showed that he, too, was scared of dying, and knew it was about to be over. But I knew I could change that. The decision, I knew, would be devastating if it went wrong – it would mean my life. I looked him in the eye, then shut mine slowly as I took a deep breath. I held up the bayonet, and the soldier turned to look away. I opened my hands, and let the bayonet drop to the floor.

'*I can't do this,*' I whispered to myself.

The soldier turned and looked, then squinted as he was coming to terms with what just happened. I knew that letting this soldier live would never make up for the soldiers' lives I had taken in the past, but somehow, I felt compelled to do it. I nodded to the soldier, then brought my clenched fist up to my chest. He continued to stare at me, as though contemplating whether he should kill me or not – I hoped like hell it was the latter.

The soldier stood and approached me, my legs now quivering as I was beginning to think I had made the largest mistake. We were nose to nose, looking at each other. Outstretching his arms, he grabbed me and hugged for a moment, then put his arm on my shoulder and nodded with a solemn look. He picked up the bayonet and exited the building, not looking back. Regardless of the small, hopeful moment that we had in the building; it wasn't enough to deter any other soldiers from the fighting – as though I was naive enough to think that each person was somehow affected by everything I did.

The sun set, the moon settled over the city, the stars glinting in the dark sky, and still the fighting raged on. The sun would rise, the sky boasting shades of pink and orange, and still the battle continued. There was no rest for the wicked – no rest for the already dead.

CHAPTER 36

October 3, 1942

They called it the fight for Red October. No soldier thought they would get out alive – we presumed that Death was calling us, whispering to us subtly, but enough for us to inch further and further to it. In the last week of September, our soldiers advanced across the ruins of the workers' settlement, and lay siege to Red October – the large industrial sector. Earnst had times where he would cry to me, hoping the tears would heal in the mourning process. He begged for Felix to come back, and I was all too familiar with it – I still missed Oskar, but I tried to convince myself otherwise.

Each time the Red Army's soldiers were cut down in numbers, it seemed to grow more. We took up positions in a ravine in the flatlands filled with bushes. Some were large enough to conceal tanks and a number of soldiers, but this one held only a few of our men. A gully sat adjacent to our location, where the tanks and a larger number of soldiers were positioned, allowing us to carry out a full-scale attack. As we waited, we could easily see the chimneys towering in the air. Dead soldiers littered the ground, and we knew this was the last great assault, and it was either going to be a sweet victory or a bitter defeat.

≡

The past two days had proven difficult to penetrate the factory sector. The Russians had machine gunners lined along the buildings, leaving us to wonder where they were getting them from. We were so certain we had crippled their defence, and yet each time more recruits sprang from what seemed like nowhere.

Our battalion had attempted to attack four times, and each time we hit the ground hard, the Russian snipers were shooting anyone so foolish to openly show their face. Our soldiers were stunned at the sight of female soldiers in the Russian army – they were mainly the snipers. Yelling in the Russian tongue, their voices were distinct from the male, and yet they seemed to be the fiercer. They bellowed orders just as the men did, and did it with such vigour and determination. We pushed furiously at the factories, hoping to make any sort of small incision that would allow us to pour our forces behind their defensive line.

I often wonder if there is such thing as good and evil – whether it is real, or whether it is just a myth perpetuated by mankind over the years. And whenever I think of the conundrum, all I have to do is look in the mirror.

The men that stand by my side have one objective – the annihilation of the Russians and the spread of Nazi doctrine – which also happens to incorporate the annihilation of my people. And yet, somehow, over the years, I find myself easily defending those who defend the doctrine. And whenever I wonder if evil is real, I look at myself now, and who I used to be, and somehow, I can't help feeling that it is real, and alive inside of me. I am part of that evil.

The failure of our army to cut off the Russian supply route via the Volga River meant that each night, Russian soldiers would receive more supplies, including soldiers. Easily identifiable with their fur ushankas and thick coats, the Russian army seemed to swarm the city, no apparent victory in sight.

The Führer had suspended all operations on the Eastern Front, except for Stalingrad – it was now the sole mission for every German soldier present in Russian territory. Our attack force on Red October was bolstered by four battalions of new engineers and experts in demolition, and in addition, we received ninety thousand men and three hundred tanks. The fight for Red October was going to be fought hard by both sides, and no one, not even our commanding officers, knew who would find victory amongst the chaos.

Our soldiers pushed at the Russians, forcing our way into the factories and laying siege to those that opposed us. The Russians had positioned themselves in the upper storeys of the large factory buildings, with snipers shooting down our men in an instant. Our men still held Mamayev Kurgan, the crucial point that overlooked the entire city from the south where the ruined residential suburbs lay waste, to the north where our soldiers pushed at the Russians in the factory district. That seemed to be our only advantage. But they knew their city, and they were more determined to defend it than we were to take it.

Within weeks we had gained the tractor plant, north of Red October. We were now coming at the Russians from the north, south and west. But to the east lay a cliff on the edge of the Volga River, and it was still at their advantage. Supplies were still carried through the Volga to the Russians that fought in the factories, and to the soldiers that were positioned on the far bank of the river across from the city.

The river stretched a mile wide, giving the Russians an advantage on the other side where mass artillery was ranged and firing on our soldiers. They were safe from our attacks as we attempted to wipe them out, but the range was cut short as we were under heavy fire from the factory district. Shells flew through the air and hit the ground as the Russian artillery continued to bombard us. The earth was constantly uplifting by artillery fire, a constant rain of dirt blinding us as the landscape continuously shifted.

As we looked to the skies for the Luftwaffe, hoping they would take them out with ease and accuracy, each passing plane was just as easily a German plane as it was a Russian plane. We no longer dominated the skies as we struggled on the ground and in the air. The artillery fired heavily down on us as we ran through the ruins of a once majestic and industrial building, only to be brought to the ground with one explosion.

I ran alongside another soldier, who kept me by his side. We ran through the crumbled buildings, ducking under broken steel structures and jumping over piles of rubble and broken clay, dodging any bullets that we could. As we ran, I could hear the sound of the distant artillery guns firing. I looked up at the sky, spotting three shells that were soaring through the air, heading straight for us. I grabbed the soldier's arm.

'Find cover!'

As I pointed upward, he looked and quickly grabbed me. We ran into a building that was crumbling, but one side had fallen on top of a pile of an already ruined building that had previously stood and allowed enough shelter for a few soldiers. A large metal beam ran along the ground as we made our way inside. I don't know how – I had kept my eye on it the whole time – but as I stepped on the beam, my boot slipped and I fell to the ground, smashing my knee on the hard metal. I screamed out in pain, but the soldier cupped his hand over my mouth, muffling any noise that was made. I squeezed my eyes shut and breathed heavily, trying to make the agony go away.

'You're going to be fine,' said the soldier. 'Just breathe.'

I continued to breathe heavily, then limped over to the pile of dirt and clay that had mounded up and sat quietly. We waited, hearing yelling outside.

'Get to cover!'

'Artillery!'

Within a few moments of those screams, the building rocked and the earth beneath us shook as the shells hit the ground. The explosions ruptured the ground and the deafening sound seemed to make the air vibrate. The ruined structure began to groan, and the soldier looked at me.

'We have to get out of here. This building will collapse any second.'

I stood up, taking a few moments as I hopped on my good leg, then began to limp for the exit. The building continued to creak and moan, until the top wooden beam that held most of the roof, collapsed. The heavy wood hit the ground hard, and along with it came a scream from the soldier. I stood there, trying to see through the dust.

As the dust settled, my eyes became fixed on the soldier as he lay on the ground, with the wooden beam pushing firmly down on his stomach. Blood had begun to seep, and the wood soon became stained in red. I ran over to the soldier and attempted to lift the wooden beam off, but it refused to move. Grunting in pain, the soldier looked at me.

'It's not going to move.'

'It will, we just need more men,' I replied anxiously.

He shook his head.

'No, we don't. Even if it does lift off, my stomach is crushed. I'm not getting out of here alive.'

I bit my lip in frustration, fighting off the tears.

'But do me one favour,' the soldier continued. 'Get out your pistol.'

I began to shake my head.

'No, I won't do it.'

'Please. Do this for me.'

'You can't ask me to do this. I won't. I can't.'

'What's your name?'

'Hans,' I said quietly, after a moment's thought.

'Hans, I am asking you to grant me a quick death. Please. I won't hold it against you in the afterlife, or wherever we may be. But please grant me this.'

I shakily pulled out my pistol and aimed it at the soldier's head, clenching my teeth as I let my emotion run free.

'I'm sorry…'

'Rikard.'

'*Rikard.*'

My finger slowly pulled back the trigger, until the shot was fired. A large bang, amidst the chaos outside, loudly ringing inside the small enclosure. I wanted to sob, but was cut short as the building continued to collapse around me. Wiping away any noticeable tears, I rushed for the exit and dived outside. The building collapsed, and as I looked around, our soldiers were still running through the ruins, not giving a second thought to anything that had happened. I rubbed my face and ran on.

≡

Pontoons ran across the river, connecting the islands that were opposite the factory district to the riverbank, allowing Russian soldiers to move across the river far more easily. By late October, large ice floes began to drift along the Volga, southward. As large as ships, the ice floes were unstoppable and made the river completely unnavigable.

The temperatures dropped to well below zero as the snow began to fall and the water froze over. We had experienced the harsh Russian winters before, and we knew how devastating they were. The sharp icy winds blew against our faces and numbed our lips, our fingers unable to move when the frost set in. Our faces began to peel as the winds blasted us, fighting to hold us back.

Accompanied by a tank that we escorted through the streets, a group of our soldiers pushed forward through the workers' suburbs, just south of Red October. Our orders were to make our way through the streets of the southern suburbs, eliminating any enemy at all costs, and bring the tank to the point of Red October, from the south. Having a presence from the south would mean that our forces would be attacking from the north, west and directly south, forcing the Russians into one small location on the cliff edge.

The Russians no longer screamed, *'For the Motherland!'*. No, they crept in the shadows and hunted us like animals in the streets, patiently walking with our guns cocked in the air and ready to fire.

We were in a small street with two-storey buildings on either side towering above, as we slowly walked along the brick paved road, looking in every direction. The slightest sound in the distance would set one of the soldiers off as they whipped their heads around and aimed, only to find it was a piece of a crumbling building that had finally fallen out of its loose socket.

As we walked, the tank rolling close behind, the guns still fired in the distance. Every plane that passed by, we looked up to confirm it was one of ours, or face the risk of a bombardment, had it been the Russians.

I was unfamiliar with all the soldiers, only recognising a few faces from a few months ago, but not enough to converse with. But in these times, talking wasn't an option as we crept around, waiting for unsuspecting Russian soldiers to jump out and shoot us down. The buildings that stood were badly damaged; walls missing, blast holes apparent and debris covering the ground. Dead bodies lay everywhere, and sometimes we had to move them from the roads. We had become accustomed to the smell of death, but even as we moved a corpse, the lifeless body almost killed us with a pungent odour.

We continued walking and reached a crossroads, deciding to turn left and head northward, closer to Red October than we were beforehand. But as we turned, gunfire erupted from a two-storey building across the road, no more than thirty feet away.

Diving for cover, I managed to crawl to the doorway that led into a building opposite where they were positioned, overlooking the road and building. Several soldiers followed and clambered inside as they ducked their heads and wove around, trying to avoid the bullets. We opened fire, protecting the tank at all costs. Burning bottles were thrown to the ground, the bricks catching alight as the bottles smashed into thousands of crystals, sending the liquid spraying. They called them 'Molotov cocktails' and they were lethal if you were standing close. The alcohol burned and fire began to spread rapidly, heading straight for the tank.

'Get the tank out of the way!' yelled the leader of our small party. 'Move!'

'Yes, sir!' replied the rest of the soldiers.

Making our way outside, cracks of sniper rifles sounded.

'Shit! Snipers in the upper levels,' exclaimed one soldier. 'We have to take them out!'

'Our snipers will deal with them. Radio the tank and tell them to aim their fire at the base of the building, towards the structural columns.'

The soldier nodded and radioed the tank, who agreed. Aiming at the base of the building, with three fires of the thick shells, the building slowly toppled to one side, crashing into the next building that stood on a large angle, with only one other building supporting it from collapsing. The Russians inside the building slid down the sloping floors and crashed into the end walls, giving us enough chance to move out of our building and up to the next without their defensive gunfire.

The tank kept moving, with several soldiers posted at the front and the back. I was ordered to walk in the front with the twenty-seven other soldiers. When we finally reached the end of the workers' suburbs, the chimneys of the factory were towering to the sky. The smoke, which at first seemed to be coming from the chimneys, spread wider than just a few brick structures atop a number of buildings, and we soon realised the cataclysmic damage of our forces had already begun.

By the end of November, our forces had occupied ninety per cent of the city, but the other ten per cent was still held by the Russians. The fighting in the factory district became animalistic, as guns were no longer used for fear of shooting our own men in the small spaces.

It was dark and musty, the gunpowder lingering in the air as we made our way through a factory that had half collapsed. A large mound of rubble was in the centre of the building, from where the ceiling had caved in, and a large metal beam arched over, attached only to a small rung where the little piece of the ceiling still remained.

The Russians had hidden themselves in the far corners, and our soldiers were hit hard with gunfire as we ran inside. They had lined the entrance up in their sights and proceeded to open fire the moment we entered.

As night fell, more Russians crept in slowly, shadows appearing larger until they were finally absorbed with the rest of the darkness. A grenade went off to our left, and every soldier dived out of the way. After the explosion, smoke filled our noses and soldiers tried to muffle their coughs with their uniforms. The silence was unnerving, and every sound was seen as a potential threat and obliterated with gunfire.

The night was long, with most of the soldiers lying about silently, hoping the other side would make the first move. But that was the fault – neither wanted to make the first move, and so for the entire night we lay awake, our eyes feeling heavier and heavier and our breathing greater and greater, waiting for someone to make the first mistake.

During the daytime, the fighting was reduced to nothing more than attempting to stab at each other with knives and bayonets. I was climbing the large mound in the centre when a Russian soldier leaned down from the top and lunged his knife forward, missing me by only inches. He growled as he retracted his knife and screamed something in Russian. I deliberately let go, knowing I was no use fighting on the mound, and fell to the ground. A sharp pain shot up through my back, but I only let out a small grunt as I staggered up. I was numbed to most pain by now, not even noticing the cuts and grazes all over my body as they bled without a moment's notice.

Retreating to the back, I watched as a number of our soldiers attempted to climb the mound, hoping to gain the higher ground. The Russian soldier who had attempted to stab me lunged for another soldier who was climbing up. The soldier grabbed the Russian's arm and pulled downward. The Russian fell face first into the ground and was soon surrounded by our soldiers who bludgeoned him to death. I turned my head and closed my eyes, blocking out any sign of barbarism – though this whole war was exactly that, an act of barbarism, just on a larger scale.

I watched on as the fighting continued, soldiers of both sides falling to the ground, stabbing each other and spitting in the other's face. The ground was soaked in blood, and the place began to smell more and more of decaying bodies and heavy gunpowder. I wanted to get out, to be in the open where the wind would blow on my face and the snow under my feet – I didn't care about the freezing temperatures, I just wanted to leave. But I couldn't and watched on from the opposing wall as a group of grown men acted like wild animals.

They say that death is only the beginning, but I beg to differ; I sure as hell don't want to see what's on the other side.

CHAPTER 37

December 12, 1942

Operation Winter Storm had been delayed by an actual winter storm in the early days of the month – I laughed silently to myself at the irony. The Sixth Panzer Army was under heavy attack from the Russians. They came at full force, with soldiers and tanks moving like a river from the hills toward the city – it was a sight that kept me anxious, even days after I had witnessed it. Their objective was to encircle our troops, and they completed it by the start of December. Our new operation was to break the encirclement from the outside and rally with our soldiers that had been cut off by the Russians.

On the first day, we caught the Russians by surprise. Our air force kept most of the Russian resistance at bay, and we made considerable advancements to break the defensive barrier. The Sixth Army fought on the inner parts of the encirclement, but they were unable to break it. Our forces pushed the Russians back, defeating their efforts to push against us. They had sustained heavy losses, allowing our forces to move across to where the blockade had been set up. We were able to move twenty-five miles within the first day.

Day two was far different. Fatigued and losing all hope

of a victory in this war, our men fought with the desperation of a beast that knew it would soon die but would still rather see its attacker wounded anyway. The Russian defences were impenetrable, pushing us back as we attempted to bombard them with everything we had. Their reinforcements had come via the north, and we met heavy resistance.

The Luftwaffe attempted air drops of supplies into the centre where our men were being held, but the Russians had also reinforced their aircraft numbers and anti-aircraft artillery. The dogfights still raged on in the skies as smoke wafted around from burning engines and explosions. From a distance they looked like birds soaring through the sky, until they crashed and burned.

Large bangs sounded as the tanks shot their thick shells at each other, and when one of the tanks finally exploded, it was ideal not to be around. The noise would deafen a soldier for almost an hour with a constant ringing in his ear, and the flames licked high in the air as the fuel burned for a time.

By early 1943, our army was reinforced with new soldiers and one hundred and sixty tanks. Relieved with the new number our army had risen to, we were able to counter-attack the Russians' offensive and regain the city of Kharkov. The campaign lasted a month, from February to March as we battled against the Russian forces.

Although we were pushed out of Stalingrad, our army persisted in taking Kharkov, to serve as a base during our second attempt against Stalingrad. We had taken the city before our invasion of Stalingrad, but during the last months of 1941, the Russians had seized it, and again in mid-1942.

I was worried. I had been for months. One of the panzer divisions of our army had been encircled along with the Sixth Army, and I knew that Earnst was in there. I suspected he was under the press of the Russian forces as they encircled them and began to wipe out our soldiers.

For the entire four months that I had been separated from him, I also held a hopeful eye open that he would be standing right beside me. I would look around to see if he was present at any moment after a battle, but he was nowhere to be seen. Death was something I had considered quite a few times, but I couldn't bring myself to think he had met it, too. I needed him. I knew that to be selfish, but I couldn't bear it anymore. I didn't want any more bloodshed. I didn't want my only remaining friend to die as well and leave me with nothing. He couldn't. We needed each other.

We were told that the Sixth Army had been defeated, and that any survivors had been captured by the Russians. If Earnst had survived it all, then perhaps death was more sincere.

I wondered if I should let go. To weep, knowing he was as good as dead. If he was captured, he wouldn't make it any further. The Russians were angry, and I didn't blame them. And they would show that to our soldiers. But I thought of what had happened to me. I had escaped Death's grip so many times, it didn't seem real. Maybe I was dead, and this was my punishment. I preferred there to be nothing. It meant I didn't have to care about anything, anymore. If Death was as kind, or unkind, given this war – to let me survive, maybe Earnst reciprocated that, too. Maybe Death knew I couldn't live without him. That, too, could mean my time was near, instead.

As we were driven out of Kharkov, and further from Stalingrad, we were engaged in a bloody battle in Kursk. Lasting over one month, they had pushed our forces out and forced us into Kiev. One of the last cities we held in Soviet territory, we were tasked with defending it from the Russians.

It had been almost one year since we were forced out of Stalingrad, with the cold November winds showing no signs of bowing down. The Russians were trying to surround us in the city. We could see tanks in the distance, rolling along with soldiers to either side. We were ordered to defend the city, and we knew that if we didn't hold it, it would be the end for all of us.

The Dnieper was a bloody battle, and I'm glad that I wasn't there to see it. Reports that over one million of our men were killed came flooding in at the end of the Battle of Kiev. Although the Russians managed to retake the city, and to destroy a large number of our soldiers, taking back the Dnieper, our army managed to move back enough to stay out of the destructive line of the Russian forces.

We walked along the road, our backs to the east where the sun rose, and Stalingrad was far behind us. A young soldier walked beside me and turned to speak.

'I knew a few of the soldiers that were captured by the Russians,' he said.

I nodded. 'So did I,' I said quietly. '*Do.*'

'You haven't given up, yet?'

'No. I try not to. I try not to think about it.'

'Sorry,' the soldier said quietly.

I shook my head.

'Maybe it's best that I just accept reality and move on.'

There was silence for a time, before I felt somewhat guilty to simply give up.

'Who did you know?' I asked.

The soldier looked at me, a small smile showing in the corner of his mouth, glad that I was finally talking to him. That smile vanished quicker than it appeared, the realisation hitting him that he would no longer see them.

'I was close to a soldier called Aurik. He always looked out for me and made sure I was all right... well, as all right as you can be in this shit pile of a war.'

I nodded. 'I hear you on that. I knew someone like that. He... he died, though. But there was another soldier who looked out for me. He's the one I hope is still alive, somewhere.'

'The Russians took many prisoners. Tens of thousands. He might just be alive and well. What's his name?'

'Earnst. We weren't on the best of terms to begin with, but we formed a good friendship. You know how it is. You try to assert your dominance to the other soldiers, but they're just as scared as you, and everyone knows it. He was close with another soldier, Felix, but he died in Stalingrad. He was one of the kindest people I've ever met, and maybe ever will. He had a good heart. He would drop everything just to make sure you were all right. He was one of those soldiers. He died saving us.'

'Like a true hero.'

I slowed down and stared at the ground. I breathed heavily, as I tried to fight back the tears. We weren't heroes. We were monsters. The feeling had finally come, the feeling of reality, I suppose. Reality was a harsh thing. I had clung onto hope for too long, far too long. The noose of hope had soon wrapped itself around my neck and sent me back to reality. Tears streamed down my face, and I quickly wiped them away as I blinked the rest out of existence. The soldier put his hand on my shoulder.

'It will all be fine,' he said soothingly. 'It's not over yet. We're going back to the Fatherland.'

'My mother always said that home was never a physical place, but when you were with the ones you love. Home is always with you, as long as the people you love are there, too. I'm going into the place I lived, that's it. Without them, it's not home.'

The soldier remained silent.

I sobbed. 'He's gone, isn't he?'

The soldier said nothing. He gently squeezed my shoulder, looking to the ground, and we continued to walk on.

As the days went on, I kept to myself. Few soldiers would talk, many choosing to remain silent. They no longer gathered around the fire together and laugh like they used to. It was quiet, morbid. We may not have been dead, but it felt like whatever fire was in us had long died out and even the embers no longer glowed. There was no possibility of it coming back and I deserved every bit I got. We all did.

Dear Earnst

Dear Earnst,

I don't know if you're gone. I don't know if you're still breathing the cold air, or if you've passed on from this world. It's the not knowing that's killing me. My mind is trapped in limbo, thoughts of your death and hoping, both battling for its place in my mind. Not knowing has always been my weakness – I strive to know. If you are alive, it is only for selfish reasons that I'm joyous; you would want to die after the harsh winters of Siberia. Maybe death is better; maybe Death will be kind to you.

You were my guidance when I thought I had none. When I lost Oskar, I gained a greater friendship with you. We started with suspicion towards each other, as every soldier did. But as we fought alongside each other, you learned about me, and I, you. You accepted my objection to the war, even if you, yourself, didn't. You accepted my 'soft heart,' as you said, knowing I was not that type of person.

I do regret things, however. I may have told you some things, but I didn't tell you everything. I will always be known to you as Hans, but that isn't who I was – who I am. I often wondered what you would think – what you would say, or even do. I feared saying something because I knew you believed in the cause. That's what you were taught. But you also believed in humanity, and that confused me. If I told you, would you believe in me, or the cause? I can never tell anyone, not now. It is my biggest secret and may remain that way forever. Maybe the world will be kind one day, and then you could know.

I wanted to tell you – I wanted you to see that we're not what they tell you. I wanted to utter the words, 'My name is Johan.' I wanted to tell you of my heritage. The blood that runs through my veins, it's the same as your own. I wanted to hold you close and tell you that it would be all right – that we didn't have to do this. Whether you held me in turn, or pushed me away, I could never be sure, but I like to think it would be the former. You're a man who is wise beyond his years, and deep down I know you would accept it, and embrace it. You were raised to believe something; a cause worth fighting for. But when the cause is finished, what do you turn to, then?

Whether you are still in this world, or have moved on to the next, I know you will think gently of me. You heart is bigger than the cause. You are my brother, and perhaps you've joined Felix – reunited at last. I hope you look down on me, and know who I truly am.

Until we meet again, my brother.

Love always,
Hans

CHAPTER 38

November 3, 1945

The war finished in September.

The aftermath was the worst I had ever seen. Even the night of *Kristallnacht* couldn't compare. I hoped I would never witness anything else like it. Buildings were destroyed, crushed into a pile of rubble. They had been reduced to nothing, from once majestic structures, towering to the heavens. Whole cities were ruined as fires still blazed even after the fighting had long since ceased. The embers still glowed like the pits of hell, waiting to engulf an unfortunate soul.

In a way, I think most of the soldiers were glad to see the end of it. It started out as duty – for the Fatherland and for our families – but it soon turned into a nightmare from which we could not get out. The endless killing – they tired of it. It seemed, for them, exciting in the beginning, almost an adventure. But reality soared through, and their smiles became tears; their words became whimpers. For me, at first, it seemed like an opportunity to get Mother and Edith freed. I thought if I made the right friends, perhaps a favour could be done, and they would be free in no time. But I was wrong... so very wrong. It was a nightmare we all shared.

Word had spread that the prisoners in the concentration camps had been liberated and freed, all thanks to the Russians. I stood in humble silence, knowing the people I fought against were the liberators of my people – I had my own humble idiocy that lingered. Each day I made my way to the particular camp that Mother and Edith were held at, hoping to see their faces through the barbed-wire fence that separated us from them, but among those that I did see, their faces weren't there. The very men I had fought against – the ones I had convinced myself were the enemies, were the ones that saved us. For so long I had believed in my duty as a German and as a Jew, but was torn. I joined the men who killed people like me, and fought against men who saved people like me, in the end. I could make out the faces of the men I killed, as clear as if they were alive. I began to cry. And I knew the crying wouldn't stop for a long time to come.

I like to convince myself that joining the army was to save Mother and Edith, but it did nothing for them. I joined because I was running – I was scared. If I could change who I was, I would be safe. But I didn't like who I had to become. I became a monster that fought against the very thing Mother and Father raised me to be. I fought the evil for so long, stirring my mind and cracking my bones, that resistance became folly. I let it linger and grow, to become a disease that slowly infected my mind. Just one more. *I can kill just one more*, I would think. *Just one more.*

For the last months, I waited at the park that we went to as children, where Father would swing me around and Mother would read to us under the large willow trees. They were still recovering the bodies of the prisoners that didn't make it and making a list of who was killed in the camps.

But each day, I got up and sat in the park in the hope that Mother and Edith would step onto the soft grass and see me. Even after months, the officials had said not to give up hope, for they may yet still be alive. Many of the prisoners fled immediately to unknown locations when they were liberated by the Russians, and they may have tried to contact their loved ones. I held onto the glimmer of hope, silently calling their names – I begged them to come back.

And after each day, I would sit in the silence. I would watch the trees flutter gently in the cool wind; I watched as the sun would hide behind the clouds and the light snow fell to the ground, but they never came.

On the evening of November, the fourth, I sat alone on the seat. The silence was crisp in the air as I stared into the sky. It was pink, as the sun slowly descended beyond the horizon, and the stars began to glimmer one by one. As I gazed toward the night sky, I imagined Father, Oskar, Felix and Earnst looking down on me, smiling as they were finally released from this life. And I imagined Alina and Nikolai looking to the same sky, whispering to me, as I did to them.

I continued to gaze, until the moment was broken by a light tap on my shoulder. My heart raced and my eyes widened, as I whipped my head around to look behind me. Almost immediately, my heart sank. There was no one. Had I imagined it, purely because it was on my mind every second of every day? Or was it the tap of Death, politely letting me know that the waiting was over; that he had had the last say?

Whatever it was, I closed my eyes and let the lone tear roll down my cheek. I finally let go.

Letter to Death

Death,

You linger in the shadows and move silently but are always there. You watch as men kill one another, as widows and mothers mourn, and as children yearn to see their fathers. Men will take one another's lives, but it is you who takes the last.

I silently prayed for you to take me, to hold my hand and carry me away. I hoped that you would wrap your arm around me, protect me from what was real, and let me go to what was final – what I knew was the end.

Each day I saw men die. I saw them fall as they yelled. They fought for the Fatherland, they fought for their families, they fought for their friends, and yet they were all to go to the same place. The illusion was they were fighting for life, but what they were fighting for was to meet you.

The sweet kiss of death could be no sweeter, for if they knew in their minds they would not meet the illuminating figure that is preached, but you, they would be far more willing to cling on to life. They imagine the world after this to be of beauty, but it is no more than the eternal dark abyss – but I would rather this than the pain that the real world offers.

They say you are evil, that to wish for you is to commit a heinous crime, even a sin. But I find you fascinating; men yearn for you when there is nothing left, and they fear you when there is so much more. Yet, you are always the same. You have perplexed the generations, leaving them in wonder and, dare I say, awe.

I am not ready for you to claim me yet, and that time will not come soon. For now, I am content with your opposite, life, and I do not think I could let go of it for a moment – not now, anyway.

Be gentle, I ask.

Johan

EPILOGUE

March 23, 1957

I stood under the shade of a large oak tree, leaning against the rough bark, folding my arms and looking into the distance. I often stood in contemplative thought. It was always contemplative thought – the past, the present, but never the future. Everyone's future involves Death, and I never wanted to brush past while knowing. The cool breeze accompanied the warm afternoon sun. I sighed heavily. Pulling back my long-sleeved shirt from my wrist, I looked at the time. *Three o'clock.*

The war finished in 1945 – I was twenty-three. It was hard to believe that it had ever happened to me; that I was part of the largest assault in human history. Too many times I thought I was going to die. Sometimes I was ready, but others I wasn't. Once the Russians had defeated us, our cities lay in ruins and our men had lost everything. I finally let go of Earnst – the feeling had come that he was no longer here. But he, along with Oskar and Felix, Nikolai, and Alina, remain in my thoughts. Each time I walk among the trees, they're with me in my mind. And the greatest thing is they have never changed in my thoughts, and that's fine by me. People crossed my path and changed my life, and for that I will always be grateful. Life is a strange phenomenon – amongst the chaos, I found small pieces of hope that pushed me further and further.

Sergeant Shödler, the man who earned his name as the 'Beast' survived the war, much to my surprise. In 1946, he was put on trial for war crimes. I was there at his proceedings, purposefully watching as the judge passed down the sentence of a thirty-year prison term and hard labour. He was going to die in there and I didn't care. As he walked down the courtroom, he looked over and saw me, his eyes widening. And, in a moment of sweet poetic justice, I clutched my Star of David pendant that was given to me by the Russian soldier and let him see it. He screamed in the hall, yelling, 'I knew it! You Jewish pig!' as the officers carried him away. And that was the first time in a long time that I had smiled and it felt wonderful.

I spent the last months of 1945, up until the last day, waiting in that park. Even after I knew, deep down, that Mother and Edith weren't coming. But I still went, with a small bit of lingering hope.

I was left in wonder – had they joined Father? Wherever they may have been, it was difficult to accept. The streams of tears were never-ending. Guilt had begun to set in, as I blamed myself for what they may have endured – that I would never see them, hear them or kiss them again. I promised I would free them, but that promise was never fulfilled, and never would have been. I had conned myself. I blamed myself for the death of my entire family for too many years, until that guilt had finally come to an end.

I now stood, eleven years later, outside of a school. The cities had been rebuilt, and a new war had begun – but this one was without fighting. The Russians and the Americans. And new weapons were built, that could kill millions. I just hoped it would never come to that, again. I found myself supported by American soldiers as we were settled in West Germany – opposing the Russians once again. But I had learnt that humanity can be better, but it can also be worse. I decided not to interfere in any of the politics – I had had enough politics for one life. My cause was humanity.

Children came rushing out of the large building, running onto the lawn as the school day had finally finished. I looked out to see them smiling and waving to one another, and I smiled knowing that Death would not be as busy as it once was, even for a short time.

A small hand clutched mine and I looked down. I instantly smiled at the young boy, his locks of gold swaying gently in the afternoon breeze.

As he gazed up, his grin showing dimples in his cheeks, he spoke. 'Papa.'

'Oskar, my boy, are you ready to go home?'

Shawline Publishing Group Pty Ltd
www.shawlinepublishing.com.au